IN HER
CAGE

ALSO BY DANIELLE GRAINGER

THE DENTON HEIGHTS SERIES

Under Her Wing (Book One):
The Shasti and Madison Story

In Her Cage (Book Two):
The Jaleesa and Tina Story

Within Her Grasp (Book Three):
The Marta and Shanice Story

THE BERNADETTE SERIES

Wrecking Bernadette (Book One)

(S)mothering Bernadette (Book Two)

Becoming Bernadette (Book Three)

Desiring Bernadette (Book Four)

Loving Bernadette (Book Five)

IN HER Cage

DENTON HEIGHTS BOOK 2

DANIELLE GRAINGER

Bibi Books Publishing Company

Paperback ISBN   978-1-953734-29-7

First Edition 2023

9 8 7 6 5 4 3 2 1

Cover design by Sarah (Forcoverservice)

Published by:

Bibi Books Publishing Company, LLC

Dedication

This book is dedicated to all those dealing with addiction of any sort. Stay strong, stay focused, and by all means, ask for help.

Acknowledgments

I want to acknowledge the readers of my books especially. You are demanding yet uplifting and exactly what this writer needs. I appreciate your feedback on my work, but most of all, I appreciate your loyalty. The emails you send brighten my day and positively keep me going. Thank you.

I also need to acknowledge and thank my awesome beta readers. Jiske – thank you for letting me bounce so many ideas off of you. Your insights and suggestions are always spot-on and most welcomed. Olivia – comma and grammar queen. Thank you for continuing to point out my ineptitude in these areas. Angela M. – thank you for signing up to beta once again. You always find something, no matter how meticulous I think I've been. Tanya – thank you for sharing your knowledge and expertise in my growing understanding of "the life." Your ideas and point of view are refreshing and help me reflect on the messages I intend to convey.

Table of Contents

Chapter 1

Jaleesa

Amazed that she got the key into the lock smoothly on the first try, Jaleesa Whitmore unlocked the door and stepped into her apartment. With a fist, she reached back and grabbed her companion of the evening by the front of the jacket and yanked her inside. How she had the presence of mind to close and lock the door was beyond her. It must have been the years of bringing home one-night stands that had honed her sense of self-preservation. She couldn't remember this one's name—Jack Daniels tended to mess with that. But names didn't matter now, did they?

Still holding the woman by the lapels, Jaleesa slammed her against the back of the closed door and eliminated the space between them. Jaleesa pressed her body against the shorter woman. A soft encouraging moan came from the woman as Jaleesa's lips found hers. It was a possessive kiss. Jaleesa's thigh, made strong from years of working out, insinuated itself between the woman's thighs. Legs spread in invitation as fervent kisses continued.

Jaleesa gently moved the woman's thick Marley twists out of the way and kissed the silky bronze skin beneath. The woman shivered and arched her pelvis against Jaleesa's thigh. It was time. Time for Jaleesa to be the dominant woman she was in the bedroom. She pulled back, placed both hands on the woman's shoulders, and, in one swift move, spun her around so the woman's back was to her front. One arm snaked around the woman's waist while the other claimed her chest.

"Why are you here?" Jaleesa whispered into the woman's ear.

"Because…" Her breathing was heavy. She was clearly turned on and couldn't finish her sentence.

"Why. Are. You. Here?" Jaleesa asked in a tone that demanded a truthful answer.

"Because you're the best. They say you're the best."

"Who says this?" Jaleesa pressed. Maybe it was her ego asking, or maybe it was the whiskey in her system. Who knew? She didn't care.

"Everyone at Dominique's."

Jaleesa scoffed. "Everyone," she muttered. Mm hmm. She'd certainly taken home more than her fair share of women from Dominique's Dungeon. She unzipped the woman's winter jacket and let her hand stroke her "date's" stomach. She untucked the silk shirt and popped open the button of the slacks. Yes, it was time to take charge of this evening's events. Jaleesa almost laughed. She'd been in charge since their first exchanged glance at Dominique's. She'd let the good-looking woman know she'd been seen and admired but made no move to close in for the kill at first—that must have been frustrating for the woman in her embrace.

Let them thirst for it, Jaleesa always thought. True enough, but on rare occasions, the girlfriend of the flirting scamp would show up, and the game would be lost. It was always better to be patient than to rush in. Except now she had her prey in her arms.

The woman moaned encouragement for Jaleesa's wandering hands. She lay her head back on Jaleesa's shoulder and surrendered. Ahh, yes. Jaleesa was good at reading the signs. The woman wanted this.

Jaleesa's fingers swirled their way under the woman's panties. She stroked the trimmed mons but went no further. She stopped all motion.

"Mmmm." The woman moaned encouragement. "Don't tease." She reached over her shoulder and pressed her hand on the back of Jaleesa's head.

Jaleesa grunted. This woman hadn't seen anything yet. The traveling hand tracked lower until she found what she knew would be there.

"Somebody's wet." A statement. Not a question. Her fingers dipped through the slick nether lips and then back up to reveal a swelling bud. "Mmm. Nice, baby."

The woman's hips undulated slightly, clearly wanting more pressure.

Jaleesa would love nothing more than to have this woman burst into orgasm right there in her arms within minutes of being in her apartment, but no. It was best to check in first. Jaleesa chuckled. It was an almost evil chuckle as she denied the woman her release.

"What's your safeword?"

"Umm," the woman stammered.

Shit, was she a newb?

"I'm not sure what that means," the woman admitted.

"Say your safeword if you don't like what's happening, and we'll stop. Red is the most popular. Green if you like it and want things to continue. Yellow means we'll pause, or you need to regroup."

"Ahh, okay," the woman said and arched her pelvis, obviously encouraging Jaleesa's exploring hand to continue its exploration. "Green, please."

Jaleesa laughed and then bit down gently on the exposed curve of the woman's neck. Why not? It was right there.

A low moan of arousal filled the space. "Green," the woman murmured.

"Do you like it rough?"

"I don't know," came the honest answer.

"We'll go slow," Jaleesa said, releasing the woman from her grasp. "Hang your coat there, and then go use the restroom. I want you completely nude when you come back out."

Jaleesa almost laughed at the woman's startled expression, but she remained stoic and pointed to the bathroom door.

"Okay," the woman stammered with a shaky voice.

"And you'll call me Ma'am or Sir, depending on what works for you."

"Umm, okay."

The slight tilt of Jaleesa's head and narrowed eyes made the woman rethink her reply. "Okay, *Ma'am*."

"Better," Jaleesa said. "Go." She turned her back on the woman. She had to. The grin on her face would wreck her badass Domme persona.

The sound of the woman's shoes slapping on the tile as she hurried to the bathroom made Jaleesa smile. When the door shut, Jaleesa hung up her signature leather jacket and pulled out the futon. The waterproof mattress pad and sheets were intact, of course. Jaleesa was always prepared.

She'd snagged herself a newb. That was okay. She liked newbies. They flocked to Dominique's Dungeon on the outskirts of Cincinnati, wanting someone to help them explore the BDSM lifestyle, and Jaleesa was always happy to oblige. Hers was a caring and loving form of dominance, but it was dominance, nonetheless.

Of course, scoring an experienced submissive bottom was always welcomed, too. She hadn't given a good flogging in quite a while. It was hard to find available experienced subs these days. Most had been scooped up and collared. No, a flogging or any other kind of impact was not going to happen tonight. This woman was too raw. Too new. And besides, they were both a bit sauced. Jaleesa always thought drinking at the dungeon was a bad move, and clearly, Dominique agreed because the only thing you could buy at the "bar" was water and non-alcoholic drinks. Of course, that didn't stop most of Dominique's customers from stopping at Murph's to pound down a few beforehand or sneaking stuff in. Murph's was only a city block away. Jaleesa had to admit that she liked to oil things up with a good mixed drink or five, even if they were Murph's watered-down versions.

Jaleesa turned on soft mood lighting and fixed another drink for each of them. Jack and Coke seemed to be the woman's preferred drink, so Jack and Coke it was. She put the glasses on the side table and turned toward the opening bathroom door.

Her breath caught in her throat. This woman was ebony perfection. Her bronze skin was smooth and pure and slightly darker than her own. Her hips were shapely. Womanly. Her breasts were upright and perky. The dark areolas perfectly highlighted the erect nipples that were either announcing their arousal or reacting to the chill in the apartment. Late December could do that to bare nipples.

Jaleesa swallowed. Hard. Uh, oh. The tingles in her belly weren't all from lust. Damn. She was in trouble. "Gorgeous," she murmured, unsure if she'd meant to say the word out loud. No, she hadn't meant to. The woman looked down, obviously uncomfortable with the compliment. "Stay right where you are," Jaleesa commanded, her voice a bit shaky.

Jaleesa opened a drawer on the side table and pulled out a new collar. It was a feminine collar, just like the woman in front of her. "I want you to wear this. It will remind you that you're mine while you're here and that you are to do whatever I ask of you."

"Yes, Ma'am," the woman said meekly. She moved her hair out of the way so Jaleesa could buckle the collar on. It was red and matched the woman's "kiss me" lipstick. "But, Ma'am?"

"Yes, baby?"

"I can still say the word and stop something, right?"

"Your safeword? Yes, of course. And what is that safeword?" Jaleesa moved in front of the woman, so close that there was barely a sliver of personal space between them.

"Red to stop. Yellow to hold things up for a second. Green to go." The woman laughed. "Oh, it's like a traffic light." She chuckled again, making Jaleesa's chest bloom with feelings she hadn't felt since her one great love in college almost twenty years ago. Damn. That long ago? Caution was needed, though. She'd had these feelings before, and they never panned out.

"And what's your color right now?"

The woman put her arms around Jaleesa's neck and nuzzled against her. "Very green." She sighed a lustful sigh and then added, "Ma'am."

"Good girl," Jaleesa said.

The woman moaned at the words. Ahh, yes. Most subs loved to hear those words. It hit them viscerally for some reason.

Jaleesa guided the woman to the end of the makeshift bed in the living room and handed her the drink. She took the other for herself. The woman took a big gulp as if for courage and handed the glass back to Jaleesa. Jaleesa put her own drink down after a quick sip and guided the nude woman onto her back.

Fully clothed still, Jaleesa hovered over the lovely body below her. Without touching the breasts, she traced a line down the woman's torso with the tips of two fingers. The woman squirmed both from arousal and the unexpected ticklish spots Jaleesa caressed. Good information for later when it was time to really make her squirm. Jaleesa's fingertips glided from one hip bone to another and then down to the tightly closed legs of her soon-to-be captive. "Gorgeous," Jaleesa said, this time meaning to say it out loud. She bent lower and kissed the trimmed mound below her.

The woman's hands insinuated themselves in Jaleesa's short chunky afro and pushed her toward her area of most need. Jaleesa shook her head and grinned. It was an evil grin. Yes, this one would need restraints. But they all did, didn't they? They all wanted that. Even the soft butches yearned for it. Not that this gorgeous creature on her futon was butch. Not in the slightest.

"Tsk, tsk, baby," Jaleesa scolded with a shake of her head. She stood up and reached behind the futon's frame for the pink wrists cuffs. Pink was for newbies. The red ones were for the middle-of-the-road bottoms, and the black—mmm, for her more hardened and experienced subs. She hadn't used the black cuffs in a long time. But this was no time to get wistful. Not with an eager woman in her lair.

"Do you trust me?"

"Y-yes," the woman stammered. "I think so."

Jaleesa smirked but said nothing. She maneuvered one of the women's arms overhead and gently attached the wrist cuff. She searched the woman's reaction for any signs of stress. Breathing rate increased, but not to panic levels. Good. Jaleesa attached the other cuff and then told the woman to pull herself out.

She did, pulling one wrist out at a time. "Oh," the woman said in surprise.

"I want you to feel safe with me," Jaleesa said. "If you feel panicky, you can release yourself." Jaleesa put the wrists back into the cuffs and added, "But I'd rather you didn't."

"Yes, Ma'am," the woman said. "Will you kiss me again?"

"In time," was Jaleesa's only answer. No sense in giving this bottom any sense of power. Jaleesa was calling the shots here. In fact, maybe it was time to let her simmer.

Jaleesa picked up her drink. The ice had already begun to melt, and that was annoying. But it didn't matter. The feel-good power was still in the glass. She headed to the loveseat across from the futon and sat down. She put her feet up on the hassock.

"Come back," the woman whined. "Make love to me."

Jaleesa simply smiled and took a sip. Oh, she would "make love" to this woman, but on her terms, and the sooner the woman realized that, the better.

A full minute went by with neither of them speaking. The woman started to release herself from the cuffs but stopped when Jaleesa gave her the subtle but clear Domme eyebrow lift. Ahh, good. Message received. She was catching on quicker than most. The deeply submissive types were sometimes the toughest, though. They acquiesced immediately, and their obeisance was almost off-putting. They were hard to read—so used to letting others step on them or have their way with them without understanding that they had a say in what went on between them. That was the lesson Jaleesa tried to instill in them. To her, sex was secondary in those cases.

But not tonight. This woman was submissive, yes, but not overly so.

Jaleesa drained her glass and set it down gently on the coaster. She stood up slowly and walked over with purpose. Without making eye contact, Jaleesa traced the woman's lips with the side of her thumb. She pressed against the closed lips with the tip of her index finger. The woman opened slightly and accepted the finger eagerly. Good. She was hungry. Sexually hungry. She sucked gently, accepting the invasion. Jaleesa thrust her finger in and out gently. She was waiting for the moan. They almost always did. Ahh, there it was. She pulled out and leaned down to kiss the woman gently. Not in a lovemaking kind of way, but in a "slow down, we'll get there" kind of way.

Jaleesa thrust her tongue in and out, but not so much as to gag the woman. She never liked that from a lover, so she never did it to hers. The woman moaned in frustration as she tried to move her arms. She'd forgotten that her wrists were tethered. Who knew where those arms and hands were trying to go, but that didn't matter now, did it?

Jaleesa's lips and tongue kissed the woman on the forehead and then commenced a slow and probably frustrating journey from her sensitive neck, down her collarbone, to her breasts. The way the woman arched up to increase the pressure made Jaleesa understand how close she was to orgasm. Best not to keep her waiting too long. They had all night, didn't they? Had they discussed that? And did she have the STD-clean talk with this one? Shit, she couldn't remember. Jack had its downside, didn't it?

Jaleesa sucked the woman's left nipple into her mouth and reached over to oh-so-gently pinch the right. This was the litmus test to see how much pain she could tolerate. Pain was a means to an end. Pain enhanced the flood of mind-blowing chemicals produced during sex. The woman inhaled deeply and moaned her exhale. Excellent. A would-be pain junky. Jaleesa squeezed a bit harder, and the woman started panting.

"Yes, yes," she moaned. "Touch me, Jaleesa. You're as good as they say. Holy fuck."

They had barely begun, Jaleesa thought with a mental shake of her head. The only thing that smiled was her ego. Taking a woman to new heights was more intoxicating than that first shot of Jack every evening. No, it was more than that. It was the hunt and seduction that thrilled her. And their ultimate submission, of course. Like this woman who had no name.

Without releasing the nipple between her fingers, Jaleesa's kisses continued their trail lower. She kissed the lower belly several times but the mons only once. She chuckled when the woman groaned in frustration. With two fingers, she parted the soaked and swollen flesh to reveal the healthy, bright pink tucked away underneath. Coating her fingers with the woman's arousal, she lazily swirled them around the labia as if this was a cozy Sunday afternoon and they had all the time in the world. Grinning at the woman's obvious frustration and urgent need, Jaleesa finally circled her index finger around the now-hidden clitoris, coaxing it out from under its hood. Ahh, there she was. Swollen and hard, the little bundle of joy came out to play. Jaleesa placed a reverent kiss on the protrusion. And it truly was reverent. She admired the female form. Worshipped it almost.

The woman arched her pelvis in encouragement, her knees falling to the side, giving Jaleesa ample room to work. Lightly sucking the pea-sized nub, she slaked her fingers through the soft folds and then inserted a finger partway in. A few women didn't like too much penetration, lesbians especially. You would think the soft butches would be the biggest holdouts, but they opened their legs wider as if trusting Jaleesa with their deepest darkest secret.

The woman below her opened her legs even more. Ahh, there it was— the invitation. Jaleesa maneuvered between the woman's open legs, her broad shoulders keeping the legs separated. She reinserted the finger and slid it to the hilt. She pulled out and inserted two. Her fingers were long. The various women that found themselves cuffed to her futon appreciated that. Two was all she needed at the moment. She pulled her head back and blew lightly on the woman's clit, causing an immediate tilt of hips. Jaleesa chuckled but didn't tease. She pulled the pearl back into her mouth and flicked it with her tongue. Her thrusting fingers turned over and bent slightly, continuing their rhythmic pumping. Ahh, yes, there it was—the ribbed flesh inside most women. Her long fingers loved caressing a woman's G-spot.

"Fuck, fuck," the woman cried as her body arched up off the futon as her first orgasm slammed into her. Her legs tried to close but only ended up pressing hard against Jaleesa's shoulders. That spurred Jaleesa on, and she continued stimulating this magnificent creature under her control. The woman begged Jaleesa to stop so she could recover, but as predicted, when asked her color, she moaned and said green. That was all Jaleesa needed to hear as she drew out a second orgasm before relenting. She unclipped the cuffs from the futon but didn't take them off the woman. She had a feeling there'd be more fun in store for them that night.

Jaleesa was pleasantly surprised when the woman asked to be held. Jaleesa graciously complied. Some women folded in on themselves, embarrassed by their flood of arousal and vulnerability. Others fell asleep. But the ones Jaleesa liked best were the ones who wanted to be held. Like this woman.

"Thank you, Jaleesa," the woman murmured. "I want to see you again."

"The night's still young, baby."

"I know, but can I see you again?"

"We'll see," Jaleesa said. "There's always a reexamining of things in the morning."

"By you or by me?" The woman moved to look Jaleesa in the eye.

"By you."

The woman's grin told her everything she needed to know. There would be a repeat of this night.

Jaleesa couldn't help the deep chuckle that seemed to come from her toes. "Rest now. We've got all night."

"And you are still fully dressed," the woman accused. "Not fair. I heard you were a hotshot college basketball star or something." She ran her hand over Jaleesa's abs, still covered by the black lace shirt she'd worn to Dominque's. "Mmm," the woman moaned appreciatively. "I'd like a chance to, umm, return the pleasure."

"Ahh," Jaleesa quipped, "the pleasure will be all mine."

"We'll share in it," the woman countered. "How about that?"

"Deal." Jaleesa pulled her close and urged her to rest. She drew in the woman's soft fragrance, which somehow calmed her. It could have been the Jack Daniels, but she didn't think so.

A horn honked on the street below and tore an older Jaleesa out of the self-indulgent memory. "Fuck you, Gabby. Today would have been three years." She pounded her fist on the kitchen table. "Why did you leave?" She stood up and swiped at the tears, annoyed at her own weakness. Fuck! She needed a drink. Her hand was on the liquor cabinet before she remembered. There was no liquor in this cabinet anymore—no Jack Daniels. No nothing. She was sober. Had been for almost a year.

She opened the cabinet anyway, just to make sure. Nope. Mismatched plastic bowls and lids. "Fuck." She slammed the door shut.

A mixture of anger, sadness, and abandonment fought for control inside her. She shuffled to the living room. It was the same living room with the same futon she'd cuffed Gabby to that night three years ago to the day. She'd put up no Christmas decorations this year, not a single one. Pulling out the box from her closet would mean she'd see the ornaments she and Gabby had collected together. And they would still be in the box because Gabby hadn't taken any of them. None of those ornaments had meant anything to Gabby, had they? Just like Jaleesa had meant nothing to her either.

She turned to the sideboard and picked up the photograph she had framed of the two of them. It was a good picture. They both looked good in it. They had been celebrating their two-year anniversary. The party, as always, was right there in the apartment.

Jaleesa wiped the tears from her eyes again, angry that she couldn't get control, and then traced a finger over Gabby's beautiful smile. Her finger came back with several months' worth of dust. Jaleesa smiled at the Goddess box braids she'd done for Gabby a few days before that party. Gabby had flipped out on their third date when she learned that Jaleesa did hair. And not only did Jaleesa do hair, but she worked at Miss Bessie's

Salon, one of the busiest Black hair salons on this side of town and the most difficult to get an appointment at.

"You stayed over that entire first night, didn't you, Gabs?" Jaleesa said to the photo. "I had those scratches on my back as proof. That was the beginning of us." Jaleesa put the photo back on the dusty sideboard. "Until you ended it."

She picked up the framed photo of the New Year's Eve party over the border in Covington, Kentucky. It was a few days after the anniversary party. "That night was the beginning of the end, wasn't it, Gabby?" Anger burst through Jaleesa's core, and she flung the picture across the room like a frisbee. The breaking glass fueled her fury. She threw another and another. "None of this mattered to you, did it?" Another picture smashed against the wall. "Should have thrown these out long ago," Jaleesa growled. "Why the fuck did I think you were any different than the rest of those self-centered women?"

Jaleesa slid her socked feet into leather boots and dug in the closet for her old leather jacket—the one she'd worn the night she'd met Gabby and brought her home, not even knowing her name. She shrugged on the jacket. It was a little big. She'd lost weight since being sober.

"Couldn't handle it when things got hard. Could you, Gabs?" Jaleesa jammed her keys in her front pocket, her wallet in the back. "I hope your new butch girlfriend is everything you want." Her hand reached for the front doorknob. The familiar ache of loss squeezed her chest. A small sob escaped, and she stamped her foot. No! She would not shed tears for the woman who abandoned her three months into Jaleesa's forced sobriety. Where was the support? The sympathy? The … She couldn't think of a good word, only that she'd felt betrayed. She and Gabby had developed a great partnership together. Or so she thought. Jaleesa had even started thinking about asking Gabby to marry her.

But no. Gabby left when it got hard. She left when Jaleesa needed her the most.

"I stayed sober after you left, Gabs," Jaleesa said, heartache burning her insides. "I waited for you. I wanted you to see how strong I was. I thought you'd change your mind and come back. I just knew you would." She stifled a sob and whispered, "But you didn't."

And now, it was two days after Christmas on what should have been their joyous third-year anniversary or maybe even a few months as a married couple. But no. Gabby decided that Jaleesa was—How had she put it in her cowardly Dear Jane letter, the one she'd left on the kitchen table for Jaleesa to find after work? Oh, yes. "Different." Three-months-sober Jaleesa was different and apparently not fun anymore. "Is that baby butch I hear you're fucking now fun? Are you her shiny new toy?" Jaleesa smacked the back of the closed front door. "No, she's *your* shiny new toy, isn't she?" She yanked the door open.

"Fine." She stepped out and slammed the door shut behind her. She turned and locked it tight while muttering. "I'll show you who's fun."

Yes, the urge was back. Okay, it had always been there, and it was only three o'clock in the afternoon, but she didn't care. There was a shot of Jack Daniels waiting for her down at Murph's. After that, a trip to Dominique's. She felt strong enough to handle things if Gabby happened to be there. Of course, the strength would come from the shots of Jack at Murph's, but still. She was tired of her life being on hold.

Back in January, almost a full year ago, she'd done her seven days in that stupid jail, paid her fines, put up with that ridiculous ignition breathalyzer device, and even submitted to that bogus treatment program they'd made her go to. She'd proven to any and everybody that she could remain sober for the required six months. Shit, she was five days shy of being sober for an entire fucking year. Who cared? There was no one here to care, anyway. And, what the hell. It had been her first DUI. The cops were out in force last New Year's, especially watching those that came back over the border from Kentucky. She'd had the bad luck of getting stopped by a redneck cop without a personality.

She scoffed at the memory and double-timed the stairs down to the parking garage. She jammed the key in the ignition of her new Ford F-150 pickup and fired it up. She screeched her sober-ass self out of the garage toward Murph's and the sanity her first drink in almost a year would bring her.

"Fuck you, Gabby. Fuck you, Judge whatever-the-fuck-your-name-is." She smacked the steering wheel. "Jaleesa Whitmore is back!"

Chapter 2

Tina

Tina stood up and shook hands with the newest and probably the shortest JW Bank customer she'd ever dealt with. It wasn't every day she got to set up a savings account for a twelve-year-old. She watched with satisfaction as the girl and her mother put their coats back on and headed out the bank door.

That was cool, Tina thought with satisfaction. The young girl had been determined to set up a college savings fund for herself with the money she'd gotten for Christmas. Tina advised a savings account to start with and perhaps a CD in the future. Kids were fickle, not that she knew firsthand, but she advised keeping the $150 liquid for now. Who knew? The next greatest video game might come out, and the girl would need to drain her account to get it.

Tina smiled as she sat down. Yes, that part of her job as a personal banker was satisfying. Other parts were not. Take the recently hired bank manager, Doug Henderson, for example. True to form, he was leaving for the day, two hours before the bank closed. And they were swamped, this being the first bank day after Christmas and all. He'd come so highly recommended by the Denton Heights branch that his actions were confusing. He was a good-looking man in his early forties, maybe nine or ten years older than she was. His wit and charm had probably helped him get far in his career, but Tina wasn't fooled by it. He wasn't pulling his weight, and you'd think he'd have more to prove as the new guy. Apparently not. And apparently, no one else noticed or cared.

And without him there, management of the daily operations fell to her and the head teller. But Nancy was on vacation for the rest of the week—Christmas at Disney World in Florida or something amazing like that.

Tina wasn't exactly jealous of the Florida vacation; she had no right to be. She hadn't left Cincinnati since her senior year in high school. Yep, senior year—when the shit hit the fan, and everything changed. Ev-er-y-thing.

The familiar mixture of anger, anxiety, and shame ratcheted up inside her, so she placed both feet flat on the floor and took a cleansing breath. She straightened the stapler on her desk so it was aligned with the edge of the desk blotter. Best to keep things neat. One of her favorite mantras was "Neat Environment—Neat Mind." Sometimes she shortened it to "NE-NM." She'd written the acronym on a post-it note and placed it strategically in her center desk drawer. It was a coping mechanism she'd created for herself during years of therapy following the shitstorm. And then there was her other favorite. "Routine Brings Peace. Routine Brings Calm." Yep, "RBP-RBC" was another one in her center drawer. These acronyms helped quell her anxiety and gave her something to focus on besides the mind-sucking urge to use. And the overwhelming guilt. Every day she felt both, even after all these years.

She'd long since quit Dr. Bradley since they both felt she'd picked up enough coping strategies to manage her cravings and anxiety. And as long as she kept order in her life and kept to a daily routine, she was fine. She'd just turned thirty-one in November and had, so far, been coping as well as she deserved.

Tina jumped when a voice spoke at her office door.

"I need twenties," Amber, the newly hired teller, said.

Tina looked up slowly. "You'll need to try that again."

"What?" Amber asked, obviously not understanding how rude and unprofessional she had been. "Have you seen the line? I'm out of twenties."

It took all of Tina's strength not to show the anger she felt. "Was that a professional way to ask?"

"Whatever," Amber said and pushed off the door jam. "Just get them," the brat called over her shoulder.

Anger flashed through Tina. She had no choice; she had to get the twenties. Mr. Henderson had asked her to fill in as lead teller while Nancy was on vacation. It was a natural ask since Tina had been the lead teller for a few years before being promoted to personal banker. Well, her official title was Relationship Manager and Business Owner Specialist. That was too much of a mouthful, so she typically introduced herself as a *Personal Banker* instead.

She tried to remain calm and collected, but gosh, darn it, why was Mr. Henderson never around when this sort of disrespect happened? Tina could write Amber up for impertinence, so it went in her file, but it wouldn't matter. He wouldn't do anything about it. He was more interested in coming in late and leaving early. She wished she could write *him* up.

Tina put both hands on her desk, stood up, and let the chair roll back and hit the rail behind her. This was her tiny act of defiance. She tucked the bank keys in her skirt pocket and headed out her office door. She tapped the jam three times and then went to rectify the shortage of twenties in Amber's cash drawer. Amber didn't thank her, but Tina hadn't expected her to.

Tina checked in with the other tellers and helped out Kate, who needed more deposit slips. Once satisfied that the tellers had things under control, she headed back to her office to double-check the twelve-year-old's information before making the account official.

She left her office door open, so she would have a full view of the tellers if they needed her. She remembered those early days as a teller. She had just finished her sophomore year at Blackwell University, an all-women's college in the heart of Cincinnati. Since she had been handling the routine of school and classes well, Tina, her parents, and Dr. Bradley thought she was strong enough to handle a part-time job. Since she was working toward a bachelor's degree in Finance, a bank teller job seemed perfect. She could work her way up. Of course, the new job venture had caveats. She was not to work at a branch that would require driving near the neighborhood where she used to score. Easy enough.

After verifying the young girl's information, Tina filed it and then pulled up the electronic folder from the loan application she'd taken that morning. A twenty-two-year-old kid had applied for a car loan. All Tina had to do was verify the validity of his information and double-check his credit. It was good that he had his mother co-sign the loan because twenty-two-year-olds with little to no credit history rarely got loans from JW Bank.

Try as she might to concentrate on the loan app, her focus slid toward her next meeting. Eek! That was tomorrow! She'd promised Fran and Pastor Paul that she would be the speaker for the mixed meeting. Her last speech had been about five or six years before. She often shared her personal story, but those were typically quick sound bites containing the bare basics—quick nothings. Giving a speech meant a longer, more in-depth look into her addiction journey. She was supposed to show everyone the mistakes she'd made so that they could learn from them. Almost like "True Confessions" or a "TED Talk."

She had a vague idea of what she would say but had no clue how to be inspiring. And her nerves would get her. She just knew it. It had gotten her last time, too. Public speaking just wasn't her thing.

The tip of the middle finger on her right hand hit the hard surface of the desk three times. Tap, tap-tap. And again. Tap, tap-tap. She closed her eyes and took a cleansing breath. Tap, tap-tap.

She opened her eyes and muttered, "You're o-kay." Tap, tap-tap. One tap for each syllable. She really meant it this time.

She pulled her silenced cell phone out of the top right drawer, even though she shouldn't, but Mr. Henderson wasn't there to reprimand her, so there. Yes, another small act of defiance. The new Kroger flyer had come out. She'd already perused it on her lunch break since she would hit up the grocery store on her way home from work. She scanned the shopping list app she shared with her mother.

"What the hell?" Tina muttered. "C'mon, Mom." She looked up to make sure no one needed her. The coast was clear. She texted her mother immediately.

TINA: Krinkle potato chips, Mom?

Tina smirked when she saw the three dancing dots on her text screen. Mm hmm. Her mother worked remotely from home but must have been waiting for Tina's text.

MOM: Your father likes that kind, and they're BOGO. (shrug emoji)

TINA: I thought we were watching his sodium. (frown emoji)

MOM: We are. We'll dole out the chips sparingly.

Tina laughed but then bit down on her lip.

TINA: You literally made me laugh out loud, Mom.

MOM: (smile emoji)

TINA: Okay, I'll get them. Anything else for the list? Do we need parmesan?

MOM: We're good on everything.

TINA: Okay. I'll leave here at the regular time. Track me?

MOM: Always.

MOM: Wait! I almost forgot. Dad texted earlier. He wants garlic bread with the spaghetti tonight.

TINA: Absolutely not! Too many carbs. Tell him no. No, actually, I'll tell him no when I give him his double portion of salad later.

MOM: He will not like that at all.

TINA: (devil emoji)

"Tina?" Kate called from the teller area.
"Be right there," Tina called back and stood up.

TINA: Gotta go, Mom. Love you.

Tina hated leaving their chats so abruptly, but her mother understood that her job sometimes took her away at a moment's notice.

For the next hour, Tina let the tellers have their afternoon breaks as she filled in for them one at a time. Her own work was waiting undone in her office, but there was nothing she could do about it. She had to help out. All for one and one for all, right? So why did it feel like she was the only one at this bank with that philosophy?

After dinner, Tina tried to help clean up, but her parents told her to scoot upstairs and work on her speech. Yes, "scoot" was the actual word her mother had used. Okay, fine. She'd go.

After a soaking hot shower, she towel-dried her hair and wrapped it up high on her head. Sitting in a robe at the desk in the room she grew up in, she stared at the collage of celebrity pictures she'd tacked to her walls over the years—her very pink walls. One day she'd paint it a more grown-up color, but for now, she had other things to worry about. Like speeches.

Knowing it was a delaying tactic, she stood up, kissed her latest celebrity crush, and wondered what it would be like to be on the arm of the lovely five-foot-nine-inch Issa Rae. Everyone would see that Issa had chosen her. Issa's protective arm would wrap around Tina as they navigated Hollywood's extravagant parties.

Tina laughed out loud. "As if!" Issa was probably straight anyway. Oh, well. Back to it. She had a speech to write.

She sat down and tapped her gel pen against a fresh new legal pad. Typically, when people gave speeches like this, they spoke about how their addictions had wrecked their lives and those around them. Her chest tightened with emotion as she looked down at the blank paper. Maybe that's why she was having anxiety over this stupid speech. She would have to dredge up how much she'd hurt those two loving people downstairs watching TV. It was alternatingly confusing and amazing that they let her remain in their home after what she'd done. Maybe that's why she worked so hard to be a fully contributing member of their household now that she was an adult. To atone for...to atone....

An iron fist of shame and humiliation gripped her by the heart. She couldn't stop the sob. She shoved the collar of her robe into her mouth to silence her regrets. Her parents couldn't know. They had to believe that she was fine and that everything was going well. She needed them to believe the crap back then was merely a blip on the family radar. Admittedly, a big blip, but they had gotten through it and had come out a happy, healthy little Jenkins family. And, no, her parents would not be attending the meeting tomorrow evening because this particular one was closed. It was a mixed meeting for addicts and alcoholics only. That's probably why Tina had picked that date. If her parents did happen to hear her speech somehow, they might figure out the lie of it all. And no one could know. Not her parents or Fran or Pastor Paul. Not Harriet or Dana, two women she kind of nurtured—when they let her. All would be lost if any of them knew. Really knew.

A wave of grief passed through her. Her secrets could never be revealed in her carefully controlled world. They just couldn't.

She tapped on the desk three times as she said out loud, "You're o-kay." When tapping didn't ease her chest ache, she ripped the towel off her head and got up to turn off the light. She sat on the edge of her bed and closed the canopy curtains, creating a quiet, dark cocoon. She wiggled under the covers, which was hard to do in a robe, but she didn't have time to change. She needed relief. Now. One by one, she pulled the top sheet, the blanket, and both comforters over herself. Mindful breathing and whispered mantras calmed her. Somewhat. She forced herself to think about something other than her current worthless life.

Memories of high school softball came up. Good memories. She'd been a decent second baseman, and a good base stealer, too. At only five foot tall, she'd managed to make the second-team all-star list for Hamilton County her senior year. And then there was Nylani: her teammate and her first love. Tina had been smitten with her, but soon enough, Nylani wanted more than cuddles, hugs, and kisses. And Tina found she didn't. In fact, she'd never understood what the other girls meant when they said someone was "hot." Nylani was cute and had nice firm muscles. She was funny, and her smile was to die for, especially when directed toward Tina. But all that didn't seem enough to qualify as "hot."

Tina tried to figure it out as her senior year went on. She even started tacking up pictures of people she found attractive and wouldn't mind cuddling with to find the common denominator among them. Maybe if she found that common thing, she'd figure out what made them "hot." Funny thing—most of the celebrities she'd tacked on her walls turned out to be women. These women were beautiful, but Tina quickly learned that the kind of attraction she had for them still didn't mean hot. "Hot," according to her friends, always included a sexual factor. Those feelings or urges had never happened to Tina. Her heart had stirrings, yes, but nothing "down below" ever did. Yeah, she kept that weirdness about herself a secret from her friends and from Nylani. And Nylani? Well, she ran out of patience waiting for Tina to reciprocate sexual feelings. After graduation, they went their separate ways. Nylani found another girlfriend. And Tina found…addiction.

She burrowed deep underneath the covers as the crap memories overtook the good ones.

She'd caused a colossal mess that summer after graduation. A mess caused by her and her alone. As much as her parents tried to shoulder the blame, it wasn't their fault. How could it be? They didn't sneak out of the house at night and walk almost two miles to Skeeter's for her weekly supply. They didn't steal money from their own wallets or pawn off Mom's jewelry, including some of the heirloom treasures she'd hidden deep in her closet that Tina had no problem finding.

The day they confronted her about the missing money and other stuff was epic. It was the day Tina learned she could lie convincingly right to their faces. She lied and lied and continued to get away with it. Years later, she realized that her parents still knew but were in their own form of denial. Ahh, addiction. Fun times.

Tina rolled over in her cocoon and realized she didn't necessarily have to focus on her parents during tomorrow's speech. Maybe her focus could be about how she'd been able to stop using and how she'd managed to create a good life for herself.

Was it a good life, though? She pinched a roll of skin on her stomach and squeezed. The pain felt good. Distracting. She'd long ago decided that cutting, as attractive as that sounded, wasn't for her. There would be too much to explain. She pinched another section of her stomach. Tomorrow the bruises would be a good reminder. Of what? She was never quite sure, but seeing them always calmed her for some reason.

It wasn't all about her speech tomorrow, now, was it? Hopefully, Harriet would show up. She hadn't been to a lot of meetings recently, which made Tina worry. And Dana. She only got to see her at the joint AA and NA meetings once a month, even though they texted constantly and sent each other uplifting memes. Dana had suggested hanging out outside meeting times, but Tina wasn't ready to venture out like that. She wasn't grounded enough for Dana's flighty antics. Harriet wasn't flighty, but she was kind of unpredictable. Both had lovely souls, and both seemed a little lost. Just like Tina.

Ahh, but anyway, she'd get to the Friendship Church early as usual and clean out the coffee urns. People always said her coffee was the best they'd had at meetings, and she took pride in that. Clean urns and fresh mild-roast coffee, both regular and decaf, were the keys. Obviously, she'd set out the hot water urn with a selection of teas and hot chocolate. The pitcher of cold water would round it out. Yes, doing all of that would be enough to distract her from the spotlight that would be on her soon enough.

In her mind, she meticulously scrubbed one of the coffee urns. The rote and familiar activity, even though imaginary, helped calm her mind, and she fell asleep satisfied that something would go right the next day.

Chapter 3

Jaleesa

Jaleesa wasn't surprised to see over a dozen cars in Dominique's lot. The days after Christmas were still holidays, kind of. She locked her pickup and pulled her jacket tight against the cold midwestern winter. The studded leather jacket was meant more for style than actual warmth.

She stopped in her tracks. Shit, she had planned to go to Murph's first for a hefty dose of liquid courage. But she'd driven straight to Dominique's. Fine. Whatever. She'd go to Murph's after.

Anticipation squeezed her core as she made her way to the familiar entrance. There was no way she was going to sit alone and just watch. No way. She planned to be part of that crowd, enjoying herself. She'd prowl the rooms. She'd search. Maybe she'd find. She hadn't been to Dominique's since Gabby left seven months ago, and she almost felt like a stranger.

Yes, she'd search. She needed to find and feed on the energy Dominique's Dungeon usually offered. The hunt was on for the tug of a live woman on her hook, the landing of a new body in her bed. She needed a nameless woman who would submit to her. A woman who would give Jaleesa full control, who would cum at Jaleesa's command with Jaleesa's name on her lips.

As soon as she opened the outside door and stepped inside, that old familiar urge to stalk and pursue overcame her. She followed a white hetero couple into the entryway that funneled them to the front desk. She showed her ID, signed several non-disclosure and hold-harmless forms,

25

and paid for a six-month membership. Hers had run out while she was in forced sobriety. She waved off the coat-check nymph because Jaleesa's leather jacket was going to make a statement for her. Subs often fingered the steampunk rivets as if the hammered metal gave up her secrets or something. Or maybe it was a way to get into Jaleesa's space without getting too close. She took an overlong look at the nymph who wore skin-tight leggings and a low-cut blouse, her bare belly showing. It was good to see that Dominique hadn't changed that sexy detail.

The primary public area was named the "woodshed" and was a warehouse-sized room filled with small side tables and chairs and sectioned-off regions for impact sessions. Jaleesa was no stranger to those impact stations, the flogger being her favorite implement, of course. It could caress, or it could hurt. Sometimes in the same stroke. Harder impact with canes and switches was better at home without such a public audience.

She hesitated before going into the public room. What if Gabby was there? Stealing herself to her full six-foot-one-inch height, Jaleesa stepped through the doorway and allowed her eyes to adjust to the lower lighting. There were a few people here and there. Ahh, yes, a white guy was strapped to a St. Andrew's cross getting cropped by one of Dominique's hired Dommes. He was gagged. Excellent. Muffled screams were always more satisfying. Jaleesa recognized the working Domme from back in the day. Patrons didn't officially pay for these services but were strongly encouraged to tip and tip well. And most did. Those that didn't were politely refused service for the rest of the night and thereafter. Jaleesa had seen it happen to many a thirsty dude looking for free kicks.

Speaking of thirst, she should have stopped at Murph's first, damn it. Instead, she grabbed a small complimentary bottle of water and headed to the viewing area in the center of the communal space. She sat down in one of the leather club chairs with a grunt.

She'd hang out here for a while, and if companionship pickings were slim, she'd head down to Murph's on the corner. Murph's would have the

Jack Daniels she'd denied herself for a year because of that stupid judge. She hadn't even been that drunk when the cop pulled her over. Truly. She'd driven way more impaired than that before. Many times. That stupid cop probably saw the color of her skin, and… Nah, stop—no sense rehashing it. No need. Murph's would have the cure she needed. The cure for a new start and a new life. A life without Gabby.

The dude under the crop finally threw the red bandana on the ground—their agreed-upon signal to stop. The Domme released him from the cuffs, and then he fell to his knees in front of a woman sitting on the sidelines. The woman stroked his head and told him he'd been such a good boy taking all that pain for her. He seemed to eat up her attention and started crying. Apparently, he'd needed that physical release of pain, and his aftercare was well underway. It was a private moment, so Jaleesa looked away. Dawnn had introduced her to Dominique's Dungeon during their brief relationship in college over a decade and a half before. She had schooled her on proper BDSM etiquette. Oh, if Dawnn could see how far she'd come now.

Jaleesa hated when people used impact as punishment. Pain shouldn't be punishment. Pain should ultimately bring out feel-good sensations. It should cleanse stress and enhance bonds between partners.

The women she used to bring home before she became exclusive with Gabby were always surprised at how much aftercare Jaleesa was willing to give. There had even been that one older woman who didn't want sex. She wanted someone to give her controlled pain and then simply hold her for a while. That had been a new one on Jaleesa, but that was okay. It helped her understand that BDSM wasn't always about sex. It was also about connection and trust.

"Trust," Jaleesa murmured out loud. She and Gabby once had trust between them, like their first shared night exactly three years ago today. Jaleesa had finally walked over to that gorgeous younger woman after an hour or so of meaningful and suggestive glances. She couldn't remember the exact words exchanged the morning after that first night, but Gabby basically said she'd see Jaleesa "around." Whatever that meant. Ahh, buyer's remorse. Many women had it after an alcohol-fueled night of lust, especially the kind of lust Jaleesa offered. She had been disappointed but had to respect the woman's wishes. She still hadn't learned her name at that point. Not yet, anyway.

One week after her first encounter with Gabby, a new calendar year had begun, and they both happened to show up at Dominique's on the same night. That was when Jaleesa learned that the woman's name was Gabriella. It was a beautiful name, just like the woman, and Jaleesa made sure to tell her that.

They lasted through two drinks before Jaleesa invited Gabby back to her apartment for round two. Gabby agreed after a bit of egging on from her friends. Second dates didn't always happen in Jaleesa's world, but if there was chemistry, she'd go for it. And there had definitely been chemistry with Gabby. That second date led to a third, which became two years, three months, and fifteen days. And then Gabby decided it was done.

That second date had been hot, though. Gabby's wrists were cuffed to the futon over her head, and her ankles were cuffed and spread below. Jaleesa sensed that giving up control was new to Gabby, but she seemed willing to try. Over years of experience, Jaleesa knew not to rush. She ran her hands down Gabby's nude restrained body in an unhurried way. She avoided the ticklish spots she'd learned about the weekend before and spent more time on those places that made Gabby sigh or moan.

"Does it make you hot knowing I can do anything I want to you right now, Gabby?"

"Mm hmm," came the complacent reply.

Jaleesa massaged the soft flesh of Gabby's small breasts, chuckling when Gabby begged her to touch her now-erect nipples. She didn't. Gabby needed to learn who was in charge, didn't she? Jaleesa was in no rush to get to that final prize. She rather enjoyed making the women ache for it, ache for *her*. She skipped right past Gabby's wet and swollen flesh at the notch between her legs—a spot so obviously needing attention, and instead massaged Gabby's thighs and calves. Gripping Gabby's feet firmly so as not to tickle her, she massaged gently. Gabby's lolling head told Jaleesa that this was a woman who needed this type of touch, this type of pampering. Past lovers probably never took the time.

Jaleesa put down the foot she was holding and stood up. It was time. She grinned at Gabby. "You have choices." She went to her toy chest and bypassed the flogger and other implements of impact. Impact wasn't on the table for that evening. Third dates were typically the earliest for that sort of thing unless the woman was experienced. Gabby wasn't. Instead, Jaleesa pulled out a selection of strap-ons and brought them over for Gabby's approval. Gabby's eyes brightened at the sight, and she bit her bottom lip. She searched Jaleesa's face. For what, Jaleesa wasn't sure, but it seemed like she was gauging how far she wanted to go.

"You'll be okay, baby," Jaleesa said softly. "We won't do anything you don't want to do."

"Yeah?" Gabby took a deep breath and let it out slowly. The slight rise in her hips told Jaleesa all she needed to know.

With a slight nod, Gabby gave her approval and then selected the medium-sized strap-on. Wearing only tight black boxer briefs and a black tank, Jaleesa donned the apparatus and settled herself between Gabby's spread legs. Gabby's heavy breathing told Jaleesa all she needed to know.

Jaleesa pressed the length of the strap-on against Gabby's already wet and soaking center. Before entering, she slid the phallus up and down to coat it well with Gabby's increasing arousal. She may or may not have accidentally rubbed the phallus against Gabby's clit, causing Gabby to arch her pelvis even more.

"Look at me when I enter you," Jaleesa said. Her voice held just the right amount of authority.

"Yes, Ma'am." Gabby moaned as the tip pressed against her entrance, her eyes automatically shutting.

Jaleesa wanted her lover to be fully present. "Eyes open, Gabby."

Gabby complied but murmured, "Please, please, please." She groaned and arched her pelvis. She pulled against the restraints as if to force Jaleesa to enter her, but she had submitted, hadn't she? Submission got rewarded.

"I do love a woman that begs," Jaleesa teased, positioning her body over Gabby's. She pushed against nature's natural barrier and sank into Gabby nice and slow. Without reaching the hilt, she pulled out. Gabby's eyebrows furrowed slightly, probably worried that Jaleesa would tease her by pulling all the way out, but Jaleesa did not. She sank back in to the strap-on's full length.

"Yes, Ma'am. Yes, yes, yes," Gabby arched her pelvis and spread her legs wider, giving Jaleesa full access. Jaleesa kept a steady rhythm, only slowing when Gabby seemed ready to orgasm. Delaying was frustrating, she knew firsthand. Dawnn had done that to her. It had been quite a learning experience back then, but she'd also learned from Dawnn that she wasn't a bottom. No, she wanted to experience that same power her older teammate held over her both on and off the court. Their relationship didn't last much longer after Jaleesa's epiphany, but she drank in everything BDSM, and for that, Dawnn would always have a special place in her heart.

Jaleesa pushed in to the hilt and pressed firmly inside. Micro thrusts forced the tip against Gabby's cervix, which she seemed to enjoy, judging by her panting. The back end of the strap-on jammed against Jaleesa's very swollen and aching center. She shifted so her clit took most of the pressure. She felt the spark of orgasm ignite in her own body as she backed out and slammed into Gabby repeatedly. The shouts of ecstasy as Gabby orgasmed were a glorious accompaniment to her own. Jaleesa collapsed on top of her, spent.

"Fuck, baby," Jaleesa said as she struggled to push her one-hundred-eighty-pound frame off of Gabby. The last thing she wanted to do was hurt her.

Jaleesa allowed them the shortest of rests, but it wasn't long before Gabby was on her knees, ass in the air, taking Jaleesa's thrusts from behind. Gone were the restraints for this round. Gabby relaxed as Jaleesa got into a steady rhythm behind her.

"Don't cum until I tell you," Jaleesa commanded.

Gabby groaned her displeasure but knew enough by now not to protest.

Her clear acquiescence sparked Jaleesa's psyche, and her own orgasm spiked furiously. She thrust and came loudly. She was letting Gabby know that she was taking pleasure from her body but not allowing any in return. Jaleesa never stopped thrusting, and when she felt another climax upon her said, "Go! Cum for me, Gabby."

It wasn't exactly a simultaneous release, but Jaleesa's orgasm came within moments of Gabby's. The power she held over this woman, combined with the flood of released chemicals, made her hungry for more. But they needed rest. She guided them down on the bed gently, both of them breathing heavily. Jaleesa held her tight as they each trembled with expended lust. The phallus remained inside Gabby. This was a way for Jaleesa to show ownership, to show her dominance. They dozed this way for a while until Jaleesa woke and wanted to take Gabby again. The lion inside her had been unleashed. She woke Gabby with gentle thrusts from behind. Gabby moaned her acceptance.

Yes, there had been a lot of trust between them. Or so she thought, but Gabby left her out of the blue. She left without a discussion. A letter on the kitchen table. Really? A fucking Dear Jane letter?

Jaleesa stood up and changed chairs so she could watch an older white guy setting up to flog a younger, smaller submissive—a dark-skinned guy who looked to be of South Asian descent. India, maybe? The sub was clearly hungry for the sensations. Jaleesa glanced around. Everywhere she looked, there were pain junkies taking and power junkies giving. Is that why she was there? For the power? For the control?

What do I *need?* "I need a fucking drink, damn it!" Shit, she'd said that last part out loud.

"How's that?" a woman two chairs away asked. She looked to be at least a decade older than Jaleesa, with slightly graying dark hair. She might have been younger, but her face and body language betrayed a hard life or maybe just hard circumstances.

Jaleesa grunted. "Just muttering to myself."

"Mmm," the woman said and looked back at the flogging getting underway.

Jaleesa wondered what a woman like that was doing at Dominique's. "Do you think those two are a couple?"

The woman nodded. "Master Seamus has at least three, maybe four subs."

"I've never seen them here."

"You haven't been here in a long time," the woman said without looking at Jaleesa.

"Do I know you?"

The woman glanced over. "No."

"Then how do you know I haven't been here in a while?"

"You yield a good flogger."

"Have I ever—"

"No," the woman interrupted. "I used to watch you."

"Oh." Normally Jaleesa's ego would have inflated. Instead, she wondered who else had watched her drunk ass over the years.

"No worries," the woman said, obviously picking up on Jaleesa's discomfort. "You were good. Always good with them."

"I try to be."

"Would…" the woman shook her head and looked away. Her attention was drawn back to Master Seamus and his sub.

"What?"

"Never mind. I shouldn't have thought it." The woman didn't make eye contact.

Jaleesa was having none of it. "Look at me, please," she said in a dominant tone, one that typically got results.

When the woman turned to look Jaleesa in the eye, Jaleesa saw a need so raw that her heart clenched. "What do you need from me? I'm Jaleesa, by the way." She stuck out her hand.

The woman reached across the empty chair and shook Jaleesa's hand. "Harriet."

Jaleesa got up and sat next to Harriet. "What do you need?"

The woman sighed and then looked down. "The holidays are kind of hard, you know?"

"I do know."

"Do you think you could…I don't want sex. I just need…"

"Need to feel the leather tails of a flogger from someone you think you can trust?" Jaleesa kept her tone soft.

Harriet nodded, not making eye contact.

"Words, please," Jaleesa said.

"Yes, Ma'am. Would you honor me with a flogging?"

"Yes."

"You will?" Harriet's face lifted, and she smiled at Jaleesa.

"Yes, with one condition."

Harriet lifted her eyebrows but didn't say a word.

That was okay. This woman wasn't her sub. She wasn't Gabby. Anger flushed through her at the intrusion. She took a breath and said, "The one condition is that you allow me to give you aftercare." She pointed to Master Seamus, now holding his sub in his arms.

Harriet looked surprised but cleared her throat and nodded. Jaleesa raised an eyebrow, and the woman said, "Right. Words. Yes, Ma'am. I'll agree to aftercare. That's generous of you. Thank you. I can give you twenty dollars, but if you need more, I can—"

"No, no," Jaleesa said with a chuckle. "I don't work here. I'm happy to help."

Harriet nodded and then said, "Just let me know what I can do for you sometime."

"Helping you is enough."

They watched a member of Dominique's crew clean and sanitize the

St. Andrew's cross and all the equipment. Even equipment that hadn't been used.

"Shall we?" Jaleesa stood and beckoned the older woman toward the cross.

Harriet followed Jaleesa. Harriet took off her outer shirt and was left wearing a sleeveless tank top. They discussed particulars about safewords and places Jaleesa would and would not hit with the flogger. Jaleesa teased out of Harriet that she wanted more than a light flogging. She wanted to "feel" the pain. When Jaleesa offered the words "submit to the pain," Harriet nodded vigorously.

Jaleesa directed Harriet to put wrist and ankle cuffs on herself, but then Jaleesa took over and attached Harriet face first toward the cross.

"You will use your safewords if you need them," Jaleesa said as she trailed the tresses of the flogger over Harriet's shoulders, back, and butt.

"Yes, Ma'am," Harriet said without turning around.

"But I get the feeling you might be a bit non-verbal, so I want you to hold this red bandana and drop it if you need me to stop or slow down."

Harriet nodded but then burst out, "Yes, Ma'am," as if suddenly remembering that Jaleesa liked actual words.

As Harriet took the bandana, Jaleesa noticed her hands. They were strong and calloused and had a tiny smudge of what looked like paint on them. She definitely had a physical job of some sort. Of course, it was none of Jaleesa's business, but she wondered why this seemingly strong woman was at Dominique's two days after Christmas. And why was she by herself?

Jaleesa grunted. The same could be asked about her, she supposed.

"I'm going to touch you with my hands occasionally, Harriet," Jaleesa warned. "But not in a sexual way. I'll just be checking in and soothing your skin."

"I expected that, Ma'am." Harriet shook out her arms and body, apparently getting ready.

"Let us begin then." Jaleesa lightly flicked the strands over Harriet's back. She knew Harriet wanted it harder, but there had to be a buildup.

You had to have appetizers before the main course, didn't you?

Jaleesa made her way predictably down Harriet's back, across her buttocks, and over the back of her legs. She made good on her promise to avoid the kidneys and the back of the knees. Those areas were never meant to withstand impact. As she made her way back up Harriet's body, she changed her strokes to forward and then back, thus doubling the strokes in each section.

Harriet grunted—not in pain. No, it was more of a satisfied grunt that she was finally getting what she wanted.

"Your skin is pinking up nicely," Jaleesa said but didn't wait for a reply. Instead, she increased the intensity.

It was a natural human reaction to tense up at pain, and Harriet did at first, but then she blew out a sigh and humped her back as if inviting the pain from the flogger.

"That's it, Harriet. Take this pain. Use it." Jaleesa moved from side to side to relieve the ache in her wrists and fingers. She was out of shape. Not good.

A few bystanders had come by to watch. That was the nature of Dominique's dungeon. The woodshed was for public play, while the smaller rooms down the hall in the back were more private.

Jaleesa increased the power of her hits. Harriet yelled into the pain. Each strike elicited another outburst.

"That's my good girl," Jaleesa said, hitting Harriet again. "Let it out. Let it out."

Another yell was followed by a sudden sob.

"Five more," Jaleesa said with intensity. And then they were done. She tossed the flogger aside and gently pressed her hands on the fiery red skin, hoping to ease the pulsing pain she knew Harriet was experiencing.

Another sob emerged, and Jaleesa took the bandana out of Harriet's hand and threw it on the ground for her. She motioned silently for one of the dungeon masters to undo the ankle cuffs below while Jaleesa undid the wrists above. Harriet fell into Jaleesa's arms, a quivering mess. Jaleesa settled them both down on the padded bench and held the crying woman in her arms. She pulled her close in a Jaleesa cocoon.

Jaleesa was grateful when the DM moved the onlookers along, reassuring them that the Domme was experienced and that her sub was getting good aftercare.

Jaleesa rocked Harriet gently and murmured encouraging words. "You did so well." She stroked Harriet's sore skin gently. "You reached a good place. I'm really proud of you." Jaleesa suddenly teared up as she proudly took care of this woman, a stranger who was so obviously in need. "I am so proud," she whispered with a high tight voice as she struggled to get her own tears under control. She reached for the towel and then draped it over Harriet's shoulders. "You're a good girl, Harriet. A very good girl."

"I'm not, really," Harriet said into Jaleesa's shoulder.

"Shh, shh," Jaleesa hushed. "Let's catch our breath first."

Harriet acquiesced and nuzzled into Jaleesa's shoulder. Jaleesa rocked her serenely for a good five minutes before offering her the fresh bottled water the DM had put down next to them.

Harriet sat up to take the water and wiped at her tears. "Sorry for that." She wiped her forehead with the towel.

"I'm confused," Jaleesa said and sat back, giving Harriet her space. "You have nothing to be sorry about. Our session seemed pretty cathartic for you."

"Yeah." That was all Harriet said until she blurted, "I need a meeting. There's a mixed one at the Friendship Church tomorrow. NA and AA. Do you need one?"

"What do you mean?"

"You're sober now, aren't you? Earlier, you said you needed a drink, but maybe you need a meeting instead."

"Ahh," Jaleesa said. How could she tell this woman that her sober days were over? She wasn't a damn alcoholic. She'd done her time and played along with that stupid judge. She'd gone to the weekly meetings and gotten a sponsor—all of it. But what's done is done. "How did you know?"

She chuckled, not letting Harriet answer. "Never mind. The gossip mill, I suppose."

Harriet nodded as she took a deep, cleansing breath. "Thanks for helping me. I feel better. I might go back to those NA meetings on a regular basis. Maybe. We'll see."

Jaleesa's heart went out to this stranger. "Would it help if I said I'd go tomorrow? Meet you there?"

"Would you?" Harriet's face held so much hope that there was no way Jaleesa could turn her down.

"What time?"

"Six-thirty. Tina makes coffee. And she's the speaker tomorrow, too." Harriet looked down as if debating something. "I told her I'd go."

"Then you need to honor your commitment, don't you?"

Harriet nodded.

"And I'll be there, too," Jaleesa added. Fine. She could wait one more night to go to Murph's and have that drink. Someone needed her. And for once, it wasn't someone who wanted sex.

This would be the first meeting she'd gone to since a few months after Gabby left. As memories of Gabby niggled at her brain, she squashed each one, not allowing any of them to gain traction. Maybe it was finally time to accept the fact that Gabby wasn't coming back.

Chapter 4

Tina

Focusing on the coffee setup was wonderfully distracting because it kept the dark clouds at bay. This meeting couldn't start and end soon enough as far as Tina was concerned. "And this too shall pass," she muttered. She may or may not have been hiding out in the small kitchen off the large meeting room in the basement of the Friendship Church, but yeah, she kind of was. She poured the decaf from the decanter into the large urn. One more of those, and she'd carry the urn to the table just outside the kitchen and set it down next to the caffeinated one.

She hadn't seen Dana or Harriet yet, but it was still a bit early. Harriet tended to sneak in after the meetings started and then sneak out before they'd ended—if she came at all. It was a brilliant strategy to avoid socializing. Tina could never do that. She wouldn't want to disappoint Fran, the Narcotics Anonymous leader. Not only that, but Pastor Paul was here tonight, too, as the Alcoholics Anonymous leader, and he was a pastor at the very church whose kitchen she was not necessarily hiding in. Both of them relied on her to be their right-hand person at these mixed meetings. At this point, she'd been going to meetings at Pastor Paul's church for about ten years and knew the ins and outs so well that she could practically run the meetings herself. Not that she wanted to. Ever.

Ahh, the second decaf was done. She poured it into the urn and then picked it up. Ugh, she hated it when people congregated near the kitchen door. She headed out the door into the meeting room with her heavy load.

"Excuse me," Tina said, cursing the meekness in her voice. No one moved.

"Make room, people," an authoritative voice bellowed. People moved. Oh, to have such command. Tina wished she had that *something* in her voice that made people listen.

"Thank you," Tina said politely and looked up at the owner of the voice.

She gasped. Smiling back at her was a tall Black woman with flawless creamy brown skin and cheekbones to die for. Her eyes were bright and spoke of depths Tina had never witnessed before. Oh, her lips.

The woman cleared her throat and then chuckled. "Can I help you with that?" She didn't wait for an answer and easily relieved Tina of the heavy coffee urn. She set it down on the refreshment table in just the right spot.

"Thank—" Tina coughed to relieve the tightness in her throat. "Thank you." No other words formed in her brain as she took in this tall newcomer wearing black leather boots with pointed, kick-ass toes and black slacks that looked tailored to fit her strong, perfectly proportioned frame. The white V-neck button-down shirt, linen maybe, stopped just before her cleavage leaving everything to the imagination. That was tasteful. But it was the leather jacket with the silver studs artfully positioned on the shoulders that had her attention.

"No worries," the woman said. She reached out and put a hand on Tina's forearm. "Are you okay?"

"Hmm?" Tina took a breath and snapped out of whatever spell the tall stranger had put on her. "Yes, thank you. Fine." Oh, gosh. Was that even English? The woman's deep brown eyes kept trying to suck her in. *No, no, no. Don't smile at me like that.* "I have to—" She ripped her gaze away and headed back into the tiny kitchen. *Please don't follow me. Please don't.*

Tina's heart pounded in her ears, blocking all rational thought. Her forearm burned where the woman had touched her. Tina fussed in the kitchen until her heartbeat reached semi-normal levels. *Who was that?* her brain demanded. *She's never been here before.* Tina would have remembered. "You can't," Tina said out loud, grabbing the inside of her forearm. "There's no future in it." One good burning squeeze later had her semi-focused and ready to be her usual Pollyanna self.

She lifted her chin and headed back out. The refreshment area needed double-checking, didn't it? She poured herself a cup of water in case her throat got dry later. She scoffed out loud. Who was she kidding? It was one hundred percent going to happen as soon as her nerves woke up.

She closed her eyes, took one of her therapist's recommended deep breaths, and let it out slowly. Darn. Fran brought cake donuts again. She'd have to remind her that this mixed meeting crowd was more of a glazed and frosting crowd. Ah, well, it could keep until next month's mixed meeting. The donation box was set up, and Tina popped a dollar in the slot.

Bravely, she looked up. The tall woman had moved away from the kitchen door and was talking to Pastor Paul and Fran. It looked like she was introducing herself. Wow. It had taken Tina over four months to introduce herself to Fran and even longer than that to have a casual conversation with her. It must be nice to be so self-assured. Tina was self-assured in some parts of her life, like the bank. Maybe that's because she knew what she was doing there. And at home, too. But that was home, not out here in the wild with strangers.

Oh, there was Dana. Dana saw her and waved big.

"Cute," Tina mouthed across the room and gestured to Dana's hair. She'd worn her natural afro in two puffballs that evening.

Dana grinned, reached up, and patted them before making her way over. One hug later and Dana was yackety yacking about her week and this cute girl she'd seen at the flea market the other day. She'd been positive the girl was flirting with her.

"Slow down, Dana," Tina said with a laugh. "No rushing into things now." Dana was a sensitive soul, and at one time, Tina thought maybe Dana had a crush on her. Thankfully that seemed to have melded into a nice friendship. Tina wasn't girlfriend material, anyway, so nothing would have ever come of it. Tina was about five or six years older than Dana and found herself in more of a big sister role. She wagged a scolding finger at Dana like she'd done so many times before.

"Yes, Mom," Dana said with a laugh.

Tina chuckled and patted Dana on the arm. She was a petite Black girl in her mid-twenties who, like Tina, had discovered addiction early in life but seemed to be doing well for the most part. It did Tina's heart good to see a success story on such a sweet and vibrant girl.

They chatted for a few more minutes, and Tina was heart warmed when Dana wished her good luck and then asked Tina to say hello to her parents for her. They'd met at a non-closed mixed meeting a few years back and had sat together ever since.

A gentle clearing of a throat got her attention. "If you'll all find your seats, we'll get started in a minute," Fran said. Just like the tall stranger, Fran was another one who could get and keep people's attention. It must be something in their body language because, like the tall stranger, Fran also stood to her full height and had an ease about her that was magnetic. These types of people drew others toward them easily. Tina was okay not having that superpower. She didn't really want to associate with people. Seeing them at meetings was as far as she ever wanted to go. She had her routine that included work, home, Kroger once a week, and these meetings once or twice a week. Oh, and the three or four Ballet performances at the Center for the Arts every year. That was it, thank you. Everyone knows that routine brings peace, and routine brings calm.

Tina glanced at the refreshment station to make sure all was well there. When it was, she took a seat in the front row.

"May I sit here?" came a smooth-like-butter voice.

Tina's heart sped up. It was the tall woman—the stranger. But Tina's usual stranger-danger alarm was not going off. A different alarm was going off—the one that said, "Yes, please."

"Yes, yes, of course," Tina stammered. Yikes, how was she going to do her testimonial with Ms. Chiseled-cheekbones sitting right there?

Even sitting, the woman commanded the space around her. Magic. It must be magic. Her posture was tall and straight. Her head held high.

Fran fussed through her meeting book on the podium and patiently waited for the stragglers to be seated. Oh, yay, Harriet was there. Good. One less thing to worry about. Tina waved and threw her a big smile. Harriet nodded back and then did something weird. She nodded to Ms. Oozing-charisma sitting next to her. Tina wondered how they knew each other. Ahh, whatever. Probably a different meeting or something. It was a big world out there.

"Good evening, everyone," Fran said. "I'm Fran, and I'm an addict."

"Hi, Fran," came the automatic response.

"Welcome to our once-a-month mixed meeting of the Narcotics Anonymous and Alcoholics Anonymous groups. Pastor Paul and I created these joint ventures, no pun intended—" She had to wait while the group chuckled at her unintentional marijuana reference. "We created these mixed-group speaker meetings because, well, addiction is addiction, and we both felt that hearing recovery stories might benefit both groups. Something said tonight might resonate with you, and that's what we hope for."

Tina nodded and hoped that maybe she would say something good in her speech that would help at least one person. Ahh, there they were. Her nerves. She tapped her leg three times with her index finger. Tap, tap-tap. Her nerves were ramping up a little, but nothing she couldn't handle. It felt like the nerves she'd had before softball games in high school. She had this.

"Please join Pastor Paul and me in the Serenity Prayer," Fran said.

When Tina first started attending the meetings, she had to read the prayer off the giant cardboard poster hanging on the wall, but now she had it memorized. A peek out of the corner of her eye told her that the tall stranger beside her also knew it by heart. Hmm. Interesting.

Pastor Paul moved behind the podium and said, "I'm Pastor Paul of the Friendship Church, and I'm an alcoholic."

"Hi, Pastor Paul," the group said back.

"The Friendship Church is a non-denominational Christian church that is open to any and all. You don't have to be Christian to attend recovery meetings. The only requirement for membership is—" He held out his hands, expecting and receiving the group response. A mix of both "—a desire to stop drinking" and "—a desire to stop using" filled the space.

Pastor Paul's smile was electric. A true shepherd. "We are all here in God's love and His light." Tina listened politely as Pastor Paul went over the meeting's mission and the confidentiality expectations. "We also want to welcome any newcomers this evening, and after our speaker, we'll go around the room so you can introduce yourselves and tell us what brought you here this evening. But that is only if you choose to share. We'll pass the plate around during this time since our meetings are fully member-funded. We'll give out any milestone tokens at that time as well."

For some reason, Tina was calm. Too calm? The calm before the storm?

"And for once," Pastor Paul said, "I'm going to stop talking and let someone else have the podium. Tina has agreed to share her story with us tonight. We all know it takes great courage to admit you have an addiction and even greater courage to talk about it. So, as always, let's be kind and give Tina a nice welcome."

As the group clapped politely, Pastor Paul gestured for her to take the podium as he went to sit next to Fran.

Tina tapped her leg three times and stood up. She smoothed her dress pants, hoping they weren't too wrinkled since her mother had ironed her entire outfit for her while she was at work. She stood behind the small wooden podium. It was just a simple wooden pole with a base on the bottom, a tilted flat surface for notes on the top, and no place to hide. *Tap, tap-tap.*

Tina smiled. She surprised herself when it was a genuine smile. These people were here for support and kinship. Dana's bright smile flashed encouragement. Tina nodded at her in thanks.

"Hi, everybody," she said. "My name is Tina, and I am an addict." God, how she hated saying that.

"Hi, Tina," the group said back.

Tina gulped down the nerves that threatened to close her throat and tapped the podium again three times. "I am ten years, eleven months, and twenty-six days clean. A week after graduating from high school, I had all four wisdom teeth removed. The dentist wrote a pain prescription for oxycodone." Many heads nodded, including the woman sitting in front of her. *Yes, they all see where this is going.* "It was one prescription, but that's all it took to ruin my life." Even she heard the high tightness in her voice as emotion bubbled up to the surface. *Tap, tap-tap.*

She needed two cleansing breaths before she could continue. *God, give me strength. This is hard. Maybe I should have used note cards. Too late now.*

"Once the anesthesia wore off, my mouth hurt. Holy mother of all things good, my whole face hurt. My mother gave me the first pill, and the pain subsided. I felt better. Actually, I felt good. Really good. Not high, per se. Just peaceful. My mom gave me the oxy as prescribed for my pain. We did other things, too—cool cloths on my face, liquid foods, room temperature water. And here I am, twelve years and six months after that first pill…still recovering.

"Mom would ask if I needed a pill, and I always said yes, because I *did* need one. At first, it truly was for the pain, but after a while, it wasn't. I just liked how it made me feel. A doctor had prescribed them, so there was nothing wrong. Right? Wrong. Very wrong." More heads nodded, including the tall woman in the front row who was leaning slightly forward. She gave Tina a subtle nod as if to say, 'You're doing great. Keep going.' It was unexpected yet calming, nonetheless.

Tina continued. "After a while, one pill wasn't enough. I snuck extras. And then the bottle ran out. Neither of us realized what was happening to me, and when my mom called the dentist's office for a second prescription, they said no. Upon their recommendation, she gave me extra-strength acetaminophen. Yeah, they did nothing. I stopped taking them."

Tina cleared her throat. She looked in Harriet's direction. Harriet sat up taller and threw her a thumbs-up. "I didn't know it then, but I had begun going through withdrawal. I had chills. I was nauseous. When I got the shakes, my mother took me to our family doctor, who recommended an over-the-counter flu remedy. He said I probably caught the flu that had been going around. Well, as you can guess, that did nothing for the withdrawal symptoms. Another day passed, and I became, like, seriously depressed. My anxiety ratcheted up. I barely left my room.

"I had cravings like nothing I'd ever experienced before. They were bigger than me. They were ever-present. They were intense. No, intense is not a strong enough word. Uncontrollable? Overpowering? I'm not sure those capture what I was feeling." Tina ran her fingertips along the well-worn wood of the podium as she spoke. *Tap, tap-tap.*

"I did desperate things to get more pills. Without telling my parents, I made an appointment at a different dentist to try to get another prescription. I took out the car, lied to my parents about where I was going, and pulled into the parking lot. I never got out of the car, though. I couldn't do it. I thought they'd call my parents, and I couldn't have that. Sitting in that idling car, desperate for relief, I remembered a stoner kid at my high school. Rumor had it he was also a dealer. He was easy enough to find. He wasn't home when I drove by, but his mother said he'd be home later that evening.

"That very night, I snuck out of the house and walked almost two miles to his house. He ran his business out of a van parked on the street. I scored that very night. I think he felt sorry for me or something. I took a pill on the way home. No water. I just swallowed it. I only took the one to make sure he hadn't given me something ultra-weird. I still had a few ounces of rationality in me at that point.

"Sneaking out and going to Sk—." She stopped herself short before saying his name. "I mean, going to my dealer became a regular weekly thing. I drained my savings account. Okay, there wasn't much money in there, but I ran through it quickly. My parents never checked that account. Maybe they should have." *No, no, no. You can't blame them. They are not to blame.*

Heat flushed her face. *Tap, tap-tap.* "I needed money. My parents' wallets were easy pickings. I was conservative at first, only taking a little. They didn't even notice. But then I got bold, took more, and they stopped keeping cash in their wallets. Then there was the trip to Grandma's house. I scored big time. She had an old container of oxy in her medicine cabinet. That almost-full bottle came home in my pocket. And, to top that, I snagged over five hundred dollars hidden in her underwear drawer. I had zero remorse over it back then. But, you see, the money kept running out while my desperate need did not. I pawned Mom's jewelry. Even some heirloom stuff that we've never gotten back. Didn't feel terrible about that at the time. It got me cash, cash bought oxy, and oxy brought happiness. No, happiness isn't a strong enough word. Euphoria. That's what it brought me.

"I used to love going to the ballet. But I wasn't interested anymore. Not even the Nutcracker, my all-time favorite. My summer softball team? I didn't play, and I love softball. I didn't do much of anything except read books, play computer games, watch movies, and sleep. Even going to college wasn't important. I was supposed to go to Notre Dame that fall. I didn't."

Tina stood taller and tried to look at individual people like you're supposed to when giving a speech, but that just made her insecure. She fixed her gaze on the concrete wall behind Dana and her cute puffballs. "That euphoria wears off, though, doesn't it? My dealer told me to crush the pills and snort them. That worked well enough. At first. And then…and then there was the night I snuck out and went to his van even though I had no money. I thought maybe since I'd been such a good customer for the last six months, he'd front me some if I promised to pay him later. He was willing, but it would come with a price."

She blinked back the tears that had come from nowhere. Her chest tightened. Her throat closed. She couldn't continue. She splayed her hand against her chest, trying to keep the deep sorrow from washing over the others in the room. God, she just wanted to be free from this hell. Giving this testimonial was dredging it up for all to see. She'd wasted so much of her life on this addiction. She swallowed hard against her regret. Grief closed her throat as the tears came.

Through blurry eyes, Tina's gaze anchored on the tall woman in the front row. She blinked back tears so she could see more clearly. The woman caught her gaze and mimicked taking a deep breath. "Inhale," the woman mouthed. Tina did. The woman nodded, a smile crinkling her eyes. "Good. Again." And she mimicked breathing again. Tina did so and felt infinitely better. A small smile crept up her face, which the tall woman reciprocated. The woman's expression was warm and comforting. Tina nodded her thanks as the woman sat back, looking relieved.

Feeling strong enough to continue, Tina tapped three times on the podium and blew out a sigh. She said, "The price for deferring payment was to service him. Please, don't make me say it. You all know what I mean. When he pulled down the zipper of his jeans, I ran. I can still hear his laughter in my head. You would think that would have been enough to scare me straight, but when I took my very last pill on New Year's Eve, I remembered those horrible withdrawal symptoms. And so, I went back to him on New Year's Day, later that night, of course. I had money that I'd ironically gotten from Grandma for Christmas.

"My world was going to be alright once I got my supply. But guess what? He didn't have any oxy. He always had oxy. I didn't understand. He offered me something else. He said if I went easy on it, I could get that same high. You know what was going to be next on the Tina addiction parade? Heroin. He offered me her-o-in. Even wanted to give me a free sample. I didn't need to service him or anything, he'd said. Generous guy, right?"

She waited for the scoffs and groans to die out before continuing. "Do you know what I said to him? I said, 'no. No!' That moment right there was the beginning of me taking control of my life. The few brain cells I had left finally fired simultaneously and said, 'Enough! This isn't right. You don't want this.' Where that strength came from, I'll never know.

"I didn't exactly run home; it was more like I marched myself home. It was weird and hard to explain. All I knew was that I had gotten myself into a mess, and it had to stop." Quick glances at Dana, Harriet, and the tall stranger puffed Tina up with enough energy for the next part. A difficult part. Hell, all the parts were hard.

"I didn't trust myself to wait until morning, so I marched myself right up to my parents' bedroom and woke them up. In one giant stream of consciousness, I told them everything. I confessed absolutely everything— the cravings, withdrawals, deception. The lying, the stealing. All of it. They had to stop me several times to re-explain. Oh, the guilt they felt. There were a lot of hugs and reassurances that night. But!" She put a finger in the air for emphasis. "I had finally told the secret. My parents now understood why I wasn't going to college and why I had no desire to do anything. They said they thought I was depressed and hoped I'd snap out of it. I hadn't realized they were worried about me. When you're in the throes of addiction, you don't think about other people much, do you? At least I didn't. Not before that night, anyway.

"Somehow, I found the courage to ask for help. My biggest strength to this day still comes from the help I get from other people, even strangers at meetings—strangers who've become supportive friends." She looked back at Dana, who wore a sympathetic grin, and then over at Harriet, who had tears in her eyes. "I admitted my addiction to amazing people who understood my struggles." She looked at Fran and Pastor Paul for the first time since starting her unscripted tale. They returned her smile in kind. She looked back at the group. "If you don't have one, get yourself a sponsor. It is so important to have a sounding board like that.

"Lest ye think recovery is easy, let me tell you what happened next. I went to a live-in treatment center for over a month. I went through withdrawal there. I cried. I screamed. I cursed out the staff. I cursed the dentist and everyone in that office. I cursed the pharmacist who filled the prescription. I cursed the drug manufacturers who made it. I cursed the scientists, whoever they are, that came up with this heinous drug. It's not a medication. It's a drug and should be illegal."

She decided to save that rant for another day.

She softened her tone and said, "In rehab, I never cursed out my parents. I didn't even curse out myself. Cursing out myself came much later when the guilt and depression hit. I mean, my mom had to quit her job and stay home with me while I recovered. She eventually got a decent-paying job working from home, but I felt guilty every waking moment because she had to do that. And that they had to pay for the rehab place. I felt guilty for everything I'd put them through. Guilt became my new companion." *And is still here, unfortunately.*

"At the clinic, they started me on methadone, which eased the withdrawal symptoms, thank God. It eased my cravings and helped me feel somewhat *normal*." She made air quotes around the word normal. "But, seriously, what is normal anyway?" She paused while the group laughed and was secretly pleased that the tall stranger seemed to laugh most of all.

"But, yikes, that methadone messed up my sleep, especially at first. I was still on it when I was released from the facility. I had to go to methadone clinics after that. Have you ever been to one? I was eighteen. No, just turned nineteen at that point. I was so scared. Both parents came with me every Monday to get my week's dosage—every week for five whole years. We finally tapered off on the dosage at the five-year mark. That was a precarious time. It wasn't easy. The withdrawal symptoms came back. Lesser, but they were still there. Nothing about any of this has been easy."

She paused to take a big breath and, with as much gusto as she could muster, bellowed, "But I did it." She jumped when the group burst into applause as if they needed relief, too. She hadn't expected that. "I mean, I did relapse once. It's what we addicts do, right? Relapse?" Knowing chuckles and head nods filled the room. "About a year into being clean, I found one of my hidden stashes. I didn't think twice and snorted one. Then another the next day. But, but, but! I stopped once they ran out and got right back on the horse." She hung her head as the audience chuckled at her inadvertent reference to heroin. She smiled as she shook her head and said, "I am now clean and serene, and I think my biggest message to all of you today is that I didn't do it alone. Asking for help is monumentally difficult, but you need to. Addiction is stronger than any of us individually."

Tina was shocked to see the tall woman in the front row brushing away tears. That only spurred Tina on. She found herself directing her next comments to the woman in front. "You have to ask for help. You. Must. Get. Support." She tapped the podium in time with each word. The woman looked up at her. "Seek out help. The only way to recovery is to march head-on and through it. There's no dancing around it. You can get through it with others by your side, holding your metaphorical hand. And you all know the phrase. You can't take the elevator. You have to—" She nodded at their correct response and then repeated it, "You have to take the steps," and pointed to the sign on the side wall with all twelve steps written out in big, bold lettering.

The group clapped again, but this time she was ready. It wasn't easy, but she tore her gaze away from the emotional woman in front of her and smiled at the whole group. "I still live with anxiety, but I have strategies in place. Strategies I learned from getting help. And I have a bachelor's degree now. Go, honey badgers!" The group laughed again, and her heart swelled when she noticed the tall woman also laughing and kind of beaming at her. Not sure what to make of it, Tina said, "I have a good job and have earned two very nice promotions already."

She lifted her head higher. "As most of you know, recovery is not quick. It's not easy. Addiction is sly. It's tricky, confusing, and completely takes over your life. But with help, you can evict that addiction right out of your life. You may not realize it, but there is an army of people willing to fight for you. And they'll fight hard. You need to do the same. Fight for yourself, I mean. These meetings?" She tapped once for each of her next three words. "Keep. Coming. Back."

Tina let out a long sigh, ecstatic that she had reached the end of her sordid tale. Well, a sordid tale with a somewhat happy ending. "And that, my friends, is my ongoing, unfinished story." The group clapped, and Tina added, "Thanks for listening."

"Thank you, Tina," the group said automatically.

Pastor Paul made his way back up to the podium. Tina sat down next to the tall stranger.

"That was amazing," the tall woman said.

"Thank you," Tina answered perfunctorily without looking at the woman. She took what was supposed to be a deep breath but wasn't. She tried again unsuccessfully. Her hands began to shake.

"Oh, shoot, you're dropping," the woman said. "I'm going to hold you tightly to me. Just for comfort. Would that be okay?"

"Mmm," was all Tina could get out in affirmation and leaned into the woman whose arm was now pulling her close. Tina's body was pulled tight against the woman's warm leather jacket. She stiffened at first. She couldn't help it.

"It's okay, Tina," the woman said softly. "I have you. Just be." She paused and then repeated. "It's okay. You're safe. You're safe. I was very impressed with your story. That must have taken a lot of courage to tell your story like that."

Tina let herself relax a tiny bit as her head rested on the woman's chest near her shoulder. Tina's hands continued to shake, so the woman reached over and nestled both of Tina's hands into one of her own. *She has big hands. Big hands, warm heart.* Tina nuzzled into the warmth of the woman's jacket. It was nice. Safe. "Mmm," she murmured again, this time in comfort, and felt herself relaxing.

"Good, good," the woman murmured quietly as Pastor Paul asked the back row to start the introduction phase. "You're doing great, Tina." The big hand squeezed gently. That felt so good. Did the woman know that?

51

Tina's hands stopped shaking. "Thank you." She let herself be held for a few more moments and then sat up, feeling kind of awkward. The woman removed her arm and then released Tina's hands. Tina looked up into beautiful brown eyes that seemed to be searching her own for something.

Tina broke their connection when she heard Harriet's voice. "Harriet. Cocaine addiction. A year and eleven months clean." And that was it. Short and succinct, but that was Harriet. Tina waited for Harriet to look up again after the clapping subsided. Tina threw her a thumbs-up which garnered a smile and a blush.

Dana was also in the back row and, when her turn came, said, "Hi, I'm Dana, and I'm a raging alcoholic." She didn't get the laugh she'd been going for but continued anyway. "I am, let's see—" She counted on her fingers and then said, "I am a little over three years and seven months sober." Tina clapped along with the others and also threw Dana a thumbs-up which was returned.

The donation basket was making the rounds, and Tina was impressed when the comforting stranger tucked a twenty-dollar bill inside. Tina tossed her usual five in and then passed it along. When the introductions came to the front row, Tina said, "You all know way more about me than you probably care to know at this point." Polite chuckles followed her statement, and then it was time for the mystery woman to introduce herself.

"I'm Jaleesa. I..." The woman paused for a moment and then swallowed hard. "I'm an alcoholic." It was as if she was admitting it for the first time. Tina reached for the woman's hand in encouragement as the group said hello back to her. "I am currently eleven months and twenty-six days sober. If it weren't for a certain woman in the back of this room who encouraged me to come to this meeting tonight, I would be zero days sober. Thank you all for the boost." Words of encouragement flew about the room, along with enthusiastic clapping. Her nod toward Harriet was all Tina needed to know.

"That was brave, Jaleesa," Tina said. "Thank you for sharing that."

Jaleesa simply nodded. It was clear that she was still choked up. Epiphanies often do that to a person.

Tina turned her attention back to the front as Fran moved behind the podium. When she did so, she realized that her hand still covered Jaleesa's. She squeezed once and pulled away.

Fran took back the meeting and wrapped things up. She reminded both groups that since they were in the twelfth month of the year, they would discuss the twelfth tradition from the "Twelve and Twelve" book at their next respective meetings. She closed the meeting by giving out tokens for various milestones and then looked over the group with a twinkle in her eye. "This program works." Her smile grew wider as she opened her arms to the crowd. "Say it with me."

Tina joined the group as they said, "It works if you work it. So work it! You're worth it!" Jaleesa had apparently never heard that saying before and laughed politely at the group's enthusiasm. Fran told them to go back into the world with love and then invited them to stay for more casual conversations, refreshments, and "yummy" donuts. Ugh, she still had to talk to Fran about her donut selections.

Tina smiled politely at Jaleesa, thanked her again for her help, and then hightailed it for the kitchen. She may or may not have been hiding from the tall, good-looking stranger. She did, however, wonder how Harriet knew Jaleesa. What a pretty name. Ja-lee-sa. As Tina fussed in the kitchen, more questions than answers ran through her brain. She should really go out there and see how Harriet was doing. She headed toward the door and almost bumped into Jaleesa.

"You didn't have to run away from me," Jaleesa said, taking up the entire open doorway with her wide stance and both hands on either door jamb.

Oh, God, how did she know? Tina was about to defend herself when she looked up and saw the teasing twinkle in Jaleesa's eye. Tina wasn't sure why she did what she did next, but she fisted both hands, put them on her own hips, and said, "I'm not scared of you, you tall drink of water."

Jaleesa looked startled at Tina's response and then threw her head back and laughed a huge laugh straight from her belly.

Tina's grin matched Jaleesa's, and she laughed along with her. Heads turned in their direction, but she found she didn't care.

"I should go say hello to Harriet," Jaleesa said once they'd both recovered. "Will you be at the next mixed meeting?"

Tina nodded and then almost forgot to breathe when Jaleesa leaned down and whispered in her ear, "Mind if I bring the donuts next time?"

It was Tina's turn to guffaw out loud. "Please, yes. Please do."

"It was, uh…It was nice to meet you, Tina," Jaleesa said. "You're strong. Just remember that."

"Thank you." Tina felt herself blushing. "You are, too. It was nice meeting you. I'll see you next time, then."

Tina's blush deepened when Jaleesa smiled at her and then turned to walk out the open kitchen door.

Oh, no, Tina thought as she watched her go. *I'm in trouble.* A whole heaping big mess of trouble.

Chapter 5

Jaleesa

New Year's Eve at the salon was always busy, and it was also the sixth night of Kwanzaa, where families gathered to eat together and celebrate their shared heritage. And true to form, every appointment slot had been filled, including Jaleesa's. She only had to finish Miss Sonja and close the shop once everyone else was finished. Not that she had anywhere to go. Not that she'd been invited to anyone's Karamu feast since Gabby seemed to have gotten all the friends after the breakup.

Whatever. Jaleesa was just glad to have the distraction of work. She was one of three assistant managers at Miss Bessie's Salon, and she was the one who volunteered to do New Year's Eve. Of course, the assistant manager position didn't mean she had fewer clients. Nope. But that was okay. Jaleesa was used to pulling more than her weight.

She winked at the high school girl who had just swept up her station and returned with fresh, clean capes. It looked like the kid was also ready to be on her way. Hopefully, she wouldn't be heading to a party with drinking, and lord knew what else the younger generation was messing with these days.

"Miss Sonja is dry and ready for you, Miss Jaleesa," the kid said.

"Thanks, Cristal. Bring her over." Jaleesa took a deep breath. She would focus all her energy on Miss Sonja, of course, but all she wanted to do was think about the meeting. And Tina. Yes, she had to admit she mostly wanted to think about Tina.

"You look like a love-struck puppy, Jaleesa," Miss Sonja said with a laugh.

Jaleesa chuckled. "It shows, huh?"

"Mm hmm," the older woman said with a knowing nod. "I'll keep your secret, dear."

Jaleesa chuckled. "Ah, it's probably nothing. Just an interesting person I met this week." She patted the empty chair and draped a cape over her client once she was seated. She touched the older woman's salt-and-pepper hair to make sure it was dry enough and then sprayed a little Goddess Polish on it. "A little anti-frizz," Jaleesa said. "Makes it nice and shiny, too."

Jaleesa had already done the preliminary cut on the tapered look Miss Sonja was trying this go-around and insisted that Jaleesa was the only one she trusted to do it. That was a nice stroke for her ego, but she knew any of the other stylists would have done a fine job as well. Miss Sonja was going to a Kwanzaa feast that evening at her niece's home and wanted the new style for the party and a fresh start to the new year, which would begin in a few hours.

Jaleesa removed the ten or so rods and began the arduous process of unwinding the tight hair. As she worked, she asked Miss Sonja how her husband was doing and laughed when Miss Sonja scoffed and said he was "organizing the garage" again. It was clear to Jaleesa that Miss Sonja suspected her husband was doing something altogether different than "organizing" out there, but Jaleesa simply quipped about him needing a man cave.

Jaleesa loved this part of her job. Talking with people. Getting to know them. Being a small part of their lives. Some weren't as outgoing as Miss Sonja, but Jaleesa still valued every interaction and tried to make every person feel seen, even if they didn't appreciate her efforts to make them feel good. Kind of like Gabby, huh?

As she undid the rope twists, her thoughts strayed. Tina had looked directly at her and said, 'You have to get help.' No, no, no, she'd said you must 'ask for help.' That was hard for super-self-assured Jaleesa. She was the one in charge. She was the one who had it all together and helped *other* people. Like Gabby. Like Harriet. And in a small way, Tina. Small, lost Tina. No, it was not the other way around. She was *not* the one who asked for help.

A burst of laughter from the reception area brought Jaleesa back to the present. She smiled at Miss Sonja in the mirror and then sprinkled some mask powder to cover the thinning spots between her parts. Then she took a few moments to pull the bigger hair clumps apart to fill things out.

"Doing okay?" Jaleesa asked. Miss Sonja nodded. "Good." Jaleesa used a pick to fluff the hair from the bottom up, covering the thin spots. A little fine-tuning with the sponge brush to enhance those naturally tight curls and then a quick edge cut with the electric trimmer to even things out all around. A quick snip-snip of those straggly sprigs and then a spritz of shine and Miss Sonja was finished. Just about.

"Shake your head, please," Jaleesa instructed. Ahh, a few more stragglers. A quick snip snip, and now she was done.

"Thank you, dear."

"I'm glad you finally let me do the tapered cut," Jaleesa said. She put both hands on Miss Sonja's shoulders and looked at her in the mirror. "When your husband sees you, maybe he won't spend so much time in the garage."

Miss Sonja burst out laughing. "Your words to God's ears, sister." Heads turned in the direction of their mirth.

"Looking good, Miss Sonja," Cristal called from across the shop.

"Thank you," Miss Sonja said to Cristal. She stood up from the chair and patted her new doo. She turned and handed Jaleesa a folded-up bill. "Take your new girl somewhere special."

"I don't have a new—"

"Uh uh. No, no," Miss Sonja scolded as she shrugged on her winter coat. "Think positively. Keep your heart open. You're a good person, Jaleesa. I think it's about time the universe gave you what you needed."

Jaleesa waved her hand, holding the bill in salute. "Thank you, Miss Sonja." She cleared the sudden emotion that had snuck into her throat and said, "Have fun with your Grands. I want pictures next time. Okay?"

"Yes, yes, my dear. Happy new year and Happy Kwanzaa." She patted Jaleesa on the arm and headed up front to pay.

Jaleesa turned to clean up her station. *Keep my heart open?* She scoffed out loud. The last time she'd opened her heart, Gabby wrapped herself around it and then stomped the ever-loving life right out of it.

Jaleesa locked up after the last stylist left the shop and had an entire night ahead of her. Once upon a time, she and Gabby would either be heading to their next big party or hosting one themselves in their apartment. But that had been a long time ago.

She got in her pickup and headed back to the apartment. Once inside, she threw a frozen meal in the microwave and changed into sweats. She was amazed that her Blackwell College basketball sweats still fit her. Maybe she'd go for a workout tomorrow. That might loosen up her sore and aching joints that reminded her at age thirty-eight that she wasn't a spring chicken anymore. One of the perks of being the captain of a Midwest League championship team her senior year was getting free admission to the college's fitness center for life. Reason enough to still live near the college. Her joints would either thank her or curse her tomorrow.

"Joints," she said with a laugh as she plopped on the couch with her meal. She hit up Netflix and remembered the NA leader's slip at the last meeting. Tina had also slipped when she'd said, "horse." Everyone had chuckled good-naturedly, but the clear embarrassment tinging Tina's cheeks made Jaleesa's heart go out to her. And then when Tina called her a "tall drink of water" at the end of the night, that was too funny.

"It's like I know you from somewhere, Tina," Jaleesa said to the chilly air in her apartment. "But I don't." She should get up and adjust the heat but was too tired. And her knees ached. She found her favorite vampire drama and hit play to start the next episode, but her mind couldn't stay focused on the drama. Her thoughts kept wandering back to the short white woman who had given a very vulnerable and personal speech. She was maybe, what, late twenties? Early thirties? White girls' ages were hard to gauge sometimes. Wait, wait. She'd mentioned something about twelve years after high school. That made her at least thirty.

And then there was Harriet. She'd never seen Harriet before the night she'd flogged her, not that she remembered anyway, but she felt like a kindred spirit.

"Open your heart," Jaleesa said with a groan. "Ugh, Miss Sonja, why did you have to say that to me?" Jaleesa had been fine by herself without Gabby, living quietly, living sober, and …

"And what? What are you doing with your life, Jaleesa Whitmore?" Jaleesa demanded of herself. She swirled the last of the chicken cacciatore around in the mystery sauce and stuffed it in her face. She tossed the plastic tray on the side table and reached for the water bottle with the honey badger's mascot on the side. That was another perk of being on the championship team—more swag than she knew what to do with.

Jaleesa stared at the mascot. "This was a lifetime ago, wasn't it?" She counted back the years. "Whoa. Sixteen friggin' years since I graduated." Her parents, her father especially, had been so disappointed when she decided not to use her Psychology Bachelor's degree in counseling and instead wanted to do hair. Jaleesa kept insisting the hair gig was temporary and that she was seeking a counseling job. She wasn't. She was more interested in partying and sampling the finely wrapped morsels down at Dominique's Dungeon than looking for a real job. Not that doing hair wasn't a real job. It was. And Miss Bessie had even given her that small promotion, even though it didn't really pay much.

Jaleesa had taken her parents' concerns to heart, though, and actually went as far as to take classes to become an ordained minister. She knew back then that it wasn't a career move, but it had placated her parents, *and* she'd officiated a few weddings. Her official signature was on over a half-dozen marriage certificates. She was proud of that. But that was back in the day, right out of college. She didn't even know where those people were any more or where any of her college friends were, either.

Drinking did that, didn't it? *Getting soused was always more important than...* "everything," Jaleesa finished out loud. She muted the television. The fight scene was jarring her nerves.

"'Ask for help,'" Jaleesa quoted Tina. A melancholy sadness gripped her chest. She wiped at the stupid tears in her eyes and whispered in a shaky voice, "I don't know how."

~~~

Three days later, Jaleesa hit up the side door to the church—it was always a side door, wasn't it—and made her way down the steps to the basement meeting space. This was an AA meeting, so there was no chance of seeing either Tina or Harriet. Good. She needed to regroup. Musing over the pull she'd felt toward both women, Jaleesa thought maybe God was guiding her toward … something. She reasoned He was guiding her back to these meetings. That was probably all. Like she'd told herself a thousand times since Miss Sonja's advice to open her heart, she would do it. But she needed grounding first.

She stepped into the meeting space and noticed a nice crowd. The young Black girl whose name she'd forgotten was there still sporting the puff balls. Jaleesa stopped herself from thinking how she would do the girl's hair because the puff ball thing wasn't quite right for the mid-twenty-something girl. And thinking about her as a 'girl' was wrong, too. She was a grown-up woman.

"Too much thinking," she muttered out loud and headed over to greet Pastor Paul. After doing so, normally, she would have made her way around the room like the mayor greeting her constituents. Not tonight. She wasn't in the mood. Regrouping. That was her mood.

She grabbed a hot coffee from the urn, tucked a buck inside the box, and headed for the same seat she'd occupied at the last meeting.

Just as Pastor Paul announced that the meeting would soon begin, there was a slight commotion in the back of the room. Jaleesa followed Pastor Paul's glance. Her heart swelled. It was Tina. She and Dana were greeting each other noisily. Tina looked up, maybe sensing Jaleesa's gaze on her, and waved big. Jaleesa smiled and waved back. Tina sat down next to Dana. Was she Dana's sponsor or something? No, that didn't make sense because Dana was AA, and Tina was NA. Maybe they were friends. It was a big world, wasn't it?

Most AA meetings she'd been to had the same basic format, but this one was different somehow. Maybe it was Pastor Paul. He wasn't in a rush. The first month of meetings she'd ever gone to at the rec center—you know, the ones required by the judge—were rushed and rote and not worth much at all. As Pastor Paul spoke about the twelve steps, Jaleesa realized she hadn't been ready to receive the messages behind the steps back then. She'd been angry and somehow wronged by the system. She'd blamed the judge that had sent her to those meetings. But sitting there at the meeting, she was slowly understanding something. She hadn't been ready to admit she was an alcoholic. Not then, anyway. She just liked to have fun, she'd reasoned. She wasn't an alcoholic. She liked to be the life of the party and, as Gabby accused in her letter, the center of attention. Was that true? She looked down, her brow furrowed.

She mused about her partying days and questioned everything. And before she knew it, it was time for discussion and introductions. They didn't go around the room this time, but everyone was encouraged to speak as they saw fit. Jaleesa didn't contribute. She had too much to think about.

And then, it was time to hand out the milestone tokens for sobriety. One brave Asian man who looked barely in his twenties got a twenty-four-hour first-meeting white chip. Was he court-ordered to be there, like she had been once upon a time? She couldn't tell. He looked kind of dazed. That's probably how she'd looked at the beginning, too. She was so angry at her first meeting, deep in the throes of alcohol withdrawal, that she'd taken the white chip she was handed as a symbol for starting her journey of sobriety. Way back in February, they'd given her another chip—the one-month chip, only because the leader knew it was one month for her and insisted. Both chips currently lay dormant somewhere in one of her dresser drawers.

Pastor Paul looked right at her and said, "Anyone celebrating one year of sobriety?"

Jaleesa stood up and received the weighty metal token. Wow, she thought, this place is truly special. The cheers and clapping touched her soul. This group understood. They meant their encouragement. Jaleesa couldn't meet anyone's eye. She simply sat back down, and Pastor Paul led them in prayer and ended the meeting.

When the group stood up after the meeting, Jaleesa made a bee-line for Pastor Paul, thanked him for the token, and purchased the AA Big Book. She'd seen them before at meetings but had always waved them off. Maybe it was time to get serious about this.

"Oh, that's a good one," the young Black woman with the juvenile hairdo said. She was pointing to the book.

"Oh, yeah," Jaleesa said. She wasn't typically at a loss for words, but for some reason, she wasn't feeling strong that evening.

"Good to see you back," Tina said.

Both of these women are so short, Jaleesa thought randomly. "Uh, yes, yes," she stammered. God, what was wrong with her tonight? She cleared her throat. "What are you doing here this evening?" She directed that to Tina.

"Supporting my friends," Tina said.

"Mm hmm," the young Black woman said, linking her arm around Tina's.

Oh, maybe they were in a relationship. *Not everyone is a lesbian, Jaleesa*, she chided herself silently. "Better selection of donuts tonight, I see," Jaleesa said, pointing to the line forming for the sweet treats. She knew she was deflecting, but she had to. She was feeling all kinds of vulnerable.

"Yeah," Tina said. She leaned in and whispered, "Pastor Paul does a much better job."

Jaleesa held up her still half-full coffee cup. "This, not as good."

Tina leaned in even closer, and Jaleesa smelled Tina's freshly showered scent. It was comforting for some reason. "Mario uses the old coffee. And he doesn't clean the urns." She shook her head, but Jaleesa could see she wasn't seriously judging whoever this Mario guy was.

"That was a great speech the other night," Jaleesa complimented.

"Wasn't she so good?" the young Black woman said. "Oh, my God. I was so proud of her. I've never given a speech like that. I can't even imagine."

"Oh, gosh. Have you met Dana?" Tina asked.

"No, it's nice to meet you, Dana," Jaleesa said. "I'm Jaleesa."

"Oh, believe me. I know who you are," Dana said with a smirk and then shot a glance at Tina. She pointed at Jaleesa and said, "Congrats on making it one year. That is super awesome." Before Jaleesa could respond, Dana said, "Okay, I'm going to talk to..." she surveyed the room and then blurted, "Kadesha. Bye-ee." Again, without waiting for a reply, she skipped away. "I'll text you tomorrow, Tina," she called over her shoulder and then linked arms with a woman on the other side of the room.

"She's full of energy," Tina said with a laugh.

"I see that."

"Seriously, though. Congratulations on the one-year token. That is quite an achievement."

All Jaleesa could do was nod.

Tina spoke again, possibly picking up on Jaleesa's discomfort. "Um, I also came here tonight hoping to find you."

"Me?"

"Yes, I wanted to thank you again for, uh, comforting me during and after my speech the other night," Tina said. "I don't know why I was so shaky afterward, and if you hadn't been so kind, I might have made a fool out of myself."

"Just lucky timing on my part, I guess."

"And I also wanted to give you this," Tina blurted, handing Jaleesa a red boutique bag with white handles. "Go on. Take it out."

Jaleesa pulled out the softest, most exquisite scarf she'd ever seen. "This is gorgeous, Tina. Thank you. But you didn't have to buy me—"

"I made it."

Jaleesa was stunned. No words would come. She'd made it?

"It's cashmere," Tina said. She wasn't bragging, just stating a fact. "This jacket doesn't look very warm, so I thought you could use a scarf. It's so soft, isn't it? And I thought red would look good, but now I see that any color would look good on you."

Jaleesa pressed her lips together as she tried to get her emotions under control. "What a kind thing to do," she finally said after too long. She heard the emotion sneak out on the last word and swallowed hard.

A small hand pressed against the leather of her jacket sleeve. "You may not understand what an amazing thing you did for me. I don't let people in, but there I was, being held by you in the crook of your arm, getting comfort. Dana has been teasing me to no end about it."

Jaleesa laughed, glad for a break in the intensity.

"I'm honored to accept your gift, Tina. Thank you."

"You're welcome." Tina stepped back and said, "Well, I should go home now."

"It was nice seeing you," Jaleesa said and put the scarf around her neck. Ooh, it really was soft. And warm.

"You, too."

Tina turned to go, and Jaleesa panicked. "Tina!"

She turned back around. "Yeah?"

"Can I…uh, can I take you to lunch sometime? Or out for coffee?"

Tina glanced to the side as if panicked.

"No, it's fine," Jaleesa said, backtracking. "It's okay. I'll see you at the next—"

"Yes, you can," Tina said. "But you need to come to my house.

Sunday. I don't go out places."

"Sunday? That's fine."

"I cook Sunday dinner while my parents are at church. That okay?"

"Parents?" Jaleesa said, a grin spreading on her face. "Parents are fine with me."

Tina relaxed a moment but then said, "Oh, shoot. I can't. It's rug-cleaning day. Dad gets the equipment Saturday night, and I do the carpets while they're at church. It's kind of my way of giving back to them."

"I love rug cleaning," Jaleesa teased. "It's one of my all-time favorite things to do."

"It is?" Tina looked momentarily confused and then smacked Jaleesa on the sleeve. "Oh, you're teasing me."

"Seriously, I'd love to help." Jaleesa wasn't sure why she did what she did next, but she raised both arms and made her biceps tight. Not that you could see them under the jacket. "I'm pretty strong."

The look of longing on Tina's face went straight to Jaleesa's core.

"Is that a yes, then?" Jaleesa asked quietly.

"Mm hmm," Tina said. It seemed to be all she could get out.

They exchanged phone numbers, and Tina said she would text the address to her on Saturday.

"May I text you before then?" Jaleesa asked. Consent was always paramount in her mind.

Tina narrowed her eyes, and a mischievous smile crept up her face. "Yes. But just remember that my parents still check my phone on occasion."

"Noted."

"I'm gonna…" Tina pointed toward the door leading to the parking lot. "I'm gonna go now."

Jaleesa nodded, pulled out her phone, and sent a text.

JALEESA: Drive carefully.

Tina grinned back at Jaleesa when she heard the ding of a text go off on the phone in her back pocket. She headed out the door, and as soon as she was out of sight, Jaleesa's phone dinged an incoming text.

TINA: Always do.

Jaleesa picked up the Big Book, tossed her cold coffee remnants, and headed out the same door Tina had gone through.

Chapter 6

Tina

The knock on Tina's open office door made her jump. "You okay?" Nancy asked. "You've been kind of distracted all week."

"Fine. I'm fine," Tina said, knowing the head teller could see her face blushing red. Daydreaming about a certain tall drink of water could do that to a girl. That certain tall stranger was coming over on Sunday. Tina tapped her desk three times.

"Thank God it's not only Friday but quittin' time to boot. Am I right?" Nancy said.

"Absolutely," Tina agreed. "This has been an extraordinarily long week." She rolled her eyes. "If you want, I'll do the final counts after I lock up."

"Oh, would you? Donny has a basketball game tonight, and I need to shove food down the twins' throats." Nancy patted her chest twice, sending Tina love. "You know that's not why I came in here, right?"

"No worries," Tina said. Nancy was a not-quite-middle-aged woman with a husband and family on top of a full-time job. It was the least Tina could do to help.

Nancy leaned in and whispered, "Too bad Mr. Charm-and-Personality isn't here to do his job."

Tina groaned. "Remember the totally undeserved 'you can do better speech' he gave you on Monday?"

"Mm hmm."

"I got that one today."

"No way," Nancy scoffed. "You? This branch would have been closed long ago if it wasn't for you."

"I don't know about that, but thanks for the compliment. It's a team effort, for sure." She stood up. "I'll lock up and wait for that last customer to clear out."

"You're a Godsend, Tina."

Yeah, she wasn't sure about that either, but it was nice to be appreciated at the bank for once.

~~~

It was Sunday morning. The day had finally arrived. How Tina had been able to sleep was beyond her—maybe from anticipation exhaustion. She paced the kitchen with her second cup of coffee. The slow cooker was already purring away with the pot roast, Yukon potatoes, onions, carrots, and some beef broth. No wine. Not that there was any in the house, anyway. Later, when her parents returned from church, she'd pop some crescent rolls in the oven and call it dinner. Dessert was a pound cake she'd made on Saturday after her Zoom meeting with the Eastside Cincinnati Newcomers Group. It was an entirely online group she'd been attending since she was a newbie all those years ago. Her sponsor recommended the online meeting when she was afraid to leave the house and asked Tina to stay on as one of the moderators. She liked helping out the newbies. She liked instilling hope in them as they interacted with her. She was living proof that staying clean could be done. And tonight, her other group—the Greater Cincinnati Women's Online Group—was celebrating a big anniversary for one of their members. The leader of the group, in fact. All the members had secretly agreed to have a piece of cake or something to hold up as they sang Happy Anniversary to Josie for thirty-three years clean.

"Thirty-three years," Tina said out loud. "Oh, my God."

"Josie's anniversary tonight?" Tina's mom asked and poured herself a cup of coffee.

"Yes," Tina said and hugged her mother like she did every morning. "She's been clean longer than I've been alive, Mom."

"Quite a milestone," Tina's dad said, stumbling to the coffee pot.

"Easy on the sugar," Tina and her mother said simultaneously. The two women burst out laughing.

"That's too much pressure on your old man, TJ."

"You're not old, Dad."

"Feels like it somedays."

Tina raised one eyebrow and looked him right in the eye. "More exercise. Fewer potato chips."

"Yes, Ma'am," he said good-naturedly. "We'll go for our evening walks again when it warms up."

"I'd love that, Dad." Tina hugged him. She turned away but called over her shoulder. "Easy on that sugar."

"You have eyes in the back of your head, kid."

Tina laughed evilly and sat down in her usual spot when her mother patted the kitchen table. Tina took another sip of the medium roast breakfast blend the family had compromised on for mornings.

"When is your new friend coming over?" her mother asked. Her tone was all business. Tina would have expected nothing less.

"Nine," Tina said succinctly.

"So, we'll get to meet her before Dad and I head off to church." It wasn't a question.

"She's clean, Mom."

"I know. I know. You said." Her mother forced a smile and sighed. "It's just…"

Tina's father came to the rescue. "It's just that we haven't heard you talk much about Jaleesa before. She seems to have suddenly appeared in our daughter's life, and we're…."

"Wary," Tina's mother finished.

"As you should be," Tina said. "As *I* should be. She knows Harriet somehow, and Harriet doesn't let many people in, as you know."

Both her parents nodded. They'd met Harriet at a few open meetings and saw firsthand how closed-lipped and reticent she was. But they'd seen enough of Harriet and Dana to understand that they were good people.

"At our Nar-Anon meetings," Tina's mother continued, "they warn us about sudden new friends. That's where our concerns are coming from."

Tina nodded as she sipped her cooling coffee. "I see." She sighed and tapped the table. "I get a good feeling about her, Mom. I told you how she helped me last week during and after my speech."

Tina's father looked at her mother as he nodded in acquiescence. "Fair point."

"And the texts between you seem tame enough," her mother said. "No hidden messages or meanings."

Tina shook her head. *No,* Tina thought, *just a little bit of covert flirting.* Had they caught on to that? She hoped not. That would be *tres* embarrassing.

"I'll be okay, Mom. Please don't worry." Tina stood up. "Now, if you don't mind, I need to get ready."

"We love you, TJ," her father said. "You know that, right?"

"Yeah, Dad." Tina smiled back at her parents. "I do know that. I thank you silently every day for your continued love and support." Tears welled in her eyes as she headed up the stairs to her bedroom.

"Something's coming, Mother," Tina's father said quietly, but not quietly enough.

An hour or so later, the doorbell rang precisely seven minutes after nine. Tina ran down the stairs to get the door before her parents could and stopped for a moment to catch her breath. She took a quick look through the peephole and saw that gorgeous face on the other side. She loved Jaleesa's hair. An afro, but not an afro. It made Jaleesa look so cool and free. Oh, look, she was wearing the scarf Tina had knitted for her.

Tina whipped the door open and said, "You made it."

"Hey," Jaleesa said. "Yeah. Sorry, I'm a few minutes late. I had to find a good place to park. This is some icy hill you live on."

"Yeah, sorry about that." Tina moved to the side to let Jaleesa in. Neither of them moved in for a hug which was just as well because both of her parents were watching from the kitchen doorway. "And our driveway's packed with our cars." She gestured to herself and then to her parents to acknowledge that she knew they were there. "Let me take your coat."

Jaleesa unwound the scarf and, as she handed it to Tina, said, "This thing is so warm. Thanks again for thinking of me."

Tina felt her face flush at the acknowledgment. She couldn't trust her voice, so she simply nodded and hung up the fabulous, studded leather jacket on top of the scarf.

"No way," Tina gushed when she took in Jaleesa's long-sleeved t-shirt. "Honey Badgers basketball? Did you go to Blackwell College, too?"

Jaleesa nodded as a mischievous grin crept up her face.

"Wait, so when I said that at the meeting the other night, you knew we'd both gone to the same college?"

Jaleesa laughed, and the sound was so nice. "Yes. I figured I'd bring it up at some point today." Jaleesa cleared her throat and said, "I assume these humans are your parents?"

"Oh, gosh," Tina stammered. "Yes, yes." She stepped back and gestured to Jaleesa and then to her mother. "This is my mom, Marion Jenkins. Mom, this is Jaleesa." Shoot, she didn't know Jaleesa's last name yet. They weren't supposed to share last names at NA or AA. You know, the whole *anonymous* thing?

"Thank you for helping Tina with the carpets this morning," Tina's mother said.

Hmm, Tina thought. *That was kind of rude, Mom. You didn't say, 'Nice to meet you' or 'Tina told us a lot about you.'* Tina's radar was on alert. Did her mother not understand that Tina hoped Jaleesa would become more than just an acquaintance? That maybe Jaleesa would be her first real friend besides Dana in over twelve years?

"I'm happy to help," Jaleesa said with an easy smile.

"And this is my dad," Tina said.

"Nice to meet—"

"There's no alcohol in this house," Tina's mother blurted.

"Mom!" "Marion!" Tina and her father said at the same time.

Not taking her eyes off Jaleesa, Tina's mother said, "I just want that to be clear."

"I'm sober, Mrs. Jenkins," Jaleesa said calmly. Almost too calmly.

"A full year, Mom," Tina said, trying to keep the anger out of her voice, knowing she hadn't been successful. Her whole body tensed, and she hoped Jaleesa wouldn't turn around and walk out the door and out of her life. All because her mother had to be overprotective. "She got her one-year token on Monday."

Jaleesa waited a beat as she held Tina's mother's gaze and then pulled the token out of her pocket. She flipped it end over end in the air, caught it deftly, and pocketed it, all without saying a word. And all without breaking eye contact. Talk about smooth.

"Well, it's nice to meet one of Tina's friends, Jaleesa," Tina's dad said and reached over to shake hands. "TJ has spoken quite highly of you."

"Thank you," Jaleesa said. It was a genuine thank you, too, with a genuine smile and all. Her tone didn't suggest that at least one person in this house had manners. No, Jaleesa seemed to be taking her mother's brash boldness in stride. That was amazing.

"Marion," Tina's father said, "let's go upstairs and finish getting ready for church."

"Mm hmm," Tina's mother said. Her tone, however, suggested she wasn't happy about this stranger in her house and that she had her eye on her.

As soon as her parents made their way upstairs, Jaleesa turned to Tina and said, "TJ?"

Tina shrugged, grateful that Jaleesa didn't seem put off by her mother's aggressiveness. Or at least she wasn't showing it. "My dad likes to call everybody by their initials. Tina Jenkins. TJ."

"Got it," Jaleesa said with a chuckle.

Most of the tension in Tina's body dissolved at Jaleesa's smile. "Would you like some coffee?"

"Absolutely."

Jaleesa followed Tina into the kitchen. "My parents hate this coffee, but I think you'll like it. It's called Cool Café Blues. She handed Jaleesa the foil bag.

"Caramel, maple, pecans, and cinnamon," Jaleesa read. "Sounds interesting." Her tone was cautious.

"Ahh, a disbeliever," Tina said, taking back the bag. "Just wait. The flavors are subtle." She gestured for Jaleesa to sit at the table in the fourth unused seat and set about making the fresh pot. "How do you like your coffee?"

"Black, like my—" Jaleesa groaned. "Sorry. Habit." She looked down, and Tina noticed Jaleesa's cheeks getting a tiny bit darker.

Tina whispered, "What were you going to say?"

"Oh, nothing," Jaleesa singsonged. She clamped her lips shut, twisted an imaginary key over them, and tossed it over her shoulder.

Tina caught the imaginary object and held it up. Jaleesa's eyebrows raised up as if giving Tina the power. Tina grinned and tucked the key in her shirt pocket. Their gazes locked, and Tina felt her cheeks warm.

Tina's father cleared his throat from the doorway, breaking the spell. "We'll be off. Call if you need anything."

"Okay, Dad. Thanks," Tina said.

"Have a good day, honey," Tina's mother said to Tina. She did not address Jaleesa.

Once the front door closed and she heard the car engine start up, Tina sighed out a groan and said, "I am so sorry about my mother."

Jaleesa simply nodded. "It comes with the territory. Doesn't it?"

"You know why there's no alcohol in the house?"

"Why?"

"Because of me," Tina said and turned to get two fresh mugs. "They don't want any temptation around me."

"I get that."

"And I will remind my mother of that fact after you leave this crazy Jenkins' household."

Jaleesa simply nodded. Her lips were tightly pressed together as if she wanted to say more but was holding back.

They sat for a few minutes at the table, drinking their coffees and sharing details of their respective experiences at Blackwell College.

"So, you delayed going to college?" Jaleesa asked. "There's only seven years age difference between us, but nine years difference in college graduations."

Tina nodded. "Yep. Dealing with the shit, so to speak."

Jaleesa reached over and put her hand lightly on top of one of Tina's. "You've come a long way. It couldn't have been easy."

Tina shook her head and then cleared her throat. "Maybe we should get going on one of your favorite things to do." She grinned and gestured toward the rented rug cleaning system.

"Lead on, Macduff," Jaleesa said, took another swig of coffee, and stood up. "And just so you know, this is good." She gestured to the coffee. "I'd do it again."

"See? I knew you'd like it." Tina said. "Do you like Shakespeare?" Tina headed into the living room with Jaleesa following.

"Okay, that was random," Jaleesa said. "I do like Shakespeare. Why do you ask?"

Tina melted. There was no condescending tone—only one of interest. "'Lead on, McDuff,'" Tina quoted.

"Ahh, Macbeth," Jaleesa said. "One of my favorites. No one ever gets that reference."

Tina beamed. Had she passed a hidden test or something? "And it's often misquoted like that." Oh, shoot. Did that sound too arrogant? Darn it.

"Lay on, Macduff," Jaleesa amended. "It could apply here, too, I suppose."

"Yes, it could. We'll give it our best efforts, won't we?"

Jaleesa squatted down and read the instructions on the side of the machine. She pulled out the water reservoir and held it up, obviously asking where to fill it.

"Kitchen sink," Tina said, following her with the jug of soap.

"Indeed."

After setting up the machine, Tina was amazed at how easily Jaleesa lifted and moved the furniture, mostly by herself. Jaleesa's movements were effortless. It was obvious she had been a strong athlete. And those muscles—yes, please. Ahh, but she shouldn't ogle someone who could never be anything more than a friend. Hopefully, she'd turn into a good friend, but she was destined to be only that, nonetheless.

The loud whirr of the machine as they took turns wielding it cut any further meaningful conversation, but they worked together well as each one anticipated what the other one needed. Jaleesa was moving the side table before Tina could ask her to. Tina moved the electric cord out of the way before Jaleesa tripped on it. They did manage to talk about their favorite books, though, and even recommended a few to each other. Tina was definitely going to check out "The Invisible Man" once Sunday dinner was done and put away. "The one by Ralph Ellison," Jaleesa had emphasized. "Not H.G. Wells."

The entire downstairs area was finished in record time, and Tina debated asking Jaleesa to help her clean the upstairs carpets. Typically, she did the upstairs six months later, just so she wouldn't overdo it, but she rejected doing the upstairs for two reasons. One—she didn't want to overburden Jaleesa so early in their friendship, and two—her parents probably wouldn't want someone they hardly knew in their bedroom. And besides those two things, Tina hadn't looked at her own bedroom through the eyes of someone else. She hadn't had a friend at her house since high school. She had those pictures tacked to the walls—all her crushes. Umm, no, Jaleesa didn't need to see that. Or her journal, which was sitting out for anyone to see. Her parents read it, sure, but it wasn't for public consumption.

"You okay?" Jaleesa asked as she coiled the rinsed-out hose in the now-empty water reservoir.

"Yes, yes," Tina said, snapping out of her fog. She fanned herself. All that work had made her ultra-warm. "Let me refresh your water bottle."

"Actually," Jaleesa said, glancing at the clock, "I think I, uh, need to get going."

Disappointment soaked into Tina like syrup over pancakes. It was too soon. Wasn't she going to stay for dinner? "Oh." It was all she could get out.

Jaleesa took a step closer. "I had a good time."

Tina scoffed. "Cleaning my carpets?"

Jaleesa stepped even closer and reached out to hold each of Tina's hands in her own. "I had fun spending time with you," she said quietly.

"Oh." Tina heard the surprised lilt in her own voice.

"Let's do it again sometime," Jaleesa said with a laugh. She leaned down and kissed Tina on the cheek.

Tina melted. "Yes." Again, it was all she could get out. She desperately didn't want Jaleesa to leave and lunged forward to wrap her arms around the taller woman. "Thank you. I had a good time with you, too." Strong arms went around her back. One hand rubbed gently.

Too soon, way too soon, Jaleesa pulled away. "I have to go, Tina."

"I know." Part of her did know that Jaleesa would leave before her parents came home. Tina watched her put on the leather jacket that in no way kept out the Ohio January cold. At least she had the scarf. "When will I see you again?"

"I don't know," Jaleesa said.

That wasn't goodbye forever, was it? It couldn't be.

"How about you text me when you're ready," Jaleesa said. "We can figure things out from there.”

“Okay.” Tina opened the front door even though every fiber of her being didn't want to. “Thanks for your help.”

“Of course.” And with that, Jaleesa headed out the door. She turned outside on the front landing, said, “Bye,” and then walked away. Tina watched her pick her way down the icy driveway and then down the hill.

“You threw yourself at her,” Tina muttered as she watched Jaleesa walk away. “Idiot.” Was that the last time she would ever see Jaleesa? *No, you said I could text you.* There was hope yet.

“What kind of car do you drive, Jaleesa Whitmore?” Tina whispered into the windowpane. “At least I know your last name now. But what kind of family do you have? Are they in Cincinnati? Do you live with them? You're a hairdresser or stylist, or however you phrased it, but do you like doing that?” She wiped the condensation from the window and then closed the door. “What are your dreams, Jaleesa?”

Tina closed and locked the front door and said out loud, “What are *my* dreams?” She had no answer but then started to chuckle. One of the lightbulbs was burned out in the foyer chandelier. “I should have asked you to change that for me. I bet you could reach it without a step stool.” Tina tucked the carpet machine out of the way and headed into the kitchen to check on the slow cooker.

She was tired but still a little wired, so she got out the step stool and replaced the burned-out bulb herself. Thoughts of Jaleesa's strong presence made her both shaky and warm all at once. She'd never felt that way about anyone before. She put the stepstool back in the kitchen pantry and was just about to text Jaleesa when she heard her parents' car pull into the driveway. She tucked her phone away. She'd text later when she was in her room.

She popped the crescent roll tube open and laid the dough on the cookie sheet.

“We're home,” Tina's father announced loudly. He never did that. He was making their presence known for some reason.

OMG, did he think she and Jaleesa were up in her room with the door closed? One day maybe, but gosh, not on the first date. Oh, shoot, had this been a date? If it was, worst date ever. A do-over was needed. "But I don't go places," Tina mumbled to herself.

"Hi, Dad," Tina called to them. "How was church?" *And Mom, did you notice that I didn't greet you? Do you see how rudeness feels?*

"Always good," her father said, pulling Tina into a side hug. "How goes the carpet cleaning?"

"All done," Tina said and popped the cookie sheet into the oven.

"Where's Jaleesa?" he asked, looking around.

"Uh, she helped me do all the carpets, and then she had to go."

"Mm," her father said knowingly. "Too bad. I wanted a chance to get to know my daughter's friend better. I wanted to hear about her basketball days at B.C. We might have watched her on the college channel."

"I know," Tina said. "I thought about that." *And I will have to Google her later,* Tina thought mischievously.

Tina squelched a grin as her mother entered the kitchen. "The carpets look good. You got that stain out by Dad's chair."

"Mm hmm." Short and not-so-sweet.

Her mother glanced around the kitchen as if looking to see if anything was missing or out of place.

Are you kidding me, Mom? Tina screamed inside. *Who are you?*

"Mom, why did you have to go and say that to Jaleesa?"

Her mother's expression was kind of nondescript, almost cautious, as she said, "We don't know her, Tina. *You* don't know her."

"Just because she's an addict like me—"

"No, *not* like you," her mother snapped. "We don't know who she is. She just walked in here into our house."

Realization dawned on Tina. "Mom! Oh, my God. It's because she's Black, isn't it?"

"You didn't tell us, Tina."

"Did you think she was going to steal the silver, Mom? She couldn't do that, could she, because you and Dad removed everything of value from this house. And why? Because of me. Me! I'm the fuck-up. Me. Don't project that onto my new friend. And, Mom, when the hell did you become a racist?"

"It's just that it came as a surprise," Tina's father said quietly.

Tina groaned in frustration. *Him, too? Grr.* "Your dinner's ready. I'm suddenly not hungry anymore." She ran up the stairs two at a time. She was about to slam her bedroom door when she heard her mother speak.

"We don't know the woman, Bruce," Tina's mother said quietly. "She's an alcoholic. We don't know what she's capable of. She's probably done things."

"That's why this day was so important, Marion. We were going to break bread with our daughter's first friend in quite a while. And do I need to remind you that our own daughter has also done *things*?"

"I know." Her mother's sob slammed into Tina's heart. "I didn't ask for any of this."

"None of us did," Tina's father said. "Least of all Tina."

Tina shut her bedroom door and sobbed into her shirt. "I'm sorry, Mom." She took a shaky breath. "I'm sorry, Dad." *You shouldn't have to be saddled with…me.*

Chapter 7

Jaleesa

Pacing didn't help. Jaleesa's apartment wasn't big enough to get in more than a few strides anyway, so she stopped at her floor-to-ceiling bookshelves and ran her finger over the spines of her book collection. They ranged from classics to downright trash. Ugh, no way. Jaleesa pulled Toni Morrison's *The Bluest Eye*, *Beloved*, and *Song of Solomon* off the shelf.

She scoffed. Gabby must have done this. Ahh, yes, she'd put all the books in alphabetical order by author, which by rights, made sense. Still, Jaleesa had her books carefully sectioned off, and Nobel Laureate Toni Morrison's evolutionary works did not belong next to Amber Morris's lesbian BDSM collection. When did Gabby do this? And why hadn't Jaleesa ever noticed?

"I've been distracted," Jaleesa said to the Morrison books. "I will rectify this…soon." She laid the books flat on the shelf. She could do it now, especially because her Sunday afternoon and evening had opened up after she'd fled Tina's house. But she didn't have the energy.

She picked up the aftermath of her Hungry Hamlet's meal and tossed the fast-food containers in the trash can under the sink. Now what?

She headed back to the living room and plopped on the couch. Her hand reached for the television remote, but then she spotted the AA Big Book underneath. She'd already read a few pages since buying it at last Monday's meeting, but not enough to get pulled into it.

With a resigned sigh, she pulled the book off the side table and opened it up to the page she'd left off in the middle of Chapter 1: Bill's Story. Ugh, she wasn't interested in reading this heavy stuff right now. She closed the book.

She leaned her head back and closed her eyes. She didn't want heavy. She wanted air, fresh air. Freedom. A new beginning.

She opened her eyes and put the book back on the side table. You know what else she wanted? More hugs from that incredible woman whose carpets she'd help clean that morning. Tina's hug felt like…"like nothing I've ever felt before," Jaleesa finished out loud. She'd even gotten a few tingles of arousal as she held the dainty but strong woman in her arms.

But it could never be. Tina's parents hadn't welcomed her. Only the father had half-heartedly done so. They didn't want to get to know her. They saw her as a threat to Tina. And maybe she was.

Her hand flung into her front pocket, and she yanked out her phone. It was already five o'clock. Nope, no text from Tina. She sighed. There wouldn't be one, would there? Meeting Tina had been nice, but it was just a chance meeting, a brief connection, and now they were going their separate ways. God had simply sent a caring, thoughtful, smart, and compassionate woman like Tina Jenkins to show Jaleesa that people like that existed. Tina had helped Jaleesa set her sights back on the right path. So why did that hurt so much? A low ache settled in her chest.

And, sure, part of the reason she had taken her phone out was to see if Tina had texted, but the other part was to find an old contact in her phone.

> JALEESA: Hey! It's been a while, I know. Do you have time to talk tonight?
>
> JALEESA: Or sometime?

She tossed her phone on the Big Book and was just about to stand up and get Toni Morrison righted when her phone dinged an incoming text. Was it Tina? Jaleesa swallowed her disappointment when it wasn't.

ELAINA: Do my eyes deceive me? Hey there, stranger. Give me five minutes to get George his dinner, and I'll give you a call. Are you okay?

JALEESA: I'm okay. Thanks for getting back so quickly.

ELAINA: (Thumbs-up emoji)

ELAINA: Give me 5.

Jaleesa didn't know what to do with herself, so she went to the bathroom and then filled her reusable water bottle from the cold-water container she kept in the fridge. "Honey badgers," she read the label out loud. Tina had also gone to B.C. Her chest ache made a momentary reappearance, but she willed it away.

She had just sat back down on the couch when her phone rang. This time she didn't hope that it was Tina. She knew it wouldn't be. And it wasn't.

"Thanks for calling me back so quickly, Elaina," Jaleesa said.

"Where are you right now?"

Jaleesa chuckled. "I'm home. I'm sober, and I don't have any alcohol here."

"Excellent," Elaina said. "You knew those would be my next questions."

"I'm going to meetings again," Jaleesa said.

"Good. I noticed you weren't coming to the campus meetings anymore." Elaina's tone held no judgment, merely observation. "But I admit I was concerned when you didn't return my texts."

"I know. I thought I was above the system." Jaleesa sighed.

"I'm your sponsor," Elaina said softly. "I'm here to help. What do you need?"

"I bought the Big Book, and I was hoping you could find time to go over it with me again. And this time, I'm going to listen."

"I would be happy to help. Why the sudden change of heart?"

A certain five-foot-nothing dark blonde, white woman with endearing eyes and a comforting smile who showed me it could be done. Of course, Jaleesa couldn't say any of that to her sponsor, so instead said, "God nudged me this way, then that."

"A simple enough answer," Elaina said. "I'm proud of you for calling. When's your next meeting?"

"Tomorrow night. I'm at a new place. The Friendship Church on Vine. I like it. It has a cozy, supportive feel to it."

"Pastor Paul does great work over there. Good for you."

They arranged to meet after work on Wednesday at Jumpin' Joe's Coffee Bar, which was all coffee and no bar. Jaleesa was to have both 'The Doctor's Opinion' and 'Chapter 1: Bill's Story' read completely by then, highlighting anything that resonated with her. Elaina said she would also bring a copy of the twelve steps, and they would read each one but then focus on the first two. Yes, they had done all of this before, but this time, Jaleesa was ready to hear it—maybe for the first time.

"And, Jaleesa," Elaina said as they were wrapping up their call, "I'm proud of you for taking back the reins."

"I have to try," Jaleesa said.

"You miss every shot you don't take, Miss hotshot basketball player," Elaina quipped.

Oh, the irony of that statement. "Taking shots got me into this mess in the first place."

Elaina burst out laughing. "We do pour our own trouble, don't we?" She chuckled again and said, "I'm looking forward to hugging your neck on Wednesday. But you'll have to lean down for this old lady to reach you."

"You're forty-five, Elaina. That's not old," Jaleesa said.

"You're as old as you feel," Elaina said with a laugh. "See you Wednesday."

Jaleesa said goodbye, sat back, picked up the Big Book, and began reading 'The Doctor's Opinion,' from the very beginning.

~~~

It was Monday night, and Jaleesa sat in the front row, as usual, in the basement of the Friendship Church. She decided against Mario's coffee and grabbed water instead. She still tucked a dollar in the box, hoping it would help Tina in some small way. She took a sip and heard, rather than saw, people filling in the seats around her. The seats were arranged in a quasi-circle, three chairs deep. There was no speaker's podium this time. It was group discussion night. She remembered these from her first go-around.

She pulled out her phone ostensibly to check the time, but she was really checking to see if Tina had texted. Nope. That cute little ship had sailed. It sailed the moment Tina's mother got a look at Jaleesa. She sighed. Whatever. She was about to slip the phone back into her pocket when she laughed. She'd pulled it out to check the time but had forgotten to do so. Just as she turned it back on, a text came in. Then another.

TINA: You're not invisible to me.

TINA: Look behind you.

Jaleesa spun around so fast in her seat that she almost gave herself whiplash. She stood up, and right there in front of her was Tina. Tina's smile was sympathetic, and she almost seemed on the verge of tears.

"I'm sorry I didn't text you last night," Tina said. "I had so many thoughts swirling around in my head. And I'm not sure if I would be welcomed in your life after yesterday's disaster."

Jaleesa knew a thousand different expressions crossed her own face as Tina spoke, but she finally settled on a nurturing one. Tina needed reassurance. "Takes more than that to scare me away."

Tina visibly relaxed.

"You started reading Ellison's book, I take it?"

Tina nodded.

"Come sit with me?" Jaleesa asked and patted the empty chair next to her.

Tina nodded again and worked her way around the fold-up chairs, and they both sat down, each one turning slightly toward the other. Before Jaleesa could say anything, a boisterous young voice filled the space.

"Happy Monday, everybody," Dana announced, hair still in puffballs. She hugged her friend Kadesha and then spotted Tina and Jaleesa. "Ooh, c'mon, let's sit with Tina."

Jaleesa chuckled and then leaned in close. "Have coffee with me after this? Down at Jumpin' Joe's?"

Tina's face was very expressive. It went from terrified to questioning to determined to angry, all in two seconds. "Yes."

"Yes?" Jaleesa said, eyebrows raised. "Excellent."

"I'll have to text my parents to forewarn them, though."

"Are you going to ask their permission or simply tell them what you're doing?"

Tina thought about the question for a moment and then said with surety, "I'm going to tell them." She poked Jaleesa's thigh with the tip of her index finger as if putting an exclamation point on her resolve.

"Good for you," Jaleesa said and grinned.

Tina grinned back and then let herself get attacked by Dana from behind.

After greetings, Dana looked Jaleesa right in the eye and said, "I know we're not supposed to ask, but what do you do for a living?"

"Dana," Kadesha said with a groan. She seemed a little older than Dana and carried herself maturely, unlike the puffball kid interrogating her.

"What?" Dana said with a shrug. "Okay, fine. I told Kadesha that you have to be some kind of PE teacher or fitness trainer or a coach or something like that."

Both Jaleesa and Tina chuckled. Tina shook her head.

"No way," Dana said. "You look so…strong." Her breath seemed to catch in her throat.

Ahh, Jaleesa recognized that look. Dana was attracted to her. Okay. A little flirting wouldn't hurt. Jaleesa stood up, reached right into Dana's personal space, and smoothed down one of the puffballs. "You can do better than this," she said authoritatively. She kept a straight face as Dana melted right there in front of her.

"Yeah?"

"How old are you?" Jaleesa asked.

"Twenty-six."

"And what do you do for a living?"

"I sell indoor and outdoor plants for J&B Landscaping at the flea market. But I really want to get into the actual landscaping part. Designing yards and commercial spaces."

"As opposed to sales?"

Kadesha leaned over Tina and added, "But she's a really good salesperson."

"I'm sure she is," Jaleesa said. She turned to Dana. "Come by the shop. Let's do something about this, okay?" She stopped short of taking Dana's chin in her hand. They were not at Dominique's, and she truly didn't know this young woman very well.

"Shop?" Dana's eyes grew wide as a realization hit her. "Wait, you do hair?" She glanced at Kadesha and said to Jaleesa, "For reals?"

"Yes," Tina said. "She does hair."

Jaleesa handed Dana one of her cards.

"Holy excrement," Dana said as she looked at the card. She sat down hard on the metal chair. "I'll call your shop, like, tomorrow." She leaned over and showed Kadesha the card. It was like she'd gotten a golden ticket to the chocolate factory. Jaleesa handed a card to Kadesha as well.

As an afterthought, Jaleesa handed one of her cards to Tina. "And if you want, we can also discuss a new style for you." Tina's long dark blonde hair was healthy, but Jaleesa had a dozen styles swirling in her mind that she wanted to try, but only when and if Tina was ready. Thinking she might have overstepped, she added, "But only if you want. You're beautiful the way you are."

Tina looked like she was about to choke on the compliment, so Jaleesa simply smiled and patted Tina's hand as Pastor Paul got the meeting underway.

As the meeting drew to a close, Jaleesa vowed to speak more next time. She hadn't felt ready yet. She wanted to meet with Elaina first and get herself grounded. She and Tina said their goodbyes to Dana and Kadesha and then headed up the stairs toward the outside set of doors.

"Oh, oh," Tina said in a rush as they hit the top landing before heading out into the cold. She reached into her pocket and pulled out a pair of black gloves. She handed them to Jaleesa. "I didn't think you were a red gloves kind of person, so I knitted you black ones. 'Black, like your...'" Tina pulled out the imaginary key tucked in her shirt pocket and untwisted it in front of Jaleesa's lips. Jaleesa shook her head as a smile crept up her face. She grabbed the imaginary key and tucked it in her pocket. Nope. She'd never finish that sentence.

"Oh," Tina said in frustration and stomped the heel of her boot on the concrete landing. "I'll get that key back someday."

Jaleesa pressed her lips together and then looked at the gift in her hand. "These are gorgeous, Tina. Thank you."

"The fingertips slide back, so if you need to work on your fancy sports car, you can."

"Sports car?" Jaleesa laughed. "You think I drive a sports car?"

"My mind has gone all kinds of places."

"C'mon, we'll walk to Joe's, but I'll show you my vehicle once we get outside." She pulled her new scarf tighter around her and pulled the uber-soft gloves on her hands. So warm. "These are nice."

"I'm glad you like them," Tina said, beaming. " I finished them right before leaving for the meeting."

"You're something else," Jaleesa said. "Okay, ready to hold your breath?"

Tina nodded and made a big show of taking a deep breath and puffing out her cheeks. They slammed open the outside doors and hustled through the haze of cigarette smoke that permeated every parking lot after any and every AA meeting Jaleesa had ever attended.

As they walked together toward Vine Street and the coffee shop, Jaleesa pointed to her black pickup.

"Oh, that suits you," Tina gushed. "Aha!" She poked Jaleesa in the chest. "'Black like your pickup truck!'"

Jaleesa's laugh came from her toes. "Sure, we'll go with that. C'mon, let's hustle. It's cold out here."

They made it to Joe's in record time. Despite Tina's protests, Jaleesa paid for both of their coffees. Tina ordered a flavored medium-roast coffee and added a splash of half-and-half, while Jaleesa ordered a darker roast taking it black.

"Did you text your parents yet?"

"Yes," Tina said succinctly.

"All is well?"

Tina shrugged. "I haven't checked their response. They might not have even seen the text yet, but don't be surprised if my mother knocks down the front doors checking up on me."

Jaleesa sighed. She really had no response for what might become an actual reality. Her nurturing nature took over, and she said, "You're okay, Tina. I'll make sure of it. I'll always make sure of it."

Tina tapped the table three times and then cleared her throat as if to change the subject. "I'm glad I met you, Jaleesa Whitmore."

"Me, too. I'm glad I met you, Tina Jenkins. You've inspired me."

"Me? How?"

"Your recovery. Your ability to plow right through the terrifying stuff and seek out the clear sunny meadows."

"With a babbling brook and maybe a log cabin?"

"Shit, yeah," Jaleesa agreed with a laugh. "I, uh, called my sponsor. I'm meeting her here on Wednesday after work."

"Seriously? That is—" Tina looked at a loss for words. "That's great, Jaleesa."

Jaleesa nodded. "We're going to hit the steps again—"

"There is no elevator."

Jaleesa smiled. "Gotta take the steps. We're also going through the Big Book. Again. It didn't really take the first time."

"If you're comfortable, can you tell me more of your story?"

Jaleesa nodded. "I feel safe with you. I think I can trust you with my story." She reached across the table and patted Tina's hand once. Visions of Tina's mother bursting through the front doors flashed in her head, and she pulled her hand back.

"Thank you for trusting me."

Jaleesa relayed the events of that fateful night—the Kwanzaa gathering with friends that turned into a blow-out New Year's Eve party. She had to mention her ex, even though it was difficult in many ways, but she told Tina that since her then-girlfriend, Gabby, was so shit-faced, Jaleesa stopped drinking and switched to water. She'd even had a cup of coffee before getting in the pickup and driving back over the border into Ohio. So, even though she'd tried to be responsible, none of it mattered. She drove drunk or buzzed so often that she hadn't thought twice about it. When there was no judgment lighting up Tina's face, Jaleesa felt brave to go on.

She told the tale in a blur. She told about the flashing red and blue lights behind her and how she initially didn't understand they were for her and that she was supposed to pull over. She told how the cop did a sobriety test on her at one in the morning on the side of the busy highway. When she failed, he guided her to the backseat of his cruiser. Gabby had to go with them since she was in no shape to drive. Jaleesa then quickly glossed over her time in jail and her sentencing before the judge.

"So, I basically had no choice in getting sober," Jaleesa said. "It was court-ordered."

"Baby? I hate to break this news to you, but you always had a choice."

Baby? Did she just call me 'baby'? Jaleesa didn't know what to do with that.

"Hmm?" Jaleesa said. "I've always had a choice? What do you mean?"

"You didn't have to go to those court-ordered treatment sessions. You didn't have to stop drinking, Jaleesa. You always had that choice."

Jaleesa was stunned into silence. She looked off into space for a moment. "I never thought about it that way. You know, at the first meeting I went to, they gave me this white poker chip. It was to signify my commitment to remaining sober. Honestly, Tina, I just took the thing and jammed it in my pocket. I played along with the game. I had to, so I could get my life back."

"'Get your life back,'" Tina repeated. "So, be honest, have you had a drink since that first meeting? Since that day you got the chip?"

"No."

"Really?" There was a hint of doubt in her one-word question. "Most alcoholics and addicts relapse at least once." She put both hands up to frame her face.

"I haven't. Honest. Gabby tried to sabotage me on occasion. And then, well, she left. Just left."

"Let's talk about that another time, okay? I can tell she made a dark spot on your heart."

"Okay," Jaleesa said. "I may talk to Elaina about all of that, though."

"Good idea," Tina said and patted Jaleesa's hand. She sat back, sipped her coffee, and said, "I can't believe I'm sitting here with a white-chip wonder."

"What is that?"

"Someone who has been sober, with no relapses, since day one."

"I'm not a wonder, Tina. If I hadn't met Harriet and then you, I would have relapsed, if I'm being honest." She rubbed at her aching fingers. It had been a heavy braiding day at the shop, but Miss Bessie wouldn't hire another braider for some reason. And then there was the rumor Jaleesa had heard about another rent hike for her apartment. She was making ends meet, but barely. Having Gabby help with the rent was a Godsend, but then Gabby up and left, now didn't she?

A soft clearing of a throat brought her back to reality. Small but warm hands reached across the table and grabbed both of hers. Tina began a slow massage of one hand, asking Jaleesa's permission with her expression. Jaleesa nodded.

"A hazard of the job?" Tina suggested.

"Mm hmm." Oh, great. Now she was pulling a Dana and reduced to one-word responses.

Tina looked down at the hand she was working on and said, "Your hands are so strong."

Jaleesa had no response for that but said, "You know that cabin you mentioned earlier?"

"Mm hmm."

"It's got to have Wi-Fi."

Tina burst out laughing, her already pink cheeks turning pinker.

As Tina worked on first one hand and then the other, Jaleesa watched Tina freely. She understood how addiction could make you feel vulnerable. She'd seen Tina that way. But at the moment, Tina seemed right in her element, caring for and nurturing someone, *nurturing me.* Jaleesa felt her whole body relax. *Yes, that would be nice—someone I could take care of who would know how to take care of me, too.*

Ah, yes, another epiphany was happening right there in Jumpin' Joe's Coffee Bar. *Gabby never did know how to take care of me. No, that wasn't it. She'd tried. She'd organized my books, and I didn't even notice. It was more like I didn't know how to let someone in enough to take care of me. I'd never let my guard down long enough to truly let someone in. Yes, that was probably more like it.*

"Thank you, Tina," Jaleesa said quietly. "I should probably walk you back to your car so you can get home. Before your parents worry."

Tina nodded. Her expression said she knew they'd have to end their evening together at some point, but she didn't want to. Tina stood up, put on her coat and scarf, and then gathered the empty ceramic mugs. All without saying a word. She waited for Jaleesa to fasten her coat before heading to the dirty dishes tray near the garbage barrels.

She held the outside door open to let Jaleesa walk through first. Interesting. Most of Jaleesa's dates expected her to hold the door open for them.

"So, do you think you'll be at Miss Bessie's shop forever?" Tina asked, finally breaking her silence.

Jaleesa sighed. "I mean, I'm thirty-eight. Too late to start a new career, I suppose." A gloved backhand hit her lightly on the arm. "Hey! What was that for?"

"You're never too old to start something new," Tina scolded. "Tell me what you want to do. For reals," she added with a grin, mimicking Dana's words.

"Seriously? I'd like to scale back on actual customers. I'd like to own my own shop. One that anyone can come to. Whites, Blacks, anyone. Everyone."

"Wow. I love that. That's an admirable goal," Tina gushed. "What do you need to do that?"

Jaleesa chuckled quietly. Tina's questions sounded like one-part interrogation and one-part therapy session. That was okay, though. Not many people asked her questions like that. It was refreshing.

"I need to come up with a realistic business plan. Um, I need to get a letter of recommendation or two. Easy enough, I think. I need to show my good credit history to get a loan."

"You'll also need collateral to get that loan," Tina said, all professional.

"I guess so," Jaleesa said. "I haven't thought it all the way through. I mean, maybe my parents can co-sign with me."

"Yes, that would help," Tina said. "Would you mind if we talk about this sometime? In depth, I mean? Maybe back at Jumpin' Joe's? Over coffee?"

"Or maybe at Laurent's? Over steaks?"

Tina stopped walking and turned to face Jaleesa. "Jaleesa Whitmore, are you asking me out on a date?"

"Maybe."

Panic took over Tina's expression. "I, I, …" She took a breath and looked down at the concrete sidewalk. "As much as I want to, I, I, I just can't. I can't." She looked up. "I'm sorry." She stammered for a moment. "It's not you. It's me. And please don't think it's my parents. It's just that I don't…I'm not normal."

"Come here. Come here." Jaleesa said and drew her into a hug. "What's wrong? I didn't mean to make you upset." She wrapped her arms around the distraught woman and rubbed her back over her coat. "Shh, shh. It's okay."

"No, I owe you an explanation." And then, as Jaleesa held her, Tina's words came out in a long stream. "I'm ACE. I mean, I'm asexual. I'm not like Gabby or any of your other old girlfriends. I'm different. And if we went any further, we'd both end up hurt and frustrated. You'd be mad, and I'd hate myself for allowing myself to fall for you. Obviously, there's no way we can be together. There's no happy ending for me in a relationship, so you should move on, Jaleesa. Forget about me. Just…forget I exist."

"Absolutely not," Jaleesa tried not to roar. "Look at me." Yes, the Domme was out, and Tina looked up. "There's obviously a lot on your mind, and we need to talk more about it. Together. I can't have you make one-sided decisions for both of us. So, let's have a good open, honest discussion, okay?"

"Okay," Tina said.

Jaleesa steered Tina around and toward the church parking lot. The night cold was biting, so Jaleesa suggested they sit in Tina's car to warm up. Once in the car, Tina turned the key and got the heat going. It took a few moments, but after a while, the car had enough warmth to stop their shivering.

"Tell me more," Jaleesa said and did her best to turn toward Tina in the tiny MINI Cooper. She'd seen the car in the driveway the day before and knew, just knew, it was Tina's. And she'd been right. Tina looked up at her shyly and bit her lip. Had she become embarrassed? Did she now regret blurting out her secret because it had felt like a deep dark secret. Was it too hard for Tina to get her words together now that they were alone in a cozy space? Cozy, in this case, meant way too small for a six-foot-one former power forward, but Jaleesa didn't care.

"Talk to me, Tina."

"No one wants to date an asexual," Tina said matter-of-factly. "Sex is apparently the ultimate goal in relationships, but I have never been interested in sex."

"Never?"

"No. I still haven't figured out what my high school friends meant when they said somebody was 'hot.' There always seemed to be a sexual component to it. I'm just not into it. And it's not because of the addiction. I had this way before then. Like when I was with Nylani in high school. She wanted more than I could give her. I mean, I tried with her a couple of times. I managed to get her to, you know, climax a few times."

Jaleesa nodded but remained silent.

"But she got so mad when I wasn't even, you know, ready for her. She said I didn't love her, but I did. I did love her. So much. All I wanted to do was cuddle and kiss and hug her, though. I dreamed of long winter nights snuggling together in front of the fire. I never ever dreamed of long winter nights naked on the bear skin rug doing the down and dirty."

Jaleesa chuckled. "I've met a few asexuals in my day, just so you know, I understand. And it sounds like you like the romance and closeness of relationships, but not necessarily the jumping of bones part."

"You do understand," Tina said. "And see, someone like you, who I assume is a sexual being, wouldn't put up with no sex for too long. Or maybe you'd get so frustrated that you'd try to change me. Or maybe you'd force me."

"I would never do that, Tina. Consent is paramount in every relationship. Even in our friendship."

"Is that all we'll ever have?" Before Jaleesa could respond, Tina continued, "Yes, that's all we can ever have. I can't delude you or lie and say I can change. I can't. And I won't fake it. That's too stressful."

Jaleesa took off her new gloves and reached for Tina's hands. She tugged Tina's gloves off and held both of Tina's hands in her own.

"You've been so upfront and honest with me," Jaleesa said. "It's refreshing, actually, and I know it took a lot for you to come out to me that way. Honesty is essential in every relationship—honesty, consent, and communication. One of my old lovers in college taught me that. And I'm going to be honest right back, okay?"

Tina nodded and squeezed Jaleesa's hands. "Good. I am attracted to you, Tina Jenkins. And not just physically, although there have been tiny sparks of that, I'm not going to lie. But I'm also attracted to everything that seems to make you who you are. You're nurturing, compassionate, caring." Jaleesa let go of one hand and grabbed onto the cashmere scarf. "Who does this? Who makes a scarf for someone they just met? A nurturing person. You. You're smart and funny and downright cute."

Tina scoffed quietly and looked down. Jaleesa reached over and lifted her chin. "Nope. Nope. I want you present."

Tina looked up. Her cheeks were much redder than simply from the cold. Her expression said she was still present and ready to listen.

"I like you," Jaleesa said, reaching for Tina's hand again. "And I'd like to get to know you better. I probably shouldn't have suggested a date at

Laurent's right off the buzzer, but I'd still like to see you again."

Tina looked away again as if replaying all her arguments in her head about how they could never be in a relationship.

"Nope," Jaleesa said, this time a little of her Domme tone came out. It couldn't be helped.

Tina looked back at her. "I'm scared, Jaleesa. I've only had one real relationship and a couple of online ones I faked my way through."

"I'm sorry you felt you needed to do that. Faking it, I mean. Let's agree to be genuine with each other. All the time, okay?" She reached into her pocket and held out the imaginary key. "I'm giving you back this key so that if I ever get reticent with you or hold something back, you twist this key, and I have to spill it." Tina took the key and did something so endearing that Jaleesa felt her heart falling in love with the blonde-haired sprite in the driver's seat in a car that was the perfect size for her. Tina reached into a different pocket, pulled out her own imaginary key, and handed it to Jaleesa. "This is hard for me, but I give you the same power."

Jaleesa nodded. "This is a great start, isn't it?"

Tina nodded.

"Now, where shall I take you to dinner that allows us to get to know each other better?"

A mischievous gleam hit Tina's eyes. "My house. Next Sunday. For dinner."

Jaleesa didn't hide the surprised expression on her face. "Your mother?"

"We talked late Sunday, after my online meeting, and she and Dad said they wanted a do-over."

Jaleesa looked at her with doubt.

"Okay, fine, it was mostly Dad, but Mom agreed. So how about we try again?"

Jaleesa took a deep breath. The rewards were worth the risk. "Okay, it's a date. With you and your parents."

"It's a package deal," Tina said with a chuckle. She pulled out her phone and sent a text. At first, Jaleesa figured Tina was checking in with her parents, but then her own phone dinged. Jaleesa took it out, and her heart melted.

TINA: (key emoji) I like you.

Jaleesa chuckled and texted back.

JALEESA: (key emoji) I like you back.

Chapter 8

Tina

Sunday dinner was scheduled an hour later than usual, so Tina could make sure her parents were calm and clear-headed before Jaleesa arrived. The doorbell finally rang, and even though Tina wanted to rush and fling it open, she forced herself to stroll over calmly. No big deal. Just a friend coming for dinner. She didn't want to tip her hand to her parents that Jaleesa might be more than a friend. She'd barely allowed herself to think it. Even their daily texts bordered on out-and-out flirting. Thankfully her parents stayed in the kitchen this time and let Tina greet her guest alone. They'd be able to hear everything, anyway.

"Hi," Tina said and opened the front door. Jaleesa held something behind her back. Oh, no, what was it?

Jaleesa stepped inside and shivered off the cold momentarily as she warmed up. She handed Tina two bouquets of flowers. "This one is for you," she said. "And this one is for your parents. For the dinner table, maybe?"

"Thank you." Tina made a show of smelling them and was surprised that they even had a smell. "That was sweet of you." The grocery store flowers her father sometimes brought home to his "girls" were always pretty but never really smelled like anything.

Jaleesa stuffed her new gloves into her pockets and then hung up her scarf and coat on the freestanding coat rack. Tina took in Jaleesa's ass-hugging charcoal gray slacks and the long-sleeved button-down shirt that accentuated her body so nicely. Tina tried not to stare, but yearnings from somewhere deep inside welled up and threatened to melt her right there. She wasn't sure she had any right to them. Jaleesa would find out soon enough that Tina couldn't give her what she wanted. But for now, she'd ride it as long as she could, knowing it would end eventually.

Jaleesa chuckled knowingly. "You're cute," she whispered. A bit louder, she said, "Wow, it smells so good in here."

"We're having lasagna," Tina said. She leaned in close and said, "It's Dad's favorite."

They reached the doorway to the kitchen, and this time, Tina's dad was the first to extend his hand. "Nice to meet you again, Jaleesa." They shook hands, and he stepped back.

"It's nice to see you, too, Mr. Jenkins," Jaleesa said, and Tina secretly smiled. Jaleesa was so polite.

Tina's mother extended her hand and said, "Yes, it's good to see you again." Tina was amazed at how genuine her mother's words sounded.

Jaleesa shook the offered hand and smiled. "Thanks for having me."

Tina exhaled through her nose, somewhat audibly. It was her way of expelling the anxiety that had built up as her parents greeted Jaleesa.

"Okay, so dinner is pretty much ready," Tina said. "We usually have water or milk with dinner. What would you like, Jaleesa?" Tina opened the refrigerator. "Oh, we have Crystal Light, too."

"Water will be fine," Jaleesa said.

After Tina filled a glass with water and set it down at the seat next to hers, Jaleesa asked, "Can I help in any way?"

"No, no—" Tina's father started to say.

"Yes, actually," Tina said. "Mom, Dad? Go ahead and sit. Jaleesa and I have this."

"Oh, okay," her mother said, sounding pleasantly surprised.

After enlisting Jaleesa's help pulling the two pans of lasagna out of the oven and onto the wooden trivets on the table, Tina put a big bowl of salad between them and plunked an array of salad dressings down.

Tina almost melted as Jaleesa pulled Tina's chair out and then waited for her to sit first.

"This looks wonderful," Jaleesa said and snapped her cloth napkin to the side and placed it in her lap.

Tina almost laughed when her father grinned and then did the same.

Tina's mother chuckled at his antics.

"May I say grace?" Jaleesa asked.

"Of course," Tina's mother said.

Jaleesa reached for Tina's hand on one side and Tina's father's hand on the other. Once the hand-holding was complete all around, Jaleesa began. "Lord, thank you for the nourishment in both body and soul that you have presented us with this afternoon. Thank you for the strength and fortitude you give us every day to face our challenges, new and old. Through you, we find this strength and find others to help us on our journey through the trials and tribulations that life throws us. And it is through you that we find peace. Amen."

"Amen," the members of the Jenkins family echoed.

"That was very nice," Tina's mother said.

Tina reached over and squeezed Jaleesa's thigh. It was her way of conveying her gratitude for such a moving grace. Jaleesa's smile was close-lipped but grateful.

As Tina doled out the salad into small bowls, her father attempted to make small talk. "So, your name is Jaleesa Whitmore. JW?"

"Mm hmm," Jaleesa said. She reached for the Newman's Own oil and vinegar dressing, checked the cap, and gave it a vigorous shake.

"Jay Double-U is quite a mouthful," Tina's father mused out loud.

"No, Dad," Tina said, trying to derail her father. She knew what was coming.

"Gotta shorten that," her father said.

"Oh, noooo, Dad." Tina moaned and put her hand on her forehead. "Don't—"

"J-Dub," her father announced, quite pleased with himself.

Jaleesa laughed heartily; it was so genuine that Tina's melting continued.

"And I believe your first name is Bruce," Jaleesa countered, "making your name Bruce Jenkins, thus making your initials—"

"Nooooo!" Tina said, cutting off Jaleesa's sentence.

Everyone at the table burst into laughter.

"I was the butt of many jokes growing up," Tina's father admitted. "But I survived. It was probably why we didn't name Tina Beulah or something."

Tina rolled her eyes. "Thanks for that, you guys."

Tina's nerves ratcheted down as the dinner went on. Jaleesa seemed impressed that Tina had made a ground beef lasagna and one without meat, just in case Jaleesa was a vegetarian or something. She said it was "very thoughtful" of Tina. If they'd been alone, Tina would have confessed that Jaleesa had been in her thoughts almost constantly since they'd last seen each other.

"Here, let me help with that," Jaleesa said, standing up to take the dirty plates from Tina's mother once the meal was over.

"No, no," Tina's mother said. "Dad and I have this. You two go on upstairs and visit."

Tina's eyes grew wide. "Really, Mom?" She figured they would move to the living room, where the real interrogation of Jaleesa would begin. But that wasn't going to happen. Wow. "Uh, okay." She turned to Jaleesa and said, "Follow me then."

"Lead on," Jaleesa said, making Tina giggle. Oh, wow, they already had some inside jokes.

Once inside Tina's bedroom with the door firmly closed, Jaleesa said, "Dinner was great. Thank you for the invitation."

"It went well, don't you think?"

"I do," Jaleesa said, turning her attention to the stuff covering Tina's walls. She smiled at the anime drawings but then, as expected, zeroed in on the montage of Tina's crushes.

"Wow," Jaleesa said as she scanned each one. She tapped one picture and said, "Most people don't know who Dorothy Dandridge is. And I'm afraid I don't know who this next one is."

"Marpessa Dawn," Tina said. "She was a singer and actress. American-French."

"She's pretty. And why does Tina Jenkins have all these women on her wall? Kat Graham, Fletcher, Candace Parker, Naomi Scott, Tessa Thompson, and more." She gestured to the other unnamed pictures. "Ooh, Kehlani. Aww, you have my girl, Mary J., on your wall." Jaleesa patted her chest twice.

"Sit, and I'll tell you." Tina gestured to her swiveling desk chair while she sat on the side of her bed. Tina relayed as best she could her quest to figure out what "hot" meant and that she'd started the collection in high school and had continued to add to it over the years.

"*Hot* is obviously in the eye of the beholder," Jaleesa said, "but I would agree that you have a steamy collection of hot women here."

"I do?"

Jaleesa fanned herself. "Oh, yeah. So have you figured out what *your* definition of hot is?"

Tina's face flushed as she said, "Maybe." Her gaze took in all of Jaleesa before settling back on her face. "A body that I want to touch. Not sexually, mind you. Not that far. But strong biceps I want to feel under my hands. A soft face I want to stroke as I lean in for a kiss. Long arms going around me, holding me, loving me, caressing me." Tina felt her core clench. She couldn't believe she was saying all of this out loud.

"Mm hmm," Jaleesa said and swallowed hard.

Tina stood up and reached out her hand. Jaleesa took it, and Tina pulled her to her feet. "Caressed like this." Tina ran the back of her knuckles along Jaleesa's warm cheeks. "Is this okay?" She heard the tightness in her own voice.

Jaleesa nodded but made no move to pull Tina into a hug.

"And this?" Tina ran her hands gently down both of Jaleesa's upper arms.

Jaleesa nodded again, her eyes searching Tina's for…something. What? Permission. Oh, permission was going to be granted, but Tina was going to initiate it.

Tina moved her hands behind Jaleesa's neck and pulled her down toward her. "And this?"

Jaleesa answered by closing the distance, her lips finding Tina's. Soft lips met hers, and Tina sighed. Oh, yes. Yes, yes. Jaleesa's arms went around Tina's back and pulled her body tight to her own. So strong. As the kiss deepened, Tina ran her fingers through Jaleesa's hair. So soft. She pulled Jaleesa's mouth tight against her own until she needed air. She pulled back a little and pressed her forehead to Jaleesa's.

"That was…" Tina sighed. "All I hoped it would be."

"Me, too," Jaleesa said.

Tina's heart clenched. Jaleesa had thought about kissing her, too? Yes! "I hope that was okay," Tina said.

"It was tender and probably the most honest kiss I've ever received," Jaleesa said. She still held Tina close.

Embarrassment crept in, and Tina pulled away. She hadn't kissed another human in over a decade since Nylani. "Thank you," she finally managed to say and sat down hard on the bed. Jaleesa resumed her spot in the office chair.

"Oh, I forgot to tell you. I got a visitor at the shop on Friday," Jaleesa said, obviously changing the subject.

"Who?"

"Dana."

"No way," Tina said, leaning forward. "You know, she texted me on Friday to tell me she was doing something secretive. I thought she was meeting up with her crush from the flea market or something. So, you did her hair?"

Jaleesa nodded. "You'll see if you come to tomorrow's AA meeting."

"I was planning on it. Maybe coffee after?"

"I'd like that," Jaleesa said gently. "Dana was so nervous. I think she has a crush on me."

"She does."

Jaleesa laughed big. "I thought so. She was the one who told me to bring you flowers today. She made me come by the flea market and helped me pick out the best of the bunch."

"'Made' you," Tina said with a laugh. Tina was pretty sure that no one made Jaleesa do anything she didn't want to do.

"I think she knows I'm sweet on you," Jaleesa said.

'Sweet on me'? How old-fashioned and endearing. "Actually, she knows all about my crush on *you!*"

"Oh, I see," Jaleesa said. "That little matchmaker. She is adorable, though. You have to admit."

"She is," Tina said. "She's a good friend. And she's doing well in sobriety."

"Good."

"And so are you. How did your meeting go with your sponsor?"

"Elaina was so happy I called her. We talked about you a bit, actually."

"Uh oh."

"No, it was all good." Jaleesa swiveled the chair from side to side. "She just told me to go slow and be careful. And I think that's what we're doing."

Tina touched her lips. "Are you sure about that?"

"Yes, I'm sure." Jaleesa grinned at her. "Anyway, we mostly talked about the steps and what the first two meant to me."

"Step one says, 'I can't.' Step two says, 'God can.'"

"Mm hmm." Jaleesa nodded. "That's it in a nutshell."

"That was such a nice grace you said tonight, Jaleesa. I know part of that was a message to my parents, but you sounded like a preacher or something."

Jaleesa laughed. "Actually, I'm an ordained minister. I never really practiced, but I did officiate a few weddings. It was right out of college. I was searching."

"Wow, I think I'll let you be the one to let that factoid slip to my parents."

"I'm not a real minister, just an ordained one." Jaleesa laughed and then, at Tina's prompting, spoke briefly about growing up in Cleveland as the eldest sister of two younger sisters and a younger brother.

"Wait," Tina said, her eyes narrowing. "Does this mean you're a Cleveland Browns fan?" She whispered the last three words.

"Sure, but I like the Bengals, too. I've lived in Cincy for twenty years now. That's longer than I lived in Cleveland, and I get the feeling that if I know what's good for me, I'd better profess a love for all things Bengals right now. Is that it?"

Tina pointed to the Bengals pennant on her wall, right above her Blackwell College one.

"Observed and noted," Jaleesa said. She stood up and went back to the wall. "Who is this woman?" she pointed to one of the pictures.

"Chloe Sevigny," Tina said. "Do you consider her hot?"

"Sure," Jaleesa said enthusiastically, then added, "But out of all these women, you are by far the hottest."

"Me? No. no." Tina absolutely one-hundred and a million percent knew she was not hot. She didn't have the looks or the body to compete with her collection of women.

"Like I said, 'hotness' is in the eye of the beholder. And the only hot woman I am beholding is you."

Tina frowned and was surprised when tears welled up.

"Uh, oh," Jaleesa said. "What's happening here?" She reached for both of Tina's hands.

Tina looked around her room. At the pink walls, her computer, the closed but unlocked bedroom door.

"I'm thirty-one and still live at home. My parents read my texts and track my location. My mother searches my room on a regular basis." A sob wanted desperately to escape, but Tina pulled one hand out of Jaleesa's and squeezed the skin on her inner arm just enough so the pain got her attention.

"Whoa, whoa," Jaleesa said. "What's this?" She pulled Tina's sleeve up to reveal old and new bruises.

"Coping mechanism."

"Tell me more."

Tina sighed and looked down, not sure how much she should reveal. Jaleesa might go running for the hills. She looked up when Jaleesa held an imaginary key near Tina's lips and twisted it.

"Not fair," Tina mumbled, then said, "Okay, but remember, you asked."

"I did," Jaleesa said.

Tina had no clue how someone could look so authoritative and strong. It must be her posture or something.

"I have anxiety that overwhelms me at times. You know, ever since the *shitstorm*." Tina made air quotes around the last word. "And, I, uh…" She swallowed hard. Okay, fine. This might be a make-or-break moment, but she was going to be honest. That's what Jaleesa seemed to want. She gestured toward the bed. "I pull those curtains closed and snuggle under lots of comforters on top of me, so I feel like I'm in a cocoon." She marched to her closet and pulled out a belt. "I sometimes use this to get relief. It kind of works, but not always."

"Show me," Jaleesa said. "Gently, though."

Tina wrapped the belt around her hand a few times and swung it over her shoulder so it smacked against her sweater. "I don't usually have clothes on, and sometimes I hit other parts of my body, not just my back. Not my face, though. That would show." Tina flicked her wrist and wrapped the belt around her torso, hitting herself on the hip and butt.

Jaleesa stood up, took the belt from her, and hung it back in the closet. She closed the door and leaned against it. Putting both arms out wide, she said quietly, "The presence of Ms. Tina Jenkins is politely requested."

The melting process was complete as Tina flew into Jaleesa's arms.

Tina pressed her face into Jaleesa's shoulder and let the sobs come out. Jaleesa held her tight and stroked her back with one hand.

"You're okay, Tina. I've got you." The calm way she said the words and the way she held Tina made Tina think everything would be okay.

The door flew open. "Tina? Are you okay?" Tina's mother took in the scene and asked Jaleesa, "Is she okay?"

Jaleesa nodded and let Tina pull away. Tina swiped at her eyes.

"She's just blowing off a little pressure, Mrs. Jenkins," Jaleesa said. "She's okay."

"I'm okay, Mom," Tina said. "Having a friend is going to be good for me. I promise."

Tina's father stood in the doorway and touched Tina's mother's shoulder. "The kids are fine, honey. Tina's fine."

"I'm fine, Mom. Really." Tina stood tall, not quite in defiance. She wasn't strong enough to do that. She was trying for a confident posture. Yep, like the woman whose arms she had been in only a few moments before, which was kind of embarrassing now that she realized her parents had seen them embracing.

"All right," her mother said. The resigned tone in her voice was obvious. "But it's getting late. Perhaps you two should say your goodnights." And with that, she turned and agitatedly motioned for Tina's father to get out of the way.

"Okay, Mom," Tina said. "Just a few more minutes, and I'll walk Jaleesa out."

Once the door was closed and the sound of two sets of footsteps finished the trek down the stairs, Tina said, "Maybe next time I'll lock the door."

Jaleesa chuckled and pulled Tina back into her arms. She kissed Tina on the lips once and then pulled her close. Tina's head nestled into Jaleesa's shoulder, a spot that was quickly becoming her favorite.

Jaleesa stroked the back of Tina's head and said, "I understand your need for the belt. I do, but now is not the time to get into that conversation. Agreed?"

Tina nodded.

"Words, please."

"Yes, Ma'am," Tina said. "Agreed." The 'ma'am' that slipped out of her mouth surprised her. She hadn't said it in a mocking way. She simply responded to Jaleesa's authoritative request.

"Good." Jaleesa leaned down, kissed Tina again, and then said, "Will I see you tomorrow?"

"You smell so good." Tina let out a contented sigh and basked in the comfort. A gentle clearing of a throat inches from hers made her understand that an answer was needed. "Yes, you'll see me tomorrow, but I also have an idea."

Tina wiggled out of Jaleesa's arms and grabbed her phone off the desk. She showed Jaleesa a folder on the phone titled "Anime Art" and opened it. Inside were several genuine anime apps, but on the folder's second page was one called *Anime Chat*. "It's ostensibly a chat site for anime lovers, and I do use it for that, but it also has a private chat feature where you can chat one-on-one. My parents don't know I use it, and that's how I was able to have two online relationships, at different times, of course. My parents never found out. *ShortStuff*, that's my screen name."

"You spend a lot of time alone, don't you?"

Tina furrowed her brow. She hadn't thought about it that way. "Yes, I guess so. I mean, I watch TV with the folks most nights. You know, I take care of them."

"They seem perfectly capable of taking care of themselves."

Tina had no response for that but instead said, "When I need an outlet, I go support Dana at her AA meetings."

"And now you support me, too."

"Mm hmm." Tina smiled coquettishly for a moment but then said, "We can communicate privately on that app. I mean, if you want to."

Jaleesa nodded. "It's unconventional, but I can get on board with that. I'll come up with an obvious screen name, so you'll know it's me. I would, however, like to talk about that," she pointed to the closet, "in person. Without fear of being overheard. It's a big topic."

"Yes, Ma'am." Dang. Why were these 'ma'ams' popping out all over the place?

"Good."

Tina melted again. Right there in front of her was that confident posture. *Ugh, I am powerless over you.* "You have to go, but can I get one last kiss to last me until tomorrow?"

Jaleesa grinned and raised a suggestive eyebrow. "I would love that more than anything."

Tina flew back into Jaleesa's open arms. "I'm glad I met you," she murmured before moving in for another soul-caressing kiss from the hot woman in her pink bedroom.

Chapter 9

Jaleesa

Tina looked good in the driver's seat of Jaleesa's pickup truck. Tina took a sip of coffee, a to-go cup from Jumpin' Joe's. They'd walked to the coffee shop after Jaleesa's AA meeting, and Jaleesa suggested they grab their coffee and hustle back to her pickup so they could sit and talk privately with the heater going. Tina readily agreed. And if Tina's parents checked her location, they would find her right there in the Friendship Church's parking lot.

"What?" Tina said. "You have a weird look on your face."

"Just admiring the view."

"Flatterer." Tina put her cup into the cup holder on the driver's side door and leaned toward Jaleesa. "My lips are lonely."

"Mine, too," Jaleesa said with a chuckle. She leaned closer but didn't close the deal. She let Tina do that. Not a mind game, not at all. She just wanted to make sure Tina understood that she had power in their relationship. Whatever that turned out to be. All Jaleesa knew was that she liked Tina in her life, and she wanted more.

Tina touched her lips to Jaleesa's. The gentle pressure eased the cold in the pickup's cab for some weird reason. Tina's soft moan could have been misconstrued as sexual arousal, but Jaleesa knew it was not. As the kiss deepened, Jaleesa grabbed the back of Tina's head and pulled her tighter. She nipped at Tina's lips and then started a trail of kisses along Tina's cheeks to her neck. Jaleesa moaned, and her moan was definitely one of sexual arousal. Tina shivered when Jaleesa sucked at Tina's tender neck. She gently pushed Jaleesa away.

"Oh, my God," Jaleesa said. "I'm so sorry."

"Were you turned on?"

Jaleesa locked gazes with Tina and said, "Yes."

Tina looked away.

"Nope," Jaleesa said.

Tina looked back up. "I told you. This can't work."

Jaleesa reached for Tina's still-gloved hands. "We'll figure this out, okay? I am, indeed, a sexual being. But I can, you know, take care of things on my own. Later."

"You would do that?"

"Of course. I'm not going to pressure you into anything you don't want to do. In fact, if anything happens sexually between us, it will be completely your idea." Jaleesa said the words, but her body was still firing on all cylinders. She was used to making the first move and dominating women sexually. But that wasn't going to happen with Tina. Her body and brain just had to get used to the idea.

Tina narrowed her eyes, not quite sure if she believed Jaleesa or not. "It'll be my idea?"

"Yes, but I am not going to hide my body's reaction to you. Honesty in all things, okay?"

"Okay." Tina seemed to muse on something and then said, "Jaleesa?"

"Mm hmm?" Jaleesa took a sip of her still-hot coffee and held the cup in both hands for the warmth.

"You might be waiting a long time."

"Understood."

"You know what?"

"What?" This was good, Jaleesa thought. She and Tina were having a mature conversation about something that could have gone incredibly sideways. She considered herself lucky. Very lucky.

Tina smirked. "I think maybe you're different than the women my ACE friends describe."

"You belong to an ACE group? Online?"

"Yes, my parents have no clue about that part of me. I delete my browser history every time I go in there."

"So, what do your ACE friends say about these women?"

"The women they date say they understand the whole ACE thing, but then they'll put on the pressure to have full-on sex. Or they complain that they're sacrificing so much, and my ACE friends aren't sacrificing anything and are just being selfish and should put out every once in a while."

"'Put out?' Ugh. Were your friends honest about being ACE before getting into those relationships?"

"Yes, yes," Tina said, clearly upset. "I've spent many long nights comforting my friends when it all goes to shit for them."

"I'm sorry that happens."

"Me, too. And then my friends say their love interests sometimes demand they get their hormones checked. And they do, and it comes back normal—every time. My doctor always checks hormone levels at my wellness exams, so I know that's not it. And you know what?"

"What?"

"After finding this chat group, I realized I'm not a freak. I'm not abnormal. I'm not broken." Tina's voice broke on the last word, and Jaleesa pulled her into her arms.

"Shh, shh," Jaleesa hushed and rubbed her back. "You are not broken. Not in the least. You're an amazing woman, and I'm ecstatic you want to spend time with me."

"I still like you," Tina said into Jaleesa's shoulder.

"And I still like you back," Jaleesa said, letting Tina pull away.

"Good. And don't you forget it." Tina wagged a finger at Jaleesa and then swiped at the tears in her eyes.

"Respect is essential in any and all relationships. That and honesty, communication, and consent."

"You sound like a noble knight living under a code of conduct or something."

"Yeah, kind of. I had a lover in college, Dawnn—she taught me a lot about how to show respect and how to command respect. Not *demand* it because you can't. It's not genuine that way. You have to earn it."

"What do you mean?" Tina turned sideways and sat back against the driver's door, her feet up on the seat. Jaleesa was amazed that Tina was small and flexible enough to do that. She peered at Jaleesa over the top of her coffee as she took a sip.

Jaleesa sighed. It was time. "Let's back up and talk about that belt in your closet. The pain you give yourself helps distract you from the other things in your life, right? It helps relieve stress, anxiety, even boredom?"

"OMG, that is so true. The boredom part, too."

"I don't get the impression that you're doing permanent damage to yourself. Am I right about that?"

"Yes, Ma'am. You're right."

Whoa, this is, like, the third time she's called me 'Ma'am.' "Good. You showed your own body respect by not damaging it."

"I did the same thing when I finally told my parents about my addiction."

"Getting and staying clean is the ultimate show of respect for your whole body and soul, isn't it?"

"Elite athlete," Tina said, pointing toward Jaleesa with her coffee cup.

Jaleesa nodded, thinking about how finely tuned her body was back in college. But now was no time to be wistful or think about how her joints ached in this cold weather. Jaleesa needed to go about this next part gently so she wouldn't come across as aggressive. "In your online relationships, were you submissive to your partners?" There it was. Put it right out there, but hopefully in a gentle way.

"What does that mean? Like was I a shrinking violet or something?"

Jaleesa laughed. "No, no. Submissives are people who tend to like when more authoritative people take control of things. Submissives lean on their Dominants and show respect by allowing their Dominants to take care of them." Oops. Jaleesa didn't mean to throw the word *dominant* out there so soon, but there it was. "Although, the submissives I've known have been very strong and independent people."

"You're one of these 'Dominants?'"

"Mm hmm," Jaleesa said with a nod. "I've always had the urge to take care of people. Maybe because I'm the oldest of four kids?" She shrugged. "I don't know."

Tina took off one glove and rubbed the back of her fingers across her cheek. This must be a thinking tic. It was an endearing quirk. "I think maybe I was submissive sometimes," Tina said honestly. "Not all the time, though."

"Keep the idea in the back of your mind as you think about your past relationships, including the one with Nylani."

"Okay," Tina said in a tone that said she'd do that, but she was a little wary of where this conversation was going.

Jaleesa felt that Tina was still somewhat receptive, so she went on. "I've known a lot of people who like pain. Good pain. For some, it's cathartic. It helps them move on from whatever anxiety or imbalance they might be feeling."

"Yes," Tina interrupted. "Imbalance. That's it. That's the perfect word."

"Others like the pain-to-pleasure connection."

Tina narrowed her eyes. "What does that mean?"

"They take the pain and let it feed their sexual centers. They get aroused."

Tina's eyes grew big. Her facial expressions certainly were expressive.

"Are you okay?" Jaleesa asked.

"I just can't picture that," Tina said. "Do you like that?"

"Not receiving, no," Jaleesa let her response hang there.

It wasn't long before her unspoken meaning dawned on Tina. "Ohhhhhhh. OMG. You like *giving* that to people."

Jaleesa nodded. "Always with consent and with continual

communication. Remember that it's not always about arousal, though. Some people just want the cleansing. I've held many a sobbing sub in my arms after a flogging."

Tina's eyes grew wide again. "Flogging," she whispered. "I heard Dana use that word. She was talking to Kadesha about it, but they stopped their conversation when I walked up."

"Did she now?" Hmm. Jaleesa had suspected a brat-like submissive nature in Dana. Maybe the young woman was experienced.

"So, you flog these people?"

"With consent, yes."

"What do you get out of it?"

Jaleesa bit her bottom lip. "It depends on the reason I'm doing it. In fact, the last time I flogged someone, it was at Dominique's—"

"Yes, Dana mentioned Dominique's. I was going to look that up, but I keep forgetting. Is that like a Dominatrix lair or something?"

"It kind of is, but there's a lot more to Dominique's than that."

"Is Dominique a real person?"

Jaleesa laughed. "Yes, she's a businesswoman who owns a private membership club."

"Do you go there?"

"I, I used to," Jaleesa said. "It's where I met Gabby."

"Was she your submissive? Did you flog her?"

"Yes and yes, but I'm going to stop you right there. There's etiquette in BDSM, just like at our meetings. What goes on there stays there."

"I get that."

"And, honestly, I don't think I'm ready to talk about Gabby right now."

"Okay," Tina said. "But can we go back to something? You said, 'BDSM.' In my second online relationship, Therese was her name, she was the one that suggested the belt thing. She had me do it and then tell her how I felt. At first, I only did it when she told me to. But after a while, I liked it. It helped. I didn't know that it was called BDSM. And, wow, I have totally lived a sheltered life, haven't I?"

"Yes, you have. You live in cages. Your bed itself is a cage with those pink curtains and heavy comforters. Your room is a cage. Your house, too. Your well-defined pig trails to and from work."

Tina looked stunned as she absorbed Jaleesa's observations.

Jaleesa reached behind her into the extended cab, heaved up a box, and placed it gently onto Tina's lap. "I wanted to find the right time to give you this."

"It's heavy. What is it?"

"Open it. I didn't make it myself, but I think you might find it useful."

Tina reached into the large bag and pulled out a heavy blanket.

"This is a weighted blanket, isn't it?" Tina asked. "Dr. Bradley recommended one of these for my anxiety. We never followed up on it." She looked up at Jaleesa, gratitude etched all over her face. She rubbed the surface of the blanket. "It's so soft. And it's pink."

"Couldn't help noticing the plethora of pink in your cage."

Tina smacked Jaleesa on the knee. "Oh, don't call it that. Even if it is."

Ahh, good. Tina had accepted that her life was lived in cages. Tina spread the blanket over both their laps and then blurted, "Does flogging people turn you on? Do you flog men, too?"

Jaleesa held in her laughter at the outburst and said, "I've flogged lots of men, but only at Dominique's. Those sessions don't turn me on."

"But flogging women sometimes does?"

"Yes, sometimes. Remember, it's all about consent and communication. If we both want the arousal, then yes, it can turn me on. Sometimes I get satisfaction, not sexual, but satisfaction knowing I've helped someone through their trouble."

"Like me when I do my belt routine. I get relief from the pain, but yours is more…emotional, I guess? And this is your way of respecting these women? Your flogees?" Tina grinned at her clever word. "Giving them relief?"

"Mm hmm."

"So, um, I don't know how to ask this, so bear with me for a minute."

Jaleesa nodded. She wasn't sure what was coming next but hoped it wasn't a request for Jaleesa to flog her. It was way too soon in their relationship for that, especially with Tina's overprotective parents. Nothing good would come out of it at this present stage.

"Some people think *being intimate* means having sex." Tina used air quotes around the words 'being' and 'intimate.' "But intimacy means so many other things. Like…"

The pause was over-long, so Jaleesa quietly suggested, "Like holding hands." She reached for one of Tina's.

"Yes," Tina said softly. "Or sharing our inner fears and feelings."

"Like you and I are doing on a freezing January evening in the cab of my pickup."

"Yes," Tina said. "Hey, why did you want me to sit here in the driver's seat?"

"So, you would feel in control," Jaleesa said quickly.

Tina stroked the steering wheel with her one free hand. "Thank you. That was very thoughtful. I never would have…"

"And that's okay. I never would have thought to knit someone a cashmere scarf after meeting them once."

Tina squirmed a bit and then said, "I like what we have. It's like emotional intimacy."

"And there's some physical. I love when you lay your head on my shoulder when I hold you. I love your kisses. That's physical."

"It is, isn't it? I find that I want to feel my hands on your bare back as I give you a back massage." Tina reached out, took off Jaleesa's gloves, and began a slow hand massage. "This is intimate."

"Yes. I like when you touch me, Tina. It's nice. It's quiet. It's not urgent."

"Because it's not leading to some frenzied smash of a body against a wall as a tongue goes down someone else's throat?"

Jaleesa laughed.

"I never understood that in movies. I always thought the acting in love scenes was so over the top that it was laughable until the softball team had a movie night, and all of them except me seemed affected by the sex scene. I just wanted to laugh."

"How about together we figure out what intimacy means to us? As a couple."

Tina's massaging fingers stopped abruptly. "Are we? A couple?"

"I'd like us to be. So, let's make it official. Tina Jenkins, would you go out with me? I'd like to be exclusive with you as we get to know each other. But that would mean going *out*. Actually going places, like this little café I want to take you to near the salon. You've been cooped up in your cages, and I want to show you…everything."

"Yes," came the quick answer.

"One day at a time, though, right?"

Tina chuckled. "Mm hmm."

"You haven't seen my apartment or the salon where I work. I want to show you these places, but we're taking it slow and easy."

"Yes, Jaleesa," Tina gushed. "I would love nothing more than to go out with you. My parents, though…"

"We'll talk to your parents when I pick you up at your house to take you to dinner and then to your meeting tomorrow. It's an open one, right?"

Tina nodded and then blew out a nervous laugh. "My dad was right. 'Something's coming.' He said that to my mother right before you walked into my house for the first time."

"Good things are coming, Tina," Jaleesa said. "Good things." She leaned in for a quick kiss and then sat back. She sensed a change in subject was needed and said, "So, how about Dana's new doo?"

"OMG, I know I've already said it, but her hair looks so good. She looks so grown up now. And she loves it. She told me it took over two hours."

"It did," Jaleesa said. "When she first sat in my chair, she threw out a thousand ideas. One of those was straightening her hair. And that was the one I thought would make her look more her age. She said she'd tried to do it herself once but damaged her hair. She probably used too much heat. I took care of her."

"You sure did," Tina said. "How did you learn to cut hair? At B.C.?"

"No. My mom always had me do my younger sisters' hair, and then I went to cosmetology school after B.C."

"Even with a bachelor's degree in Psychology in your back pocket, you still went after what you wanted. That's so admirable, Jaleesa."

"Thank you." She held out her cell phone. "Please call my parents and tell them that."

Tina laughed and said, "Oh, oh, I don't know how I forgot. I printed some stuff out for you." Tina reached into her back pocket and pulled out a few papers. "Don't be mad, but I printed a few commercial real estate listings." She handed them to Jaleesa.

"For what? Are you moving?"

"No," Tina said. "For your new shop."

It was Jaleesa's turn to be stunned. She looked at the listings in her hands. She glanced through them and said, "You're incredible. So generous. So caring. This," she tapped the papers, "is intimacy."

"Oh, good. You're not mad. I didn't want you to think I was meddling."

"Never. You had good intentions."

They looked over the listings together but decided that none were going to work. Some spaces were too small, and others were way overpriced because of their locations in the heart of Cincinnati.

"Maybe we should look farther outside the city," Tina suggested.

We? Jaleesa loved that Tina was thinking of them as *we*.

"We can try, but honestly, I don't think I'm going to be able to afford to do any of this. It was kind of a pipe dream." Jaleesa heard the defeat in her own voice and handed the listings back to Tina.

"Sooo, even though I'm not really sure about this whole submissive and Dominant stuff …" Tina pressed her index finger down on the blanket covering Jaleesa's thigh and twisted it back and forth. "Can a Dominant ever lean on her submissive?" The index finger traveled up and then poked Jaleesa gently on the chest. *Was Tina accepting a D/s nature for their new relationship?*

"I suppose so," Jaleesa said evenly. She couldn't help the grin creeping up her face. "I suppose it can be done."

"Let me help you, Jaleesa," Tina said seriously. "You've been caring for me since we met."

At Jaleesa's perplexed expression, Tina said, "Coffee urn? My breakdown both during and after my speech? And I know you're all strong with those fabulous biceps and everything, but…"

Jaleesa searched Tina's eyes for what exactly she didn't know, but what she saw there was a genuine desire to support and help. Jaleesa nodded.

"Words, please," Tina said, her eyes full of mirth.

"Really?" Hmm, did Tina have brat qualities to her? No problem. Jaleesa knew how to tame brats. "Okay, I'll play. Yes, Miss Tina Jenkins, AKA *ShortStuff*, I will let you help me. We can work on this together."

"There," Tina said. "That wasn't so hard, now was it, *TallDrinkOfWater*?" She reached up and caressed Jaleesa's leather jacket where her biceps would be. "Oh, God, I can't wait to see you in a tank top."

Jaleesa burst out laughing and pulled Tina into a possessive hug. Oh, yes, Tina was a keeper.

~~~

Tuesday evening, Jaleesa sat at the kitchen table with Tina's parents while Tina was upstairs getting ready for Jaleesa to take her out to dinner.

"We've seen a different Tina these past couple of weeks," Tina's father said quietly. "And we think it's directly related to her meeting you, J-Dub."

Jaleesa tried not to laugh at his use of the nickname. "She's a lot of fun, and we're getting to know each other."

"She used to be so carefree," Tina's mother said. "Before all of…it. There used to be a hop in her step and joy in everything she did."

"Joy. That's a good word, Marion," Tina's father said, patting her hand.

"I'd almost forgotten how carefree she could be," Tina's mother said. "That joy faded when she was using and then disappeared altogether when she began recovery. But now I see inklings of it again. She's taking the stairs two at a time."

"I've even heard her humming," Tina's father added.

"And singing." Tina's mother looked directly at Jaleesa. "Now that she's met you."

Jaleesa's heart swelled. "I…" She cleared her throat of the emotion building. "She's special." A semi-awkward silence threatened to overcome them, so Jaleesa pulled out the printed map from her back pocket and pointed to the restaurant she was taking Tina to before the meeting. She also pointed out the salon where she worked. Both addresses were written in her neat handwriting on the side.

"Thank you for understanding our concerns," Tina's father said. "You're very thoughtful, J-Dub."

Jaleesa couldn't hold it in anymore and laughed. "You are killing me with that nickname."

"What? Tina can't take all the teasing around here," Tina's father said. "I've got to spread it around."

Tina's mother was smiling, but it was clear that she was still on edge and probably would be until Tina got home later that evening. "I think it's good for her to have a friend. Especially at her meetings. Harriet is spotty with her attendance, and Dana doesn't go to the NA meetings all the time."

"I'm happy to support her," Jaleesa said. "She's doing very well in her recovery."

"One day at a time, right?" came Tina's booming voice as she bounded down the stairs.

Everyone stood up.

Tina kissed each of her parents in turn and grabbed Jaleesa by the jacket. "I finally get to ride in the pickup."

"Pickup?" Tina's mother's eyes grew wide.

Before Jaleesa could answer, Tina's father said, "It's a Ford F-150, right?"

Jaleesa nodded. He must have been watching when she parked on the street in front of their house. The street was clear and dry, with no ice this time.

"Four-wheel drive? Automatic? V6? EcoBoost?"

"And a towing package," Jaleesa added with a laugh. "You know your trucks."

"He wants one," Tina said.

"Marion, that is a sturdy pickup. They'll be okay."

Tina's mother seemed resigned to it all, simply nodded, and then hugged Tina.

It took another few minutes for the Jenkins family to say their goodbyes, and you would think Tina was going to Europe and not barely ten miles away from home.

~~~

The dinner out had been delightful, for lack of a better word. Tina had been talkative, and there were no awkward moments. Even when Tina started grilling Jaleesa about past girlfriends, Jaleesa took it in stride. She didn't discuss her many and varied one-night stands, though. She had a feeling that part of her life was over, anyway, so why bring it up? Honesty in all things, yes, so maybe that part of her life would eventually come out.

Jaleesa showed Tina the salon, even though it was locked up tight. The big picture windows out front let in enough light for Tina to see Jaleesa's station. Since time was ticking, they hustled back to the pickup and got to the Friendship Church in plenty of time to set up the coffee and beverage station for the NA meeting.

They sat in the back just in case Harriet came in, and she did, right at the last minute. "There you are," Jaleesa said just before the meeting began. "I was wondering if I'd ever see you again."

"Still kicking," Harriet said. The way she said it put Jaleesa on alert. "I like it," Harriet said, pointing to Tina and Jaleesa holding hands.

Tina leaned over Jaleesa and whispered, "And apparently, we have you to thank."

"Doubt it." Harriet coughed several times into the crook of her elbow.

"Are you okay?" Tina asked.

"Never better," Harriet said and then cleared her throat. She stood up abruptly and went into the women's restroom, where the sounds of a muffled coughing fit soon emanated.

"She doesn't look good," Tina said to Jaleesa.

"No, she doesn't. And I don't mean to be rude, but she doesn't smell very good either."

"Switch with me."

They switched seats, and Tina laid into Harriet when she got back. "You're living in your car again, aren't you?"

Harriet didn't answer. She just waved her off and shoved a glazed donut into her mouth.

"It's winter, Harriet."

"I'm okay," Harriet said after swallowing her huge bite. "Doug lets me park behind the warehouse, and then in the morning, I'm all alone in the back workroom where no one can smell me." She let out a big laugh as if her situation wasn't as dire as it sounded.

"Harriet—"

"Tina, I'm okay. I'm giving my sister and her asshole husband a break from me, okay? I'm fine."

Tina harrumphed and was about to say something else when Fran, the NA leader, cleared her throat to start the meeting.

Jaleesa pulled Tina close and said, "We'll figure something out. Okay?"

Tina looked at Jaleesa and nodded. Jaleesa's heart swelled at the trust she saw in Tina's eyes. She put an arm around her and vowed to herself to take care of both Tina and Harriet. Harriet was the one who had inadvertently kept Jaleesa sober and who had put Tina in her life, after all.

Chapter 10

Tina

When the Tuesday evening N.A. meeting ended, Jaleesa stood up, effectively blocking Harriet's path before she could bolt. Not that it looked like she was about to, but apparently, Jaleesa just wanted to make sure. Jaleesa said, "I want you to stay at my place tonight."

"You'd do that?" Tina asked, placing a hand over her heart. Was Jaleesa really that generous, or was she trying to impress people? Either way, it was extremely generous.

"Of course, I mean it," Jaleesa said. "Harriet and I go way back, don't we?"

Harriet laughed a snorting kind of laugh which set off a coughing fit.

Tina still didn't know how the two of them had met, but that didn't matter at the moment. "Yes, that's a great idea. We'll take you to Jaleesa's and get you settled in." She turned to Jaleesa and asked, "Do you have cold medications there? Non-alcoholic and non-narcotic? She may be coming down with a cold."

"I do, actually. And the non-alcohol aspect is always a part of being on the program," Jaleesa said.

Tina's hand grasped Jaleesa's as she smiled sympathetically.

"I don't know what you two are planning," Harriet said, "but I'm not going home with anybody. I'm fine. The heater works in the car, and Doug opens the warehouse at six thirty."

"Yeah, no," Tina said firmly. "Not going to happen on my watch."

Harriet frowned at Tina for a moment and asked, "Since when am I on your watch?"

"Since the day I met you, right here, in this back row a year ago," Tina said. "But today, I have backup." She jutted her thumb toward Jaleesa.

Jaleesa stood tall, crossed her arms, and said, "Yeah," in a deep, comical voice.

Harriet smiled. "I'm not going to get out of this, am I?"

"Nope," Tina said. "You'll follow us to Jaleesa's apartment."

Harriet nodded and let out a resigned sigh.

Softly, Jaleesa said to Tina, "Call your parents and let them know what's going on, okay?"

Tina nodded. That would be a tough conversation, but it had to be done. No way was Tina going to let Harriet spend one more night sleeping in her car in the middle of winter.

Jaleesa put a hand on Tina's arm and said, "Harriet and I will break down the beverage and snack station once everyone's had their fill. You can check our work after."

"Thank you," Tina said. The gratitude she felt couldn't be expressed right then, but she'd be sure to show Jaleesa later.

"C'mon, you," Jaleesa said to Harriet. "Let's be of service tonight, shall we?"

Harriet nodded and followed Jaleesa like a lost puppy. It was kind of endearing.

The call to Tina's parents was difficult. Tina's mother wanted to drive to the church and take over the situation.

"Mom," Tina said firmly. "I'm okay. I'll call you once Harriet is safe in Jaleesa's apartment."

"I don't like this," Tina's mother said.

"I know, Mom, but I want to do this for Harriet."

"Is she high? Is she using?"

"I don't get the feeling that she is, but Jaleesa and I will be sure to find out."

There was silence on the phone, her mother obviously displeased with the night's events. "Fine," her mother finally said. "If you feel tempted by anything, Tina, call home. We'll pick you up."

Tina smiled. "I'll be fine—"

"I want Jaleesa's address and phone number."

"Okay, I'll get the address from her before we leave here."

"Does she have medications? You need to ask. Does she have guns in her apartment?"

Guns, Mom? Really? And plural? More than one? Holy— No, Tina refused to think about the reasons her mother might think Jaleesa had guns. Another day. Maybe.

"I'll ask," Tina said, her voice sounded halting and stiff to her own ears.

"Okay. Good."

"But Mom?"

"Yes, honey?"

"Don't come by unannounced. You can come by if you want to, we're not hiding anything, but let me know, so I'm not embarrassed. Okay?"

Tina heard her father talking in the background but couldn't make out his words. Her mother finally said, "Call when you get to Jaleesa's."

"I will. Thank you for trusting me."

"Be safe," Tina's father called from the background.

"I will," Tina said. "I'll call you once we get Harriet settled."

They said their goodbyes, but before Tina ended her side of the call, she heard her mother say, "I don't like this one bit."

Tina ended the call and let out a frustrated sigh. She heard Jaleesa teasing Harriet good-naturedly about something, which furthered Tina's resolve. Her friend needed her. She wouldn't go off the deep end and relapse if she helped Harriet. But maybe that wasn't what her mother was worried about. As she walked back over to her friends, she realized what it was. Her mother was anxious about her spending time with Jaleesa and about her going to Jaleesa's apartment. That had to be it. Tina grunted. Well, too bad. Jaleesa had been a Godsend—probably a literal one.

Tina looked toward Jaleesa, who must have sensed her gaze and looked up. The smile that lit Jaleesa's face went straight to Tina's heart. Tina smiled back and threw a thumbs-up that all was well, even though it kind of wasn't.

On the drive to Jaleesa's apartment, which overlooked the gorgeous B.C. campus, it was Tina's job to make sure Harriet's car was always right behind them. It was. Tina never doubted it. Harriet looked so tired and defeated at the meeting that the offer to stay at Jaleesa's must have been her own Godsend. Funny how that was a common theme around Jaleesa. As they drove, Tina stole a moment to take in Jaleesa's strong features. She was exceptionally good-looking, which made Tina wonder why at age thirty-eight, the woman hadn't been snatched up and tied down already.

"What?" Jaleesa said from the driver's seat, sensing Tina's gaze.

"Just admiring the view," Tina said.

"Flatterer," Jaleesa quipped.

After parking, Tina and Jaleesa met Harriet at her car. It was a small, seen-better-days, four-door car that seemed jam-packed with everything Harriet owned.

"Got your wallet? Keys? Phone? Glasses?" Jaleesa asked.

Harriet nodded at each one, and Tina linked arms with her as they followed Jaleesa to the stairwell and up two flights to her third-floor apartment. They had to stop once while Harriet had a coughing fit, but they made it the rest of the way without much trouble.

Tina wanted to take in more of the environment around her, but she was rather tunnel-visioned helping Harriet. Once inside Jaleesa's apartment, though, Tina allowed herself to take in the space. There were no clutter piles, only a neat and tidy functional space. A neat environment means a neat mind, doesn't it? The curtains covering the windows were black, brown, and tan, and although masculine, they complemented the throw rugs and furniture nicely in the nice-sized living room. There were two open doors off the living room. One looked to be a bedroom, and the other a bathroom. The whole place seemed clean, inviting, and totally Jaleesa. There were a few pictures and pieces of art on the walls, but Tina didn't have time to check them out.

Tina took the helm. "Do you have a pair of sweats and maybe a t-shirt she can change into?" This she said to Jaleesa, who nodded. "I know you'll swim in them, Harriet, but they'll be clean and warm."

"Mm hmm," was all Harriet said.

"Actually, I have some clothes that might fit her," Jaleesa said, guiding Harriet to a kitchen chair. "Let me get you some water."

"Thank you." Harriet sat docilely, apparently resigned to her fate that evening.

While Harriet sat at the kitchen table and Jaleesa was off in search of fresh clothes, Tina opened one of the kitchen cupboards. She stopped herself abruptly. She should ask permission first. *Consent is paramount,* she heard in her mind. It was something Jaleesa had said a few times.

"Jaleesa, can I look around your cupboards for something to feed Harriet?"

"Of course," came the immediate answer. "Pantry is to the left of the sink."

Tina found the pantry and was ecstatic to find cans of soup and crackers. Harriet settled on chicken noodle, and Tina started the preparations.

"Perfect," Jaleesa said as she came back into the kitchen and gestured to the soup on the stove. "I put some clothes, including warm socks, in the bathroom. I figured a nice hot shower would do you good. Oh, and I also pulled out a fresh toothbrush and toothpaste. You'll see them."

"You two…" Harriet said and blinked back a sheen of tears. "Thank you." She was definitely choked up, which totally pinged Tina's heart center.

"You're worth taking care of, Harriet," Tina said softly and then presented her with a bowl of soup and a pile of saltine crackers on a plate. "I saw cheese in the fridge. I can cut a slice or two for you if you want."

"This is plenty," Harriet said and moaned when she took her first spoonful of soup. "So good."

"Good," Tina said and moved on to the next item on her mental list. She turned to Jaleesa. "Where will she sleep?"

Jaleesa curled her finger in a come-hither motion, and Tina followed her to the bigger of two couches in the living room. Oh, it was a pull-out couch. No, it was a futon. Jaleesa removed the dust cover, pulled out the futon, and revealed a nice-sized mattress covered in what looked like clean sheets.

"Comforter and pillows live in here." Jaleesa moved a book off the hassock and pulled up the top. Tina couldn't help noticing that the book was the AA Big Book. Good for her. She was taking her sobriety seriously. Inside the hassock was a gorgeous comforter. It didn't exactly match the curtains, but the browns, blues, and soft greens complemented them well. Two pillows followed.

Together, Tina and Jaleesa put the comforter on the bed and tucked in the corners. The pillows were placed just so, and then Jaleesa did something so endearing that Tina wanted to hug her silly. She reached up to a high shelf of her gorgeous floor-to-ceiling bookshelves, which Tina couldn't wait to peruse, and pulled down a teddy bear and placed it between the pillows.

"Everybody needs something to cuddle," Jaleesa said.

"I'm keeping you," Tina said softly.

"Sounds good to me," Jaleesa said.

Wait, was that a tinge of blush on her cheeks? Was Jaleesa Whitmore a softy? This must be explored further, but not right now. Tina went over to the bookshelves, neatly organized yet packed with books. Hardcovers and paperbacks. Non-fiction and fiction. Ooh, and some cool-looking textbooks on Psychology. She ran her finger along one row at eye level and stopped at a certain title.

"I'm still reading it," Tina said, holding up *The Invisible Man*. "It's very thought-provoking. He's not literally invisible. It's just that people don't give him the time of day or try to get to know him. If they look at him at all, they don't bother to get to know the *real* him. Inside. Ugh. It's pissing me off that no one sees him."

Jaleesa took the book from Tina's hand and reshelved it. "When you're finished, we'll talk about it, okay?"

"I look forward to it." Tina inched closer to Jaleesa. "You're pretty unique, Ms. Whitmore."

Jaleesa's arms went around her as Tina had hoped. "As are you, Ms. Jenkins."

Water running in the kitchen broke their connection, and they headed back.

Jaleesa grabbed a tissue box on the way and plunked it on the counter where Harriet was drying her hands with a paper towel.

"Thank you," Harriet said.

"Difficult question coming," Jaleesa said.

"I was expecting it."

"Have you been using?"

"No, Ma'am," Harriet said. "Can't afford it, anyway." She scoffed at herself and said, "God—" she reached over and took Jaleesa's hand in her left and Tina's in her right. She cleared her throat and asked, "Will you both join me in the Serenity Prayer?"

"Of course," Tina answered.

When they finished, Harriet squeezed each of the hands she was holding and then brushed the tears from her eyes. She looked up at Jaleesa. "You said something about a shower?"

"Right this way," Jaleesa said, leading Harriet to the bathroom.

Tina stayed in the kitchen to wash up the soup pot. Harriet had already washed and dried her dishes and spoon. Tina knew that Harriet was a kind and caring person, and washing her own dishes when she was exhausted was proof of that.

Tina heard Jaleesa say, "I pulled out shampoo and conditioner for thin hair. Let the conditioner sit in for a while, okay? And then, if you want, maybe not tonight, but at some point, I can give you a trim or a different style altogether."

"I can't pay you."

"I'm not expecting payment," Jaleesa said. "It's something I can do, so I'm offering."

Tina couldn't hear the rest of the exchange, except when Jaleesa said, "You'll be alright, Harriet," and then closed the bathroom door.

Tina rushed over and threw herself into a hug around Jaleesa's body.

"Oof," Jaleesa said as Tina squeezed the life out of her. "What's this for?"

"For being so awesome."

Jaleesa wrapped her arms around Tina and chuckled. "I'm not so sure about that, but I do like a beautiful woman in my arms. It's been a while."

"How long?"

"Uh uh," Jaleesa said with a shake of her head. "Tonight is about Harriet. We'll talk more about my exes another day."

"Okay," Tina said. "Thank you for doing this for Harriet."

"It was a no-brainer. I've got the room and the resources, and she needed help." Jaleesa guided Tina to the loveseat. Tina kicked off her shoes and then turned sideways on the couch with her feet tucked underneath her. Jaleesa turned so she was facing Tina and said, "You need to call your parents."

Tina was still a bit miffed at her mother's reactions on the phone, so she waved off Jaleesa's suggestion with a flick of her hand.

A deliberate clearing of a throat from the other occupant of the loveseat got Tina's attention. She took in Jaleesa's expression and instantly felt bad that she'd been so cavalier. One of Jaleesa's eyebrows raised up as she said, "Tina." That was it. Just the one word, but the way she'd said it made Tina instantly remorseful.

"Okay, fine," Tina said. There was no way she was going to challenge that eyebrow. Jaleesa was only helping her do the right thing. *Oh, shit.* An epiphany was happening. "Wait, is this you being, like, dominant on me?

If it is, it's okay. I think. Maybe. Sometimes."

Jaleesa nodded. "You know you need to call them."

"Yes. You're right." Tina took her phone out of her pocket as a bloom of something good seeped through her chest while Jaleesa watched her. Whatever it was seeped right into her core, her heart, her head. What was this feeling? She wasn't sure, but she really, really liked it.

After checking in, Tina reported that her parents seemed to have settled down and even said they were glad Harriet was okay.

"Once we have Harriet settled," Jaleesa said, pointing to the futon, "I'm going to drive you home."

"No," Tina said.

Jaleesa laughed. "No?"

"I'm staying here." Tina had decided that two seconds ago.

"I would love that, Tina," Jaleesa said gently. Okay, almost too gently.

Was she coddling Tina? Tina was not a child. How could she get anyone to understand that?

"You have work tomorrow," Jaleesa pointed out.

Tina gestured toward the bathroom, the shower still running. "She is going to call in sick because she truly is sick. I'm calling in, too. I haven't taken a day off since I had the flu a few years ago."

"If you do this, your parents are going to flip," Jaleesa said.

Instant regret hit Tina right in the heart. "They will, won't they?" Jaleesa had a valid point. Her mother was going to flip out that Tina wouldn't be coming home. But it was for just one night. *And I am not a child.*

"No, you're not a child," Jaleesa said.

"Oh, shoot, did I say that last part out loud?"

Jaleesa nodded and reached for Tina's hands. "Baby, I know you want to help, but I can take tomorrow off easily and stay with Harriet. She'll be in good hands."

Whoa. She just called me 'baby,' didn't she? Tina poked Jaleesa in the arm. "You're right."

Jaleesa picked up the hand that had poked her. She kissed the palm, all four fingers at once, and then the one finger that had just poked her. "This poking? It's a form of micro-aggression. I'd rather you use your words instead. I can see that there's so much inside you that needs to be expressed and let out, but tonight is not the night. Do you agree?"

Tina's face felt blazing hot as Jaleesa scolded her in a very calm but serious way. "Yes, Ma'am." *OMG, again with the Ma'am.* Even Harriet had said it earlier. The words tumbled out before Tina could stop them. "What is this power you have to make people call you Ma'am?"

Jaleesa laughed but never broke eye contact. "You're showing me respect. I think you're reacting to my gentle dominance."

"Hmm," Tina said. This was going to take more thought. "Okay, how about this? Once Harriet is settled, I'll call my parents to pick me up."

"I can drive—"

"No, I'd feel better if you stayed here with her. And my parents will feel better if they saw where and how you lived."

"There is wisdom in that, I suppose," Jaleesa said. "But I think we should preserve Harriet's dignity tonight by not having your parents here. I'll drive you home tonight, but I have an idea if you're amenable. I'm going to suggest that Harriet stay with me for a while until we can figure out how to continue helping her, but that's only if she wants to, of course."

"Of course," Tina said.

"My idea is this. How about I invite you and your parents over for dinner tomorrow night? This way Harriet has a chance to get used to the idea, and I have a chance to clean."

Tina chuckled. "Your home is immaculate, but I love your idea." She crossed her arms and said, "I'm sorry for poking you."

"It's okay. Just me being honest. And I expect the same from you."

"If honesty is what you're after," Tina said, "then I would honestly like a kiss from you. Or twelve. Right here on this tiny couch of yours."

"Gladly."

Jaleesa pulled Tina into her arms. She ran the back of a knuckle over one of Tina's eyebrows, down her cheek, over Tina's lips until finally cupping Tina's chin. She tilted Tina's head up.

Tina sighed. She understood it for what it was. Jaleesa was making love to her in a way that Tina would understand. And, oh, yes, she understood.

When Jaleesa's lips landed on hers, Tina was done with gentle and threw herself on Jaleesa, knocking her back on the couch. Tina wiggled her way on top, with one foot on the floor for balance. She loved the feeling of Jaleesa's warm body under hers and the possessiveness of Jaleesa's arms around her back. Tina wasn't sexually aroused, but she was…something.

"You kids having a good time?" Harriet teased.

Tina leaped off Jaleesa.

"Absolutely," Jaleesa said from where she still lounged on the couch.

Tina's heart was racing. In their fervor, she had forgotten about Harriet. Tina looked from Harriet to Jaleesa and back again and then burst out laughing. "Busted. So busted."

"Oh, c'mon," Harriet said. "Everybody knew it was happening."

Tina grimaced. "Everybody?"

"You two are like love-stricken puppies in each other's presence." Harriet sat on the edge of the futon that was to be her bed. "I think it's great that two amazing people have found each other." Her smile for them was genuine, but so were her yawn and drooping eyes.

Jaleesa stood up. "I'm going to take Tina home. I expect you to be here when I get back."

"I'll be here."

"Giving me your car keys will guarantee that."

Tina was flabbergasted at Jaleesa's request. How can she demand something like that? Harriet barely knew Jaleesa. Wouldn't Harriet worry that she and Tina would steal her car or something? Tina was equally flabbergasted when Harriet simply nodded and handed over the keys.

"Thank you," Jaleesa said softly. "I know that took a lot of trust."

Harriet looked away. "Thank you both for caring for me even when I don't feel I deserve it."

Tina and Jaleesa sat on either side of Harriet, and Jaleesa pulled Harriet into her arms. "Remember how we did this? A few weeks ago?"

"Mm hmm," Harriet said, emotion clear in her voice.

"You were a stranger to me then, but still worth taking care of," Jaleesa said.

Tina was confused but knew it would be the very first question she'd ask Jaleesa in the pickup on the way home.

Harriet pulled back and looked into Jaleesa's eyes. "I see what Tina sees in you."

Tina nodded and squeezed Harriet tight. "I have to go now. You're in good hands." She stood up and refused to let the tears that wanted to sprout come out.

Jaleesa also stood up and said, "Now, as soon as this one," she pointed toward Tina, "gets in the pickup, she's going to ask me how you and I know each other. Would it be okay with you if I tell her?"

"Yes, Ma'am," Harriet said. "Thank you for asking. You're a very considerate Domme."

Jaleesa patted Harriet on the shoulder. "Before we leave, I'll need you to call your boss. Doug. Is it?"

Harriet nodded.

"Call Doug and tell him you won't be in tomorrow."

"Yes, Ma'am."

Tina and Jaleesa moved to the kitchen to give Harriet some privacy.

Jaleesa said, "And you are going to call your parents now and tell them I'm driving you home."

"Yes, Ma'am," Tina said and grinned.

The 'ma'ams' were spilling out of her mouth way too easily. She would absolutely be researching this phenomenon of dominance and submission as soon as she got home. She was tired, for sure, and should probably go right to bed, but this was too important. What was developing between Jaleesa and her felt too strong and important to mess up. She'd done enough messing up in her lifetime.

Chapter 11

Jaleesa

Saturday afternoon was bright but cold. Januarys in Cincinnati tended to behave that way, the cold part especially. Harriet had so far stayed four nights and was currently at work, having recovered enough from her cold. Harriet refused any cold medication besides a couple of cough drops and seemed to feel better every day. Jaleesa didn't know the woman that well, but there was now a brightness to her eyes that hadn't been there that first night.

Jaleesa compromised with Miss Bessie and worked that morning until her lunch break. Now she was home and sitting on the couch in her oddly quiet apartment reading from the Big Book. Since she'd had to cancel with her sponsor, Elaina, on Wednesday evening, she promised to continue reading and making notes. And she was, except her thoughts kept drifting back to the big dinner Wednesday night right in that kitchen there.

The dinner with Tina, her parents, and Harriet went smoothly. Tina came earlier than her parents because she had to stop at Kroger to pick up a few things for the dinner. When she got there, it was clear that Tina was in charge. When Jaleesa tried to help, she was unceremoniously kicked out by Harriet. So, Jaleesa set the table instead after getting permission from Harriet. The gleam in Harriet's eyes when Jaleesa asked for that permission was priceless. It was nice to see there was a playful spirit inside the obviously beaten-down woman.

As preparations went on for dinner, it became uber clear that Tina and Harriet worked well together and enjoyed each other's company.

Maybe that's why they counted each other as friends, even though they'd only interacted at meetings. And, Jaleesa noted, it was uber-obvious that both women liked taking care of others. Jaleesa was still trying to piece together the things that made Harriet tick but thought maybe Harriet missed having someone to take care of.

Wednesday morning, well before the family dinner, Harriet had opened up to Jaleesa. She told her about the divorce from her husband. It had been amicable, and he had been pretty fair about everything, but the rejection still hurt. Harriot said she'd been okay with his philandering as long as he did it elsewhere and not in their home. He wanted the house in the divorce to move his mistress in, so she let him keep it in exchange for half of his retirement assets. She'd been shocked when he agreed.

Harriet brought up her job as a middle school art teacher and her inglorious fall from grace. The fall that had gotten her fired. Basically, what happened was that a seventh-grade girl and her mother stopped by the art room after school at just the wrong moment. The moment? Right when Mrs. Harriet Monroe had chosen to do a line of coke on a mirror at her teacher's desk. It had been very late in the afternoon. No one should have been around. She hadn't heard them coming down the hall. The worst thing? She finished the line. Her career was over, she knew it, so she finished the damn white line in front of a twelve-year-old kid and her mother.

She told Jaleesa that she never ratted out the young hip art teacher that had introduced her to cocaine in the first place. Initially, he'd told her it would lift her up. It would bolster her creativity, he'd said. And she confessed that it had seemed to, but she felt disconnected from the pieces she'd created while high. She'd sold a few, but she wasn't proud of them.

Unfortunately, Mrs. Harriet Monroe, fallen art teacher, was made an example of by the school district and the county. Harriet said it was on local and even national news, and Jaleesa vaguely remembered hearing about it. Like Jaleesa, Harriet had been forced into recovery by a court order. Unlike Jaleesa, Harriet had been arrested, handcuffed, and hauled out of her classroom the very next morning as she was packing up her career. The worst part was that the classroom had been full of eighth-grade children at the time. It seemed like Harriet was more upset about that than anything else.

Harriet said she couldn't go anywhere without someone recognizing her. Thankfully, she'd had a good lawyer that convinced the judge a second chance was in order, so she didn't serve a day of prison time beyond those first few days. She didn't go into what kind of names and taunts were thrown at her by ignorant people, but Jaleesa could tell it hurt the caring teacher deeply then and still did now. Jaleesa held her while she cried and then ordered a nap which Harriet didn't fight.

Once Tina arrived with the groceries that Wednesday evening, she gushed over the haircut Jaleesa had given Harriet, even though it had only been a trim. That was Tina, Jaleesa was figuring out. Tina noticed you. Tina made you feel seen and, best of all, made you feel needed.

The pan-seared chicken, broccoli, and rice were delicious during that Wednesday evening dinner, and everything seemed fine on the surface. However, Jaleesa still felt hesitation around Tina's parents, her mother especially. Were they afraid Tina's burgeoning independence was going to end in disaster? Were they afraid Jaleesa would be the cause? Or was it the elephant in the room—that their white daughter was dating a Black woman? Hopefully, the more they got to know Jaleesa, the better they would understand that she cared deeply for Tina and only had her best interests in mind. And, yes, she was indeed finding herself caring deeply for Tina. Even though it had happened quickly, it felt pre-destined or something.

Jaleesa's phone dinged an incoming text bringing her back to the present Saturday afternoon. Ahh, good. It was Tina, finally. Since that Wednesday dinner, Tina had hinted that she was going to take Jaleesa somewhere on Saturday afternoon but wouldn't tell her where they were going or what they would do.

Fine by her. It didn't matter where they went because if she were with

Tina, it would be fine. Harriet was all set up with an apartment key and plenty of food in the kitchen, so that wasn't a worry. Jaleesa had even taught her how to use the remote controls for the television and DVR system so she wouldn't be bored. At some point, though, they would have to decide if they wanted to make this a permanent arrangement. Jaleesa had some soul-searching to do in that regard. Bringing home one-night stands was definitely over. Being with Tina had kind of ended that anyway, hadn't it?

TINA: I'm here.

JALEESA: What do I need to bring?

TINA: Wallet, phone, sunglasses, apartment keys, your smile, and those biceps of yours.

Jaleesa laughed and shook her head. Tina had a great sense of humor, that was for sure.

JALEESA: Be down in two.

Jaleesa folded herself in the passenger seat of Tina's car and leaned over for a kiss. "I like kissing you on a Saturday afternoon."

"And in the morning and the evening," Tina said.

"Ain't we got fun?"

Tina's mouth fell open. "No way. No one ever finishes that when I say it. Except my dad, of course."

"My grandmother loved her some Peggy Lee."

"Mine did, too, except it was my grandfather," Tina said. "I think he had a crush on her."

They looked at each other perplexed. Jaleesa figured Tina was wondering the same thing she was. Was this a sign sent from above?

Jaleesa looked up and pointed toward the sky twice. Tina nodded. Yes, she had been thinking the same thing.

Before Tina pulled out of the parking lot, she said, "Oh, my dad wants to know if you're still on for the Bengals playoff game tomorrow at our house."

"Absolutely. Wouldn't miss it."

"Cool. Let me just text him. Meanwhile…" Tina handed Jaleesa a folder. "This is where we're going." Tina sent the quick text, got an immediate reply, and pulled out of the spot.

"Denton Heights?"

"Mm hmm," Tina said without looking at Jaleesa. She was intent on driving. "Remember how we thought we'd need to look outside Cincinnati? This listing looks promising, and a realtor is meeting us there in half an hour."

"Denton Heights is one of those expensive suburban communities, isn't it?"

"Yes, but the realtor said it's a buyer's market for commercial properties right now because growth in that area has been stagnant for a while."

"Hmm," was all Jaleesa could get out. She wished Tina had shown her the listing earlier, so she could have looked it over and felt more prepared. *Sure, and then you would have come up with a dozen reasons why it wasn't possible. Let her help you,* she scolded herself. "Okay, but it's kind of far, Tina."

Tina glanced in her direction as she pulled onto the onramp for I-75 northbound. "Far from what?"

"Far from you, Tina."

"Awww," Tina said and whimpered the cutest little whimper. "You are so sweet. It's not that far. Let's give it a chance, okay?"

"Okay, okay," Jaleesa said, trying not to find those dozen reasons for not moving to far-away Denton Heights.

They rode in silence for a while as Jaleesa read the listing. "Am I reading this right? This listing is for the entire building?" She looked over at Tina. "All three commercial spaces?"

"Yes, it's a small strip mall," Tina said. "That price is for all three. You'd be the landlord over the other two. There was a pizza restaurant on one side, but it's no longer there."

"Why not?"

"Not sure," Tina said. "That will be a question to ask the realtor, I guess. But, get this, there's a nail salon on the other side."

"Seriously? A nail salon? One-stop shopping. And If I could somehow attract a new pizza restaurant—" Whoa, was she letting herself think this could be a possibility?

"Or some other small café or something," Tina suggested.

"Right, right," Jaleesa mused. She still didn't believe the asking price was for all three spaces. She'd believe it when the realtor confirmed it. And, of course, the place was probably a dump full of rats and mice and cockroaches and snakes.

"Hello?" Tina said. "Where'd you go?"

Jaleesa laughed big and said, "Nowhere. Just not quite believing that this price is real. Like there should be another zero on the end or something."

"We'll find out. Make that one of your first questions."

As soon as they pulled into the strip mall parking lot, Jaleesa immediately saw some issues. The filthy dumpsters were the first thing you noticed, and the parking lot had seen better days. The Northcentral Plaza sign was in major disrepair. It was beyond fixing and would have to be replaced. As far as the building itself, the paint was chipping, and there was evidence of water damage around some door frames, probably due to poor drainage.

"All of this is fixable," the cheery realtor said as she approached them.

Jaleesa stuck out her hand and said, "I'm Jaleesa Whitmore, and this is—"

"Tina Jenkins," the realtor interrupted. She shook hands with Jaleesa and pulled Tina into a hug. "It's so good to see you again."

"Thanks, Penni." Tina hugged her friend and then held her at arms' length. "It's good to see you, too. It feels like we're still in high school. You haven't changed a bit. Except for that swanky coat covering an equally swanky suit."

"Thank you. And you haven't changed either, my friend. You look good." Penni turned to Jaleesa and said, "I'm Penni Pepper. Yep. That's my real name. So, what kind of business do you want to open? Tina told me a little, but not much."

They stood in the cold parking lot for a few more moments as Jaleesa explained what she wanted to use the space for. Penni nodded and, in true realtor fashion, said that it was all doable. Jaleesa would have to determine that for herself, of course. And the asking price? Yes, it was legit for the entire building, with all three commercial spaces and the apartment upstairs.

Once inside the space, Penni found and turned up the thermostat so they could get warm enough to "think," as she put it. The main area was spacious, about the size of Miss Bessie's salon, if not bigger.

"What kind of business was in here prior?" Jaleesa asked. There were several rows of outlets in the floor as if maybe a bunch of desks or workstations had been there. That would be perfect for stylists' stations.

The realtor opened her zippered leather portfolio and rifled through a few papers. "I know I have it in here somewhere." She pulled out a printout. "Here it is." She handed the paper for Jaleesa and Tina to see.

"Oh, wow," Tina said. "A sewing and alterations shop." She looked around the large space. "Quite a big space for that sort of thing."

"Was it a dry cleaner as well?" Jaleesa scoured the paper. She didn't even want to think about the kind of chemicals that could be lurking in the walls and floor. *Maybe that's why—*

"Stay with us, Jaleesa," Tina whispered. "Together, we'll get everything answered."

Jaleesa nodded. Funny how she was supposed to be the strong one, but this whole surprise venture was threatening to overwhelm her. And Tina sensed it. A small hand snaked itself into hers. Jaleesa squeezed Tina's hand and let out a sigh. Yes, Tina was right. She had to chill the frick out.

She relaxed a bit when Penni assured them that, no, it had not been a dry-cleaning establishment. As the tour continued, Jaleesa was having a tough time finding anything wrong with the space. There were no signs of bug or rodent activity, thank goodness. She kicked beams and even jumped up and down on the floor to see how sturdy it was, making Penni quip that Jaleesa looked like a building inspector.

As they walked the space, Jaleesa detected no smell of mold or mildew. Except for the exterior door frames, there was no evidence of flooding or water damage. There was a back room outfitted with a kitchen that had obviously been used as a breakroom. There was even an old refrigerator, empty but clean.

"Ooh, look, babe," Tina gushed as she opened a door off the break room. "This is a bathroom."

Jaleesa grinned, but she wasn't grinning because of the discovered lavatory. She was grinning because Tina had called her *babe*. And in front of her realtor friend. Funny how just that one small word of endearment filled her core with fuzzy warmth.

"This must be for the workers back here," Tina said.

"And there are restrooms up front for for customers," the ever-helpful Penni added.

"Great," Jaleesa said. The space looked promising, but she'd need to get a look at the other two spaces, including the currently occupied nail salon next door and the empty space on the other side. "May I take a quick look out this back door?"

"Of course," Penni said and gestured to the door off the break room.

"I'll stay here where it's warm, honey," Tina said.

"I'll be quick."

'Honey?' Is she trying out pet names for me? It's nice, and I kind of like

145

it. With that thought wrapping around her heart, Jaleesa headed out the door. As she turned to close it behind her, she heard Penni say, "I'm straight, Tina, but phew, she's a hotty."

Jaleesa muffled a laugh, so they wouldn't know she'd overheard and walked out on the small landing. She headed down a set of sturdy wooden steps into the alley behind the building and took a deep, cleansing breath of cold air. She hoped she was putting on a good face in front of Tina and her friend, but in truth, she felt way in over her head. She didn't have enough money for a large down payment this type of venture would need. She had decent credit but didn't own much to put up as collateral.

She looked skyward and asked, "What are you doing to me?" She believed in spiritual bumps, but this was a helluva lot more than a little bump. This was a shove. Could she handle this? Would Tina be disappointed if she didn't even try? The simple answer to the last question was yes. Would Jaleesa herself be disappointed? The jury was still out on that one.

The space truly was incredible and almost a little too hard to believe. But it was just what she'd been dreaming about since her first day in cosmetology school. No, it was before that, way before that. It had started when she'd sat in a chair for the very first time in her life at the *Tangle and Curl* in Cleveland. Her mother wanted something that would keep her rambunctious five-year-old daughter's hair out of her face and would last a while. Artful cornrow braids were the result. Jaleesa couldn't stop looking at them. Yeah, Jaleesa was hooked, not only hooked on how she looked but on how the gentle stylist had done it.

"Yes," Jaleesa said to the overgrown driveway behind the building. "Yes, I can do this." With new eyes, she surveyed the snowy empty field behind the building and made a mental note to look into who owned the field and what was going to happen with it. And look, there was plenty of room to hide those eye-sore dumpsters behind the building. She would have to check into that as well.

"Hey, goofball," Tina called out the backdoor. "Did you freeze solid out there?"

Goofball? Fine. I'll one up that. "I'll be right in, doofus," Jaleesa called back.

With renewed energy, Jaleesa followed the realtor as they explored the old pizza restaurant and were surprised to see that the ovens were still there. The manager of the nail salon and the nail technicians were delighted to see their potential new landlord and had a lot to say, not all good, about the previous owner. Jaleesa drank in every word and put them in the overflowing box of things to think about.

Jaleesa's head was swimming as they returned to their respective cars. She took Penni's business card and asked, "Again. This price. Is it seriously for the entire building? All three units?"

"Yes, the way I understand it, the owner moved his business into Cincy itself." Penni hesitated and then said carefully, "This is a bit of a depressed area, even though it has the Denton Heights address. You're surrounded by lower-income and controlled-rent housing. I'm not trying to talk you out of making an offer, just keeping it real."

Ah. Jaleesa understood. Before heading home, she'd ask Tina to drive around so that her suspicions about what Penni meant could be confirmed.

Jaleesa and Tina asked a few more closing questions and then said their goodbyes to Tina's friend. Once back in the MINI Cooper, Tina blew out a sigh. "That was a lot to take in, wasn't it?"

"It most certainly was. But the space looks sound."

"So, you like it?" Tina said, her entire face hopeful.

Jaleesa nodded but said, "There's a lot to consider, Tina. Like how far away this place is from you."

"I have an idea," Tina said as she adjusted the car's heater. "Let's go into the main town of Denton Heights and look around. They have to have a coffee shop or something. We can review what we saw and figure out more questions to ask Penni." She pointed out the front windshield toward the building and said, "Like, what is that room up there?"

Up above the vacant center shop, there was a row of windows.

"Storage space, maybe?" Jaleesa offered.

A quick text to Penni revealed a quick answer.

"No way," Tina said. "It's an apartment. Oh, shoot, she did say that when we first got here." She read more of the text. "She says it's a rentable studio apartment and that she completely forgot to take us up there."

"An apartment?"

"Babe, you can live up there. You'll own the building."

"I don't own anything yet," Jaleesa reminded, but the thought of not having to pay rent was extremely enticing. "Hey, while you were texting Penni, I found a coffee shop right in the heart of town. It's called Rikki's Coffee Shop."

"Perfect," Tina said.

"Would you mind driving around these neighborhoods first? I want to get a feel for the area."

"Excellent idea. Navigate on, McDuff."

They both chuckled and headed into town through several neighborhoods surrounding the shop. The houses were eclectic. Some were small, some larger. Some were in disrepair, while others looked cared for. As Jaleesa suspected, the houses seemed owned or rented by mainly brown and Black humans. The apartment complexes as well. Jaleesa intended for her shop to service any type of human—melanated, white, and everything between and beyond. These neighborhoods weren't a minus. No, they were a plus as far as Jaleesa was concerned.

The town of Denton Heights itself was quaint. That was the best word. They still had their Christmas decorations up, and the quiet calm about the town almost equaled the feeling she'd had in her own neighborhood growing up.

Tina found a parking spot on Market Street in front of a furniture store just beyond the coffee shop. As they were about to get out of the car, Tina's phone dinged.

"Oh, it's my mom," Tina said. "She wants me to call her. It looks crowded in there, so why don't you go on in, get my usual, and find a table? Or a couch. This place looks like it would have couches."

"Kiss first?" Jaleesa leaned over and got what she asked for. She stroked Tina's cheek, pink from the cold, and said, "See you inside."

Jaleesa opened the door to the coffee shop and got in the short line. She checked out the list of items available on the overhead menu. Ooh, blueberry muffins. Yes, please. She was a little hungry. Too bad the shop didn't have anything of more substance to fill their bellies. Oh, well.

"Wow, you're so tall," a voice behind her said.

Jaleesa turned around to find a young woman of East Asian descent staring up at her with wide eyes. "Thank you?"

"Do you play volleyball? Oh, sorry." The woman looked down. When she tucked a stray lock of hair behind her ear, Jaleesa saw a bracelet with a triskelion symbol. That was the symbol for BDSM. "That was presumptuous of me. I bet you hate people assuming you play volleyball just because you're tall."

"Basketball."

The woman's eyes bugged out as she said, "No way."

"Yes, way," Jaleesa said with a chuckle and moved up as the line moved. "That was a long time ago at this point. In college."

"Mistress says I have to stop blurting things out just because my brain thought of it." The young woman gestured to a good-looking woman of South Asian descent sitting on one of the couches. Aha! Tina was right. On the back and side walls were couches, separated expertly into small sitting areas so friends could have private spaces for visiting. Perfect. This place was very homey.

"I like your bracelet," Jaleesa said, but before the young woman could respond, she added, "Is that your Mistress on the couch there?"

The look of utter love and devotion that spread over the young woman's face was indescribable. If only that feeling could be bottled.

"Yes," the young woman said reverently.

"She's hot," Jaleesa whispered out of the corner of her mouth.

A shriek of laughter flew out of the young woman's mouth, startling everyone around her. The mistress on the couch looked up concerned. Jaleesa mouthed to her, "It's okay," and put up a calming hand.

"Okay," the hot mistress answered. She looked like she was about to bolt out of her seat and take the situation in hand.

The young man in front of Jaleesa finished his order and stepped out of the way. Jaleesa ordered two coffees and noticed only one blueberry muffin on the tray. "Do you have any more of these?"

"No," the blonde barista said. She looked to be somewhere in her late twenties and was obviously a manager-type. "Diego already went home. This is all we have."

"Okay, I'll take the one."

A not-so-quiet groan sounded from the young woman behind her, and Jaleesa turned around. "What's the matter, bucko?"

"Mistress said I could get a muffin."

Jaleesa narrowed her eyes. "How about we split it?"

An instant smile lit the young woman's face. "Yes. Thank you, Ma'am."

Jaleesa turned back to the barista. "How about a plastic knife and four plates to go with that muffin."

"Yes, Ma'am." The barista nodded, and Jaleesa couldn't help noticing her amused smile. She was amused at the young woman's antics, no doubt.

"Thank you, Lydia," Jaleesa said after making a show of reading the woman's name tag. A pink hue grew over the barista's cheeks when she asked for Jaleesa's name to write on the cups.

"I'll bring your coffees over to you, Miss Jaleesa," Lydia said as she handed over the muffin, plates, and plastic knife.

"Excellent. Thank you," Jaleesa said.

The young woman behind her blurted, "The usual, Miss Lydia."

"You got it, Madison."

A warm, comforting feeling spread through Jaleesa's core. There was a clear Dominant and submissive hierarchy going on here. The barista

150

named Lydia seemed to understand that Jaleesa was a Dominant. Without knowing her. And the young woman named Madison was clearly a *little,* and her mistress was her Mommy Domme.

Boxes that Jaleesa didn't even know needed to be checked were getting checked up here in this small bedroom community called Denton Heights.

"Come sit with us, Miss Jaleesa," Madison said and tugged on her arm.

"Hey, babe," Tina said. "Making new friends already?"

"Apparently." Jaleesa introduced Madison to Tina and let herself be tugged over to the now-curious hot mistress on the couch.

"I see you've met Madison," the hot mistress said. "This one has never met a stranger." She took a breath and looked skyward as if this was the bane of her existence, but Jaleesa saw the amusement in her expression. Oh, yes. This mistress was a Mommy Domme, indeed, and clearly smitten with her *little* as well.

"Jaleesa Whitmore," Jaleesa said. "This is Tina Jenkins."

"Have you ever been to the zoo, Miss Tina?" Madison asked as she bounced on the couch.

Tina chuckled. "It's nice to meet you, Madison. And, yes, I have been to the zoo. I grew up in Cincy."

"No way," Madison said wide-eyed, as if growing up in Cincinnati was the most amazing thing.

"Come join us," the mistress said. "I'm Shasti Balakrishnan." She stuck out her hand, and Jaleesa shook it.

It wasn't long before the four coffees arrived, brought by Lydia herself. "Thank you, Lydia," Shasti said.

"You're very welcome, Miss Shasti," Lydia said. She turned to Jaleesa and acknowledged Jaleesa by saying, "Miss Jaleesa," with a slight nod. And then she did something that made Jaleesa's chest swell with pride. Pride for a woman she didn't even know. Lydia took three steps backward and then turned on her heels to head back to the counter.

"She's a good girl," Jaleesa said to Shasti.

"She is, but she's a bit down at the moment," Shasti added. Ahh, Shasti was an observer. Well, duh. She had to be. She was a Mommy Domme, after all. "Her Dom just released her."

"Oh, that's too bad," Jaleesa said, wondering why these people assumed she was one of them and that talking to her about their obvious power relationships would be okay.

Tina jumped in and said, "Sometimes your soul needs a new start."

Her words seemed so deep and meaningful that no one spoke for a moment...until the resident *little* broke the silence.

"Miss Jaleesa," Madison groaned. "May I please have my one-quarter of a muffin now?" Much couch bouncing commenced at the request.

Miss Shasti rolled her eyes and nodded to Jaleesa that it would be okay.

Tina caught on quickly and set out the four paper plates and then handed Jaleesa the plastic knife.

Jaleesa threw Madison a grin and said, "You got it, bucko."

Chapter 12

Tina

"We're going upstairs, Mom," Tina called toward the kitchen. "We'll be down for the second half." Tina beckoned for Jaleesa to follow her up the stairs. She felt a little bad because Jaleesa looked like she'd become one with the couch.

"Okay, honey," her mother answered from the other room. "Sloppy Joes will be ready when you come back down."

"Thanks, Mom." Tina looked at her father and wagged a finger at him. "Dad, you've had your snacks, so no eating dinner early. Wait, okay? We have company."

"O-kay," her father said, sounding like Eeyore. "But, J-Dub, I'm looking for you to make sure you're back here for the start of the second half. The Bengals have the lead, and we can't do anything different."

"Superstitious much?" Tina said with a laugh.

"Will do, Mr. Jenkins," Jaleesa said.

Hmm, Jaleesa still hadn't gotten up from the couch. "Do you need help?" Tina joked.

"Yes, actually." Jaleesa scooted to the edge of the couch. "This couch is kind of low, and my knees…" She didn't finish her sentence as Tina and her father each grabbed a hand and helped Jaleesa unfold herself from the couch. The unmistakable groan of pain had Tina on high alert.

"Thanks," Jaleesa said. "My old basketball knees." She said this, though, while rubbing her elbows and then her hands. This was more than knees. Something was wrong.

Tina kept a smile on her face and reached for Jaleesa's hand. Nothing like a Sunday family gathering to let the parents know that she and Jaleesa were becoming more than friends. She watched as her father tried to hide his grin. If he suspected before, he knew now.

Jaleesa's trek up the stairs was slow but steady. Once inside the bedroom, Tina said, "You might feel better if you lay down." She gestured toward the bed.

Jaleesa raised both eyebrows in surprise, but pulled open the princess curtain, sat on the bed, and lay down. She stretched out her full length, which was considerable. She slid closer to the wall, allowing room for a certain girlfriend.

"My goodness, you are a long drink of water," Tina said with a laugh and dove onto the bed next to Jaleesa.

The bouncing must have made something hurt because Jaleesa winced.

"Honey, what's wrong?" Tina reached over and kissed Jaleesa's cheek. She was afraid to touch anywhere else.

"Just the weather, maybe." Jaleesa closed her eyes, obviously tired or in pain or both.

"Excuse me," Tina said. When Jaleesa opened her eyes, Tina took an imaginary key out of her shirt pocket and unlocked Jaleesa's lips.

Jaleesa sighed and said, "You're right. I sometimes get this way. I'm not sure why, but every joint aches. I thought maybe it was arthritis. Maybe from my ball-playing years. And I did work out this morning because, you know, someone in this room has a fetish for my biceps."

"Yes, she does," Tina said with a laugh. "This sounds like inflammation, babe. Have you gotten it checked out?"

Jaleesa nodded. "He said it wasn't arthritis and gave me a prescription for painkillers."

Tina knew the blood drained from her face.

"I never filled it. I shredded the stupid script."

"I wish doctors..." Tina sighed. "Never mind. Anyway, my grandma used to do hot baths to ease her stiffness. Sometimes Mom would set her up with warm compresses when her hands got achy."

"I've done that and cold treatments, too. They help a little. I didn't want to ask you for an ice pack because that would have been weird."

"And you didn't want me to know you were in pain." Tina hoped her scolding expression was enough because she really wanted to poke Jaleesa on the nose.

"Yes, yes. Next time I'll ask."

"Good." Lecture over, Tina snuggled up against the long drink of water on her bed. She lay her head on Jaleesa's shoulder. "Is this okay?"

A strong arm went around her. "Always."

Tina lay her arm across Jaleesa's chest. Her hand rubbed just underneath Jaleesa's throat. "That couple we met yesterday—they were so interesting, weren't they?"

Jaleesa chuckled. "Yes. Did you understand their relationship?"

"Not then, but it made sense when you explained it on the way home. It's a power exchange dynamic, like the Dominant-submissive ones you've told me about, right?

"Yep, but in this type, the Dominant is a caregiving parent-type figure."

"That was obviously Shasti."

"It doesn't weird you out?" Jaleesa stroked Tina's hand.

"No, not at all. Love is love. That Morgan, no, her name was Madison. Madison was the cutest, most endearing thing I've ever met. I'm tempted to take her up on the offer to go to the zoo together. She was so excited to tell us about the annual passes Shasti got them for Christmas."

"Maybe we should go. We all seemed to get along well. Why not make new friends in Denton Heights?"

Tina bolted upright. "Does that mean you're considering buying the Northcentral Plaza?"

Jaleesa's smile was so big that Tina squealed and landed on top of Jaleesa as she kissed her face all over, only slowing down to savor those soft lips against hers. A small groan of pain sent Tina flying off the bed. "I'm sorry, honey. I forgot."

Jaleesa adjusted her body and patted the bed. "It's okay. Come back."

Tina carefully eased herself back on the bed.

"After you dropped me off last night," Jaleesa said, "I did a little internet searching about the property and the entire area. That big field behind the shop is a farm. Soybeans and corn."

"That's good."

"I also researched building inspectors specializing in strip malls and commercial spaces and made a list."

"Baby," Tina whimpered. "I'm so pleased. Should we text Penni?"

"Yes."

"That simple?"

"Mm hmm," Jaleesa said. "I mean, I obviously need to make an appointment at a bank to see if I'd even qualify for a loan."

"I know a banker," Tina teased.

"You do?" Jaleesa teased back.

"Yes, indeed. And we'd make sure there was no conflict of interest. You should come in this week to get that ball rolling." Tina was already musing on how she would go about it, but then a thought intruded. Was she being too pushy? Her father told her she could be bossy at times. "Of course, if you don't want me taking a deep dive into your financials, then you can go to somebody else. I didn't mean to overstep."

"No, no, it's fine." Jaleesa stroked Tina's back. God, that was the best feeling in the world. "I'll text Penni when we're done here and then arrange for half a day with Miss Bessie sometime this week so that I can come by the bank."

Jaleesa pulled Tina back on top of her and wrapped her arms tightly around Tina's body. Their kisses were soft and sensual at first. And then Tina felt the switch. Jaleesa moaned, and it wasn't one of pain. She was aroused again. A tiny sense of pride filled Tina, knowing she could do that to the gorgeous woman beneath her. Another moan and strong hands moved lower to cup her buttocks. Jaleesa moved rhythmically beneath Tina. Her hands stroked Tina's body.

Jaleesa's moan of pleasure turned into a groan of frustration. She broke off the kiss and turned her head to the side. She was a little out of breath. She gently moved Tina off her and, with a few grunts, turned onto her side. "You affect me, Tina. I'm not going to lie. I want so much more, but I know you can't. And I would never do anything to ruin what we have. I love our friendship, but what we have is turning into much more than friendship for me."

Tina didn't know how to respond as a million thoughts raced through her brain, some wonderful and some worrisome. When Jaleesa pulled out an imaginary key and unlocked Tina's lips, Tina said, "I feel it, too." There. That was the honesty Jaleesa wanted.

"I guess all we can do is go one day at a time." Jaleesa smiled gently.

"Where have I heard that phrase before?" Tina teased. She reached up and stroked Jaleesa's face. "You've been so respectful, Jaleesa. I didn't mind your wandering hands, but please understand that I might mind in the future."

"And you would tell me, and I would stop immediately. Physical touch is intimacy, but only if it's wanted."

Jaleesa started to say something else, but Tina put a finger over her lips to shush her. "Not right now, but sometime I would like to help you out with your, um…"

"With what?"

"Your arousal. I've done it before. With my ex. And it was fine."

"You would do that?"

"Yes. Maybe not every time. I don't know. But you have to understand that when you're in the throes of passion," this she tried to say with a jovial lilt, "I won't be. I won't ever be, so you can't try to give back. I won't want you to touch me the same way I'll be touching you."

"I understand," Jaleesa said. "But promise that if I overstep, you'll correct me."

"Oh, I will."

"You are something special, Tina Jenkins. Are you planning to go to my meeting tomorrow night?"

"Of course, I wouldn't miss it."

"I know it's a work night, but would you like to come back to my apartment for a couple of hours?" The vulnerable tone of Jaleesa's voice made Tina understand what Jaleesa was implying.

Tina kissed Jaleesa softly and said, "Yes." She kissed Jaleesa again but then remembered. "What about Harriet?"

"She's going to her sister's for dinner and then grabbing a few more things to bring back. She said she won't be home until ten."

"Green light then. Nice." Tina felt the stirrings of nerves in her chest. It would be a big step in so many ways. Was she going to be an adequate lover? She hoped so, but the bigger concern was whether or not Jaleesa would try to touch her in return. "And, just so you know," Tina said. "I'm not sex repulsed."

"I know, sweet thing," Jaleesa said. "C'mon, we should get back down there."

"Okay, my mom might barge in any minute anyway."

"That has got to stop," Jaleesa said but then put both hands up in a helpless gesture as if to say she didn't mean to overstep. Tina understood. But she had begun to feel the same way about the whole barging-in thing.

~~~

On Monday evening, Tina got to the church basement early. A force of habit, she guessed. And wow, Dana and Kadesha were already there. They were deep in conversation on the far side of the chairs, so Tina decided not to interrupt them. It was kind of hard not to hear them, though.

"Why you always gotta do stupid things, Dana?" Kadesha was asking.

"It's just an auction. I did one before," Dana said, clearly on the defensive.

"Why you like them women to tie you up and hit you with sticks is beyond me but live and let live. I guess."

"It's not sticks," Dana said. "It's...different."

"But this will be a stranger. A stranger that will tie you up and do Lord knows what to you."

"Naw," Dana said. "The online auction people vet everyone, including me. And besides, I already paid my seventy-five dollars. I won't get that back unless I attend at least three of the five sessions. And I'll need all five to show my worth to attract a good Domme."

Tina was stunned at what she was hearing. She wasn't sure what it all meant, but she agreed with Kadesha. It sounded dangerous and downright stupid. What should she do? Should she intervene?

"When is it?" Kadesha asked with a resigned sigh.

"It starts on the first Saturday in March. They have them once a quarter, but I had to sign up this early to get a spot."

Kadesha sat down hard on one of the chairs. "Do you have to post pictures for everyone to see?"

Dana sat down much more gently. "Yep. I'll post two pictures of what I look like. Those will be just me from here up." Tina was purposefully rifling through the pamphlets on the side table, so she hadn't seen where Dana gestured. "But then when a Domme, oh, they don't have to post their pictures until we agree on a week-long in-person dynamic, and then I get to see them. But after someone checks my box—"

Kadesha burst out laughing. "Your '*box*,'" she repeated.

"Shut up," Dana said. "This is serious. So, after someone checks *the* box on my profile, I can choose to check theirs, and that's when it gets fun. We talk privately online and exchange pictures and...stuff."

"You play with them online?" Kadesha asked, her voice low.

"Of course," Dana said. "That's how we know if we're compatible or not. If someone chooses me and I like them, then I have to follow through, and we meet."

"A stranger."

"Not really, because we've already interacted online."

"Without seeing their pictures."

"Sometimes they send you one, but they don't have to. They're the Dominants, so they get to do whatever they want."

"Doesn't seem fair," Kadesha said.

Two strong arms wrapped around Tina from behind. "Hi, babe," Jaleesa said. "You look gorgeous."

Tina swiveled in Jaleesa's arms and landed a kiss on Jaleesa's cold lips. They had agreed to "come out" as a couple at the meetings.

Dana shrieked when she saw them arm in arm. "I knew it," she yelled and ran over to them. When she looked up at Jaleesa, a clear blush filled her cheeks, and she looked away.

Oh, yes, Dana still had a major crush on Jaleesa. *Don't we all?* Tina wanted to say.

"It was the flowers, wasn't it?" Dana said to Jaleesa and waggled her eyebrows.

"Yes, I believe that is what did it," Jaleesa teased.

"I told you. I told you," Dana said to Kadesha as she hopped around in front of them.

"Congrats, you guys," Kadesha said. "That's cool."

"Thanks, Kadesha," Tina said.

Jaleesa still had one arm wrapped around Tina. She squeezed and said, "I got lucky."

Kadesha simply smiled and pulled Dana away by the arm. "C'mon, I have an hour to talk some sense into you."

"You can't. I already signed up." But Dana let herself be led away anyway, and Tina told Jaleesa she would tell her what that was all about later.

Tina always liked January meetings because the theme reverted back to step one and tradition one. They reminded her how strong she had been to admit she had a problem and ask for help. That had turned out to be the easy part. The real hell began when she not only had to heal her body but her mind and spirit as well. It took quite a while as she learned to absorb the next eleven steps into her soul.

The AA meeting that evening went amazingly quickly, and Tina loved having Jaleesa's arm draped over the back of her chair possessively the entire time. As Pastor Paul wrapped things up, Tina remembered the first time Jaleesa had taken her to dinner by the salon where she worked. Jaleesa had confided then that she hadn't truthfully admitted to having a drinking problem until a couple of weeks after Gabby left her. And even then, she'd said she was still going through the motions, waiting for some epiphanic miracle. Tina couldn't help thinking that maybe, just maybe, it had happened that night they'd met—the night of Tina's sharing speech. The night the tall stranger pulled Tina close and soothed her like no one else had ever done before.

"You okay, babe?" Jaleesa asked.

Tina came back to the present. Everyone was standing. "Oh, sorry. Lost in thought." She stood up and stretched and then made a show of wrapping her arms around Jaleesa's neck. It must look comical at how high five-foot-nothing Tina had to reach, but she didn't care. "Baby?" she said low.

"Yes?" Jaleesa said and dipped her head.

"Take me home. To your home, I mean."

"You sure?" Jaleesa searched her face.

"I'm sure."

They stayed just long enough to seem sociable, said their goodbyes, and then bolted to Jaleesa's pickup. Once inside the apartment, Jaleesa got them both water from the fridge. They sat on the loveseat in the living room for a while and talked about nothing and everything. They discovered their mutual love of the online *Words with Friends* game and exchanged info. Tina scoured the bookshelves, and Jaleesa pulled out a few for Tina to borrow some time. Tina was still reading *The Invisible Man* on her e-reader and didn't want to take a physical book until she was ready.

Finally, it dawned on Tina. Jaleesa was nervous and was stalling. Tina took matters into her own hands and led Jaleesa to the couch. When Jaleesa sat, Tina shook her head. "How can I lay on top of you if you're sitting? Lay down, please."

Jaleesa's amused expression was precious, but Tina was serious. She clapped her hands and said, "Chop, chop." Jaleesa did as commanded, and Tina shimmied her body on top. She kissed Jaleesa the way Jaleesa had kissed her in the past, starting at various places on her oh-so-lovely face, ignoring her lips, and making a trail to her earlobes. A gentle suck made Jaleesa moan. Oh, yes, Tina thought. She was doing it right. She trailed her kisses lower. The slight turn of Jaleesa's neck gave Tina more room to work.

More moans followed until Jaleesa pulled Tina's lips to her own and kissed her passionately. Jaleesa's tongue sought out Tina's. It wasn't something that did anything for Tina, but it obviously did for Jaleesa. She let Jaleesa win the tongue war and then let her take over the kissing. Tina pulled away when Jaleesa started to kiss her roughly.

"Sorry, baby," Jaleesa said. "Sorry."

"Mmm, no worries," Tina said, letting her thigh insinuate itself between Jaleesa's. Nylani had done that to Tina back in the day, thinking it would turn Tina on. It didn't. But now, here in the present, Jaleesa arched her pelvis and sighed the most satisfying sigh Tina had ever heard. Oh, good, she'd hit the mark.

"You okay, baby?" Jaleesa was breathless.

"Yeah, yeah," Tina said. She wasn't going to fake being "turned on" just for Jaleesa's sake, but Jaleesa's reactions kind of amused her. *Sex is so weird.* Tina squelched the thought instantly, trying to stay in character.

Jaleesa let out an exasperated sigh and let her body go flat. "I can't do this."

Shoot, Tina thought, *my attitude must have bled through*. "You can. Aren't you aroused? Excited?"

"Oh, God, yes," Jaleesa admitted. "But this is so not fair to you."

"No, no," Tina insisted. "I want to do this. I—" Oh, God, she had been about to say, *I love you.* Was that true? "Take me to your bedroom. I'm going to undress you."

When Jaleesa hesitated, Tina insisted. "I want to see you."

Jaleesa searched Tina's face and must have found an acceptable answer because she nudged Tina up and off her lap, picked her up, and carried her to the bedroom. Tina giggled the entire way. Jaleesa plopped her on the queen-sized bed, making Tina bounce delightfully.

After firmly closing the bedroom door, Jaleesa started to undo her own shirt when Tina intervened. "I want to do it."

Tina stood up and looked right at the buttons on Jaleesa's shirt. Once she'd gotten the first one undone, she looked up at Jaleesa's face. Uncertainty was written all over her expression. Tina flashed a reassuring smile and continued her work. When the shirt was completely undone, Tina sighed and ran her fingers over the lace of the black bra covering Jaleesa's breasts. Jaleesa leaned down, nudged Tina's chin up for a quick kiss, and then shrugged off the shirt.

Tina was glad when Jaleesa didn't demand equal undressing. Maybe she'd reveal her body at some point, but not tonight. Tina was too nervous for all of *that.* Tina moved in and kissed the beautiful swell of Jaleesa's breasts that weren't hidden beneath the bra. So smooth and silky.

"You're gorgeous, baby," Tina said almost reverently.

"I need," Jaleesa began and then moaned in obvious frustration. "I need to touch you. It helps me…"

"Get yer sexy on?" Tina offered.

Jaleesa nodded. She unzipped her jeans and stepped out of them, leaving on her cute boyish panties. She then ran her hands over Tina's back and pulled her close. She walked Tina backward toward the bed, and in one smooth move, Tina was on her back with Jaleesa climbing on top. Oh, right. Jaleesa liked to be the Dominant one.

"Tell me what you need," Tina murmured in Jaleesa's ear.

"Mmm, I will," Jaleesa murmured. "Stop me if I go too far."

"I will."

Jaleesa positioned herself so that one of Tina's thighs landed between hers, much like they'd been on the loveseat, but this time Jaleesa was on top. Jaleesa lay her full length on Tina, which was exquisite, even if Tina was still completely dressed. She must have been holding herself up somehow because Tina wasn't becoming a pancake underneath her lover.

Her lover, Tina squealed inside as Jaleesa kissed her skin. *OMG. I have a lover.*

Jaleesa leaned up and tugged on the hem of Tina's t-shirt, asking permission with her eyes. Tina nodded. Yes, that was okay. Once the t-shirt had been thrown unceremoniously on the floor, Jaleesa unclipped her own bra and threw it in the same general direction. And with the athlete's grace Tina was coming to love, Jaleesa somehow relieved herself of her boy shorts and was now completely naked. Tina reached up and touched Jaleesa's firm breasts. How lovely. The dark areolas were so perfectly symmetric around Jaleesa's nipples as to be almost otherworldly. Jaleesa's breathing got a little heavier as she locked her gaze onto Tina's, her nipples hardening under Tina's touch. Jaleesa guided Tina's fingers to her nipple and pressed the fingers together, pinching the tender skin between them. Jaleesa's eyes closed, and her head tilted back as an unguarded sigh of desire escaped her lips. Tina pinched the other nipple without help, eliciting another moan.

Jaleesa made small whimpering noises as she opened her eyes to look at Tina. There was so much longing in Jaleesa's dark eyes. This is what desire must look like—a desire for Tina's touch. Lustful desire. Jaleesa seemed hesitant, so Tina asked gently, "What do you need?" She wished she knew how to make love like this. Or was this just sex? No, it was more than 'just sex,' even she knew that.

Jaleesa's grin gave Tina strength. Jaleesa maneuvered them both, so Jaleesa ended up on her back with Tina on her side. The slight sheen of sweat glistening on Jaleesa's bronze skin tightened Tina's core. Tina was turned on, too, but in a more sensual way. She really did seem to have a fetish for Jaleesa's biceps, but this? Jaleesa's long torso, tight abs, and innie belly button? This was enthralling. A secret view meant only for Tina.

Tina leaned down and kissed Jaleesa's tight abs and made her way back up to her breasts, taking one nipple at a time inside her mouth. She sucked gently and was rewarded with a hand pushing her head down firmly, urging her on. She flicked the nipple with her tongue, causing the woman beneath her to squirm.

But then Jaleesa pushed her away for some reason. Jaleesa's eyes were deep and dark, filled with full-blown lust. Tina had desire, too, but it was a different desire than Jaleesa's for sure. Being able to touch Jaleesa this way was the most intimate thing she'd experienced with her.

Jaleesa reached for Tina's free hand and kissed it. She placed her own hand on top and then guided their combined hands down her torso—over her stomach, belly button, and lower abs. And then she stopped. She looked up at Tina, questions in her eyes. Tina answered by taking over and sliding her hand lower, fingers first. She cupped Jaleesa's trimmed mons, so pretty. And then went lower. Jaleesa's legs widened in invitation. Her fingers made their way between Jaleesa's legs and cupped the heat there.

Jaleesa pulled Tina into a passionate kiss and then released her. She took over the hand movements and helped Tina's fingers slide between her slick folds. Tina felt pride that she had caused such obvious arousal. She let her fingers be guided as they slid between the outer and inner folds and then completely between the inner folds. Tina curled her fingers and penetrated Jaleesa slightly, but Jaleesa pulled them out and maneuvered them to her swollen little nub. Ahh, yes, it was time. Jaleesa guided Tina's fingers in a circular motion around the base of her clit and then on top. She did this several times and pulled her hand away as her hips rocked against Tina's hand.

Oh, oh! Jaleesa wanted Tina to take over. *Oh, God. Okay. I can do this.* The low sounds of passion coming from Jaleesa's throat, the undulating hips, the arching of her back—all of it made Tina's own senses come alive. She was doing this to her lover. Her. The asexual. Ha!

165

Tina must have been doing something right because Jaleesa's cries became louder and longer until the world stilled for a split second, and then she cried out, "Tina." It was a desperate shuddering release. It was a surrender. Her hips continued to rock, so Tina continued to stroke. Jaleesa, so vulnerable beneath her, made Tina's breath catch in her throat, and tears blur her eyes.

Jaleesa's hips slowed their movement, and the long breathy moan that followed made Tina giggle. Jaleesa's languid eyes looked up at Tina, and she smiled. She pulled Tina's hand away from her slickness and popped the wet digits into her mouth. Tina giggled again; she hadn't been expecting anything like that.

Jaleesa reached over, pulled a tissue from the box on her nightstand, and dried Tina's fingers and hands. "Why are you giggling, my love?" She cleaned her own fingers with a second tissue.

"Because that was so epic."

"No kidding." Jaleesa tossed the tissues over the side of the bed and blew out a sigh. She tapped her shoulder in invitation, and Tina gladly settled in at her side. "Thank you, sweetheart."

"Aww," Tina whimpered shyly. "I like when you call me that. But what are you thanking me for? I loved this."

Jaleesa reached down and pulled the top sheet over them. Tina snuggled in tighter.

"I hope it was okay for you," Jaleesa said.

"Are you kidding?" Tina leaned up to kiss Jaleesa. "I loved it. To be able to give you such pleasure was…."

Jaleesa waited while Tina tried to find the right words.

"I felt so trusted and protective of you, baby," Tina said softly. "I imagine it takes a lot to let yourself be so exposed in front of another person. And I don't mean literally exposed, although that kind of applies, too."

"I wanted to do this with you," Jaleesa said, "but I have to tell you that I'm not used to being the one made love to." She sighed as if regretting something. "I think all those women I brought home were mostly about sex and power dynamics, not love-making."

"What about with Gabby?"

Jaleesa was quiet for so long that Tina was afraid she'd overstepped.

"It was all about sex at first. For quite a while, actually, but then things kind of smoothed out, and I thought maybe we were making love after a while."

"You don't know?"

Again, Jaleesa was quiet for an inordinate amount of time. "Maybe I was the only one who thought that. But this? What we just did? I have no doubt we were making love."

"Oh, baby," Tina gushed. "I thought so, too. I loved it."

"Sooooo," Jaleesa said, her eyebrows raised expectantly. She gestured over Tina's whole body. "Anything happening here? Anything I need to take care of?"

"No, no," Tina said. "I'm so content right now. Your body is gorgeous, and you are a magnificent creature that has wiggled her way into my heart."

"I'm a creature, am I?"

"Mm hmm," Tina said, trailing lazy circles over Jaleesa's stomach under the sheet.

"Okay," Jaleesa said with an exaggerated sigh. "Just as long as I'm in your heart because you're in mine, too."

Was this their way of saying *I love you* to each other without actually saying the words? If so, that was okay. She'd only known Jaleesa for a month. Saying I love you should wait a little while longer, right? Tina had no clue how these things went.

"Hey, babe?" Tina said. "What's an auction?"

"How do you mean?"

Tina relayed Dana and Kadesha's private conversation and apologized for eavesdropping, but she was concerned about her friend.

Jaleesa said, bolt upright in the bed. "This is not good. You were right to tell me. You said she already paid into it?"

"Yes, do you know what this auction stuff is all about?"

"It's risky business. I participated in a couple of auctions right after Dawnn, my first real lover, broke up with me. I bought a one-week submissive and then went back a few weeks later. I don't even know why I went back the second time. It wasn't for me."

"Is Dana at risk?"

"Yes, she is," Jaleesa said.

"I see." Tina formed an immediate plan. "So that's why we're going to buy her without her knowing it's us."

Chapter 13

Jaleesa

It was Thursday evening, and Jaleesa sat at her kitchen table with her laptop open to the auction site. Normally, she'd be on the couch with her feet up, but she'd moved to the kitchen to give Harriet some space. Harriet had carved out an area in the living room to put a small easel and was happily working on something. She'd said the apartment had 'good vibes' when she'd asked Jaleesa if it would be okay. "Of course," Jaleesa had said. It did her heart good to hear Harriet humming softly as she worked.

It had been a little over two weeks since the evening Tina made love to Jaleesa. The days had gone by quickly but slowly. Jaleesa's workdays were slow because they stood in the way of seeing Tina, and then the evenings with Tina went by much too quickly, just like tonight would. They hadn't reprised their first physical lovemaking session in those two weeks, though. Although Jaleesa had enjoyed herself that evening, it had felt so one-sided that she didn't want to put Tina out again. That weighed heavily on her mind. She had to find a solution if she wanted a long-term relationship with Tina.

Jaleesa had done some soul-searching during those two weeks and knew that, yes, she did want a relationship. She and Tina had so much in common. They laughed together easily and brought new things to each other. Jaleesa had never read some of the books Tina had recommended. One of them was on her nightstand as a loner. Gabby had never been interested in anything like that.

Jaleesa loved the gentle nurturing Tina gave Harriet whenever she came over. Jaleesa's heart was so full that she even attempted to make dinner for the two of them last week. A hamburger noodle casserole, practically the only thing she knew how to make, was set on the table in front of them one night. They both seemed to enjoy it, and Tina especially made a big fuss over the effort Jaleesa had put in for them. Tina cooked for them again another night, too. Oh, how she had tsk-tsked Jaleesa about her freezer being overstocked with pre-packaged meals in boxes and breakfast burritos in plastic. At least Jaleesa didn't drink pop or sugary stuff, which was a plus, Tina said. Oh, yes, Jaleesa had swelled with pride whenever Tina seemed pleased with something she'd done. For some reason, pleasing Tina had become important. Very important.

Much of Jaleesa's time was spent thinking about ways to make her happy, including this particular Thursday evening in mid-February with Valentine's Day only four days away. Is that what love was? Wanting to spend all your time with a person and make them happy? Jaleesa wasn't sure. She thought she had been in love with Gabby, and maybe she was in her own way. Gabby wasn't the enemy, Jaleesa was coming to realize, but her heart had taken a major ding when Gabby left. Back then, Jaleesa had begun to put Gabby into some big-picture plans in her mind. She'd even picked out an engagement ring. She never bought it, though. Gabby's cowardly relationship-ending letter was left on the table before she could get up the nerve to actually buy the thing.

Thankfully the doorbell yanked her out of that Gabby rabbit hole she was heading down. Her heart fluttered as she put her laptop into sleep mode, and she practically ran to the front door. Tina would be on the other side. A quick check through the peephole verified the truth, and she flung it open wide.

"What's all this?" Jaleesa asked, relieving Tina of several grocery bags.

Tina gave Jaleesa a stern look and said, "Your new start." Tina's long hair was loose, disheveled, and in her face. Tina flung it behind her shoulders with an annoyed gesture. "Hello, Harriet," she called toward the living room.

"Hey, Tina," Harriet called back.

"Umm. before a girl gets a 'new start,'" Jaleesa said, "can she at least get a kiss?" She set the bags down on the kitchen counter and opened her arms.

Tina ignored Jaleesa and totally left her hanging. Tina opened the freezer because that's always the first thing a girlfriend does when entering a lover's apartment, and then handed Jaleesa a fifty-dollar bill. Tina then unceremoniously took every boxed and bagged pre-packaged meal out of the freezer and wordlessly tossed each one in the trashcan she'd pulled out from under the sink.

Jaleesa carefully placed the fifty-dollar bill on the table as if it would ignite and stood back to watch her girlfriend lose her mind. Harriet sauntered into the kitchen, presumably to say hello to Tina but said nary a word as she stood next to Jaleesa watching the show. Apparently done with the freezer, Tina headed to the pantry. She didn't take every last item out, but the food that did come out went into bags she'd set on the floor. "Donate." That was all she said, and she put away the new groceries she had brought. Jaleesa's fridge and freezer had never had so many green things in it. She wasn't afraid of vegetables; she just liked them from a can. She'd grown up eating them that way. They tasted good and were convenient.

Jaleesa tried to help but got a single finger wagged at her once. Jaleesa backed away slowly and almost laughed at Harriet's amused expression. Harriet leaned over and said softly to Jaleesa, "We still on for later?"

Jaleesa nodded. Apparently, it had taken several days for Harriet to work up the courage to ask for another impact session. Jaleesa readily agreed. It had been a while since she wielded the flogger, and she was kind of itching to get back to it. Jaleesa was a bit disappointed with herself because she hadn't seen the signs that Harriet was off-balance. She supposed she'd been too preoccupied with falling for Tina. Yes, she needed to be more aware of the people in her care. Harriet wasn't officially her sub, but Jaleesa would care for her as reasonably as possible. In fact, Jaleesa enjoyed Harriet's company and had extended an indefinite invitation for her to reside in the apartment as long as the pull-out futon in the living room was acceptable. Harriet said she couldn't afford much but would pay her what she could.

Harriet grinned at Jaleesa and mouthed, "Good luck," and returned to the living room.

Tina whirled around and demanded, "Have you eaten?"

Jaleesa didn't dare speak. She simply shook her head.

"Words, please." The look on Tina's face was so no-nonsense that Jaleesa obeyed instantly.

"No, I was waiting for you."

"Good," Tina said and turned her back to Jaleesa. She looked over her shoulder. "Ask Harriet if she wants to eat with us."

"I've eaten, thank you," Harriet called from the living room. Yeah, the apartment was small like that.

"Set the table, please." Oh, it wasn't a request.

Okay, Jaleesa had had enough. "I will, but I need you to stop."

Tina turned, her expression stoic.

"Seriously, Tina," Jaleesa said softly. "I'm going to perish if I don't at least get a hug."

Tina's hard expression softened, and she let Jaleesa pull her into a hug and hold her.

Jaleesa petted her hair and pulled it back behind her shoulders. "Are you okay, baby? You're ultra-large and in charge right now." Jaleesa purposely didn't use the word *bossy*, although it fit, because Tina once said she didn't like when her father accused her of it. "You're a whirling dervish," Jaleesa said. "And I'm sensing that you're upset."

Tina's silence confirmed Jaleesa's suspicions.

"Sit for a moment." Jaleesa guided Tina to the kitchen chair that had quickly become her designated seat. Jaleesa sat in her usual seat. "What's on your mind?" Soft classical music began in the living room. It was probably Harriet's way of offering them some privacy.

More silence ensued, but Jaleesa knew how to wait someone out. It was one of her best Domme tricks.

"I'm okay," Tina said, her gaze darting downward.

"When someone says, 'I'm okay,' that can mean they either can't quite put their distress into words, or they don't want to face whatever's bothering them."

Jaleesa watched as Tina's face turned pink. Ah, yes, clearly, there was something. "Your parents?"

Tina was quick to roll her eyes and let out a frustrated sigh. "Mom barged in on me again. I had just opened that auction link you sent me. I got the window closed fast enough, but I'm tired of that. Maybe I needed the constant surveillance at one point, you know?" She looked up at Jaleesa, her face a fiery red of frustration. "But…"

"But you feel strong enough to manage your own life now?"

"I think so. I don't know."

Jaleesa remained quiet. But so did Tina. There was something else on Tina's mind.

"What else is bothering you?" Jaleesa asked softly, breaking the silence.

"Penni," Tina said right away. "She keeps texting me and calling to ask when you're going to put in a bid. You were supposed to come to the bank two weeks ago to see about a loan, and you haven't, so maybe you didn't want my help to begin with, and I shouldn't have bothered looking up listings and calling my high school friend to show us that property." She huffed and added, "And and you haven't taken your *Words with Friends* turn in, like, three days."

"Oh, honey," Jaleesa pulled her into a hug. Tina resisted at first but then let herself be loved. "I'm so sorry. I should have communicated better. I guess you haven't completed that mind-reading course yet, have you?"

Tina laughed into Jaleesa's shoulder. "No." She pulled back, took the imaginary key out of her pocket, and twisted it over Jaleesa's lips.

"Fair enough," Jaleesa said. "I wasn't lying when I told you Miss Bessie wouldn't let me take time off. She said I've already taken off more time than usual and that she's seen how distracted I've been lately. She told me in no uncertain words that she would have no trouble making an example out of me by letting me go. And even though I've been with her for a long time, she would do it. I've seen her do it." Jaleesa took a breath and then allowed her vulnerability to show. "Truth is, Tina. I'm scared. I see the amazing possibilities in Denton Heights, but I'm not sure I can pull it off."

"We."

"Hmm?"

"We. You and me. We can do this," Tina said. "*We* can pull it off. I want to help. I can loan you money if you need some."

Jaleesa put both hands up. "Oh, no, no, no. I appreciate you wanting to help, but I can't take money from you."

"I don't want you to miss out on your dream, baby."

Jaleesa melted every time Tina called her a pet name. She couldn't help leaning over and cradling Tina's chin with one hand. Jaleesa hoped her expression conveyed the love she felt for Tina. "May I kiss you now?"

Tina nodded, and Jaleesa sealed the deal.

When they broke away, Tina said, "So Mom and I were talking about your joint pain and inflammation. We thought you might try eating real whole foods instead of that crap." Tina gestured to the mound of pre-packaged foods currently melting in the garbage.

"Your mom? You told your mom?"

"She saw how you struggled that day you came over for the football game. She and dad were both concerned," Tina said gently. She stood up and opened the freezer. "Mom and I made a bunch of homemade meals for you." She took out two of the many sealed containers.

"Your mom?" Jaleesa was stuck on the fact that Tina's mom had softened a bit toward her.

"Yes, honey. She does have a heart." Tina grinned to let Jaleesa know she was teasing.

"Your mom," Jaleesa said. "Huh."

"These two are baked ham with peas," Tina said. "Real peas. Not canned peas swimming in formaldehyde. But if you don't want ham, we also made turkey with carrots meals and hamburger with green beans. Dad wanted us to put mac-n-cheese in with the hamburger." She shook her head as if she couldn't believe her father's cluelessness. "You can't freeze a salad, but I can throw one together for us if you want."

"Thank you, but the ham meal is more than enough," Jaleesa said. "Please thank your mom for me, and I will, too, next time I see her." Jaleesa's heart squeezed with emotion. She had always been the one who did the taking care of. Never the other way around. This was different. This was nice. "You're incredible. Thank you for taking care of me."

Another blush flushed Tina's cheeks, but it was for a good reason this time. She responded with a smile and then set about putting the frozen meals in the microwave. Jaleesa set the table as originally asked, and as they ate, Tina talked about Jaleesa's new eating plan. If eating whole natural foods didn't alleviate Jaleesa's flair-ups, more drastic measures might be needed, like removing dairy, gluten, or both from Jaleesa's diet. Jaleesa knew better than to protest, but seriously? Was Tina going to take away her ice cream? That might be a deal breaker, but not really. Eliminating those things might help. It was okay to get help sometimes, wasn't it?

After eating the homecooked meal and setting the dishes in the sink to soak, Jaleesa put the tea kettle on. Harriet declined, so Jaleesa only set out two cups for herbal tea.

"I like when you do things like this for me," Tina said when Jaleesa placed the steaming cup in front of her.

"Do you now?"

"Mm hmm."

"Well, I like doing things for you." Jaleesa took a sip of her tea and woke up her laptop to show Tina the auction site on *Kinks.com* for the Cincinnati area. "This is my Domme persona," Jaleesa said, pointing to the website auction page she'd filled in.

"I can tell that's you," Tina said, pointing to the one and only picture Jaleesa had uploaded. "I recognize that body under all that leather. And those hands. That looks like a riding crop in your hand."

"It is a crop." *Some subs like nice and stingy impact,* Jaleesa thought but didn't dare say it out loud. "Hopefully, Dana won't recognize me."

"I doubt it," Tina said. "Are the auction people okay with you not showing your face?"

"It's kind of expected that Dommes remain hidden. It's all about the subs."

"I can tell you've done this before."

Jaleesa nodded.

Tina, looking back at the page, started chuckling. "Is this the name you go by at Dominique's? 'Mistress Thorn?'"

"No, I had to make up something for the website."

"Even beautiful roses have thorns," Tina said coquettishly. "So, maybe it's fitting."

"You have yet to see my thorns, baby," Jaleesa said, liking the direction the conversation was going.

"Maybe I will one day," Tina said shyly. "I've been feeling the need to use my belt."

An idea popped into Jaleesa's brain. If Harriet was amenable, Tina could get a firsthand look at what impact play with Jaleesa was like. "I can help you out with that, baby."

"Okay," Tina said. This time the 'okay' was one of shyness, not necessarily fear.

"Thank you for trusting me."

Tina grinned and then totally changed the subject by pointing to Jaleesa's profile. "Whoa, I love this. 'Yes, Ma'am, is the only correct answer.' It says you are a 'gentle and loving but firm Domme.'" Tina narrowed her eyes. "I can see that."

"Oh, is that so?"

"Mm hmm. You're, like, a force but a calm one. A calming force. You didn't get mad when I came in here like a 'whirling dervish,' whatever that is. You made me slow down and tell you what was bothering me. You were kind. But you were also firm with me. And...I think maybe I needed that from you."

Jaleesa pulled Tina into a quick hug, pleased that Tina liked her form of dominance. Some people responded well to the type of guidance and nurturing Jaleesa offered.

"Can we go to Dana's page?" Tina said, letting Jaleesa navigate the site.

"Sure." Jaleesa opened the page and let Tina's expression speak for itself. "Hot, hmm?"

"She must have had a professional glamour shot done or something. She looks stunning and much older than twenty-six. Dana shares a lot of things with me, but not this side of her. She must think I wouldn't approve or understand." Tina turned to Jaleesa and said, "She is really doing this, isn't she?"

"Desperation makes you do crazy things."

"Wow," Tina said. "Look at this pic of her on her knees as if she's bowing down to someone. Do you have your subs do that for you?"

Jaleesa knew questions like that would come up, but she was surprised that Tina had used the present tense. Did she think Jaleesa still had submissives? Was she not serious about their relationship? "You know..." No, she wasn't going to lie. Honesty was supposed to be paramount. "Sometimes I have them kneel—especially if they're being bratty. Some subs don't want that type of subjugation, and others do. I suspect Dana wants to feel subjugated. Some subs even like humiliation like name calling or being forced to wear misgendered clothing. Once the auction starts, I'll have to find out what she needs."

"Have you had a lot of subs?"

Honesty, right? Jaleesa nodded.

"How many?"

"I don't know." Jaleesa sat back. Apparently, looking at Dana's page was on hold for a bit. "When I was a sophomore, right there at that college you can see from the living room window, one of my older teammates introduced me to *the life*. Dawnn was a senior and very confident and sure of herself. I had a bit of swagger back then, too, but she took me under her wing and made me understand true dominance."

"Was she your lover?"

Jaleesa nodded. "And I was her submissive."

Tina's eyes grew wide. "You?"

"Mm hmm. She saw my dominant nature and knew I would eventually find a way to incorporate BDSM and power exchange into my life. I didn't know what she was talking about at first, but she took me to Dominique's and to clubs in other cities when we had away games. I was to be seen and not heard unless spoken to by a Dominant."

"I can't imagine."

"She sometimes made me crawl when I was in her apartment, although she let me wear knee pads. I had to sit on a pillow on the floor at her feet. She'd reach down, pet my head, and tell me I was a good girl. I loved the attention. But she also taught me how to accept her discipline when I messed up."

"Ooh, what did you do?"

"Mainly, I forgot myself. Meaning I forgot the role I was playing while in her presence. After a while, though, it wasn't a role, and I found myself needing her guidance and sure touch. She taught me how to receive her crop, her flogger, and the cane. She taught me how to service her other Domme friends."

"She abused you."

"No, it wasn't abuse. I wanted it. I craved it. Those other Dommes weren't from the college. Dawnn was very careful about protecting us. When I first got with her, I thought I had a submissive nature until she made me realize that those things I was feeling, that lust for her, the longing, and the cravings were all the things my future submissives would feel and desire. She wanted me to experience it all so I would know later when I grew into my dominant role. She'd cage me to teach me lessons. I told you how she took my clothing away, but only in her apartment. She tried the humiliation thing on me early, but we both realized I couldn't handle it and didn't want that kind of subjugation. That's why I'm not that into humiliating submissives. I'll do it, but only if they want it. I've had a few subs along the way that craved it."

"Humiliation?"

Jaleesa nodded. "They wanted me to write nasty words on their bodies and do so many other things, and I did within reason, but later I praised them for how well they took it. That seemed to bolster them more."

"Do you have a sub now?" Tina asked quietly.

"No. I'm with you, silly bear."

Tina grinned. "Maybe…"

Jaleesa waited, but when Tina remained silent, she prompted, "Hmm?"

"Maybe I'm sub-material."

Jaleesa reached for and kissed the back of Tina's hand that was closest to her. "I think part of you is. But then there's the part that storms into my kitchen and throws away my food because she doesn't think I'm eating right."

Tina laughed. "Yeah, I did that, didn't I?"

"Yes, you did, baby. But I think there are times you're submissive and times you're dominant. We all have to take the lead and be in charge at some point in our lives, right? Like you at the bank. Or with your dad." She lowered her voice and said, "And how you take care of Dana and Harriet." In a normal voice, she added, "But there are other times you seem to look to me to make decisions, like about what we do when we're together."

"So, you're saying I'm a bit wishy-washy?"

"No, no," Jaleesa chuckled. "There's a word for it. I think you're a switch. People like you are quite capable of being submissive, but it has to be for the right person and situation. But you also need to be dominant in certain aspects of your life. Again, with certain people and situations."

"It sounds so black and white."

"There's a lot of gray in it," Jaleesa said. "Now, Dana here." She tapped the kneeling picture of Dana on her screen. "I think she is a total submissive who needs to feel safe. She yearns to be seen and heard but guided." She lowered her voice and said, "Harriet is also submissive, but she's an independent submissive. She can hold her own but feels safest when someone strong is at the helm. That's just my feeling about her. I could be wrong."

"You haven't known any of us that long." Tina gestured toward Harriet on the other side of the wall. "And yet you seem to know all of us well."

"Dawnn said I have good instincts both on and off the court."

"I think that's true." Tina pointed back to Dana's picture on the screen. "So how are we going to save her from herself?"

"I have to play the dominant part true to my style. She'll spot me as a phony if I don't."

"I get that."

"So, that means I have to entice her." Jaleesa didn't see understanding in Tina's expression, so she clarified. "I will probably have to interact with her sexually online. This is what she wants if you read her page."

"She says she's 'willing to try' a lot of things. Like these—'foot fetish, humiliation, watersports, polyamory.'"

"To me, that says she is willing to do a lot of things out of her comfort zone just to attract a potential Domme."

"What's 'polyamory?'"

"It means many things to many people, but it basically means she's willing to share her potential Domme with others. She may think the potential Dommes in the auction already have a sub or two and is letting

them know she's okay with that."

"Oh." Tina took a moment to absorb the information. "So, Dana might not pick you if you don't play with her online?"

"She might not. And look, this isn't me just trying to 'get some on the side.' I have to show my dominance quickly. In these auctions, you don't have much time to make an impression or convince someone they should pick you, so I'll have to assert my dominance immediately. The *play* aspect means I may need to…" How awkward was this? Explaining to her girlfriend that she needed to have sex with one of her friends in order to help her.

"You need to have online sex with her." Tina filled in. "I get that. Like my two online relationships tried to do with me."

"How did that go?"

The red now tinging Tina's cheeks spoke volumes. "I faked it in my first relationship. I told Myrna I had orgasmed when I hadn't even touched myself at all."

"And the second?"

"Therese was more understanding. At that point, I had started to understand that being ace was a thing and that it was okay to be this thing. I think it wore on her after a while, though, so she drifted away."

"Did she ghost you?" Because if so, Jaleesa was going to track down this Therese character and give her a piece or two of her mind.

"Oh, no, no. We actually still chat now and then, but we don't consider ourselves in a relationship anymore."

"How do you feel about me paying so much attention to Dana once the auction starts?" Jaleesa asked. This could be a deal breaker for Tina.

"I'm trying to wrap my head around it. Honestly, you having online sex with someone isn't an issue. For me, it's kind of like you saying you're going out to play tennis with somebody. I never liked playing tennis in PE, so I'd say go for it. Have fun but come back to me when you're done."

"But there is something that's bothering you," Jaleesa said confidently.

"Well, only that Dana will fall in love with you, and then maybe you'll fall in love with her, and because she can give you sex, you'll give me my walking papers." It all came out in a rush.

Jaleesa had expected something like that but was still stunned that Tina had come right out and admitted her fears.

"I'm so proud of you for telling me. You spoke your truth."

Tina scoffed and looked down, clearly uncomfortable.

Jaleesa held Tina's hand. "Look, even though I can't say one hundred percent what will happen on Dana's side of the equation, I can honestly say that I don't know Dana that well to know if an attraction will manifest. My focus, attention, and thoughts have been on you ever since I heard your speech."

"That soon?"

"Mm hmm."

"My thoughts have been on you, too. Ever since you helped me breathe when I was trying to have a meltdown during my speech."

"Love at first meltdown?" Jaleesa quipped.

Tina chuckled and stood up to put their teacups in the sink. Jaleesa knew better than to try and stop her from washing the dishes, so she made her way over and wrapped Tina in her arms from behind.

"I've made a decision," Jaleesa said. "Do you have time for me tomorrow morning?"

"At the bank?" Tina swirled in Jaleesa's arms. Her back was now resting on the edge of the countertop.

Jaleesa nodded.

"I do, actually. Does this mean…"

"Yes. Let me call Miss Bessie and tell her I need the morning off." After giving Tina a soft peck on her equally soft lips, she released her. "I know there's no point telling you to leave those dishes for me."

"None whatsoever." Tina grinned and went back to her task.

After talking to a very displeased boss, Jaleesa returned, ready to refocus her energy. Harriet was more than willing to have Tina watch their impact session but cautioned Jaleesa that she might need to give them both aftercare.

"True enough," Jaleesa said. "True enough."

Chapter 14

Tina

In fifteen minutes, Jaleesa would arrive. Tina squirmed in her office chair, adjusting things on her desk so they were just so. Her heart was beating fast, too. Nancy had already commented on Tina's nervous energy that morning, but Tina didn't let on. They'd all see soon enough when she walked out with Jaleesa to go out for lunch. Would Jaleesa reach for her hand? Would they all see who had picked her? Tina? The one who lived a secluded life and still slept in her pink childhood bedroom?

A knock on her closed office door sent her heart racing. Jaleesa was early. Tina looked up and was disappointed to see Mr. Henderson at her door. Just as he opened it and stepped inside, Tina saw Jaleesa walk into the lobby. She beckoned for Jaleesa to come to her office.

"I'm heading out for lunch now, Tina," Mr. Henderson said. "I may not be back, so you're in charge. You eat at your desk, so you're as good as any."

Tina's furnace fired up and boiled to a dangerous level. Jaleesa was close. She'd overhear everything. She could be that wrong kind of submissive right now and bow down to his unfairness, or she could rise up and empower that dominant part Jaleesa said she had.

"No, actually," Tina managed to say without anger. "After I finish with this next client, she's taking me out to lunch." He looked surprised when she didn't just say, "Yes, sir," like she usually did. And since she was on this roll, she added, "And I need you to look over those maintenance requests. The restrooms need repair, and those new landscapers aren't doing a good job, if any job at all."

His bemused expression infuriated her further, but rather than get herself fired, she said to him, "My customer is here, so if you'll excuse me." She politely gestured toward the door.

"I'll ask Nancy," he said.

Crap. Sorry, Nancy. Tina looked up and caught Jaleesa's concerned expression. Tina simply rolled her eyes and sighed.

"Come on in." Tina gave Jaleesa a quick hug. She wished it could be more. She closed the door to her office and gestured for Jaleesa to sit on the other side of her desk. She hated the plexiglass partition separating them, but that was the trend these days with the recent pandemic.

"What was that all about?" Jaleesa gestured subtly toward the closed door with her head.

"He's not a good manager," Tina said bluntly. "He takes advantage of our good natures."

"Privileged white male in charge?"

Tina burst out laughing. "Something like that, I guess."

"You handled him well," Jaleesa said firmly.

"Thank you. I was mad. He was going to take my time away from you. Unacceptable."

Jaleesa leaned as far forward as the partition allowed and said, "I agree." She sat back. "Okay, let's get this thing going. Be honest with me, and no special favors."

"I actually can't give you special favors," Tina said. "Like I told you, the computer has certain parameters that must be met before allowing me to give you a loan. But we're going to be optimistic."

For the next forty-five minutes, Tina hammered Jaleesa with questions about startup costs, anticipated gross income, and a host of other details. Jaleesa was prepared with her business plan and had the answers and necessary documents ready. Tina had to teach her some of the terminology, but there were absolutely no shortcuts or favoritism.

"Very thorough, Ms. Whitmore," Tina said with a grin. "I'm

impressed. This is the fastest I've ever been able to do a small business loan app."

Jaleesa grinned wide. She seemed proud of herself. No, it was more than that. She seemed proud that she'd pleased Tina. Maybe there was something to this *switch* thing.

"Okay, big question," Tina said. "And it's a personal one. You're not asking for as much as I thought you would, especially knowing the cost of the strip mall. How are you making up the difference?"

"My brother," Jaleesa said. "I talked to him last night after you left. I thought about calling my parents, but they're still paying off four kids' college loans. Lonnie is single, has this amazing tech job, and still lives at home. He's an absolute computer nerd who said he'd be happy to loan me the amount I needed. He's now my favorite brother."

Tina laughed. "He's your only brother."

Jaleesa chuckled.

Except for the 'absolute computer nerd' part, Jaleesa might as well have been describing her. She lived at home, had few expenses, and had invested her money well over the years. Still, she was a bit disappointed that Jaleesa didn't want her financial help. Maybe it was for the best, though. No one could accuse her of anything untoward or self-serving, even though it kind of was. And, if the brother's help fell through or wasn't enough, Tina could always offer again.

"Ready to find out?" Tina asked, her fingers hovering over her keyboard.

Jaleesa crossed her fingers on both hands and held them up. Tina ran the information through the final algorithm, and the results popped up. She couldn't help her grin. "You got it, baby. You got the pre-approval."

"I did?"

When Tina nodded, Jaleesa slumped back in her chair and blew out a sigh to the ceiling. "I really got it?"

"Yes, but don't forget the bank has to do the property appraisal before they let us know if they'll give you the amount you're asking for." Tina turned the screen toward Jaleesa and pointed out the approval stamp.

"Thank you, baby," Jaleesa said. "Let's finish up here, so I can take you somewhere to celebrate." Before Tina could tap in the few required bits, Jaleesa said, "Wait, there's no pre-payment penalty or anything like that on the loan, is there? Because if I can pay this thing off sooner, I want to."

"Nope," Tina said. "Nothing like that." Tina allowed herself to feel the excitement. And it looked like Jaleesa was feeling it, too.

Once Jaleesa signed all the paperwork, Tina printed out the officially stamped pre-approval letter that the seller of the strip mall wanted before agreeing to anything. She would fax the pre-approval to Penni that afternoon.

Tina stood up, grabbed her wallet, and said, "Ready?"

"One second," Jaleesa said. "Just texting Penni with my offer."

"Ooh, ten percent under the asking price?"

"Mm hmm," Jaleesa said. "It's a bit lowball, I know."

"Penni told me there have been no offers whatsoever on that property, so she thinks he'll bite at anything."

"And…done." Jaleesa stood up to her full six-foot-one height and tucked the phone in her pocket. "Do I get to hug you here or in the car?"

Tina locked the door behind them as they left her office. "In the car, but we can do this." She reached for Jaleesa's hand and held it.

"Perfect," Jaleesa said.

"Nancy," Tina called to the head teller. "We're heading out for lunch."

"Okay, fine," Nancy said without looking. She glanced up and did a double take. "Fine," she said much more enthusiastically. "Take your time. I've got things under control here. You go on now. Have fun." Nancy was clearly stalling as she took in all that was Jaleesa. The questions burning in her eyes would be burning in Tina's ears the moment she got back.

"C'mon," Tina said with a laugh. "The curiosity is going to kill them for the next hour."

Once in the pickup, Jaleesa visibly deflated. "That was nerve-wracking for me. Thank you for being gentle."

"You did most of the work by being so prepared. Thank you for trusting me with your personal financial information. Your credit score is phenomenal, and you have zero debt beyond the small balances on your two credit cards."

"I try," Jaleesa said and pulled out of the parking spot. "Your hug awaits you in the parking lot of the Elm Street Diner."

"Ooh, I love that place. They have the best eggs benedict. Served anytime."

"Sound good."

"Jaleesa," Tina said shyly, "I am so awed by what you and Harriet did last night. Your session."

"Impact looks harsh to the outsider."

"But Harriet seemed to like it. I mean, she grunted a bit and then cried a lot."

"Like I said before, impact can be really cathartic. Harriet has a lot bottled up inside. You know her story. She lost her husband, career, and dignity all at once. All of that on top of her addiction. I hope I'm helping her release some of that anger, sadness, frustration, helplessness."

"I imagine she does feel all that," Tina said. "Can I try sometime? I mean, not today. But sometime?"

Jaleesa pulled into a newly vacated spot at the diner and put the pickup in park. She looked over at Tina and pulled her into the promised hug. "Yes, baby. If that's what you want." She rubbed Tina's back and then maneuvered her way in for a kiss which Tina gladly gave. When she sat back, she added, "But we'll go light, and we'll go slow. Remember that Harriet is an old pro at this and can take a lot more. Okay?"

"Okay. I promise to use my safeword like she was supposed to. And I can hold the red napkin you gave her. That was incredible how you stopped instantly when she dropped it."

"I knew she was getting close," Jaleesa said. "Thank you for helping with her aftercare. She seemed to appreciate your arms around her. Would you want Harriet there when we do your first time? Might be a good idea."

Tina nodded. "Yes, I think so. I trust Harriet, and I trust you."

That brought out a big smile to Jaleesa's face. It was almost as big as hearing she'd gotten the loan pre-approval. "C'mon, let's go in. I'm starving."

So am I, Tina thought. *In more ways than one.*

~~~

Things were happening quickly with regard to Jaleesa's new venture, and Tina was just as excited as Jaleesa seemed to be. In addition to playing *Words with Friends* online, they chatted every day over their secure chat line about the future of the business from the smallest detail, like the type of shampoos Jaleesa was going to use to bigger details, like replacing the strip mall's signage out front. Neither of them knew how to do that, but Tina was learning from Jaleesa that even if you didn't know something, it didn't mean you were stupid; it simply meant you had to research it and learn. Big things didn't seem as daunting that way.

Not only had Jaleesa gotten the business loan for the amount she wanted, but the strip mall's owner accepted her lowball offer and even agreed to pay all the closing costs. Penni had been right. He was hungry to unload the property. It made both Tina and Jaleesa wary as to why, but that was okay because the final sale was contingent on the inspection.

Tina was impressed with the way Jaleesa made calls to various licensed inspectors, making sure they specialized in commercial properties. She'd weeded out quite a few and finally settled on the inspector they were currently walking through the property with. He was a rugged-looking middle-aged man with well-worn boots and a flannel shirt. He was clearly no stranger to this kind of work. He even had the confident, no-nonsense air about him like Jaleesa had. He and Jaleesa communicated easily, and Tina was impressed. She was taking mental notes on their interactions. Maybe that would help her with Mr. Henderson or even that bratty teller Amber who had been rude to Nancy every day last week. Since Mr. Henderson wasn't doing anything about Amber's nastiness, Tina decided that she would try. She just didn't know what to do short of firing the pest. Ahh, but there was time to fret over that another day.

Even though it was an overcast Saturday afternoon in early March, the day was full of hope. They were almost done with the full inspection, including the quaint and cozy upstairs apartment. Although they both liked the apartment, it was too small to expect two people to live there comfortably. Jaleesa made no mention of moving in by herself, but Tina figured that's what would happen.

Inspection complete, they headed back outside, and Penni locked up the front doors and took her leave. The inspector shook his heavy clipboard and said he'd work on it that evening and have it ready tomorrow. His overall feeling, though, was that the building was sound and safe. He would get the water samples analyzed that very afternoon, too. Tina thought maybe Jaleesa had paid extra for an expedited report, but she wasn't sure.

Once the inspector drove away, Tina let herself be scooped up in her girlfriend's arms, complete with kisses that felt full of future and happiness.

"This is really happening, Tina, isn't it?" Jaleesa said, releasing Tina back to herself.

"I think it is." Tina wrapped an arm around Jaleesa's waist as they walked toward the pickup. Jaleesa's arm went around Tina's shoulders. "I have an idea. How about we go to that Indigo Café we passed by the last time we were up here and then hit up that cute coffee shop."

"I love the way you think," Jaleesa said. "As long as you don't mind me going over all my notes about this." She gestured to the strip mall she might soon own.

"Of course, I don't mind," Tina said. "I have my own thoughts. But we have to make sure we're home by eight for the auction to start."

"Yes, yes. Thank you for keeping us on track." Jaleesa paused before getting in the pickup. She looked over the building from the nail salon to the vacant restaurant and said, "I can't believe we're doing this."

Tina's heart thumped harder in her chest. Jaleesa had said, 'we.'

~~~

Tina's face lit up when she saw young Madison and her girlfriend, Shasti, sitting in the same area of the coffee shop as last time. Was it presumptuous to simply join them? Yes, she supposed it was. Ahh, but as she'd been learning, Jaleesa typically handled that sort of thing. It wasn't that Tina had social anxiety exactly. It was more that she felt uneasy in new situations, probably due to her relative isolation since her addiction started. But having Jaleesa meant she could simply follow.

As they stood in the line to order, Tina squeezed Jaleesa's hand and leaned into her. An epiphany was forming. Is this what submissives want? Someone to lead the way Jaleesa does?

Jaleesa pulled Tina's hand up to her lips and kissed the back of it. She smiled at Tina and said nothing, but the smile was enough. It said all kinds of things to Tina, but the biggest message seemed to be, 'I see you, and we're in this together.'

"Miss Jaleesa," came a soft call from across the coffee shop.

Tina and Jaleesa turned toward the voice. Madison was using the arm of a stuffy to gesture for them to come over and join them. Was that a sloth? How cute. Maybe those two were regulars at the coffee shop.

Jaleesa threw her a thumbs-up and said, "We'll be right over."

When they got to the counter, Jaleesa gave her order to a very tired-looking barista. Her long auburn hair was pulled back but in disarray. It didn't detract from her beauty, though, or the clear sense that she was in charge. She was definitely a manager of some sort. It was interesting how she gave Jaleesa a knowing nod. Not that Tina understood it, but it seemed like the barista acknowledged Jaleesa as a kindred spirit or something. Oh!

Epiphany number two was on the way. They were both dominant and confident people and recognized it in each other. Yes, it was just like Shasti and Jaleesa had interacted the last time they were at the coffee shop. It was like they understood and deeply respected each other, even though they had just met.

Tina loved it when Jaleesa ordered for both of them. It made her feel special like she belonged to Jaleesa, and now everyone, including the cute barista, would know it.

"I like this place," Jaleesa said.

Tina wasn't sure if Jaleesa meant the coffee shop or the whole town in general, but it made Tina feel good either way.

Jaleesa greeted Shasti as they approached and said, "You remember Tina."

"Oh, yes," Shasti said. "This one hasn't stopped talking about you two since we met a while back. Good to see you both again. And that is a gorgeous scarf." She reached out and touched Jaleesa's scarf.

"My Tina made it for me."

Before Shasti could respond, Madison blurted, "Hi, Miss Jaleesa. Hi, Miss Tina."

"Hey, bucko," Jaleesa said and tousled Madison's hair. Tina grinned. The move had been unexpected but was endearing.

Madison bounced up and down on the couch, so much so that Shasti had to give her a 'mom' look. It seemed like something she often did, and Madison obeyed immediately. Madison took her stuffie and made it walk over to Tina.

"Very cute," Tina said. She was focused on Madison, but she heard Jaleesa telling Shasti about the property she was looking to buy and the new business she was setting up. "Have you seen the sloths at the zoo?" Tina asked Madison.

"Yes," Madison said. "Lightning is going to have a baby next summer. She lost her first baby, though." The severe frown on Madison's face tugged at Tina's heartstrings.

"Hopefully, this baby will thrive, right?"

Madison nodded but still seemed to be down.

"Have you seen Fritz yet?" Tina asked.

Madison's eyes lit up. "Bibi's new baby? Yes, of course. Mistress saw him, too. And Billy. He's huge. Fritz the hippo, not Billy the human." She looked embarrassed for a second, but her self-deprecating laugh made Tina smile. "All hippos are huge, I guess," Madison added.

Tina nodded as she chuckled. Madison was a darling little creature, probably in her early- to mid-twenties, but she had a child-like quality that made Tina want to scoop her up and hold her.

Madison velcroed the sloth's hands together around her neck so it hung down. She said softly, "Miss Tina, why do people have to die?"

The conversation right next to them stopped abruptly.

Tina sighed. The question was serious and needed a serious answer. "It hurts when you lose someone. Dying is part of life, I guess."

"The whole circle of life thing?" Madison asked.

"Yes," Tina said, wanting to hold the young woman who was obviously struggling with something. A recent loss, most likely. "I try to focus on the good things about the person that passed. The things we did together, how they made me feel. That sort of thing. And even though our heads understand the concept of passing, our hearts still hurt, don't they?"

"Yeah," Madison said, tears forming in her eyes.

Madison sighed so miserably that Tina couldn't help herself. "Come here." Tina patted the space next to her on the couch and opened her arms.

Madison didn't hesitate, flew into Tina's arms, and let herself be cradled.

"Shh, shh, shh," Tina said as she rocked the young woman. "I've got you."

"We've suffered a few losses recently," Shasti said. "A beloved matriarch in our community passed away recently."

"Miss Tilda," Madison said. "Miss Rikki's aunt."

Shasti pointed toward the tired-looking barista. "She's been having such a hard time. They were very close."

It dawned on Tina that the tired-looking barista was Rikki, the owner of the coffee shop. All of them were focused on the barista when it became obvious that something was wrong. The barista backed away from the register, her hand over her heart. Her already pale face became ashen.

Shasti leaped to her feet. "Another one. Damn it."

Shasti shot a pleading look at Jaleesa and Tina. Tina nodded, but Jaleesa said, "We have this. Go, go."

Shasti nodded and handed her phone to Madison. "Call Miss Lydia and tell her to come in." Without waiting for a response, she ran over to Rikki and put an arm around her. The look of relief on the barista's face was almost tangible, but Tina had no clue what was happening to the woman. Shasti took Rikki through a side door Tina hadn't noticed before.

"Miss Lydia?" Madison said into the phone. "It's me. I'm at the coffee shop. Here's Miss Tina." She handed Tina the phone.

Tina almost handed it to Jaleesa, but there was no time to waste.

"Lydia?"

"Yes," came the guarded answer.

"This is Tina. I'm a friend of Madison and Shasti. Shasti asked Madison to call and see if you could come in this afternoon, like right now. Rikki seems to be having a health issue, and Shasti is helping her."

"Gotcha," Lydia said. "I'm putting on my coat now. I can be there in about fifteen. Can you put me on speakerphone?"

"Oh, uh, sure." Tina tapped the speakerphone icon. "Okay, you're on."

"Madison," Lydia said, "Miss Tina is going to look after you, okay? Let Miss Shasti help Miss Rikki. Do you understand?"

"Yes, Ma'am," Madison said. "I think Miss Rikki is having another panic attack."

"Oh, my goodness," Lydia said. "Okay, I'm in the car. I'll be right there. I'm ending the call now."

"Okay, Miss Lydia," Madison said and closed the phone app on

Shasti's phone. Tina gestured that she should tuck the phone in a secure pocket.

An angry voice at the front counter got all their attention.

"I'm on it," Jaleesa said, moving powerfully to the confrontation between a customer and the young barista taking his order.

Tina rocked Madison gently as she watched Jaleesa act as if she were the shop's manager. She placated the customer quickly, throwing the young barista a wink. One by one, Jaleesa talked to each of the shop's workers, and they each, in turn, nodded their heads and seemed to move more quickly and with more purpose. Jaleesa stood by, helping out where she could. Yes, yes, Tina thought, she needed to keep this woman in her life.

"What did you and Shasti do for Valentine's Day?" Tina asked, trying to get Madison's mind off troubling things.

"Went to Miss Tilda's funeral."

Oh, crap. Wrong question, Tina. "I'm sorry to hear that. Would you like to hear what Miss Jaleesa and I did for Valentine's Day?" It was strange referring to her as 'Miss,' but it seemed like the right thing to do for Madison's sake.

Madison turned toward Tina and nodded. She wiped at the tears in her eyes, and Tina hunted down a tissue in her purse for her.

"Magic tissues," Madison murmured.

"Hmm?"

"Nothing."

"Okay, well," Tina began, "Miss Jaleesa and I usually go to a meeting together on Monday nights, but she decided we were going out to dinner instead."

"Where did you go? The food court at the zoo?"

Tina chuckled. "No, she took me to a romantic dinner at Laurent's Steakhouse in Cincy. Have you ever been there?"

"No, I've only been in this area for a little over a year."

"Oh, we'll go some time, okay?"

Madison nodded and stroked the foot of the fuzzy sloth still hanging around her neck. Jaleesa was currently bussing tables. It was so amazing how the staff took to her leadership immediately. She really was a gentle Dominant.

"So, this place is so romantic," Tina continued. "Low lighting. Candles on every table."

"White tablecloths and warm bread with butter?"

"Mm hmm," Tina said. "You sure you haven't been there?"

Madison giggled. "No."

"So, anyway—"

"Did the waiter bring wine and two glasses? Did you toast your undying affection for each other?"

It was Tina's turn to giggle. "We're not wine-drinking kind of people, but yes, Jaleesa—I mean, *Miss* Jaleesa said some very nice things to me during dinner that made me feel all warm and fuzzy inside."

"That's the best," Madison said. "Mistress makes me feel warm, too. In really good ways."

"I'm glad. It's nice when you find someone who makes you feel that way." Tina held up the bracelet on her wrist. "Miss Jaleesa gave me this that night." The silver bracelet had one charm dangling from it. A tiny key. Jaleesa said it was Tina's to use if Jaleesa ever held things back or if Tina needed reassurances.

"She has the key to your heart?" Madison asked softly.

Tina chuckled. "Yes, I guess she does."

"What did you give her?"

"Well, she once told me that as a Dominant, no one ever thinks to give her flowers."

"Ooh," Madison gushed. "Did you give her a dozen red roses? To signify she's your true love?"

"Yes. How'd you guess?" Tina was amazed at how intuitive Madison seemed to be. "I'd had them sent to the restaurant ahead of time, and the receptionist brought them to the table.

"Aww," Madison squeed. "I washed Mistress's car once to show her I loved her. Maybe I should get flowers for her, too." Before Tina could react, Madison blurted, "Do you guys live here? In Denton Heights, I mean?"

Tina relayed Jaleesa's venture into buying the Northcentral Plaza and starting her business.

"Are you going to move up here, too? With her?"

"I don't know yet."

The look Madison threw her hit her in the gut. It was a look of disbelief that said, 'Two plus two does not equal four.' Madison lifted her head, took a glance at Jaleesa, and said, "She's nervous about moving."

"Who? Miss Jaleesa?"

Madison nodded. "She wants a life with you, but maybe you like Cincinnati too much to move." Madison shrugged and then looked down at her sloth.

Tina sat back. This young woman might be childlike, but she was observant. And smart. And she just might be right.

Chapter 15

Jaleesa

After making sure Rikki from the coffee shop was okay, and their services were no longer needed, Jaleesa and Tina bought a couple of to-go coffees and headed back down the highway toward Jaleesa's apartment. They had to get back in time for the auction.

Tina seemed to be tracking their progress on a map app as if gauging how far Denton Heights was from Jaleesa's apartment. Jaleesa decided not to ask her about it because maybe she, like Jaleesa, was trying to figure out how to make their relationship work if they lived far apart. They needed to talk about it, but Jaleesa was waiting until the final go-ahead from the inspector came through to even think seriously on the subject. Hopefully, she would get the report tomorrow.

Once in Jaleesa's apartment, they exchanged pleasantries with Harriet and then holed up in Jaleesa's bedroom with the laptop. It was almost auction time.

"We need snacks," Tina announced and leaped off the bed where they had set up shop.

"You do you," Jaleesa said, knowing she sounded distracted because she was distracted. Tina might witness Jaleesa's sexualized Domme persona that evening, which might make things awkward between them. "One more minute," she mumbled to herself. The auction site would allow official entry at precisely eight o'clock. No sooner.

Tina came back in and shut the bedroom door securely behind her. She offered Jaleesa a cherry-lime flavored sparkling water.

"Perfect," Jaleesa said, taking a sip. This time she gave Tina her full attention. "Thank you."

"I made a veggie platter with ranch dressing in this bowl and humus in that one." She placed the platter on the far nightstand, the one that used to be Gabby's. Was it Tina's now?

The auction screen refreshed itself automatically at eight o'clock, and Jaleesa was in. She hit the submissives tab, found Dana's listing, and saw that Dana's eight to eight-fifteen slot was still open. She clicked that. She wanted to fill in the seven other time slots so that no other Dommes could chat with Dana, but the auction administrators wouldn't allow that. Too many thirsty Dommes tended to ruin it for everyone. And that wasn't fair to Dana.

"Is she on?" Tina asked and bit into a baby carrot. Funny how she preferred the hummus while Jaleesa preferred the ranch.

She is observant, came a thought outside of Jaleesa. Ahh, yes. A subtle reminder that Tina was watching.

"I won't know if she's on unless she accepts my chat request. Whoa, which she just did." Jaleesa hit the private chat button that became enabled once the submissive accepted the request. This auction site truly is geared toward keeping submissives as safe as possible. She hadn't registered that fact when she'd used the site over a decade ago.

> MISTRESS THORN: Good evening, Dana_sub. I hope
> you had a good day. Is it okay to call you Dana?

"Aww," Tina said. "That was a nice opening. Getting the ball rolling?"
"The first few exchanges set the tone," Jaleesa said.

> DANA_SUB: Yes, you can call me Dana. Thank you
> for asking. And, yes, I had a nice day. And you?

> MISTRESS THORN: Excellent day, thank you. And

thank you for accepting my chat request. The photos
you posted are … intriguing.

"Why the three dots?" Tina whispered as if Dana could hear them
talking.

"To indicate a pause, as if I was looking at the pictures or thinking
about them."

"Oh, brilliant."

"Sometimes it's hard to discern tone and intent in a chat." Jaleesa
reached over Tina, grabbed a yellow pepper slice, and dipped it in the
ranch. Tina handed her a napkin so she wouldn't make a mess. For some
reason, this small gesture tugged on Jaleesa's heart, and she reached over
to stroke Tina's cheek with the back of her hand. A quick kiss for
reassurance and then back to being Mistress Thorn.

DANA_SUB: Thank you. How shall I adress you?

Jaleesa chuckled. "She's nervous."

"How do you know? By the typo?"

"Maybe, but her language is overly formal. Do you ever use the word
'shall?'"

Tina giggled. "Not often."

"She's also very polite and attentive."

"You picked up a lot in such a short exchange," Tina said, clearly
impressed. "And you haven't responded to her question."

"I know."

Tina narrowed her eyes. "Oh, you're making her wait, aren't you?"

"Mm hmm. Okay, that's long enough."

MISTRESS THORN: Ma'am will do. Might you do me
a favor, Dana?

DANA_SUB: Yes, Ma'am.

MISTRESS THORN: Take a breath. Breathe in deep, hold it for three seconds or so, and then release it slowly. SLOWLY.

DANA_SUB: Yes, Ma'am.

It was funny how Tina also took a breath and let it out slowly.

DANA_SUB: Done, Ma'am. I feel better. How did you know?

MISTRESS THORN: Auctions can be stressful. Since we don't have much time together, and I'm sure you have other appointments, I'd like you to tell me why you think you're submissive. Only what you want to share. Would you do that for me?

DANA_SUB: Yes, Ma'am. I thought some Dommes might ask. So, I am pretty indapendent. But all my life, I have felt anxious about being in charge or making decisons. I think I need giudance or a boost or someone to…I'm not sure what. But someone I trust who respects me and won't treat me like I'm stupid or feeble. I am a good follower.

DANA_SUB: I have a job ajasent to what I want to do for a career, but I can't seem to get up the nerve to ask anyone for help. Or when I do, I don't get taken seriously or respected. Sorry this is so long.

DANA_SUB: One more thing (sorry). I want to give my Domme whatever she needs from me or requires (within hard limits, of course). A leash has two ends, and I know she would need me to help her with things in her life. Sex is one thing (a big thing, of course), but it's not everything. Okay, dubble sorry for rambling.

MISTRESS THORN: Thank you for sharing your truth with me, Dana. And there is no need to apologize for doing so. I would require honesty and forthrightness in a submissive. Always.

MISTRESS THORN: I understand your clear need for guidance. It's the flip side of my need to guide and help you feel empowered, so you can do what you want and need to do. So you can grow.

MISTRESS THORN: Two more items on my list, and then you will have the floor to ask me anything.

Jaleesa could tell by Dana's typos that she was either a sloppy typist, still nervous, or had some kind of learning disability. Or maybe it was a physical issue with typing. Tina's silence told Jaleesa that Tina was captivated by the chat exchange. The following parts might upset her, but as she'd said earlier, the ball was already rolling. Jaleesa wondered if what they were doing was fair to Dana. Before actually logging in, it had sounded like such a good idea, but now? Not so much. Dana didn't know she was talking to Jaleesa. Dana also didn't know that her good friend Tina was witnessing the exchange. Dana might not want Tina to know these personal things about her. Too late now, Jaleesa thought. The ball was rolling, and the clock was ticking.

MISTRESS THORN: First item: Sex. Sex often drives thirsty Dommes and thirsty subs to these auction sites. I want you to understand that although sex is important and fun, there are other aspects of a power exchange relationship I find essential. And they are: Communication. Honesty. Consent. And just so you understand, I believe that submissives in my care are my equal. We would be EQUALS. We simply have different roles.

MISTRESS THORN: Now, just so you don't think sex isn't important to me. It is. I am a fan of Impact play, Bondage, Edging, and Denial. All these and more (which we can discuss at another time—if there IS another time) are important aspects of my play. You've seen my page. You've read the list, I'm sure.

MISTRESS THORN: Second item: I'd like to know your experiences as a submissive. Again, only what you're comfortable sharing. And while I'm on that track, never lie to me (the Honesty aspect above). You can say that you're uncomfortable answering a question, or you can maintain radio silence but never make up something you think I (or any Domme) might want to hear. Okay, Dana?

DANA_SUB: Yes, Ma'am. Honesty is the best policy, isn't it? LOL

Jaleesa chuckled. Dana was relaxing. Good.

DANA_SUB: I suppose a first chat isn't the place to discuss all my/yours/our sexual apetites and needs, is it? But, yes, you're corect when you say I looked at your page. I have two screens and forgot to tell you that I like your picture. I can sense your confidence and strengh in the photo, although that may be me projecting my desires onto it. And I must mention that I have felt the sting of the crop like the one you are holding in your hand in the pic. I like it.

DANA_SUB: In a nutshell, I have had four Doms. One dude and three women. All at diferent times, of course. It started in high school with my boyfriend (before I understood that girls were my jam). He introduced me to bondage. I liked it. The anticipation. The helplesness. He liked to gag me, too. I liked that because he wasn't using my mouth for stuff. I hope you understand what I'm saying. Anyway, the helplesness I felt only worked because I trusted him completely. TRUST. That's important. My next was with a woman. I don't want to badmouth her, but let's just say she was kind of a bully, and I didn't feel valud in the relationship. (Phew, I found a nice way to say that). My next female Domme was nice, but she was way older and just wanted to watch TV after work. I guess I got bored. I don't know, but it wasn't right for me. My last Domme was from an auction like this, and it was fun for a minute, but it was only sex. All the time. So, when you said earlyer that there should be more to a D/s relatonship than sex, I AGREE!

DANA_SUB: P.S. I know I've made some speling mistakes. Please forgive me. It's not my best thing. Have I answered your questions, Ma'am?

MISTRESS THORN: You have, indeed. And I'm sorry your prior relationships haven't worked out for you. Hopefully, you learned something from each one, though. That is a great example of a task I might ask you to do at some point—find something you learned from each of those relationships. (But I am not assigning that to you right now. It's just an example).

MISTRESS THORN: Thank you for being so forthright. If you are amenable, Dana, I would like to chat again tomorrow night. Would that be okay? Same time, if possible? If you would rather not, please say so. Honesty always. It won't do either of us any good if you agree but truly don't want to continue.

DANA_SUB: I want to.

DANA_SUB: Ma'am. (Sorry I forgot your honorriffic) Thank you for being so nice and not making me touch myself at our first chat exchange. That tells me a lot.

Tina whimpered, "Aww," and then squeezed Jaleesa's arm that Jaleesa just now realized she'd been holding onto the entire time.

MISTRESS THORN: Respect comes in many forms. Thank you for your time this evening. I enjoyed our exchange. And will you do me a favor during your next seven chats? (Yes, I noticed that all your chat slots are filled for this evening, you popular woman!)

DANA_SUB: (Smiling) What would you like me to do, Ma'am?

MISTRESS THORN: Before each one, breathe. Like you did for me.

DANA_SUB: Oh! Of course. I thought you were going to comand me to tell the other Dommes something.

MISTRESS THORN: No. Of course not. You have free will. I do, however, encourage you to ask these Dommes questions. Unfortunately, I didn't leave us much time for that. How about tomorrow evening? Ask me anything you want. The honesty clause will be in effect, but I do reserve the right to defer an answer.

DANA_SUB: You're diferent. Ma'am. You said my pictures intrigeed you? Well, our whole exchange has intrigeed me. I'll be here tomorow evening, too. Good night, Ma'am. And thank you.

MISTRESS THORN: Goodnight, Dana.

The chat window closed on its own, and Sunday's chat appointment window opened. Jaleesa clicked the eight o'clock slot and then closed the entire auction site. Honesty. She made a big deal about that to Dana, and here she was, not being honest with Dana about who she was. She heaved a sigh and said to Tina, "Thoughts?"

Tina didn't speak right away, so Jaleesa looked at her. "Baby, are you okay?" She used her thumb to wipe away Tina's tears. "What happened?"

"I want to be you. To be able to say those things to Dana." Tina looked into Jaleesa's eyes. "But I also want to *be* Dana, and you hear you say those things to me."

Jaleesa pulled Tina into a tight hug. "I haven't formally said those things to you, baby. They were implied. Except for the sex stuff."

Tina's response was a light smack on Jaleesa's arm, followed by a quick, "Sorry. I know you don't like that."

"I do prefer words."

"I want to please you, Jaleesa. I want to help you like Dana said she wants to do for a Domme."

"You have been. There's no way I would be sober right now without you and Harriet. There's no way I'd have that building or the loan to buy it with. God pushed you into my life, I think. To help me. To guide me."

"I feel the same about you," Tina said, snuggling close. "You smell so good, baby."

Jaleesa chuckled. She kissed the top of Tina's head. "So do you, sweetie."

"Sunday dinner tomorrow? My parents' house?"

Jaleesa grunted in surprise. "That's the first time you've called it that. Your 'parents' house.'"

"Is it?" Tina shrugged.

"Yes, I'll be there. Can I show up early and have some alone time with my girl before the work week steals her away from me?"

"Yes," Tina said with a sigh. "They leave at nine-thirty for church."

"Have the coffee brewed and ready for me."

"Absolutely. I have to have you highly caffeinated. We're doing some high dusting tomorrow." Tina laughed and added, "No one in my house can reach the ceiling fans."

"I see how it is," Jaleesa said. "That's all I'm useful for. High dusting. Lightbulb changing."

"My dad only asked you that one time."

"It'll happen again," Jaleesa teased. "He blames me for the Bengals losing the AFC playoff game because I wasn't there to watch with him. Oh, the trouble I've seen," she sang, making Tina giggle.

"Oh, you hush now," Tina reprimanded. "It's high time you kissed me."

Jaleesa answered by pulling Tina on top of her and letting their bodies meld together. She let Tina lead.

~~~

Sunday's visit to Tina's for high-dusting and dinner with the parents went well. Tina's parents seemed to accept Jaleesa in their lives, allowing Jaleesa to relax more in their presence. Of course, it didn't hurt that Tina's father had recorded a Blackwell College women's basketball game to watch after dinner. Although the coaching staff was completely different now, the players' uniforms were the same blue and black, and the gym was exactly the same. Even the sounds of the game were the same. It was surreal watching the women on the screen play the game she loved. She admired their strength and grace and couldn't help reliving some of her old glory days in her mind.

A weird feeling settled in her chest. It was an uneasy feeling, but one smile from Tina made her understand that even though her literal days as a hotshot athlete were over, life was pretty damn good right now, with an amazing future ahead. Bonding with Tina's father over the sport and the team she'd put her heart and soul into for four years felt good. During halftime, Jaleesa realized that finding the game was his way of reaching out to her. Yes, that felt good, too.

Jaleesa went home alone after they'd watched the game. Tina said she needed to catch up on sleep. Although that might have been true, Jaleesa thought maybe Tina was giving her space to interact one-on-one with Dana during their second auction chat. And truth be told, that second session with Dana felt much more intimate. Maybe because Dana felt more relaxed with Mistress Thorn.

Dana's questions on Sunday evening weren't too intrusive, and Jaleesa was able to answer each one truthfully, with one exception. Dana wanted to know Mistress Thorn's feelings about exclusivity and polyamory. The questions had thrown Jaleesa. She had always expected to be the only lover in someone's life. That night, though, she told Dana it wasn't something she'd ever done before and would have to think about it. Did Dana know that Mistress Thorn already had someone else? Or did Dana have another Domme on the hook?

Jaleesa was surprised to find a small kernel of jealousy blooming in her chest. She joined the auction to save Dana from herself, but Jaleesa was developing strong feels for the mid-twenty-year-old. Ugh. It wasn't fair to lead her on like this. Dana would be expecting a relationship of some kind.

Mistress Thorn was making herself look so attractive that Dana was sure to pick her. But then what? If Jaleesa didn't have Tina, she would date Dana in a heartbeat. But she *did* have Tina.

And to complicate things, the inspection came back good. There was the issue of the water damage out front that she would ask the seller to address, but other than that, the inspector gave the green light. Even the water samples were acceptable. So, here she sat in her pickup on Monday afternoon during her lunch break. She had her cell phone in hand, ready to punch in Penni's number to give her the go-ahead to finalize a closing date. But she couldn't do it. How could she move to Denton Heights and leave Tina in Cincinnati? Despite Tina's insistence that Denton Heights wasn't that far away, it was. The distance was far enough to kill the relationship. Jaleesa had seen it before. And she couldn't ask Tina to move up there with her into that tiny studio apartment. What would her parents think? She couldn't exactly afford to pay rent on a bigger apartment now that she had this huge loan to pay off and a business to fund.

And now there was Dana. That ball was rolling and never should have been. And she couldn't forget Harriet. What would happen to her? Back on the streets, living in her car?

Jaleesa swiped Penni's number off her screen and punched in Elaina's. Maybe her sponsor could help her make sense of things.

~~~

Monday evening, alone in her bedroom, Jaleesa fired up the third auction chat with Dana. Tina had attended the AA meeting that evening, and they were both amused to overhear Dana hammering her friend Kadesha with details about how amazing, awesome, and perfect Mistress Thorn was and how she hoped Mistress Thorn wouldn't need the full five days of the auction to pick her. No, Dana had said at the meeting a mere hour ago that if she were lucky, Mistress Thorn would pick her that very night. She was even glad about the twelve-year age gap between them because that meant her hopefully new Mistress was experienced. And real.

Jaleesa was real, all right. And here Jaleesa sat on her bed, confused about what picking Dana would mean. No time to think about it as the chat opened up. They exchanged pleasantries, and then Jaleesa's true nature overtook her. She couldn't take it anymore. Her thorns came out.

> MISTRESS THORN: Are you alone in your apartment, as you said you would be?

> DANA_SUB: Yes, Ma'am.

> MISTRESS THORN: Undress.

> DANA_SUB: Oh! Yes, Ma'am. Thank you.

Jaleesa scoffed. *This is what we both want, isn't it, Dana?* She tucked thoughts of Tina into the back of her mind because to think of Tina was to admit she was cheating.

> DANA_SUB: Done, Ma'am. I've left my socks on. Is that okay?

> MISTRESS THORN: Yes.

> MISTRESS THORN: I won't let you greet me as I come into your room because I slam you against your bedroom door and press my mouth to yours in a greeting-ending kiss. You obeyed my request to be nude as you waited for me, which shows obedience. I like obedience, Dana. And now that you fully understand who's in charge, I have a decision to make.

> MISTRESS THORN: My first option is this. I can bind

your hands and lift you onto a hook embedded in your ceiling. Your toes will touch the floor but just barely. The spreader bar I placed between your ankles leaves me quick access to your most interesting parts. Perhaps I'll tuck Ben Wa balls inside and tell you to hold them in. Should one or both fall out, my crop is within easy reach.

MISTRESS THORN: Or…

MISTRESS THORN: I can throw you on the bed, face down. The leather cuffs I attached to your wrists are now fastened to your headboard. Yes, yes, this is the one I prefer this evening. You are mine this evening. Do   you   understand,   Dana?

DANA_SUB: Yes, I understand, Mistres.

Jaleesa's arousal was immediate and deep. She pressed her legs together to heighten the sensation growing there. She was hungry for this. Hungry to assert her dominance over a willing and eager submissive like Dana. She had denied herself for far too long. She couldn't have this with Tina. But she could with Dana.

MISTRESS THORN: I run my hands over your smooth ass and delight in the gooseflesh I create. I touch you close to your need, but not quite all the way. This makes you squirm. The flat of my hand presses against one cheek. My hand raises high in the air. You anticipate its fall, yet you still yelp in surprise when it does. Why is that? I smack your delicious ass several more times. It is now warm to my touch. Do you want this, Dana?

211

DANA_SUB: Yes, yes. Oh, yes, Ma'am. Please. I will be good for you. I'll take whatever you give me.

MISTRESS THORN: Within your hard limits, Dana. Always insist on that. But I do expect obedience. A spanking like this is not punishment. Spankings, like the one I just gave you, are to enhance the experience. You will use your safe words if you need to pause or stop. What are they?

DANA_SUB: I don't know. I've never been asked that.

Anger seared Jaleesa's soul. This was exactly why she needed to be here. She needed to save Dana from those poser amateur Dominants who put submissives at risk. And that was completely unacceptable.

MISTRESS THORN: We'll use the stoplight system. It's easiest. Red means immediate stop. Yellow means pause, ease up, or you need a short break. Green means go go go.

DANA_SUB: GO GO GO, Ma'am. LOL (And I understand the systim).

MISTRESS THORN: Is my sub for the evening wet and ready for me?

DANA_SUB: Oh, God. Yes, Ma'am. Permision to cum? I'm close.

Jaleesa laughed. She wanted to quip that Dana didn't need to call her 'God,' but they didn't have much time left.

MISTRESS THORN: No, you do NOT have

permission to cum. That was a silly question. I turn you over on your back and run both hands down your body.

DANA_SUB: Your hands are warm, Mistres.

MISTRESS THORN: Your skin is warm, too, my luscious beauty. Your nipples. They're erect and excited that I am here. I circle one with my index finger and then pinch it gently between my thumb and middle finger. I squeeze harder until you exhale to relieve the pain. I do this to the other. My lips reach down and kiss one nipple and then the other bringing them relief. I pull one into my mouth and suck. Your back arches for me. You like this.

DANA_SUB: Mmm. Yes, Ma'am.

MISTRESS THORN: My hands slide down your body, glistening in the low lighting in your room. You encourage my exploration by arching your back. My finger, just one, dips into your folds. Yes, my sub is wet for me.

Jaleesa shuddered as a wave of arousal shot through her own body. If only this were real.

DANA_SUB: So good, Ma'am.

MISTRESS THORN: That one finger is naughty and splits your folds finding a warm cavern to explore. Another finger follows it inside. They travel in and out. In and out. Over and over. But then they slide out and find a lovely pearl peeking its head out. Those two very wet fingers explore this pearl as it shines into its fullest girth.

Jaleesa noticed that they had less than a minute left to their chat. Damn.

> MISTRESS THORN: My fingers leave the pearl and explore their cavern once more while my kisses take their place on your pearl. My tongue polishes her. My fingers explore in and out and over again.

> MISTRESS THORN: You have permission to cum, my dear Dana. Say my name when you do.

> MISTRESS THORN: Meet me here again tomorrow (Tuesday) evening, same time. Have some toys out and ready to describe to me.

Jaleesa hit the send button a split second before the chat window closed. She slammed her laptop shut and jammed her hand down her boy shorts. She was as wet as Dana must be. It took less than a minute. She bit her sweatshirt to muffle the cries as she came. She imagined Dana cumming at the same precise moment, which sparked another shimmer of arousal rushing through her. As she caught her breath, she lay with her eyes closed and tried to figure out what the hell to do. She hadn't claimed Dana yet. Luckily, she had two more evenings to do so. But was it the right thing to do?

Jaleesa groaned and headed for a shower—a cold one.

~~~

Jaleesa walked out the door of Miss Bessie's salon on Tuesday afternoon. It had been one of the longest days at the salon ever. She'd purposely left her phone in the pickup all day, ignoring communication from everyone, including Tina. She needed time to think. She'd probably see both Tina and Dana at tonight's mixed meeting, which would further add to her misery and confusion.

Her hand hit the door handle, and she paused. She wanted Tina in her life. Things felt right with Tina by her side. And now, in mid-March, almost three months after they'd met, Jaleesa didn't know what to do. She wanted a life with Tina, but Dana had woken up that part of Jaleesa that just could not be denied.

"It's like changing seats on the Titanic," she muttered to the universe. *No matter what I do, I'm going down!*

Jaleesa jumped when one of the other stylists called over to her, "You going to get in that truck or what?"

Jaleesa chuckled for the woman's sake. "Yep, yep. Just figuring some stuff out before I get on with it."

"Go with your heart, Jaleesa. That'll make you happiest," the other stylist said as if knowing Jaleesa's dilemma. She waved and got in her car, leaving Jaleesa nodding in response.

Jaleesa jumped in her pickup and unlocked the glove compartment. Funny, actual gloves were in there. They were the ones Tina had made for her. There were reminders of Tina everywhere. Like her used to-go cup from Rikki's Coffee Shop that still sat in the passenger cup holder. With a sigh, Jaleesa pulled out her phone and powered it up. She had at least twenty texts, all from Tina.

Jaleesa started at the bottom. There was a 'good morning' reply to Jaleesa's initial greeting. And then a few questions about that night's meeting and what they'd do afterward. Another asked how things went with Dana the night before, followed by the big question as to whether Jaleesa had gotten the inspection back and was ready to give Penni the go-ahead to buy the strip mall.

"And the answer to that last one is, 'not yet' because I'm clueless about what to do," Jaleesa said out loud.

And then there was Tina's text that came in around noon asking if everything was okay and that Tina was worried because she usually heard from Jaleesa by then.

Texts with several links from the same website followed that one. A real estate website. Jaleesa clicked on one, then another, and a third. They were links to houses for sale in Denton Heights.

Why was Tina sending her listings? The final three texts answered this question.

> TINA: As you've noticed, I've sent you houses for us to look at in Denton Heights. I know we should have talked before I went gung-ho and started searching. I know all your money is invested in the business, but I have money to invest, too. In us. In a house for us. I want us to make a life together. Yes, I know. We need to talk about this.

> TINA: I hope I haven't scared you away. You must be very busy today. So, I won't panic (yet).

> TINA: I'll see you at the meeting. Can we go back to your place afterward and talk? This silence from you has me scared.

Jaleesa's heart was racing. Tina was trying to make the decision for her, but Jaleesa wasn't sure it was the right one. She turned the key, revved the engine, and tapped open her phone. She knew the number by heart.

"Hello?" came the quick pick-up.

"Mom? Can I come home?"

Chapter 16

Tina

Tina opened her phone for the millionth time. She had a strong signal but hadn't gotten a single text from Jaleesa besides her initial seven a.m. greeting earlier that morning. She should be finalizing her last customer's account, but some things were more important, like texting her mother.

> TINA: I'm going straight to the meeting after work. I have to set up the coffee station.

> MOM: (Thumbs-up emoji)

> MOM: Will you be getting something to eat afterward with Jaleesa?

> TINA: (Thumbs-up emoji)

Tina didn't typically use emojis as text responses. It felt lazy and rude, but the only reason she had texted her mother was to make sure her phone was working. Obviously, it was. Maybe Jaleesa's phone wasn't working, or she'd left it at home. Or lost it.

Or, and this was much more likely, Tina had blown it by pushing Jaleesa too hard with the house idea. She'd done the same stupid thing with the business property, which had thrown Jaleesa way out of her comfort zone. Just because Jaleesa would probably buy the property now didn't mean that Tina should throw a house and herself at her, too. *I'm an idiot and too bossy for my own good.*

"Let me move in with you," Tina muttered to herself sarcastically. "Take over your life. I know we just met, but I'm a princess locked away in a castle. Save me. Save me." She groaned and put her head down on the desk at the precise moment someone rapped on the door. *Jaleesa?*

Of course, it wasn't. *That was pathetic, Tina.* She tucked her phone into her desk and beckoned for Amber to come inside.

"I need a few days off," Amber said.

"I'm not—"

"Next Thursday and Friday," Amber interrupted. "All day. Both days."

Before Tina could respond, Amber let herself out and closed the door behind her. Amber was a good teller, efficient and energetic. Tina wished she didn't have to be so gruff and rough around the edges.

What Tina had been about to say was that she wasn't the bank manager. Whatever. She'd relay the information to Nancy, who could handle it from there. Tina wasn't Amber's manager in any shape, manner, or form. Tina tapped her desk three times as she said, "You're o-kay." The problem was she didn't quite believe it.

When quittin' time finally came around, Tina did her final rounds since Mr. Henderson had left early. Apparently, he had a part-time job, Tina thought sarcastically. After locking up the vault, checking the alarms, and locking the front doors behind her, she realized she was doing a lot of Mr. Henderson's job. He was the bank manager, not her. She did it because it needed to be done. A sinking feeling hit her. Mr. Henderson was taking full advantage of her and the rest of the bank personnel. And he'd had the absolute nerve to tell her and Nancy they could "do better." Why? So you can take more time off? *So we can make you look good?*

Anger fueled her as she stomped to the car. It had to end, but she didn't know what to do. Henderson was going to get a piece of her mind tomorrow, Wednesday, and if he still left early, she would report him to

Corporate. Maybe that had been in the back of her mind all along because she'd jotted down his late arrival and early department times since he'd been hired. Enough was enough. Yes, she was well aware that she had dropped the title 'Mr.' in front of his last name because that would show respect, and she no longer held any for him.

That decided, she hopped in her car and rechecked her phone. She called Jaleesa's number. It went right to voice mail as if her phone was off. They hadn't gotten around to tracking each other on their phones, so Tina had no idea if she was still at the salon. Maybe she should drive over there. No, that was pushing things and would show her insecurity. And, besides, she didn't want to be late setting up the beverage station. She pulled onto Elm and headed toward the church. You know what? It was high time someone else took over that damn beverage service. Tina had covered it for over a year, so why would anyone bother to help?

A niggling thought entered her mind. Jaleesa would advise her to ask for help or a break from it instead of waiting for someone else to notice and offer.

"Honey, where are you?" Tina asked the universe. She refused to go down the rabbit hole of calling hospitals to see if Jaleesa had been in a car accident or something. Hopefully, Tina would see Jaleesa in less than an hour, and if not, Harriet should be at the meeting, and she could get more information then. Ahh, and then there would be Dana. Maybe Dana had some information. Oh, oh! Maybe she and Mistress Thorn had met today, which was why Jaleesa hadn't responded.

Tina took a deep breath to calm her nerves. Jaleesa would have advised her to do that anyway.

She pulled into the church lot. The familiar black pickup wasn't there. No worries, it was still early. She went inside and greeted Pastor Paul and Fran and then set about brewing the coffee. While it was brewing, she made a decision. This would be her last time doing the beverage station. She put the second pot to brew and headed to the main room to inform Fran. Fran was surprised but didn't seem disappointed.

Epiphany number two thousand dawned on her as she returned to the kitchen. Tina was afraid to disappoint people. Fran, just now. Her parents, Jaleesa, even Harriet, and Dana. Henderson at first, but no longer. He was the one doing the disappointing.

"I have to live unafraid," Tina muttered as she fussed in the kitchen. She stopped all movement. That's precisely what she had been trying to do by sending Jaleesa the house listings. She'd just messed up the order of things. With a big sigh, she picked up the heavy urn. She heard voices in the main room and couldn't help remembering the first time she'd met Jaleesa, but this time Jaleesa wasn't there to clear everyone away from the doorway.

As she set the urn on the table, she looked around. Jaleesa wasn't there. But she knew that. Tina had a radar for Jaleesa's voice, for Jaleesa's presence, and that presence wasn't there.

She hustled to set up the rest of the beverage station and then made a beeline for Harriet.

"Have you heard from Jaleesa?"

Tina's nerves spiked when Harriet didn't answer and led Tina to a seat. She opened her phone and showed Tina the text she'd just gotten from Jaleesa a short while ago.

> JALEESA: Harriet, I'm going to Cleveland. My family is there. Can you please tell Tina I won't be at the meeting tonight.

Tina searched Harriet's face. "That's it? No other message?" When Harriet shook her head, Tina pulled her own phone out. No texts. No messages. Not even on their secret chat channel. "Maybe there's a family emergency. Why didn't she call me? Or text me?"

Harriet's face was sympathetic when she said. "She seemed perfectly okay this morning when she left for work. And she didn't say a thing about a family emergency or anything. I'm sorry I can't be of more help."

"Cleveland's four or five hours away, right?" Tina looked at her watch. "So, if she left right when she sent you the text, she probably won't get there until nine or ten tonight. Maybe later because of rush hour."

Tina must have looked so lost that Harriet said, "Hey, how about after the meeting, we go back to the apartment and catch up? We haven't done that in a while."

Tina chuckled. "Sounds like something I'd say to you, isn't it?"

Harriet smiled. Tina loved Harriet's smiles. There seemed to be more of them lately now that she was living with Jaleesa. *The Jaleesa-effect*, Tina thought with a smirk.

Just then, the door flung open, and Dana blew in, yammering a mile a minute to Kadesha. Dana was saying, "…had sex last night."

"In person?" Kadesha asked wide-eyed.

"No, no. Online in the auction. In our stupidly short fifteen-minute chat time."

"And?" Kadesha smacked her friend on the arm. "Why you leavin' a girl hanging?"

"It was really good. She—"

"No. No. Never mind." Kadesha put a hand up. "I don't want all those lezzie details."

"You're such a prude."

"And yet I still hang out with you."

"We're meeting on the auction site again tonight. She told me to have some toys out." Even though Dana whispered the last part, Tina still overheard it. And she wasn't sure what to do with it.

"Tina," Dana said and stormed over for a hug. "Where's Jaleesa?"

Tina's voice stuck in her throat, so Harriet said, "Family thing back in Cleveland."

"Oh," Dana said, clearly disappointed. "Okay."

Did Dana know that Mistress Thorn was Jaleesa? No, it didn't seem like it. She was just disappointed that her crush wasn't there. *Like me*, Tina thought.

Tina didn't share at that evening's meeting but was pleased when two people volunteered to take over the Tuesday night beverage station. It was nice that Fran thanked her publicly for her service. She hadn't been expecting that. It felt good knowing someone appreciated her efforts.

And, no, she wasn't referring to Jaleesa blowing her off. There must be some valid reason—

"Stop," Harriet said in a whisper.

"What?" Tina looked over at her friend.

"You're worrying. I'm sure she's fine."

Tina nodded and heard nothing from the rest of the meeting. When it was over, she gave Dana and Kadesha big hugs and then followed Harriet back to Jaleesa's apartment. It was strange being there without Jaleesa. A quick look around revealed nothing out of the ordinary. There was no memo pad with a phone number jotted down because Tina would have called it immediately. There was nothing to indicate anything.

"Tea?" Harriet asked as she put the kettle on.

"Sure." Tina sat at her usual spot at the kitchen table. Maybe Jaleesa's laptop was in her room. But no. She would not stoop to nosing around in there. Consent had not been given. But, Tina vowed, if she or Harriet didn't hear anything by tomorrow evening, Tina was going to take matters into her own hands and show up at the salon. If Jaleesa didn't want to see her, fine. At least she would know where she stood.

It was the sex thing. It had to be. And maybe some of it was the house listings thing. Yes, it was both. Jaleesa needed sex. She'd even said so. The kind Tina had offered recently clearly wasn't enough.

Obviously not! Tina shouted in her head. She tapped the surface three times. *You're o-kay.* And again. *You're o-kay.* She didn't believe it, though.

Harriet set the teacups on the table, followed by an assortment of teas, honey, and lemon slices. Aww, that was sweet. Harriet remembered how Tina liked it. Harriet poured the hot water and sat in her usual seat.

"So, this apartment is small," Harriet began, "and I overhear things. I don't mean to, but with Dana's announcement about her liaison with someone online last night, the final puzzle pieces fell into place. I'm assuming this Mistress Thorn is Jaleesa, and she is pursuing Dana online?"

Tina groaned. "Yes."

Harriet nodded. "And how do you feel about that?"

"It was my idea."

Harriet looked so surprised that it must have stunned her into silence.

Tina wasn't sure how much to reveal, but she would do it if it gave her a clue as to where Jaleesa was.

"I want Jaleesa in my life," Tina began. "You know, as a life partner. She's easy to be with and makes me feel good about myself. But I'm just not that interested in sex, like with anyone. And as I'm sure you know, she likes a certain kind of sex—the kind I can't give her. I just don't feel…I can't muster up…I can't fake it, Harriet. Don't get me wrong. I'm attracted to women, but not sexually. Romantically, I guess. Intellectually, affectionately. Sex never enters my equation."

Harriet's smile was kind. "I understand. May I share some insights I've garnered from my married life?"

"Of course," Tina said. She fixed her tea just the way she liked it and took a sip. Perfect.

"When Phil, my husband, realized I wasn't interested in sex anymore, he strayed. Honestly, I was never that interested in it before then, either. For me, it was one of those wifely duties or something. We never had children. It wasn't something either of us wanted, despite our families' urgings." She chuckled at the memory. "Anyway, I figured out pretty quickly that he was having an affair and confronted him on it. He didn't deny it. I was ready to show him my evidence, but he told me the truth. It was a client who came in on a regular basis. She started flirting, and he liked the attention."

"Is that the one he's with now?"

"No," Harriet said with a laugh. "There were a few more. But I gave him some ground rules. He was never to sleep with them in my house or bed. He agreed."

"He was probably just relieved that you gave him the green light."

"Probably," Harriet said with a laugh. "There were other requirements. He had to tell me where he was going and who he was with. I didn't think he'd go for it, but he did. And I wanted him home every night. He had to shower and sleep with me in my bed."

"And he did that?"

"Yep. And then he fell in love with one of those women."

Tina reached over and put her hand on top of Harriet's. "I'm so sorry that happened."

"Thanks. It was right about then that the cocaine started flowing." Harriet paused for a moment and said, "I think it was time for me to move on from him anyway. Hindsight being twenty-twenty and all."

"Mmm, maybe." Tina squeezed Harriet's hand and let go. "Why did you share this with me?"

Harriet set her cup down on the table and looked directly into Tina's eyes. "You and Jaleesa belong together. And if you have to share that part of Jaleesa with someone else, then maybe…" She put her hands up in a helpless gesture.

"Maybe it's a way I can have her in my life," Tina mused out loud. "Maybe she can feel fulfilled in those things I can't give her."

"It's something to think about, isn't it?"

"Jaleesa always talks about honesty, doesn't she?" Tina said.

"Yes, she does."

"I need to figure out if I'm willing to do what you did. And there's the other thing. She might not feel the same way about me as I do her."

Harriet burst out laughing. "Uh, she does."

"Really? How do you know? What did she say?"

Harriet waved off the question. "Just the way she looks at you. The way she smiles after you two get off the phone each night. Listen, you're just going to have to believe me when I say that she does."

"That's why this is all so confusing," Tina said, her tea abandoned. "I mean, where is she? I'm glad she texted you, but why didn't she text me, too? What's going on?"

"I have no idea. Truly, I don't. But the only thing I can tell is that Jaleesa has had a lot of new things thrust on her all at once since she met you." When Tina tried to protest, Harriet interrupted and said, "I'm not saying that's a bad thing, but hear me out. Did you know that she's lived in this same apartment since she was a junior in college?"

"No way. That's like eighteen years or something."

Harriet nodded. "Although she's amazingly strong and confident, she might not know how to..."

"Evolve?" Tina offered. "No. That's a stupid word. Umm, grow, maybe?"

"Maybe. I don't know. Maybe she just needed to clear her head. Total conjecture. And who knows? There might actually be a family issue back in Cleveland." Harriet shrugged. "Or..."

Tina looked up. She didn't dare think it. "She just got her one-year chip. She wouldn't."

"Addiction is a cruel mistress."

They sat silently until Harriet added, "All I know is that I've felt taken care of ever since I met her. I've felt useful to her. And—" Harriet couldn't finish her thought because emotion got the better of her momentarily. "Like you, I want her in my life. Not like a life partner, just nearby. I can't explain it."

"I know the feeling," Tina said wiping at her own tears that had sprung up. "Look at us. Two blithering softies." *The Jaleesa-effect*, she thought again.

"Tina," Harriet said after wiping her eyes, "I'm sure she's okay. If I hear anything, I'll call you immediately. I'll wake you up if I have to. Would that be okay?"

"Yes, of course. And I'll do the same." Tina stood up and put their cups in the sink. "I should get home. If you think of anything else, please let me know."

"I will."

Tina nodded and found herself in a rare Harriet hug.

They said their goodbyes, and Tina walked down to the parking lot. She paused before getting in the car, hoping to see Jaleesa's pickup pull in, but that was wishful thinking. Jaleesa was in Cleveland with her family. Tina got in her car, turned on the engine, and rechecked her phone. Nothing.

Once home, she ate some leftovers and explained that Jaleesa had to go to Cleveland. Something with her family, she'd said. She'd been honest when her mother asked. Her mother didn't use actual words, but her expression spoke volumes. She was not pleased that Jaleesa had upset her baby.

Before Tina could get roped into any kind of discussion, she claimed tiredness and went up to her cage with the princess curtains and pink walls. She propped up her phone and turned the volume up to maximum. She didn't want to miss the ding of an incoming text. She locked her bedroom door, undressed from work, and put the clothes in the hamper. Saturday was her laundry day. She was going to try that new fabric softener she'd bought at Kroger with that coupon.

"And you're totally stalling," she muttered. The blinds and curtains were already fastened shut. She only opened them on the weekends.

She put her pajama bottoms on but laid out the top on her bed. She grabbed the belt from her closet, the belt she used to attempt to bring balance to her life. With a couple of clicks, the music app on her computer played some techno dance music. You could rely on techno to drown out any sounds, mainly because the constant thump thump thump of the beat never let up. Her parents wouldn't be able to hear the slaps of the leather on her skin. They wouldn't be able to hear Tina exhale in pain. And they certainly wouldn't be able to hear her tears when the belt forced them out.

Thwack, thwack, thwack, she hit herself. Three more times in succession. "Empty your mind," she said out loud. Three more. And again and again and again. Over and over, she flung the belt over her shoulders and around her hip to sting her flesh. Yes, the tears had finally begun.

When she couldn't snap the belt anymore, she threw it in a drawer and lay face down on the bed. Her back pulsed. She lost herself in the pain, her thoughts only on the throbbing. It wasn't until she imagined Jaleesa's cool hands pressing against her welts like she'd done for Harriet that she started crying in earnest. She buried her face in her pillow and cried until she fell asleep.

A knock on her bedroom door woke her.

"TJ, it's late," her father said from the other side of the door. "Maybe you can use your headphones?"

"Okay, Dad," Tina said, bolting out of bed and turning off the music. She threw on her pajama top and turned off the lights. Opening the door slightly, she said, "Goodnight, Dad. Sorry about that."

"Goodnight, kid," he said, using the childhood nickname he'd had for her.

"Night," she managed to squeak out as emotion bubbled back up.

She listened for the sound of her parents' bedroom door closing and then blew out a sigh. She snuck into the bathroom off the hallway and washed her tear-streaked face. She did the rest of her getting-ready-for-bed routine and headed back to her bedroom. The door got locked. The small desk light got turned on, and her desk chair got sat in.

It was midnight. Her phone revealed no texts or calls from Jaleesa. She hit up the private text app, not sure what she was about to say, but she had to say something.

> SHORTSTUFF: Harriet told me you went to Cleveland. I hope everyone in your family is okay. And I hope YOU are okay. Having said that …

> SHORTSTUFF: Why didn't you contact me? I'm confused. And, frankly, hurt. Why haven't you responded to any of my texts?

SHORTSTUFF: You like honesty, right?

SHORTSTUFF: So, I'm thinking I bulldozed my way into your perfectly fine and acceptable life and wreaked havoc with it. I'm sorry. I guess that's something I need to work on. I'm not sure why you aren't talking to me right now. I've gone over all of our conversations and time together and can't figure out what I did or said to make you run. It must have been the house listings. I scared you away. I'm sorry. That was stupid of me. I need to stick to my lanes. My 'pig trails,' as you called them once. Do what I'm good at, and don't deviate.

SHORTSTUFF: Sure, maybe it's not about me at all, and you really do have a family emergency. Communication is important to you, too, though, isn't it? So, when you get a chance, please send me a message because you've moved into my heart, Jaleesa. If you have to use Harriet to deliver your message, that's okay. I'll understand.

Tina paused in her texting tirade to wipe at her tears. She couldn't decide if they were tears of anger or frustration or sadness. Yeah, it was all three.

Right then, as she sat in her juvenile pajamas in her juvenile room, she made a decision. No matter what happened between her and Jaleesa, Tina needed out. Here she was at thirty-one years old, having basically thrown away her entire twenties. She'd gone nowhere—no vacations, friends' houses, nothing. She needed to get on with life and get her own apartment. If Jaleesa moved away to Denton Heights to live in the studio apartment above her new salon, Tina could move in with Harriet. Harriet could have the bedroom. Tina would take the futon. She didn't care.

She rubbed the key charm on her bracelet that Jaleesa had given her on Valentine's Day as she gathered her thoughts for one last text.

SHORTSTUFF: I saw a small glimpse of what my life could be beyond this pink cage I keep myself in. And even though that version might be gone, you showed me I am strong enough to get out. (Maybe. That jury is still out.)

SHORTSTUFF: Goodnight.

She flicked out of the app and lay her phone on her bedside stand. She took off the bracelet Jaleesa had given her. That was ironic, wasn't it? The key stood for communication, one of Jaleesa's basic rules to live by. But the key to unlocking Jaleesa wasn't working anymore. Mistress Thorn must have changed the locks.

"Time to grow up, Tina." This she muttered to her room as she ripped down the first picture from her wall. She knew what *hot* was now. It was Jaleesa, not these women. She ripped each one to shreds and stuffed them deep inside her pink garbage can. In one way or another, it was time to start over because this had been the worst Tuesday ever.

Chapter 17

Jaleesa

Jaleesa arrived at her childhood home that Tuesday night around ten. The entire Whitmore nuclear family was there to greet her—both parents, her first younger sister Nat, next younger sister Bleu, and the baby of the family, brother Lonnie.

Of course, everyone was polite and waited for Jaleesa to let on why she'd driven five hours on a whim to come home. No one out and out asked, so she said she needed some advice about the new business and wanted to see her family before she was completely engulfed in building her business. Her mother wasn't easily fooled and raised a slight eyebrow at the tale.

Lonnie, of course, was utterly clueless, thinking she'd come up to see him about the loan. She hadn't, but they managed to hammer out some details and terms while she was there, so it was a win-win situation.

The impromptu reunion was a balm to her soul, and even though it was already after midnight, she was saddened when her sisters had to leave. Both of them hinted around for free hair appointments at the new salon, and Jaleesa reassured them the family comp deal would always be in full effect. When she hugged Nat, her childhood partner in crime, she asked if they could meet for lunch the next day. Nat laughed knowingly and said, "This is about a girl, isn't it?"

Jaleesa nodded and let Nat hug her again as they set the time and place to meet without being under the watchful eye of their mother.

After her sisters left, her father hugged her again and excused himself to go to bed. At Jaleesa's mother's insistence, Lonnie also headed up the stairs.

"What's wrong?" her mother said simply and sat back down at the kitchen table. She pulled her sweater tighter around herself.

There was no way around it. Black moms always knew when you were lying or up to no good. Jaleesa had to confess. "I met a girl, Mom. A woman, I mean."

"Does this woman mean something to you?"

Jaleesa nodded, feeling like she was back in high school being interrogated. No one could stand up to an interrogation from Ruth Whitmore, ruler of the Whitmore clan.

"What's the trouble?"

"She's pushing hard."

"Mm hmm," Jaleesa's mother said. "Do you love her?"

"Yes," came the quick answer. Jaleesa had known she was falling for Tina for a while now. On the lonely car ride north, her heart informed her brain.

"What's the problem then?"

"I don't know. Gabby—"

"Gabby wasn't right for you," her mother said quickly. "You gave and gave in that relationship. Did you ever get?"

Jaleesa was a bit taken aback by her mother's sharp words. She looked down at the old kitchen table and the myriad scratches from countless family meals, homework sessions, arts-and-crafts projects. She knew her parents, especially her mother, were "concerned" when she showed up without much notice. They didn't bring up the year-old DUI or her subsequent launch into AA, but Jaleesa noticed that the liquor cabinet had been cleaned out, and there was not a single bottle of wine in the still-cold wine fridge. She wouldn't have been tempted. She liked to think that, anyway.

"I'm not sure I've figured out what happened with Gabby," Jaleesa admitted. "I thought I loved her."

"She left when the party life left."

Jaleesa nodded. "Life got real for me when I got pulled over that night."

"And now, over a year later, you've got another woman on the line. Is she worth reeling in?"

Jaleesa laughed. "Really, mom? Fishing analogies?"

Her mother laughed conspiratorially. "Had to get your attention somehow. So, does this woman take care of you? Do things for you? Or is it all about her and her needs?"

Memories of everything Tina had done for her flashed through her mind. "She knitted me a scarf after meeting me once. She knitted gloves for me, too. She and her mother cooked food for me and put them in these microwavable containers. Tina brought them to my apartment and personally put them in my freezer."

"You've met her parents then."

"Yes. I've spent a bunch of time at her parents' house. Tina still lives there, too. And before you ask, she's thirty-one."

Her mother frowned. "And still lives at home."

Jaleesa didn't feel it was right for her to share Tina's situation, so she didn't. She simply nodded.

"Does she have a job?"

"Yes. A really good one. She's a personal banker at JW Bank in downtown Cincinnati. She's a Blackwell College grad, too."

"Go, honey badgers," her mother said, waving an imaginary flag. Her mother narrowed her eyes and said, "She asked you first, didn't she? She asked you to move in together before you knew if you were ready. That's it, isn't it?"

"How do you always know?" Jaleesa asked with a laugh. There was so much more to the story, but she had to let her mother believe it was only cold feet.

"Something isn't clicking with this story, but I know you'll tell your almost-twin everything tomorrow at lunch."

"You're scary psychic, Mom."

"Mothers always know." Her mother stood up from the table. "I have to get some sleep. I have to work in the morning. Lonnie made up the couch for you, but you'd better check it. You know where the extra blankets are. And Jaleesa?"

"Yes, Mom?"

"You have a good head on your shoulders, but don't forget to listen to that big heart of yours, too."

Her mother's words hit her in the solar plexus. Her mother was the second person that day to give her that advice. She nodded as she hugged her mother.

"Thank you, Mom. Thank you for being patient with me."

Jaleesa's mother cupped her chin, smiled, and then headed up the stairs for bed.

Jaleesa woke up the next morning stiff and sore from sleeping on the too-short couch in the living room. Both of her parents had to hustle out that morning to get to work, so Jaleesa said her goodbyes to them then. She meandered through the house, reminiscing about her formative years spent there. The basketball hoop was still in the backyard, and if she were staying longer, she'd challenge her dad to a game of Horse. They'd spent countless hours together in that yard honing Jaleesa's game—he correcting her shot, she absorbing every word. Her father was the main reason she'd gotten good enough to get the four-year athletic scholarship to B.C.

When it was time for her to leave, she knocked lightly on Lonnie's bedroom door and opened it when he beckoned her in. He was in the middle of a Zoom meeting or something, so she just waved and then hugged herself as if she were hugging him. He smiled big, made a heart with both hands, and went right back to his call troubleshooting somebody's tech problem. Her heart was full. Her brother was doing so well. Her sisters were, too. Nat was a successful accountant helping non-profits keep their status. And Bleu was rocking it as an elementary school teacher and the mom of two kids about to enter middle school. Everybody was killing it.

Her sister Nat had already arrived at Jaleesa's favorite diner and had ordered for the both of them. Their mother was right, Nat was only ten months younger and an inch shorter, but she was practically her twin in all things. She was single and kind of bisexual. Jaleesa always said, "kind of," because even Nat didn't know. She called herself a "kinky pan-sexual" because sex and gender didn't matter to her. She'd always say, 'touch her heart and mind.' and she was yours. And that was kind of the way Tina was affecting Jaleesa. Jaleesa slid into the booth in the back of the diner.

"Okay, you are so out there," Nat said. "What's her name, and how'd you meet her?"

"Cut right to the chase, why don't you?" Jaleesa laughed. She placed her phone face down on the table. "Tina. I met her at an AA meeting. Well, she's NA. It was a mixed meeting, and she was the speaker that night."

"Whoo hoo," Nat screeched, garnering looks from other people. "It was love at first sight, wasn't it?"

Jaleesa nodded. "Yeah, kind of."

"Spill. All of it," Nat said. "And not that crap you told Mom last night."

And Jaleesa did. She felt bad giving up Tina's addiction, but she needed clarity from the one person in the world who understood Jaleesa to the core, even more than Jaleesa did. She omitted a few details but mentioned the asexual aspect and the auction.

"Oh, shit," Jaleesa said, putting her head in her hands. "I left poor Dana hanging last night. Mistress Thorn was supposed to woo her for another whole fifteen minutes."

"You are out of your mind," Nat said with a laugh. "So, back up. What did Tina say when you told her you were bailing and crying home to Mommy?"

"I didn't. I texted my roommate and asked her to tell Tina."

"You what?" Nat screeched even louder than before. "You can't do that, J-Dub," she said, using the nickname Jaleesa told her Tina's father had given her.

The waitress came at just that moment and set down their club sandwiches. They both thanked her at precisely the same time, making the waitress smile. "Twins?"

Nat nodded, even though it was a lie, and then looked the waitress up and down. The waitress giggled and walked away.

"You're a bigger flirt than I am," Jaleesa said.

"Hey, I learned from the best." With a french fry dangling from her mouth, she said, "You're not getting out of this. Why haven't you texted Tina? Or called? Has she texted you back?"

"I don't know."

This time Nat didn't screech. This time she let her head fall back against the booth and said, "You're hopeless. You're a gifted athlete, the smartest one in this family after Lonnie, but you can't manage your women. And before you say anything, Gabby wasn't right for you. She was a fun two-year fling, but that's all it would ever be. If I were a betting woman, which I'm not, I would have given it ten months. But this Tina you're telling me about? Without having met her, I'd say she's a keeper. She sounds like a lifetimer."

"But what about, you know—." Jaleesa leaned closer. "The sex part?"

"She's into impact, you said. She's willing to help you out when your lady parts get needy. It's not a total loss."

"But it's a loss, right?"

"Find a compromise. I'm sure she's going to have to compromise some things to be with you, too. I don't know what, but your relationship doesn't have to succumb to your vision of it. This woman might just fulfill your needs. Needs you didn't realize you had."

Jaleesa was stunned. Nat always knew what to say to get past Jaleesa's mental blocks. She mused on Nat's words while they ate in silence for a moment.

"Jaleesa," Nat said, pointing to Jaleesa's phone with a mayonnaise-covered fingertip. "Check your texts. Right now."

Jaleesa wiped her hands on a napkin and powered on her phone. Several dings sounded, including some from the private chat channel she shared with Tina.

The one text from Harriet said calling Tina would be a good idea. Immediately. Tina was upset, she'd said. The rest of the texts were from Tina. The texts her parents might see were fairly innocuous, like the one that said she hoped her family was okay. Jaleesa switched to their private chat. Her heart broke when she heard the confusion and sadness coming through loud and clear. Anger and despair followed.

"Oh, my God," Jaleesa sputtered. "She thinks I'm breaking up with her."

"Duh," Nat said, eyes wide. "You text her every day, all day and night, and then bam! Nothing." A little more softly, she added, "You're ghosting her, Jaleesa. C'mon. Deal with your shit and call her. Drive back down there and sweep her off her feet like the woman deserves. Knitted you a scarf? And gloves? Food in your freezer? Bosses you around? A dream come true for you, sis. Someone who actually cares about the real you and not what they can get from you."

Jaleesa drank in every word. "I need to go."

"Yeah, you do. Show me her picture first."

Jaleesa scrolled and found one of the two of them.

"Oh, wow," Nat gushed. "She is adorable. Pixie cute." She clucked her tongue. "And she's white. Did you tell Mama that she was white?"

Jaleesa shook her head.

"Wouldn't matter to her anyways," Nat said. "She just wants you happy and settled. And the way you're looking at Tina in this picture? Yeah, you gotta keep that feeling in your life." She gestured to the food, most of which Jaleesa didn't eat. "You get going. I'll get this."

Jaleesa slid out of the booth and said, "I love your hair. I might copy it."

"Twist-outs with a fade. I was thinking of having Marlene do a lightning design on the sides next time.”

“You do you, sis.” Jaleesa reached down and hugged her sister. “Thank you for knocking some sense into me.”

“Call her on the way home,” Nat said evenly, her expression stern.

“I will. I love you. Gotta go.” And with that, Jaleesa turned and headed out the diner door.

She burst out laughing when she heard Nat yell, “Go get the girl.”

Jaleesa picked up speed and practically ran to her pickup. She waited until she got on the actual highway before using the hands-free feature and called Tina. She still hadn’t figured out what to say and was almost relieved when Tina didn’t pick up, and the call went right to voicemail.

“Tina!” Jaleesa said with urgency. “I’m coming back. I need to see you. I’m so sorry I ghosted you. I’m an idiot. I was confused. But not anymore. I’m heading straight for the bank. We need to talk. Okay? Don’t hate me.” She wanted to say more but didn’t know what.

She texted Tina pretty much the same message, saying she would wait in the bank parking lot. She also remembered to add that everyone in her family was fine. After that, she texted Harriet and told her she was fine and that she had contacted Tina and was going directly to Tina’s bank to make amends. Harriet got back to her right away.

> HARRIET: Good. I hope you two will be okay. I’ve grown quite fond of both of you individually and as a couple. See you later tonight.

Wow. That was a lot from Harriet. She usually wasn’t one to give her opinion unless directly asked, and here she was telling Jaleesa to get her head out of her butt and make things right with Tina. Okay, she didn’t say it in those exact words, but Jaleesa knew Harriet well enough by now to know that’s what she meant.

Somehow, Jaleesa made it back to Cincinnati in record time but had to wait for the bank to close. She thought about going inside but didn’t.

Tina might be as mad as hell. Tina might break up with her. That thought had plagued her all the way home.

After a while, Tina's was the only car left in the lot besides Jaleesa's. When she saw Tina walk out, her messenger bag draped over her body, Jaleesa's heart melted. Tina looked so professional in her tailored gray business suit, and her hair pulled up into a bun. How could she have ever hurt this beautiful soul? She wanted to run and scoop her up but held back. She had to let Tina come to her.

Tina turned to head toward her car and stopped in her tracks when she saw Jaleesa. They looked at each other silently. Tina's slight head lift meant she was evaluating her options.

"Can we talk?" Jaleesa said. She pointed to her truck.

Tina stood on the sidewalk in front of the bank and took a cleansing breath. She was deciding. Relief flooded Jaleesa's body when Tina nodded once and made her way over to the pickup. Jaleesa ran to the passenger side and opened the door. Tina stopped, her expression neutral, and looked up at Jaleesa as if deciding how many ways she was going to flay Jaleesa.

"I'm sorry," Jaleesa said as Tina got in the pickup. Tina said nothing. She only opened her mouth to take a breath. "I am really sorry," Jaleesa said again slowly as she held onto the passenger door.

"Get in." Tina gestured to the driver's seat. She looked straight ahead out the windshield.

Jaleesa got in the driver's seat, but Tina lit into her before the door was even closed.

"I thought you'd gotten into an accident or something. You texted Harriet? Not me? Don't I mean anything to you, Jaleesa? I don't understand." A flood of tears she'd obviously been holding in burst out, and Jaleesa reached over to pull her close. Tina pushed her away. "No, you don't get to do that." She shot laser beams with her eyes. She poked the air between them and said, "I'm not sure who you are anymore. I kept waiting for the smallest tidbit from you. A tiny little 'I'm okay' text. Or, heaven forbid, an actual phone call letting me know where you were or what you were doing. I was just about to drive to the salon to find you or ask them where you were. And," Tina pounded her leg, "what's almost worse is that you made Harriet worry." She sighed forcefully and looked out the passenger window. She'd said her peace.

But was she truly finished? Jaleesa wasn't sure. She took a chance. "I panicked, Tina. You were right when you said communication and honesty are important to me. I completely failed at both. I'm usually the one that leads in a relationship, and when you sent the house listings, I…panicked."

Tina huffed but said nothing. She still wasn't looking at Jaleesa, but at least she wasn't getting out of the pickup.

This was it. She had to say it. "I…" Emotion choked the words out of her mouth. "I love you, Tina Jenkins." She let the words hang there. Tina turned to face Jaleesa. She brushed tears off her face. Jaleesa continued, "I want that life with you. I want the house and the yard. And a cat. A dog? Both?" Jaleesa shrugged. She was heading into unknown territory. She was grateful when Tina chuckled quietly. "You told me once that you weren't sure what the word 'hot' meant when it came to being attracted to other people. The attraction we have for each other is *hot*. And I don't mean it in a physical way. The way we talk books, share deep feelings, share concerns."

Tina raised both eyebrows and looked at Jaleesa for the hypocrite that she was.

"No, you're right. I'm still working on that sharing my concerns thing." Jaleesa allowed herself a nervous laugh. "I've realized something, though. I realized that love is stronger than sex. I understand that now. Intimacy is when you're the one in my thoughts, no matter what I'm doing. You're the one I want to build a life with and keep safe. I want to revel in your successes and share in your failures—may those be few and far between."

The nod Tina gave Jaleesa turned on Jaleesa's waterworks for some reason. Ugh. She was supposed to be the strong one. Gentle caring arms went around her neck and pulled her close. "Jaleesa Whitmore," Tina whispered, "I love you, too."

"Thank you," Jaleesa said as she pulled Tina closer. They held each other for a few moments, and then Jaleesa pulled back so she could look Tina in the eyes. "I love you back, baby." Jaleesa kissed Tina with so much passion that they were both breathless when they broke apart.

Jaleesa took a breath and said, "Baby, from the moment I saw you, even before we'd officially met, it was like my soul breathed a sigh of relief and said, 'Oh, there you are.'" It was Tina's turn to cry, and Jaleesa pulled her close. "I mean it," Jaleesa whispered in Tina's ear. "I want a life with you, no matter how that looks."

It seemed like Tina was struggling to get her composure, and when she did, she managed to say in a high tight voice. "Me, too. When you held me after my speech that night we met, I thought you were a knight coming to save me. I still live in my pink bedroom in my ivory tower, but I needed someone strong like you to help me understand that I am tough enough to leave it."

"I don't think your mother is, though," Jaleesa quipped.

"No, not at all."

They sat back in their respective seats, and Tina said. "I am going to need reassurance from time to time, Jaleesa. It'll seem irrational sometimes, but you have to remember that I'm new to an actual real-life relationship."

"You got it, baby."

"And, and there's another thing." Tina sighed and then took an overlong moment to gather her thoughts. "I have some thoughts about polyamory. You know that sex with me isn't really my jam. But sex without some kind of love is just mechanical. I mean, you can do that with a vibrator." She laughed and said, "I'm not saying this right. Okay. Here it is. I want you to have sex with other people, but it needs to be someone you care for. Not just mindless sex with strangers. It should be someone who will lift your spirits, not just your hormones. I know you're attracted to Dana—she bragged at Tuesday's meeting about you two having online sex—so I'm okay if you want to be with her, but here's the deal. I have conditions."

"No, Tina." Jaleesa couldn't believe what she was hearing. It sounded like a trap. "Absolutely not. If I'm with you, I don't want to be with anyone else."

"A little hush now," Tina said with a grin making Jaleesa chuckle. What the heck was going on in Tina's mind? "Like I said, I have conditions. You can go have sex with Dana, but if we move in together, then you have to come back to me every night. Like, to sleep with me. I mean, just sleep. Every night."

"Every night," Jaleesa repeated, trying to make sense of what she was hearing. Why was Tina willing to do this? Sacrifice like this? Share Jaleesa? Why? Jaleesa was sure she would never accept this preposterous scheme, but Tina was making it sound intriguing, and actually, it just might alleviate the big sex dilemma between them.

"You'd have to shower when you got home, of course. And and, you have to tell me where you're going. Like an actual address and, um, oh yeah, I need to know who you're with. If it's not Dana, then whoever it is. And, again, I'll need reassurances that you still love me and that I'm number one in your life."

"Tina, Tina." Jaleesa grabbed both of Tina's hands in her own to get her full attention. "Look, I appreciate all of this. I mean, it seems like you have it all thought out, but I can't do that to you."

"You can."

Jaleesa was so confused by this turn of events that she didn't know what to say. All she knew was that she couldn't go along with it. Tina would only end up getting hurt. "Look," Jaleesa said, "I've always been the one who sets the tone in every relationship I've been in. I'm the dominant one. And what you're proposing is a rule that I would never make. I mean, come on."

"How's that working out for you?"

Jaleesa burst out laughing at Tina's blunt response. It was Jaleesa's turn to look away. "Not that well. Until you. You're a force to be reckoned with." She looked back. "Aren't you?"

"Yes. And just so you know, Harriet gave me the idea. She had a similar arrangement with her ex-husband."

"Harriet, huh? She's quite the matchmaker around here."

"Oh, yes. She's quiet, but still waters run deep, you know. And we have to remember something extremely important when it comes to Harriet."

"What's that, babe?" Jaleesa said.

"She taught middle school."

For the second time, Jaleesa burst out laughing. It was true. Harriet was a tough cookie. "She's championing our cause, isn't she?"

"Oh, yeah."

"Well, listen," Jaleesa said, "I'm starving. Can I take you out to dinner?"

"Of course, you can. Let me text my parents to *communicate* with them about my plans."

"Oh, that was a dig, wasn't it? A little sarcasm between friends?"

"Yeah, you should probably look up the word 'communicate.' Find out what it means." Tina's grin was the most adorable thing Jaleesa had ever seen. Oh, yes. Jaleesa had met her match, all right.

"Touché." Jaleesa pulled onto the road and headed for the Elm Street Diner. After a moment, she said, "Tina, I have to think about your incredible offer because it's not something I've ever done or ever considered. It feels like cheating."

"Well, listen, babe," Tina said, "you don't have much time to think about it because poor Dana_sub will be waiting at eight o'clock for Mistress Thorn to scoop her up and rock her world."

Jaleesa's entire soul dropped. She'd forgotten about the auction. "Fuck."

"Exactly," Tina quipped as she grabbed Jaleesa's hand.

Chapter 18

Tina

The singing competition Tina watched religiously with her parents every Wednesday night was only halfway over when she announced she was heading to her room.

"Don't you want to know if Tamara makes it to the next round?" her dad asked.

"I do, but…" Tina glanced up the stairs where she really wanted to be.

Her father chuckled and said, "We'll keep the recording. Going to call J-Dub?"

"She's calling me. How'd you know?"

"Because you've been walking on air all evening," Tina's mother said. Her soft expression told Tina she was okay with it.

Tina had no words. She simply smiled. Actually, it was more like a grin, and then she blushed her way up the stairs.

She propped her phone on her desk and put techno music on but kept it at a lowish volume. She absolutely did not want anyone to overhear this particular conversation.

She double-checked her phone's volume buttons, reassuring herself they were turned up to maximum so she wouldn't miss Jaleesa's call. She then opened up the real estate website she'd quickly become an expert at using. "Two-bedroom homes in Denton Heights," she muttered as she clicked the search feature. "Two bedrooms because one will, obviously, become my craft room." This was stated to the universe as a non-negotiable fact.

A host of listings came up, but she was kind of clueless about what Jaleesa wanted. Right. She was getting ahead of herself again. Both of them were not very good at this whole communication thing, were they? Maybe Jaleesa would want to get an apartment first. But that wouldn't work because the better investment was a house. Tina wanted a yard like she had here. She needed a vegetable garden in the back during summer and birds at a birdfeeder all year round. She needed to see Jaleesa at the grill wearing an apron—not too girly—and flipping burgers or hot dogs. Oh, oh, they could invite Shasti and Madison over for a barbeque. They would be their first guests, of course. And Penni, too.

"Harriet?" Tina mused out loud. "Where do you fit into all of this?"

Tina's heart leaped when her phone rang. It was Jaleesa.

"Hi baby," Tina said before the phone reached her ear.

"Hi," Jaleesa said succinctly. "Am I on speakerphone or in your ear."

"My ear. Oh, my God," Tina blurted. "Tell me what happened."

She heard Jaleesa blow out a sigh. "Okay, well, let's say that both Dana and I are physically satisfied at the moment." She laughed into the phone.

"How in the world do you do that? You only had fifteen minutes."

"Skill," Jaleesa said and then laughed big.

"A woman of so many talents," Tina said. "So? Did you tell her who you are?"

"Not yet, no."

"Did Mistress Thorn ask her out? Or pick her? Or whatever it's called?"

"Yes, I did. Mistress Thorn is meeting Dana at Jumpin' Joe's Friday night, and you are going with me."

"I am?" Tina refused to let herself panic. "What do you mean?"

"We are going to confess everything."

"Everything?"

"Yes. Including the arrangement you've offered me. Tina, it's unconventional, but the way I look at it, we've both been dealt weird hands in life, so why not make it even weirder? We don't need to be conventional."

Tina was quiet for a moment, and before she could get anything out, Jaleesa said softly, "I just took your key out of my pocket, the one close to my heart, and I'm turning it to unlock you."

Tina exhaled into a chuckle. "This will be a huge moment. She could freak out."

"Yes, she could, and that's why I want to break it to her alone. She may not believe your proposal, so I'll need you there to corroborate. I mean, I didn't believe it at first, either."

"And I need to be there to apologize for our very intrusive scheme in the first place."

"It was done out of love for her," Jaleesa said softly. "But you're right, we shouldn't have deceived her that way. Mistress Thorn told her she needed to bring a friend, so I fully expect Kadesha to be at the coffee shop. Incognito, of course. "

They discussed the details of Jaleesa's scheme further until Tina mustered up the courage to whisper, "Will you sleep with her Friday night?"

"No," came Jaleesa's quick answer. "I'm sleeping with you."

"What?"

"Just sleeping, darlin'. Maybe a little cuddling." Jaleesa's voice had a happy lilt, as if maybe she was warming up to Tina's crazy scheme. And, so far, Tina had no regrets about the scheme, but time would tell, wouldn't it? "Tina, I want us to return to my apartment after we reveal ourselves to Dana. We can kick back with Harriet. You know she's going to demand details."

"She won't ask," Tina said.

"No, she probably won't, but we owe it to her since she seems to have gotten dragged into our mess somehow."

"Yeah."

"So, baby," Jaleesa said, "how would you feel about our first sleepover? No monkey business, I promise."

"Oh, gee, I don't know," Tina lied. "I have to think about it. Okay!" she burst, not having to think about it at all. She wanted this. She wanted to wake up in Jaleesa's arms and watch her wake up. She wanted to make Jaleesa coffee just the way she liked it. She wanted to make breakfast for Jaleesa, too.

Jaleesa was still laughing when she said, "No hesitation, I see. It's supposed to be sunny and fairly temperate on Saturday, and I thought you and I could go on a hike. There's a trail at the back of the campus I used to run when I needed to think."

"Will you need to think on Saturday morning?"

"Yes, because on Friday, I might ask Dana for a date Saturday evening or Sunday. But I won't bring her back to my apartment. That's why I want to establish you in my bed there first. Make it *our* bed. I always come home to you."

"Every time."

"Yes. Every time. It's up to you whether you want to be waiting for me Saturday night at the apartment."

"Oh. That's going to take some thought. I mean, maybe you want to be alone. Think your thoughts."

"My only thoughts will be of cuddling you in my bed."

"You make it sound very enticing." Tina thought she heard a noise in the hall and said, "Hold on." She turned her music down and listened. She heard nothing but noticed a distinct shadow under the door sill. Yes, someone was standing right outside. How long had they been there? What had they heard? Part of her wanted to leap up, throw the door open, and demand privacy. Another part of her decided that maybe this was a softer way to let her parents know a few things. She kept the music low and said, "Yes, Jaleesa, I would love to stay over Friday and Saturday nights. It's about time, don't you think? We've been together for almost three months already. And, oh, did you ever call Penni?"

"Everything okay, babe?" Jaleesa said into the phone pressed to Tina's ear.

"Oh, yes. Will I see you tomorrow?"

"Uh, yes," Jaleesa said slowly, obviously not believing Tina. "After work. I want to take you to this amazing little Cuban place called the Havana House. Ever been?"

"No, I don't think I've ever had Cuban food."

"What?" Jaleesa sounded stunned. "We'll rectify that tomorrow night. And, since we're on the subject of food, may I take you to lunch on Friday? To our favorite diner?"

"Yes, indeed. I love when you take me to lunch. Everyone at the bank is jealous that I'm the one on your arm." *There, Mom,* Tina thought. *Now my love life is crystal clear.* Tina almost laughed out loud when the shadow moved away from the door. She sighed. It was time to talk to her parents about her plans with Jaleesa. She and Jaleesa had talked extensively at dinner that evening over their future plans, and Tina felt bolstered and stirred by her new possibilities that she almost couldn't contain it. Jaleesa did love her. They weren't just words. The love was there.

"Excellent," Jaleesa said. "Miss Bessie will fuss at me for not working through my lunch hour, but I want to take my girlfriend out. And yes, I texted Penni right before the auction window opened tonight. I have an official closing date."

"Ooh, tell me." Tina stomped her feet getting out her nervous energy.

"May eighteenth. A week and a half before the Memorial Day weekend."

"I know what we'll be doing Memorial Day weekend," Tina said. "If not before."

"What's that?"

"Moving you into that apartment."

"Ah, yes, well, that's something you and I need to discuss. Soon." Jaleesa yawned big into the phone. "Oh, sorry. I don't know where that came from."

"You started your day in Cleveland, remember?"

"Oh, right. I guess I need to shower and hit the hay. I love you, Tina."

Ooh, how Tina wished her mother was still standing outside her door to hear her say, "I love you back. See you after work."

"You got it. Sleep well, my love."

"You, too," Tina said. They said their goodnights, and Tina hugged herself. Things were going her way for a change.

Tina closed out the real estate pages and powered down her desktop. After getting ready for bed, she hopped in the bed, excited that she was finally going to know what it would be like to wake up with Jaleesa's arms around her.

~~~

"You're chipper this morning," Nancy said as Tina walked by after using the restroom.

"Got a date tonight. And tomorrow." Tina patted Nancy on the arm and headed back to her office.

Amber cut her off, and Tina had to stop her forward motion to avoid plowing into the young teller. "Did you give me those days off?"

Tina was about to make a snide comment about Amber's decorum but bit her tongue. "I'll check into it, Amber." Amber grunted and turned to leave, but an idea popped into Tina's head. "I notice you eat lunch here in the break room."

"Yeah, so?"

"Well, I'm eating here today, too. It's high time we got to know each other better, so perhaps we can eat lunch together at your usual time. Eleven?"

Amber narrowed her eyes as if wondering what Tina was up to. Funny thing, Tina was wondering the same thing.

"Okay, whatever," Amber said and headed back behind the counter.

Tina flew into high gear in her office, finished her work, and even took a moment to research the proper way to file a grievance against a superior in the JW banking system. Henderson had left early again yesterday. Tina had logged it in her book. And sure enough, just as she stood up to meet Amber in the breakroom, he was headed out again. She jotted down his departure time, knowing she probably wouldn't have a return time to write down.

Tina grabbed her sandwich and baby carrots from the fridge and sat across from Amber. "So, how are you settling in here?"

"Okay, I guess," Amber said, forking the poor excuse for food in her microwaved boxed meal. It looked like honey chicken chunks with rice. "Why?"

Tina's stomach lurched. Good God, this woman was rude. She channeled Jaleesa's calmness when she said, "Nancy says you're doing a great job, and from what I can see, you're holding up your end pretty well."

"Oh," Amber said, sounding surprised. "Thanks."

"Nancy also said you have your two days off next week."

"Oh, good. My mom…"

"Everything okay?" Tina took a small bite. She hated talking with food in her mouth.

Amber sighed, and then the floodgates opened. "My mother has to have surgery, and my stepfather's a drunk, so I have to be there for her. My sisters live too far away. But maybe now she can get some relief."

Tina asked appropriate questions and made all the right sympathetic noises. "Caring for someone you love is hard, especially when so much is out of your control."

"Exactly," Amber said. She scraped the last of her chicken meal onto her fork and into her mouth. "You're not like other bank managers."

"I'm not—"

"At my last two banks, none of them even knew my name."

"Is that why you're a little defensive?" Two can play at the directness game.

Amber shrugged. "Maybe. I guess. My boyfriend laughs and says I always go in with guns blazing before taking in the full situation. Take control early, I tell him." She laughed, and Tina got the idea that Amber was laughing at herself.

"Now, I want to tell you something," Tina said. She had to get the woman's attention first.

"Okay."

"I'm not the bank manager or even an assistant manager."

"No shit? You act like one."

"I handle accounts and small business loans," Tina said. "I used to be head teller until I moved up."

"Well then, who the fuck—" Amber put a hand up. "Sorry for that. Who the heck is the bank manager? Didn't I interview with you?"

Tina laughed. "You did because the manager left early that day and wasn't here. Just like he's leaving now. She pointed out the small window in the break room toward the parking lot.

"You're kidding. That guy? That tool? That asshole who cornered me right there and pressed himself up against me is the manager?"

Tina's jaw dropped open as she processed Amber's accusation. "I'm so sorry that happened. And, yes, that's Henderson. That's the bank manager."

"I reported him, you know. To Corporate."

"Wait. Why didn't you come to me if you thought I was the bank manager?"

"Bank managers don't do anything about that kind of shit. Why do you think I'm on my third bank?"

"Amber, I am so sorry this happened. Have any of the other tellers complained?"

"No, but they all have goo-goo eyes for him because he's so 'good looking,'" she mimicked their words.

"Did you tell Nancy?"

"I wanted to. She'd listen to me, I think, but I said, 'Fuck it' and called Corporate."

Tina asked a few more questions and said, "You know what's

interesting? I was about to call Corporate myself about his early departures. And now I get to add this to my complaint."

"You know, sometimes his girlfriend gives him blowjobs right there in the parking lot. I've seen his hands on the back of her head, pushing as she bobs up and down. It's disgusting."

Tina was speechless, and it must have shown on her face.

"Ah, you didn't know that did you? He's a skank."

Anger boiled up from the bowels of the earth, shot through her body, and erupted as steam poured out of her head. "I'm sorry you had to experience sexual harassment here," Tina said as evenly as she could. "Was it just the one time?"

"Just once. I pushed him away. He laughed when I did that. Asshole."

"Yes, he is," Tina agreed.

"You should be the bank manager, Tina," Amber said. "You'd be really good at it."

"Oh, thanks. Something to think about, I guess."

Before their lunch break was over, Tina asked for more details on the date and time of the incident. They chatted more casually after that, but Tina reassured Amber that she would call Corporate before the workday was through. Before then, though, she would talk to every single woman in the building, one at a time. Someone had to stop him, and it might as well be her.

~~~

"An investigation?" Jaleesa said, wide-eyed. It was Friday, and they were having lunch in what was fast becoming their favorite booth at the Elm Street Diner.

"Yes," Tina said and dapped a napkin at the corners of her mouth. "When I called Corporate yesterday afternoon, they told me he had already had several complaints from the employees at the bank. Not one or two, but 'several.' They want me to be the point person but not to tell anyone else that they're sending people down from Corporate to investigate."

"Without telling him?"

"They're going to act like customers and job applicants and things like that. They want to see how he handles it."

"They need to straight up fire his ass, Tina," Jaleesa said. "What he did to Amber is unacceptable. I don't even know her, but that shit ain't cool. He hasn't done that to you, has he? Be honest."

"No, he hasn't."

"Are you safe there?"

Tina beamed. "I love when you get all protective." She made googly eyes at Jaleesa and watched her girlfriend melt right there in front of her. "Yes, baby. I feel safe."

"I may just stick around when I drop you off after lunch."

"Aww, you don't have to do that."

"I know, but no one messes with my stuff."

Tina leaned closer. "Am I part of your 'stuff?'"

Jaleesa cradled Tina's chin and said, "Yep. Mine." She squeezed Tina's chin and then let go.

It was Tina's turn to melt. She cleared her throat and said, "What's the plan for later?"

Jaleesa sat back and let out a sigh. "Well, we have to be ready for this whole thing to blow up in our faces. Dana may not appreciate our good intentions. And the fact that Kadesha will probably be there might add to her embarrassment. So, I have some soul searching to do between now and seven o'clock to find just the right words."

"You will, baby." Tina hated seeing Jaleesa upset, so she changed the focus. "Should I eat at home with the folks and then meet you at the coffee shop?"

"Yeah, eat with your folks. Let them know you love them because this will be the first time you've not slept at home in a long time. But come to the apartment after that. We'll drive to the coffee shop together." Jaleesa pushed the remnants of her club sandwich away, obviously done, and added, "Dana's going to be early, so we'll have to be earlier."

"How do you know she's going to be early?"

"Eagar submissive. She'll want to please Mistress Thorn."

A look came over Jaleesa's face. It was one of dominance and power. She was thinking about Mistress Thorn's relationship with Dana. Yes, Tina thought. Jaleesa needs these kinds of interactions in her life.

"You know," Tina said. "I've done some research."

"Oh?"

"It's called 'ethical non-monogamy.' You'll be going off to be with Dana while you're in a relationship with me. 'Consent and communication are key,' the website said."

"And I'll be coming home to you each and every time. That's why I want you to spend the weekend with me. Are you having regrets?"

"Not yet," Tina said with a laugh. "But I'll need reassurance. I don't want you to fall in love with someone else and leave me."

Jaleesa reached for Tina's hand, picked it up in her own, and kissed the knuckles. She then kissed the back of Tina's hand, turned it over, and kissed the palm. "You're my girl, baby. You're my number one. If at any point you decided that this ethical non-monogamy thing isn't working, then you tell me immediately, and it stops."

"I love you."

"I love you back, baby." And then, as if Jaleesa needed a change in subject, she sat tall and said, "You will not antagonize this Henderson asswipe or act weird around him."

"Hard to do, but I'll do my best." Tina laughed. "He's never there anyway."

"C'mon, I have to get you back. There's a lobby I have to sit in for a while."

"Oh, and that won't look weird."

Jaleesa just winked at her, and they got up to leave. As usual, Jaleesa paid the bill. Tina stood behind her at the front register and took in

Jaleesa's chiseled features, her healthy athlete's grace, and her sure and confident demeanor. Jaleesa turned as if sensing Tina's gaze and smiled at her. The melting of Tina began instantly. Oh, yes, Tina definitely understood what 'hot' was, and she was standing right in front of her.

Chapter 19

Jaleesa

Jaleesa and Tina sat at a table in the farthest corner of Jumpin' Joe's Coffee Bar, each nursing their favorite coffee. They'd been there for fifteen minutes when Kadesha walked in. They'd purposely chosen a table far from the door and had their heads bent together, hoping Kadesha wouldn't see them. And she didn't at first, taking up a table near the counter.

"Hey," Jaleesa heard someone call. She turned toward the sound only to see Kadesha stand and head toward them. Kadesha wasn't the one with the date, but it seemed like she had also dressed up for the occasion with a long tan wrap-knot side sweater hinting at cleavage, but not quite. Her gold pendant necklace nestled perfectly just below her collarbone. Jaleesa would love to see Tina in a sweater like that, but maybe not. That might unnecessarily sexualize her, something she might not like.

"Kadesha," Jaleesa said, trying to sound somewhat surprised. "Good to see you. Join us?"

"Sure," Kadesha said. "Dana's coming, too. She's meeting a date here, though, and asked me to sort of chaperone. You know, from a distance. Can't be too safe."

"Absolutely," Tina said and hugged Kadesha. Jaleesa simply nodded and pointed to a seat in invitation.

"Oh, there she is now," Kadesha said, looking toward the door.

Standing in the doorway was a version of Dana that Jaleesa had never seen. She was stunning in her nervousness as she looked around the shop, trying to spot someone, anyone, that could be Mistress Thorn. Her black mid-length moto jacket was wrapped tightly around her body, showing off her curves. The red blouse Dana said she'd be wearing peeked out from underneath. Jaleesa's own red button-down shirt was hidden underneath her signature leather jacket. She'd open it once she had Dana alone. Dana's loose hair and little makeup made her look enticing and sensuous. But the one thing that caught Jaleesa's heart was the expectant look in her eyes. Would Dana find her true love that evening? Or just another flop?

"Poor kid," Jaleesa muttered. She was about to get blindsided.

"Yeah," Kadesha agreed. "She's nervous."

Jaleesa almost laughed. That wasn't what she'd meant, but let Kadesha think it was. The relief on Dana's face when she saw her friends at the far table was priceless. Jaleesa wanted to pull her into an embrace and make her feel safe, loved, and cared for all at once. But she couldn't. She didn't know if she'd ever be allowed such privileges with the woman she'd duped.

"You're okay," Tina said softly.

Jaleesa shot her awesome girlfriend a grateful look as Dana approached their table.

"Ooh, don't you look nice," Tina gushed and hugged her. Jaleesa just sat there with a grin, looking dumb as a thousand different thoughts battled in her head.

"I have a—" Dana started.

"I told them," Kadesha interrupted.

"Okay." Dana took a breath as she stood there. She took off her coat, and Jaleesa's eye was drawn to the swell of her breasts and the curves of her waist beneath the tight silk blouse. "Are you guys, like, going to stay here?"

"Just for a little while," Tina said. Jaleesa loved her at that moment because Jaleesa wasn't sure how to answer. So much for being the confident one. Jaleesa was nervous about hurting Dana. But honestly, the sooner she told the truth, the better it would be all around. At least, that's what she told herself.

"Okay, cool," Dana said and sighed nervously. "She said she was going to wear red, too. And she's bringing a rose for me. We even set up secret words we have to say to each other just to be doubly sure." She looked back at the door, obviously looking for her date, and then turned around. "She's so romantic." She clenched her teeth and squeed like a kid in a candy store. "I'm going over there to the section where she told me to wait. Wish me luck."

After three sincere well wishes, Dana turned her back and headed for the aforementioned section. Jaleesa and Tina made small talk with Kadesha for a short while. Once it was officially seven o'clock, Jaleesa waited precisely one minute more and felt a hand squeeze her thigh. Yes, it was time. She stood up and said, "Excuse me," to Tina and Kadesha. What Kadesha was thinking was beyond her brain capacity at the moment. Tina was going to explain things to Kadesha at the same time Jaleesa explained it to Dana. Jaleesa walked tall, with as much confidence as she could muster, and put her game face on.

She walked straight up to Dana's table and said, "Mind if I sit?"

"Oh, my date might be, uh, …" She glanced toward the door and then back at Jaleesa.

Jaleesa unzipped her leather coat, revealing the red shirt underneath. She reached inside for the single red rose she had carefully tucked inside. She handed it to Dana.

Dana didn't reach for it. She looked from the rose to Jaleesa and back again, obviously confused.

Jaleesa continued to hold the rose toward Dana as she said, "Green avocados are my favorite."

Dana inhaled sharply as understanding dawned on her. She searched Jaleesa's face for answers.

"Seriously, Dana, may I sit?"

Dana nodded. She was in shock.

"You may take the rose, sweet girl," Jaleesa said, trying to keep her voice even and calm.

Dana took the offered flower and smelled it.

"If you allow me to explain, I can clear all of this up."

"Are you Mistress Thorn?" The words were barely whispered.

"Yes."

"You? I've been chatting with you every night? You?" Dana sat back, looking terrified. "But we…"

"Yes, we did," Jaleesa said, knowing the grin on her face was reflected in her eyes as she attempted to put Dana at ease.

Dana searched Jaleesa's face again. "But what about Tina? I don't understand."

"This whole thing was Tina's idea."

Dana scoffed. "Okay, now I really don't understand. A threesome? Like poly?"

"Mmm, not exactly," Jaleesa said. "May I explain?"

"You're going to have to because I don't know whether to be ecstatic that someone as hot as you bid on me at the auction or hopping mad at both of you for fooling me." At the moment, Dana was definitely leaning toward anger when she said, "Oh, my God. You let me babble on at Monday's AA meeting about meeting someone. And all this time, it was you. Was Tina there for all the sessions? Did she see those things we said to each other? Did she see what we did?"

"No, no, no," Jaleesa said, reaching for Dana's hand. Jaleesa wasn't sure if she was surprised or not when Dana didn't pull away. Jaleesa relayed how upset Tina had been when she overheard Dana's plans to join the auction. She told Dana how they'd schemed to bid on her so she wouldn't end up in a dangerous situation.

"So, you lied to me the whole time. Both of you." Her gaze shot toward Tina. Tears filled her eyes.

Damn. Anger was winning out. Jaleesa had to act fast. This could be the turning moment. "The only thing I lied about was who I was. Everything else? I meant every word and every action. Everything we did was done honestly and with love."

"Except for the whole 'you have a girlfriend thing,' and that girlfriend was my friend long before you came along."

"I understand that, but you see, Tina wants you and me to be together."

"Yeah, no. I don't think that's true. She's in love with you, Jaleesa. How can you do this to her?" Dana pulled her hand away and banged the table with the side of her fist. The fist bang wasn't hard enough to garner any attention but enough to let Jaleesa know that Dana wasn't happy.

"Remember the part where I said it was Tina's idea?"

Dana rolled her eyes, conveying that she didn't believe it.

"I thought you might react that way," Jaleesa said softly and then lowered her voice to share that Tina was ace and had come up with the ethical non-monogamy idea. "Dana, I didn't believe her at first either. Or second. Or third. It's just not what's done, right? But she insisted. She saw that I had needs she wasn't able to fulfill. It was an amazing gesture on her part."

Dana still looked troubled, but she didn't look as angry.

"I do like you, Dana. And I know what I'm proposing sounds preposterous and might not be ideal for you, but I'd still like to date you. I'd like to continue doing those things we started online. And if I recall correctly, you were the one that asked me how I felt about polyamorous relationships during our auction chats. Right?"

Dana shrugged. "All my Dommes had other subs besides me. Even my boyfriend had another girl. I thought maybe I'd finally get somebody all to myself."

Jaleesa had no words. She sighed in disappointment for Dana.

"Why did you ghost me Tuesday night?" Dana demanded, changing the tone instantly.

"Ahh, that. What I told you on Wednesday is partly the truth. I did go home to see my family. Basically, I panicked."

"Over me?"

"Yes. You were definitely part of it. I felt guilty seducing you during

260

the auction. Another reason I lost my mind was that Tina wanted to make things more serious between us. And the next thing I knew, I was running away."

"Did she ask you to marry her?"

"No, no. She wants to move in together."

"Serious stuff."

"I know, and I panicked. I'm only human," Jaleesa said with a chuckle. "I just needed a minute to gather my thoughts. I didn't know how to contact you as Mistress Thorn, so I just…didn't. And that was unforgivable on my part. I'm truly sorry for making you feel ghosted."

"But you're back with Tina now?" Dana shot a glance Tina's way.

"We never broke up. She wasn't happy with me for running away. I kind of ghosted her, too. I behaved badly. But all is well now, and we're making big future plans to be together."

"You guys are awesome as a couple," Dana said, then looked down at the table. "I appreciate you trying to keep me safe, but there's no way I want to be fuck-buddies when my girl, Tina, is right there. You know? I mean, I can't be in some kind of relationship with you, knowing you're my friend's girlfriend." A strange expression crossed her face. "She doesn't want to watch or anything weird like that, does she?"

Jaleesa wanted to burst out laughing but toned it down to a deep chuckle. "No. She does not. She's not sex-repulsed, though. She seems to understand that I need…more. How about I ask her to come over and talk with us?"

Dana nodded. "And Kadesha, too. I need my bestie to hear things I won't."

"You got it. Jaleesa pulled out her phone and texted Tina. Within a minute, both were seated at their table.

"Crazy-sounding, isn't it?" Tina said as she sat diagonally across from Dana.

"I don't understand it. Like. At all," Dana said. Her anger seemed to be receding somewhat. What prevailed now was confusion and worry.

Worry about hurting Tina and about getting hurt or used or whatever words were ticking along in her head.

Tina turned to Jaleesa and said, "I think Harriet would be okay if I shared?"

Jaleesa nodded. "Yes, she said it would be okay."

"Harriet had a similar arrangement with her then-husband," Tina said and filled in the particulars that Tina required if Jaleesa and Dana were to pursue a sexual relationship.

Kadesha's eyes were wide as if she couldn't believe what she was hearing. To be honest, Jaleesa still couldn't believe it either.

Dana looked troubled as she said, "Oh, God, I need me some city gin."

Jaleesa laughed at Tina's shocked expression and quickly said, "Water. She means water."

"Oh, I almost had a heart attack." Tina pushed out her chair. "I'll get some for everyone."

Tina hustled to the counter and brought back four bottled waters just as Dana was saying to Jaleesa, "So, you wouldn't be allowed to stay over with me? Like actual sleep-sleep with me?"

It was Tina that shook her head.

"What about dates?" Dana asked, looking directly at Tina. "Am I allowed to be seen with her? Or am I some hidden secret? I don't want to be a secret. I hate when they do that to me. I want someone to hold my hand or put her arm around my waist."

"All that is fine with me," Tina said. "But that part would be up to you and Jaleesa. Right, babe?" Tina looked to Jaleesa.

"I would love that," Jaleesa said. "I don't want to hide you. I just have to go home to number one every night."

Dana scoffed. "So, I would be number two."

"Let's not think about it that way—"

"Look," Kadesha interrupted, thrusting both hands in front of her. All discussion stopped. "This is my girl, right here. And I don't care 'bout any of these details. I just don't want her hurt. I don't want her used and abused and tossed aside because you," she poked a finger toward Tina, "suddenly decide you don't like the arrangement. Or because you," this time the air poke was directed at Jaleesa, "get bored of your little side fling and toss her aside." Angry tears filled her eyes. "This my girl, you guys. C'mon. You can't mess her up. She's doing so well in her sobriety. She's doing good in life now. You can't fuck that up."

Silence shrouded the four women sitting together at a table in the back of Jumpin' Joe's Coffee Bar.

Jaleesa was the first one to break the silence. "You're right, Kadesha. Matters of the heart are serious." She turned to look at Tina. "I think we've overstepped, babe. We've made a mess of this." She turned back to face Dana and Kadesha. "We apologize for any harm or angst we've caused. That absolutely wasn't our intention. We're both fond of you, Dana, and we've fluffed it up trying to help you." Jaleesa splayed a hand over her chest. "Neither of us intended to use you. And just so you know, neither of us took this proposition lightly. It may not seem like it, but we honestly did have good motives in mind."

"We should go, babe," Tina said and pushed back her chair.

"No," Dana cried. "Wait. I haven't said no yet. I have a confession, too." She glanced over at Kadesha as if not wanting to share her confession with her best friend, but she continued. "The Dommes don't have to show their faces on that auction site, so what I did was picture Jaleesa as Mistress Thorn." Dana looked at Jaleesa, tears filling her eyes. "When Mistress Thorn and I got intimate in the chat, I pictured you. And now that it actually is you, my head is spinning. To hear you say you want to be with me? It's the stuff of dreams. But this," she sighed. "This arrangement is throwing me for a loop. I need to think about it." She wiped away her tears and took a shaky breath. "Yeah, I need to think about it, okay? Because it wouldn't just be a relationship with you." She looked from Jaleesa to Tina. "It would also be with you."

"It's uncharted territory for all y'all," Kadesha said. "And, I agree, she needs time to think."

Dana nodded.

Tina reached over and held Dana's hand. When Dana didn't resist, Jaleesa put hers on top and said, "We only wanted to take care of you, Dana. I promise." She squeezed the two entwined hands underneath hers and let go. She pushed back her chair and stood up to her full height. "We're still interested, and the offer is still out there."

Dana nodded. "Okay. Thank you. And, um, thank you for trying to take care of me. I'll let you know. Because, as Mistress Thorn says, 'honesty, communication, and consent' are the most important things in a relationship.'"

Jaleesa chuckled and put her elbow out chivalrously for Tina to take.

"Goodnight, both of you," Jaleesa said. Goodbyes were exchanged, and then Jaleesa guided Tina toward the front door.

~~~

The instant the front door to the apartment was closed, Tina burst into tears for the second time that evening. The first had been the moment they'd gotten into Jaleesa's pickup outside the coffee shop.

Jaleesa wordlessly wrapped Tina in her arms and let her cry it out. Harriet joined the hug, and together they coaxed Tina to the loveseat. Harriet got some water, but Tina refused to drink.

"I'm so stupid," Tina said. "Why did I think this would work? We could have helped Dana in a thousand other ways, and now she hates us."

Jaleesa filled Harriet in on the details of the meetup at the coffee shop.

"Uh, you guys?" Harriet said. "Dana didn't say, 'no,' right?"

"What?" Tina said, lifting her head. She took the tissue Jaleesa handed her and then fell back against her, obviously looking for comfort. Jaleesa obliged and wrapped Tina tightly in her arms.

"She didn't run out or throw coffee in your faces, right? You just told me she was going to think about it."

Tina took a few shaky breaths and said, "I don't want to contribute to her drinking again. I won't be able to take that. She was so upset. She's very confused."

"If you think about it, babe," Jaleesa said, "we've had a lot longer to think about this whole arrangement."

Tina nodded.

Jaleesa continued, "And she has Kadesha with her. You can text Dana tomorrow to make sure she's okay."

"Or tonight," Tina said and sat up. She pulled out her phone.

"Yes, yes," Jaleesa said softly. "But not right this second. She may misinterpret that as harassment. Let's give her an hour or two at least. I prefer waiting until tomorrow."

Tina nodded and, for some reason, handed her phone to Jaleesa, who took it and put it on the side table. Tina looked directly at Harriet and said, "Will you stay? I'm going to ask Jaleesa in a minute if she'll help me refocus myself with—" She pointed to the bookshelves where the wrist cuffs were attached to the wall hidden behind some books.

"I'll stay if that's what you want," Harriet said and reached for one of Tina's hands.

Tina nodded.

"But now you actually have to ask her," Harriet said with a chuckle.

"I know. I'm working up the courage."

Jaleesa, sitting next to Tina on the loveseat, tried not to grin as Tina turned toward her.

"Baby," Tina began. "Would you—" She looked down at the throw rug. "I think I'm out of balance. Can you help me by doing that impact stuff on me?"

"Of course, baby," Jaleesa said. "Let's go freshen you up first. Personally, that coffee's gone right through my system, and I need to get rid of it."

"You don't buy coffee. You rent it, right?" Harriet quipped, which made Tina laugh.

"Exactly," Jaleesa agreed.

"I'll get out the cuffs and a couple of towels," Harriet said and moved to the bookshelves.

"Thank you." Jaleesa reached for Tina's hand and pulled her off the loveseat.

In Jaleesa's room, Tina removed her clothes and put on a tight tank top, just like Harriet had worn during her impact session. She also pulled on tight running shorts, unlike Harriet. It was the first time Jaleesa had gotten a real hint of Tina's body. A flash of arousal hit her, but she knew this impact session wasn't about that. It was about healing.

Once they had taken a few moments to individually and collectively regroup, Tina reassured Jaleesa that she wanted to experience impact at her hands and, yes, she would use her safe words. They headed back out to the living room.

Harriet hugged Tina and said, "You'll be fine. Just remember two things. One—you can take more than you think you can, and two—it's okay to use your safewords or toss the bandana." She pulled away and handed Tina the red bandana. "You have the best and most conscientious Domme I have ever met, so you will be okay."

"Okay," Tina said. "Thank you." She took a cleansing breath, smiled at Jaleesa, and then placed one of her wrists in one of the cuffs.

Jaleesa placed Tina's remaining wrist in the other cuff tethering her to the sturdy built-in bookshelves. Tina faced the wall of books, and her neck muscles clenched. She was way too tense. Jaleesa stood behind Tina and wrapped her in a hug. "I need you to relax, sweetie. Take a few breaths for me." After Tina did so, Jaleesa said, "Red means what?"

"Stop. Yellow means stop for a moment or slow down. Green means go."

"Color?"

"Avocado green."

Jaleesa kissed Tina on the cheek and then showed her the flogger's soft leather tails. Tina had already seen it during Harriet's session, but Jaleesa liked to remind her impact partners what they were getting into.

Harriet sat on the far side of the living room on the loveseat. She probably wanted to give them space.

Jaleesa ran the tails over Tina's shoulders and told her where the flogger would and would not hit her. "Just a warmup now, so you feel comfortable." She dragged the flogger over Tina's back and buttocks gently, soft brushes against the tight clothing and what little exposed skin there was. At some point, she hoped both Tina and Harriet would feel comfortable exposing more skin. Impact on bare skin was so much more effective. Ah, but everything in its time.

Jaleesa mouthed to Harriet for some music. Harriet turned on the same classical symphony she'd played during her own impact session. There were neighbors to think of, and she didn't want to have to gag Tina during her first time.

The flogger left the skin only to return in a gentle sweep from one side to the other. There would be sensation but not pain. Jaleesa let Tina get used to the motions and the feel of the leather on her skin.

"Color," Jaleesa asked, expecting green as a response and getting it.

The contact of leather to skin increased. She stroked a little harder, but the pace remained slow and easy. Tina jumped at the next stroke and the next, but Jaleesa kept the same rhythm. Tina was adjusting. A yelp filled the room on the next stroke, but Jaleesa knew better than to stop. Another yelp, followed by low grunts. Oh, yes, her baby was feeling it. She was figuring out how to take in the thuddy pain. Jaleesa knew how to make her flogger sting, but she would reserve that for later or next time.

"Yes, baby," Tina said, grunting with the next hit. "Yes, yes. There." She lifted her buttocks and said, "Back to my ass, please, baby." With another grunt, Tina's head hung down. Jaleesa stayed on Tina's ass for a bit but then moved on. She had a sixth sense about sensory overload in any one area. She traveled down the hamstrings, not hitting as hard since this was a new area, and then back up to the ass. She couldn't wait to rub her hands over that smooth ass, all in the name of soothing. *Mm hmm. Keep telling yourself that.*

Tina lolled her head back. "My back, baby. Please. Please."

Something in the pleading tones undid Jaleesa, and a mammoth surge of arousal shot through her. She moaned out loud. She couldn't help it. She thought she could separate Tina's impact session from one that aroused her but no.

"Slower," Tina begged.

Jaleesa slowed down the intensity and pacing of her strokes. "Color?"

"Yellow. Please. Just slower. Don't stop."

Tina had no way of knowing, but the words 'Don't stop' were an instant aphrodisiac for the Domme side of Jaleesa, and she moaned again as power flooded her body and gathered in her sex. Jaleesa was well aware now that Harriet had changed her focus from Tina to Jaleesa. Jaleesa was too far gone to care.

"Red, red, red," Tina gasped. She threw the clutched bandana to the floor.

Jaleesa tossed the flogger and splayed her hand on Tina's back over the tank top. Tina moaned at the touch, and if Jaleesa didn't know she was ace, she would have thought Tina was aroused. Maybe she was aroused, but not in a sexual way. Hopefully, in a healing way.

"Color?"

"Mmm," Tina mumbled.

"She's in subspace," Harriet said.

"She is." Jaleesa grinned. That was amazing for her first time. "Help me get her down?"

Since Tina was a tiny little thing, it wasn't a struggle to uncuff her from the wall and then walk her to Jaleesa's bed. They placed her face down. Jaleesa said her goodnights to Harriet and closed the door.

"Shirt," Tina said. "Off. All of it. Off. Please."

Jaleesa helped Tina pull off the tank top and peel down the body-hugging shorts. Tina now lay completely nude on Jaleesa's bed. Jaleesa's yearning to devour the woman on her bed was overpowering, yet she resisted. She had to. She lay next to Tina and pressed her hand against the red, welt-covered back. Tina's encouraging moan filled the room, and again, it wasn't a lustful moan, just one of satisfaction and calm.

"Feeling good, baby?" Jaleesa asked softly.

"Yes." Tina dragged out the word like a sigh. "Feels good. Your hands, I mean."

"Mm hmm." Jaleesa caressed Tina's skin gently. Her hands moved lower. When she heard no protest from Tina, she cupped Tina's ass gently. It wasn't meant to be sexual, but Jaleesa was only human, and a frustrated moan escaped her lips.

"Baby, did you get aroused?"

"Mmm," Jaleesa said. "Yes."

Tina rolled to her side, facing Jaleesa, and tugged at Jaleesa's red shirt. "Off. All of it."

Tina sure could be bossy, but in this case, that was a-ok with Jaleesa.

Once freed of her clothes, Jaleesa lay on her back at Tina's direction. Tina leaned down and kissed Jaleesa firmly on the lips. "Thank you, baby," she whispered, then planted another kiss. She pulled away much too soon but then ran an exploratory hand over Jaleesa's breasts. "Is this okay?"

Jaleesa moaned in affirmative answer. Her breathing was labored, and she knew Tina was reading the signs correctly.

"Help me like last time, baby," Tina urged.

Jaleesa didn't have to be asked twice. She grabbed Tina's hand and thrust it to her need. Using Tina's strong fingers, she stroked herself. Tina shrugged away Jaleesa's hand and took over. Jaleesa's hips rose, her legs spread. What was happening? She had never let herself be this open and vulnerable before. The fleeting thought left as fast as it came. She undulated her hips as Tina's fingers stroked harder and faster.

"Fuck, fuck," Jaleesa wailed when she came. Short gasps and cries of passion escaped her throat. She pulled Tina's face to hers and kissed her passionately, thrusting her tongue and then letting her head fall back on her pillow so she could catch her breath. She reached down and pulled Tina's fingers away from her center. She'd become too sensitive for more contact. Oh, God, what was that? She'd never opened herself up this much before. But guess what? Jaleesa found she was okay with it. Tina had her. She was safe in Tina's arms. Safe.

"That was beautiful, baby." Tina caressed Jaleesa's cheek with her other hand.

"I love you so freakin' much," Jaleesa said, pulling Tina close. The feel of Tina's breasts threatened to undo her again, but she managed to squelch it. "Your body is beautiful, baby. Are you okay with both of us this way?"

Tina nodded. "Yes."

"Good, because I love it." She pulled Tina's wet fingers into her mouth to clean them and then dried them by running them over her own torso. "Thank you."

"I love you back, baby." Tina snuggled in close. "I'm going to fall asleep in your arms now."

"You do you," Jaleesa said, languishing in her afterglow. She pulled the top sheet over both of them and pulled Tina possessively closer. "Think Harriet heard any of that?"

"Mm hmm," Tina said with an amused lilt. "She'll get used to it."

"Yep, I'm keeping you," Jaleesa said and kissed Tina's forehead.

"Duh. That's what I've been trying to tell you all along."

As Tina snuggled in, Jaleesa let herself be loved.

Chapter 20

Tina

Tina hated to do it, she really did, but it had to be done. "Babe, babe," she said, jumping on the bed where Jaleesa was still sleeping. "Dana texted me. She wants your phone number. Should I give it to her? Do you think it means she's no longer mad at us, and you can fulfill all your kinky desires now? You know, the ones I can't give you?"

A hand went over her mouth. Another went around her waist and pulled her into the bed. Tina found herself underneath a still nude former basketball player who now peppered her with tiny kisses here, there, and everywhere. Tina would have told her to stop, or maybe she did, but she couldn't get much out because she was giggling too much.

Jaleesa gave her one last sloppy kiss and then leaped off Tina and off the bed. "First rule of life with Jaleesa. Never wake her up unless there's a fire, blood, or a bug."

"I can wake you up if I see a bug?" Tina said, still lying in bed.

"Obviously, since you're the princess, and I'm your knight in—" Jaleesa looked down at her naked body.

"My knight in beautifully bronzed skin with biceps I want to hang off of."

That got Jaleesa laughing as she put on her robe. "Harriet up?"

"Yep."

"And is that coffee I smell?"

"Of course, sleepy head," Tina said.

"Okay, gotta go make room for it." Jaleesa headed out the bedroom door, presumably to the bathroom, and then called back. "When I get out, tell me about the text."

Tina started to read the message only to have Jaleesa cut her off. "When I get out."

"Okay, grumpy," Tina murmured and flung herself off the bed.

"I heard that."

"Dang," Tina muttered with a laugh.

Once Jaleesa had her coffee in front of her with exactly three sips consumed, Tina read the text out loud. Jaleesa gave Tina the go-ahead to give Dana her phone number. Dana's text dinged Jaleesa's phone almost instantly.

> DANA: If you guys are still cool with your offer, I think I'm in.

> JALEESA: Excellent. We are. Did some soul-searching last night?

> DANA: Yes, Kadesha came over, and we hashed out everything. She told me to go with my gut, and my gut says I'd kick myself if I turned down a chance to be with you.

> DANA: And!!! Tina has to tell me it's okay, though. One more time.

Jaleesa showed Tina the message, and Tina texted Dana immediately that she was still okay with the arrangement.

> JALEESA: Can I call?

> DANA: Y

JALEESA: Try again.

DANA: ???

DANA: Oh!! Yes, Ma'am. Yes, you can call. (Better?)

JALEESA: Much better.

"Ooh," Tina said as she read the text exchange. You're in Mistress Thorn mode already."

"Thank you for understanding that I need this."

Tina simply nodded and pointed to the bedroom. "Go call her."

"Yes, Ma'am," Jaleesa said with a grin. She picked up her coffee and headed to the bedroom. "Good coffee, baby," she called over her shoulder.

"Thanks, hun," Tina said. A feeling of something warm ran through her. Love? Contentment? Happiness? She decided it was all three. As she poured her second cup of coffee, she remembered that she'd had the same warm feeling when she woke up that morning. Jaleesa's front had been pressed to her back with her arm possessively draped around Tina's waist. Life was good.

"Harriet," Tina called softly into the living room.

"Yes?"

"I don't want to disturb you while you're painting, but would you like some fried eggs and grits? I know Jaleesa likes that for breakfast."

"Sure," Harriet answered. "Let me just….There. Done with that part. I'll come help you."

Together she and Harriet threw together breakfast, and the quick grits were just about finished when Jaleesa burst out of the bedroom. "I've got a date for Sunday afternoon. We'll go to her apartment after I take her out for lunch."

"Oh, honey," Tina said, "did she forgive us?"

Jaleesa nodded. "She did. And I figure that you'll be needing—" She stopped her sentence short when she noticed the set table and the breakfast currently being plated by Harriet. "I think I'm keeping both of you. Breakfast. Wow. What can I do to help?"

Tina laughed. She liked pleasing Jaleesa, especially because Jaleesa seemed to genuinely appreciate it. "You can help by finishing your sentence. Sit."

"What was I saying?" Jaleesa started to sit but then stood with her empty coffee cup in hand.

"Sit, I said," Tina said again and grabbed the coffee decanter to fill up Jaleesa's cup.

"Bossy," Jaleesa muttered. "Thank you, baby." She batted her eyelashes, asking Tina to forgive her for calling her bossy.

Tina rolled her eyes and said, "You were saying I need to do something."

"Oh, yes. Tomorrow, you should be home with your folks doing your usual Sunday thing. I'm going to whisk you away from them soon enough."

"Getting serious, you two?" Harriet asked.

"Mm hmm," Tina said. "With Jaleesa starting her new business up in Denton Heights, we figured we should look for a place to live together up there." As Tina spoke, her joy was tempered by the fact that it would mean Harriet was out of the equation. She was about to suggest that maybe Harriet could take over Jaleesa's apartment when Jaleesa intervened.

"We're still in the talking stages at this point, Harriet," Jaleesa said. "You are certainly part of our discussions. We want to make sure you're also taken care of. If that's something you would want, that is." Jaleesa sighed and said, "This one and I have had a bit of trouble butting into other people's businesses lately."

Tina felt that warmth again as she watched Jaleesa expertly take control of what could have been an awkward conversation. She had been so focused on Jaleesa that she was startled when Harriet started crying.

Tina wheeled around and watched as Harriet lowered herself onto her knees in front of Jaleesa and cried. Tina was amazed when Jaleesa calmly laid a hand on the crown of Harriet's head and said, "It's okay. I understand."

Harriet leaned down even further and lay her forehead on Jaleesa's bare feet.

"Yes, yes, my Harriet," Jaleesa continued. Her attention to Harriet was unwavering. "Okay, okay. Come on up. Up up."

Harriet sat up but stayed in a kneeling position. Jaleesa reached over and cupped her chin. She leaned forward, her face close to Harriet's, and said softly, "Are you saying what I think you're saying?"

Harriet nodded.

Jaleesa let go of her chin. "I'll have to hear the words."

Tina knew better than to move or make a sound. She was barely breathing because something monumental was taking place.

"Miss Jaleesa, I would like to be of service to you. I would like to be one of your official submissives. In the short time I've known you, you have taken care of me in ways no one ever has. You've made me feel like I have worth and that I matter to someone. There's a lot I can offer you."

Jaleesa reached down to help Harriet stand. "I would be honored to be your Dominant, Harriet. I take your request seriously. You do understand that I'll need to discuss this with Tina first."

"Yes, Ma'am. Of course."

"If you look at Tina's face, she hasn't got a clue."

Harriet smirked and lowered her gaze.

And that would be correct. Tina had no idea what was going on.

"Tina and I are going to ditch our hike and drive up to Denton Heights today to check on my building and maybe drive through some neighborhoods," Jaleesa said.

"We are?" Tina finally joined the conversation. "Can we go to Rikki's Coffee Shop after?"

"Pfft, yeah," Jaleesa said. "Hopefully, our new friends will be there. Tina, would you go ahead and bring over the breakfast plates? I'm suddenly starving."

"Sure," Tina brought the plates of food and, after a moment, realized that in all the meals the three of them had shared, Harriet had never started eating before Jaleesa did. Tina folded her hands in her lap and also waited. It seemed strange but right at the same time.

Jaleesa took forever to mash her fried eggs into the grits, making an almost disgusting-looking soupy mixture. Tina was thinking that a girl could starve around here if this were to be the new protocol. She exchanged an amused glance with Harriet and then laughed when Jaleesa looked up and said, "What? Why aren't you guys eating?"

Harriet stifled a laugh behind her hand, picked up her fork, and held it at the ready. She made no move to actually put food on it.

"Oh, seriously?" Jaleesa said. "Both of you, eat! We'll talk about protocols and etiquette another day. But I thank you for the gesture." She looked at Tina. "That includes you, ShortStuff."

Tina grinned and dug into her breakfast.

~~~

The ride to Denton Heights was eye-opening, that was for sure. To read about dominance and submission from the website Jaleesa had recommended weeks ago was one thing, but to see it in action with Harriet's obeisance that morning was another.

"So, you've had submissives before?" Tina asked as they took the exit for Denton Heights. It had taken the full twenty minutes of highway for her to muster up the courage to ask.

"Of course. Some were only into service submission, like Harriet, and others were into sexual submission. Some both. There are many ways to offer submission."

"Why would these women—"

"And men."

"No way. You've had guys be submissive to you?"

"Mm hmm. Not much sexual going on with them. Most of them liked humiliation. Some were service oriented."

Tina was quiet for a while as she drank this in. Her life had been so routine and boring that to hear about Jaleesa's incredible history was fascinating.

"I try to help each one in whatever way I can," Jaleesa continued. "I have a need to nurture, guide, instruct, and train submissives."

"Train?"

"Yes. I suspect Dana will need training to be a proper submissive. And before you ask, I can already tell, based on that phone call I had with her this morning, that she's heading into sub frenzy, and I'll need to curtail that. New submissives are sometimes so excited to be in a D/s relationship that they go off the rails trying to please their new Dominant. They ignore their own limits and agree to anything the new Dominant suggests."

"So," Tina mused, "we were right in saving her from that auction."

"We were. I honestly didn't think we would talk her out of participating in it." Jaleesa pulled into the Northcentral Plaza parking lot. "Whoa. Do you see that, Tina?" Jaleesa pointed to the storefront of the central unit. "They replaced all that rotting wood like I asked."

"You have a way of getting things done, Jaleesa," Tina said as she got out of the pickup. And it was true. Jaleesa's confidence made other people want to please her. Pleasing her made them feel good about themselves, making them work even harder. It was a God-given power.

"Penni was the one who relayed my concerns. She was the force behind this."

"Mm hmm," Tina said, knowing otherwise.

Not having keys yet, they had to make do with walking around the outside of the building. Jaleesa said she was glad there were still no signs of vermin or bugs. She also pointed out that there were no signs of vagrants living in the back or drug use, either.

"I would never have known to look for those things," Tina said.

"You were the one who pointed out the non-GFCI outlets in the apartment upstairs. I never would have thought to look for that," Jaleesa said. She reached for Tina's hand as they rounded the last corner and headed back to the truck. "That's why we make a great team."

Tina stopped walking, and even though they were standing right in front of the nail salon full of people, she demanded a kiss from Jaleesa. It was gladly given, and much to her surprise, the salon workers' muffled clapping broke them apart. Tina was mortified, but Jaleesa handled it well. She bowed her head, tapped her heart twice, and pulled Tina into a side hug. The people inside laughed, threw thumbs-ups, or made hearts with their hands. It was so cute.

"That was nice," Tina said. "All those people got to witness how much I love you. And having said that, I want to know what my place will be in your life. And Harriet, too. And Dana."

"Let's drive around the neighborhoods around here to get a feel. We can talk about things as we go. How about that?"

"Okay."

"And, by the way, those people witnessed my love for you, too."

Tina grabbed onto Jaleesa's arm and held it as that warm feeling coursed through her again.

They had driven through some of the neighborhoods before on the day they'd first looked at the property, but this time they were looking with a completely different lens.

Tina had tried to be stubborn about the house purchase and insisted on paying for it herself, but Jaleesa would have none of it. She calmly informed Tina that she would make a consistent financial commitment to the venture but didn't want her name on the deed just in case her business tanked. Creditors might look at the house as an asset to be seized. Tina saw the logic in that and accepted Jaleesa's insistence. So, with that part figured out, they settled into a nesting frame of mind.

There seemed to be more than a reasonable number of homes for sale in the neighborhoods they drove through. Tina jotted down house addresses, realtor phone numbers, and website addresses of the interesting homes they drove by. A few had tubes attached to the for-sale signs with actual paper flyers. Tina took it upon herself to fly out of the pickup and get the papers. They drove by small two-bedroom, one-bath cottages on up to bigger five- and six-bedroom executive homes in a neighborhood they rejected immediately.

"We can't afford these houses," Tina said, looking at the flyer she'd plucked from a for-sale sign. She showed Jaleesa the price.

"Are the fixtures made out of gold or something?"

Jaleesa drove on. The farther they got from the strip mall, the less dense the population and the more dilapidated the houses. Jaleesa burst out laughing as they drove by one such property. "What in the trailer-trash hell is that?"

Set back from the road was a single-wide mobile home leaning precariously to one side as if the foundation was sinking. A full arrangement of couches and chairs surrounded a firepit in the front yard

"It's not a place I want to live, baby," Tina said. She knew people lived like that, but to see it up close and personal was scary. "Let's head to Rikki's, okay?"

Jaleesa groaned as she turned the pickup around. They rode along in silence for so long that they were almost back at the strip mall when Tina couldn't stand it anymore. "That bothered you, didn't it, baby?"

"It did. It does. I feel helpless knowing people live like that. You know that helping people is my gig. But I wouldn't know how to begin to help them."

"You can't save everyone," Tina said softly. "And, besides, they might be happy living that way."

Jaleesa threw her a closed-lipped smile. It was as if she had also come to those same conclusions.

"But you think you know how to help Harriet, don't you?" Tina asked. It was as good a segue as any, Tina supposed. "Hey, baby, pull onto this side street. I want to talk about this face to face."

Jaleesa pulled onto a side street leading into a neighborhood they'd missed. She parked on the side of the street but left the engine running.

"So, you want to understand more of what Harriet was asking of me?"

"Yes."

"She was basically offering to take care of me in exchange for me taking care of her."

"How?"

"Kind of like I'm doing now," Jaleesa said. "Shelter, food, companionship. And the occasional impact and aftercare."

"Would you require her to get a job?"

"That's something she and I would have to discuss. I can't support her outright, so she'd probably need some kind of outside income coming in."

"You've been so good to her. And for her," Tina said. "She would be your submissive."

"Yes. And I would be her Dominant. Obviously, there would have to be discussions about what specifically that would mean in our case. Sometimes people draw up contracts, but however we do it, you must be part of that."

"What happens if we find a house all the way up here? And…" Tina wasn't sure how to ask the question. As she searched her brain for the right words, Jaleesa seemed to know to wait. Jaleesa had amazing instincts like that. "And," Tina stammered, "what about me?"

"Babe?" The look on Jaleesa's face conveyed confusion. It was kind of what Tina was feeling at the moment, too.

"What am I? I thought I would be the one taking care of you."

"Our relationship is very different than the one I have with Harriet. She would have more of a service or domestic kind of role. You and I are romantically involved and plan to meld our lives together. We would be each other's number ones. We'd be partners."

"So, I would be like the wife, and Harriet would be the housekeeper or whatever?"

"Simply put, yes. There are more subtle nuances to the whole thing, of course. And every relationship is different."

"Harriet seems calmer and more centered since living with you."

"I noticed it, too. She's painting more. And you've been much more carefree, too, baby." Jaleesa reached for Tina's hand.

"I have. You've been more relaxed, too. Maybe because you now have people to take care of?" Epiphany number twelve hundred was on the way. "You seem to thrive when taking care of someone directly and intimately."

"I guess you—"

"And the whole Dana thing," Tina interrupted. "For you, it really is more of a matter of helping her than getting sexual gratification, isn't it?" She interrupted Jaleesa again when she tried to answer. "And me. At that first meeting, you saw a frightened little bird about to crash land during my speech, and you helped me. And I liked that help. I liked your strong arms around me. And I liked your biceps, of course. I liked your attention. So much so that I wanted to please you and take care of you in return. I get it now. I get what Harriet wants to do for you." Tina looked into Jaleesa's sympathetic eyes and said, "And I also get what you want to do for her. It's what you've been doing for me. Sometimes in a subtle way and sometimes overtly, like sitting in the lobby of my bank for an hour making sure I was safe from my boss, the sexual predator."

Jaleesa kissed the back of the hand she was holding.

"Jaleesa," Tina said, warmth spreading throughout her body, "I want to be your submissive, too." Tina knew in her heart of hearts that having Jaleesa take the lead in their relationship was not only the right thing to do, but it was also what she needed.

"You'd always be my equal," Jaleesa said. "But we'll need to talk about how being my official submissive might change our relationship."

"Like what?"

"I would be the one making the decisions. I would always ask for your input and feedback, of course, but I would make the final decision on things."

"Like buying a house?"

"Well, that one is different because it's your money."

"Well, like what then?" Tina needed an example before fully committing to something she probably shouldn't have committed to before knowing more.

"Let's say you wanted to go out for dinner. Either I'd expect you to leave the decision up to me, or I'd ask you to present me with two or three restaurant choices. I would expect these choices to include someplace you'd like to go to, but I would be the one to pick it."

"Hmm," Tina said. "What if I wanted to paint the living room optic orange, and you wanted boring antique white?"

"I'd ask you to give me your reasons for picking optic orange because I may not have considered something important, and I mean both important in general and important to you. Once I hear you out, I will make the decision. Could be optic orange, could be antique white, although I prefer painter's white if I'm being pushed to pick white."

"You picked me," Tina said coquettishly. "And I'm white."

Jaleesa laughed. "I sure did. So do those examples make sense?"

"They do. It's kind of scary, though."

"It is. Trusting someone to always have your best interests in mind is scary. But it's also a two-way street. I expect any submissive of mine to take care of me, too. Like seeing to my needs and desires that we agree upon."

"Like Harriet may be for general household stuff and Dana for the sex?"

Jaleesa chuckled again. "It's not as black and white as that, Tina. People don't like to be put in generic boxes. You helped me out with the sex thing last night if I recall."

"That was nice. I liked watching you unravel like that."

Jaleesa narrowed her eyes. "I don't usually. I just felt safe with you, I guess."

"Safe? With me? Like, I'll make sure you're okay? That I'll take care of you, too?"

Jaleesa nodded.

"Baby, that's so sweet. You're cute when you're vulnerable and all squishy-gushy." Tina was melting inside but was still a bit unsure what she had offered Jaleesa. "I don't know about this kneeling thing."

Jaleesa burst out laughing. "Baby, I would never make you kneel unless you felt that was the right thing to do. Sometimes subs like Harriet kneel because it helps them keep a submissive mindset."

That was food for thought. Tina was going to have to muse on that concept. "Hey, baby, we have to look for a bigger house. If Harriet and Dana are going to live with us—"

"Whoa, whoa," Jaleesa said, her eyebrows pinned skyward. "Who said anything about Dana living with us?"

"Cart before the horse?" Tina said sheepishly.

Jaleesa nodded. "Big time."

"Dana will be your third submissive, baby. You're going to have a harem." Tina laughed and then wondered what the hell her parents would say to all of this. Good thing it wasn't their decision.

"Come on, you," Jaleesa said. "I need caffeine and maybe one of those blueberry muffins at Rikki's."

"If Madison hasn't snagged the last one," Tina joked.

~~~

Tina was disappointed that their new friends weren't at the coffee shop. Oh, well. She and Jaleesa got their usual coffees and a blueberry muffin each and sat down on one of the couches in their friends' usual section. The owner Rikki noticed them and came over to say hello.

Jaleesa stood up and introduced herself. "Jaleesa. And this is Tina." They shook hands, but Tina only waved hello. She normally would have stood up as well, but she was content letting Jaleesa take the helm.

"Nice to meet you both." Rikki sat down in one of the chairs and blew out a sigh. "I'm glad you came in today. I needed to thank you both for handling things when I was a bit indisposed that day. Madison told me all about Tina's comforting arm around her." Rikki looked directly at Tina.

"That's what she called it. 'Her comforting arm.'" She looked back at Jaleesa. "And my staff told me all about you stepping in to manage. Brittany thought I'd hired a new assistant manager."

They all chuckled, and Jaleesa said, "Glad to do it. Weren't we, Tina?"

"Oh, yes, Madison and Shasti are lovely people. And we love your shop. We try to come in every time we're up here."

"So, not Denton Heights residents?" Rikki asked, brushing a stray lock of her gorgeous red hair off her face. Even sitting, the woman was regal. She seemed a few years younger than Jaleesa, maybe thirty-five or - six?

"Not yet," Jaleesa said. "I'm looking to buy the Northcentral Plaza and start a hair salon there. If the sale goes through, we'll look for a house to buy in this area."

"That's excellent," Rikki said, her smile infectious. "I'm always glad to have great neighbors. And I know that plaza. My Aunt Tilda used to have her tailoring done at the alterations shop there."

"We heard about her passing, Rikki," Jaleesa said. "A loss like that is devastating, and you have our deepest condolences."

"Thank you," Rikki said. "I'm still reeling. And on top of that, Eileen…" She got too emotional to continue.

"Eileen is?" Jaleesa asked gently.

"My sub. No, my ex-sub, who took advantage of me and skipped town. I'll leave it at that."

"Sorry to hear that," Jaleesa said.

Rikki looked over her shoulder at the growing line and said, "Guess I should get back to work. It was nice meeting you both. Shasti said they were going to come by this afternoon. Oh, there they are."

Madison frantically waved when she saw them and yelled across the shop, "Hi, Miss Tina. Hi, Miss Jaleesa. Hi, Miss Rikki."

Shasti leaned down and said something to Madison, and poor Madison's smile immediately left her. She must have been chastised for something.

"It was nice meeting you officially, Rikki," Jaleesa said, standing up to shake hands again.

Madison skipped over to them as Shasti got on the long line. Madison walked right up to Jaleesa and hung her head. "I'm sorry, Miss Jaleesa. I sometimes forget to greet the Domme before the sub. You can suggest a punishment for Mistress to give me."

"You know what, bucko?" Jaleesa said. "Since this was the very first time you made that mistake, I think you can be forgiven."

"Really?"

"This time."

"Yes, Ma'am." Madison hung her head again, waited a beat, and said, "Hi, Miss Tina. Did you guys move up here yet?"

Both Tina and Jaleesa laughed, and Jaleesa said, "Not yet. I don't close on the strip mall until right before Memorial Day."

"Ooh, you have to come to our masquerade ball on Memorial Day weekend. Rikki is the matriarch now that Miss Tilda passed. It's an event for our community," Madison said and bounced on her feet. Madison turned and looked toward Rikki and said, "Can I be right back? I have to apologize to Miss Rikki, too." She waited until Jaleesa nodded and then zoomed her way to Rikki taking orders at the counter. Rikki seemed less than pleased by Madison's transgression. Maybe it was a common occurrence.

"Protocols seem big around here," Tina said.

"Yes, they do. It's refreshing." Jaleesa looked over at Tina and lifted her head slightly.

"What?"

"If you are to become my submissive, you'll have to learn some protocols, like addressing the dominant partner before the sub. And by using the word 'Miss' or whatever they prefer in front of their name. It shows respect and that you understand and honor the power differential."

"So, I should call Shasti, *Miss* Shasti, when she comes over?"

"Yes, but you'll need to let me address her first. Just follow my lead."

Tina laughed. "That's what I'm supposed to do as your submissive, isn't it? Follow your lead?"

The conspiratorial look Jaleesa threw Tina turned Tina's insides into absolute mush. "I'm lucky to have you," Jaleesa said.

"Oh, yes, you are," Tina said, waving a finger. "And don't you forget it."

Jaleesa put both hands up defensively. "I wouldn't dare. Speaking of protocols, you can also wake me up if there are puppies. Or kittens."

Tina laughed and leaned into Jaleesa. Tina wasn't exactly sure what getting cozy with Jaleesa would mean in the long run, but they were on an amazing trajectory, and she was all in for the ride.

Chapter 21

Jaleesa

Waking up wrapped around Tina for the second morning in a row felt so good, so right. Something was awakening in Jaleesa's soul. She didn't quite know what it was, but she could tell it was coming.

Tina stirred, probably sensing that Jaleesa was awake, so Jaleesa kissed Tina's back once, twice, and then again.

"Mmm," Tina murmured sleepily.

"I can get used to this," Jaleesa said, holding Tina tight for a moment.

Tina rolled over and brushed a lock of hair off Jaleesa's face. She blinked the sleepiness out of her eyes and smiled. "Me, too." Her eyes widened as if something had just dawned on her, and she said, "Today's the big day. Oh, my God. What are you wearing? I have to look over your outfit," she said sternly. "And you don't have time for a haircut, do you? Your chunky fro is looking a bit too chunky there, baby."

"As far as the hair, I've been thinking of a new style. But I'll run that by you later. As far as what I'm wearing to Dana's, I hadn't thought about it."

Tina scoffed. "You have to make a good impression, babe. C'mon. You have to look all dominant and in charge, right?"

"Are you always this chipper in the morning?"

Tina laughed. "Well, the grouch factor slips in once a month or so."

"Noted." Jaleesa yawned big and stretched her one free arm and both legs. "Hey, babe, you know what?"

"What?" Tina ran her fingers back and forth between Jaleesa's exposed collarbones. They'd both slept in pajamas last night, something Jaleesa was definitely not used to when a woman was in her bed.

"I have not been achy or sore for quite a while now. I think your home cooking is helping."

Tina leaned up on her elbow. "I've noticed that you get off the couch more easily. I kept meaning to ask how you were feeling." As she spoke, her fingers continued their journey and traced their way around Jaleesa's neck and chin, around one ear and the other. She smoothed Jaleesa's eyebrows and then stole a kiss.

"Mmm, woman," Jaleesa said with a soft growl. "You do things to me."

"Well, good. You can go to Dana's and get all that out of your system."

"Nope," Jaleesa said, letting Tina trail her fingers along her arms, following the cut of her biceps. Tina sure did have a thing for arms. "I don't think I'll ever get you out of my system."

"Aww," Tina gushed. "We should get up, I guess." She then spouted off the zillion things she had to do that morning before Jaleesa left for her date with Dana. Surprisingly, one of those things was to help Jaleesa shower. This would be after the clothes were picked out, which would be after coffee and breakfast, naturally. Jaleesa had never given that much thought to her morning activities, and it was nice that someone else was doing it on her behalf. She could get used to this.

Coffee and breakfast consumed, Jaleesa promised Harriet that they would have a serious discussion later that evening about what each might expect from a D/s relationship. She'd come home for dinner, and they could talk then. There was no sense venturing into a D/s relationship with Harriet if they were on different pages. Harriet agreed and, after doing the dishes, excused herself to get ready for a day of painting since she'd have the apartment to herself for a while.

Jaleesa made a mental note. Harriet needs quiet moments and

privacy. Something she definitely wasn't getting while camping out in the living room.

When Tina finally dragged Jaleesa back into the bedroom, she tore open the closet door and started rifling through Jaleesa's clothes. Jaleesa hadn't exactly given her permission to do that, but it amused her, so she let it continue and sat on the edge of the bed watching.

"No, no, no," Tina said repeatedly as she shuffled through the garments. "These are nice clothes, but, ugh, are you a banker or something?" She laughed big and continued to lambaste the wardrobe. "Okay, you're going to have to help me out here. "You're not planning to wear one of those bustier corset things, are you? Or whatever it's called?"

"Do I look like a corset kind of gal?"

"No. But I'm going to need some help here. What's your go-to Dominatrix outfit?"

Jaleesa laughed. "I am not a Dominatrix. That's the stuff of porn." She stood up and said, "Can I show you?"

"Yes." Tina sounded exasperated.

Jaleesa moved her work clothes to one side in the small closet and uncovered her going-out wear. She pulled out a long-sleeved button-down rayon utility shirt. It had straps sewn in, which were handy for keeping rolled-up sleeves out of the way. She liked it for impact play, especially.

"No. Too drapey. We have to accentuate your assets." Tina hung it back up.

"My assets?" Jaleesa was becoming more and more amused. Here was her girlfriend picking out her clothes for a date with another woman. It was heady stuff, but since Tina seemed okay with it, Jaleesa decided to be as well.

"Mm hmm," Tina said without turning around.

The Tina machine rejected more shirts. Even Jaleesa's favorite satiny low-cut collared blouse was dismissed. When Jaleesa whined at the rejection, Tina narrowed her eyes and said, "Maybe for the second date."

"Yay," Jaleesa said, sounding like Madison, that cute twenty-three-

and-a-half-year-old kid from Denton Heights. Dana was a few years older. Twenty-six. Jaleesa hoped the twelve-year gap wouldn't be a problem for Dana. Or for her.

Tina muttered, "You have to be able to move to do your impact with her. Wait, does she even like impact?" Tina whirled on Jaleesa for an answer.

"That might be more information than she wants me to share, babe. And, besides, I really don't know yet."

"I hope she likes it," Tina said. "Because it's amazing. Highly recommend. And Harriet likes it, too." With her hand still clutching a rejected shirt, Tina said, "We should have a dedicated but private space to do impact. You know, in the new house? And maybe a cage."

"A cage?"

Tina nodded enthusiastically. "For me. For when you're not home, and I feel angsty. But then maybe we should just get curtains around our bed. Can we make it a nice bed? A king size? With satin sheets? But we'll need cotton or—" She inhaled big as a revelation hit her. "Yes. Flannel sheets in the winter. Oh, babe. This is going to be so much fun."

"What is? Playing house?" Jaleesa stood up and pulled Tina into a reverse hug. Tina's back was now nestled against Jaleesa's front. Jaleesa's arms were wrapped around Tina's body, holding her tight. Her lips kissed Tina's neck, causing her to giggle.

Tina wriggled out of Jaleesa's grasp and turned around for a proper hug. "Yes, playing house, as you call it."

"And when we get stressed over playing house, because I'm sure we will, we'll stop, take a breath or five, and regroup." Jaleesa could see Tina losing her mind over house details.

"In it together, right?" Tina murmured against Jaleesa's chest.

"Yep."

"You and me and Harriet and Dana."

Jaleesa had no response. Tina had this vision of Dana living with them. It was definitely too soon to tell. They hadn't even had the first date yet.

"Okay, Vera Wang," Jaleesa said. "Let's get this outfit picked because time's running short here."

Tina dove back in the closet and, within minutes, held up what she called "the perfect outfit."

~~~

Jaleesa pulled up to Dana's apartment building, expecting to park and meet Dana at her actual unit, but Dana had other ideas. Dana stood up from where she had been sitting on the edge of a planter box near the front entrance and waved, her big grin making Jaleesa smile. She wore the same curve-enhancing coat she'd worn to the coffee shop two nights ago, which had a similar lovely effect on Jaleesa's libido.

Jaleesa pulled up alongside Dana, but before Jaleesa could do anything chivalrous, like open the door for her, Dana jumped into the passenger seat. Something weird pinged Jaleesa's heart as she greeted her passenger. Dana was in Tina's seat. This feeling would take some serious examining. Later.

"Hi, Jaleesa," Dana said, her smile beaming. Her makeup was flawless, and this time she wore lip gloss. A very lovely kissable shade of lip gloss.

"Hey, gorgeous," Jaleesa said, reaching for Dana's hand and kissing the back of it. "You look lovely this afternoon."

Dana giggled and said, "I'm nervous."

"No need. It's just me." Jaleesa put the pickup in drive and headed to a restaurant Tina had assured her that her parents would never go to. The night before, they'd talked about how much openness they wanted to be free to express in their relationships, but they both agreed that Tina's parents wouldn't understand. They didn't know about Tina being ace, which she absolutely did not want to discuss with them. Talk sex with your parents? Eww, Tina had said with the cutest scrunched-up face.

It was difficult, but Jaleesa shook thoughts of Tina from her mind and said, "I know a nice café on the west side where we can get to know each other better. Sound good?"

"Sure. I have to admit that I'm still not sure about this arrangement."

"What do they say on Monday nights?"

Dana laughed. It was the cutest laugh. "One day at a time."

"That's it."

Once settled at a back table in the café, Jaleesa purposely avoided topics like kink, protocols, and any references to BDSM. She didn't ask Dana if she liked pain or how much. She didn't ask if blindfolding or gagging would be a problem or how much bondage she could tolerate. Nor did she ask more personal questions about the types of penetration she preferred or whether or not anal was on the table. None of these things did she ask. Instead, she kept it light and breezy. They joked and laughed with each other.

"I tried college," Dana was saying. "But my dyslexia put a halt to that. I couldn't keep up the pace. I didn't even know I had dyslexia until one of my community college teachers asked me to read in her office one afternoon. She was the one who suggested I get tested."

"High school would have been a lot easier, I suppose," Jaleesa said. "I mean, if you'd had some coping strategies back then."

"I guess."

"Have you worked on reading?"

"Oh, I can read. Don't get me wrong. I can do it. It just takes a long time. Longer than most people have patience for. Back home in Columbus, that professor hooked me up with a course designed to help people with learning differences like mine prepare for college. I did well in that course, but I was already so discouraged that my parents said I could take a break. And then Tee and Marie moved here, and I tagged along. And besides, I want to grow things and design landscapes. Not read from textbooks." Dana then launched into the various design elements and principles of landscaping. She seemed to relax as she spoke lovingly about different plants and trees, most of which Jaleesa had never heard of.

"And so why aren't you designing landscapes now?" Jaleesa asked. "You seem to know a lot about it and seem to love it."

Dana sighed and shrugged. Jaleesa waited. Dana shrugged again and looked down. Both hands fell into her lap.

"Nope, nope, nope," Jaleesa said. "Look up."

Dana did, but her eyes darted to the side, not looking directly at Jaleesa. Okay, something was going on here.

"You told Mistress Thorn that you had difficulty asking for help and guidance, right?"

"Yes, Ma'am."

Ahh, the submissiveness was manifesting. Or maybe it was just shyness. No, Dana wasn't shy.

"As your Dominant, I would be the person you would come to for help and guidance. Correct?"

"Yes, Ma'am." Dana's gaze was now fixed on Jaleesa's. That was a good sign.

"So, here's one thing I want you to do this week. I know you're a busy gal, working and going to meetings and chatting up mistresses at night."

Dana scoffed but had a smile on her face. "After the first night, it was just you," she protested.

Jaleesa's ego sighed contentedly. "I want you to search for schools or online programs that offer landscape design. You used another phrase earlier." Jaleesa narrowed her eyes as she tried to recall it. "Architect. Landscape architect. Look that one up as well. Can you do this? Print out the information to show me?"

"Yes," Dana said. She'd dropped the Ma'am. But that was okay. She was feeling empowered by this simple assigned task.

"Excellent. And then when you've done this, we'll sit down together and try to make sense of it."

Tears welled up in Dana's eyes. Jaleesa leaned forward and clutched one of Dana's hands in hers. "You're okay, ladybug. I've got you."

"Thank you." Dana wiped at her tears with her free hand.

After another beat, Jaleesa asked, "Roommates gone?" She released the hand she'd been holding.

Dana pulled out her cell phone, presumably to check her texts. "Yes, both Tee and Marie texted to say the coast is clear. They're so excited for me."

"Excellent. Results?" Jaleesa was glad when she didn't have to explain what she meant.

Dana tapped her phone a few times and then held up the results of the STD testing she'd done at Mistress Thorn's request.

"Good girl," Jaleesa said and then held up her own results she'd gotten done that week.

"Thank you for thinking of that, Ma'am," Dana said. "No one has ever—"

"I know," Jaleesa interrupted. "Imma pay the check now, and then I'm going to take you home. I'd like to get better acquainted. Would you like that?" Jaleesa signaled the server for the check.

"Yes." Dana took a nervous breath. "Yes, Ma'am."

Jaleesa took the bill from the server, glanced at it, and handed over her credit card. Once the server was out of earshot, Jaleesa asked, "How much did you tell them?"

"My roommates? Nothing about our arrangement with Tina, but I hinted there might be a little kinky flair to my afternoon."

Jaleesa laughed. "Good for you. Be open and upfront about your needs."

Bill paid, Dana's hand in hers, they headed back to the pickup. The ride back to Dana's apartment was not quiet as Dana chattered away. Jaleesa enjoyed Dana's youthful exuberance and outlook on the full life ahead of her. It was refreshing. Once in the cozy, quaint apartment, Dana hung up their coats by the front door and got them both bottled waters.

"I like your clothes, Ma'am," Dana said. "They make you even hotter."

"Thank you, Dana. You're sexy yourself." Jaleesa couldn't wait to tell

Tina that the three-quarter sleeve tailored-fit button-down cream shirt and tight black Sloan pants she'd picked out for Jaleesa to wear were a big hit. Before it could get awkward, Jaleesa reached for one of Dana's hands and said, "which of these three doors is yours?" In the other hand, she clutched her bag of implements she might use that evening.

Dana giggled again, most likely due to nerves. She pointed. "That's Tee and Marie's room. That's the bathroom. And that's my room."

Dana barely got the last word out as Jaleesa pulled her toward her room. A glance around showed a very organized and clean space. Tina would love this room. It was neat with a lot of pink. Dana closed the door behind her, and Jaleesa tossed her goody bag on the single bed. She whirled around to press Dana against the back of the door gently. Jaleesa wasn't quite at the fervor stage, but she was definitely aroused. She wasn't sure what state Dana was in, but she was about to find out.

Jaleesa laced her fingers loosely in Dana's and then lifted her arms up and overhead, pressing them against the door. Dana was effectively pinned. Jaleesa moved her face closer to Dana's. The dilating eyes, shallow breaths, and yearning expression were the signals she needed. Jaleesa closed the gap and kissed Dana's full soft lips. Dana moaned and tried to move her hands, maybe to wrap around Jaleesa's neck? Not yet. Jaleesa kissed those soft lips with fervor, her own breath quickening. She moved on to kiss Dana's neck, earning shivers in response. An earlobe got nibbled, a chin got kissed, and a tongue got thrust. Dana thrust back but let Jaleesa command the tongue encounter. Jaleesa pulled back abruptly, releasing Dana's hands. She stepped back into the dimly lit bedroom and pointed to a spot to the right of what looked like a clothes dresser. "Kneel."

"Yes, Ma'am." Dana kicked off her flats on the way to the spot and then sank to her knees.

"Good girl." Dana's sharp intake of breath at the praise told Jaleesa this phrase excited her. Good to know. "Nadu."

At Dana's confused expression, Jaleesa said, "I want you to learn poses. One word from me, and you get in that pose. Eventually, we'll replace that with a hand signal. Nadu," she said again. "Kneeling. Back straight. Head up. Good. Yes, shoulders back like that. Do you see what delightful assets you now present to me?"

Dana looked down at her breasts underneath her clothes, thrusting toward Jaleesa. She blushed and smiled at the same time. "Yes, Ma'am."

Jaleesa stepped closer. She was so close that the hem of her shirt touched Dana's chin. More softly, she said, "Do you also see how your current position could serve my very special needs?"

Dana swallowed hard. "Yes, Ma'am."

Jaleesa stepped back. "Spread your knees apart. Ah, beautiful. This pose will allow me to see all of your beauty. We'll do this again later, but I recommend you practice it several times daily. It takes strength to kneel for any length of time."

"Yes, Ma'am."

"What was that kneeling pose called?"

"Nadu," Dana said. The lack of the word Ma'am would get a reprimand another time.

"Good. Safewords?"

"Like we discussed on the phone. Red, yellow, green." Again, there was no Ma'am. Maybe there would have to be a hard lesson this afternoon.

Jaleesa asked Dana to define each color, and when she was satisfied with the responses, she reached into the front pocket of her pants and pulled out a thin blue collar. She'd purchased it explicitly for use on Dana. Dana's expression melted at the sight. "This is your play collar. I will put it on you while we're playing. This collar can also be construed as your consideration collar. I am considering you as a submissive, and although I don't wear a collar, you are considering me as a Dominant."

At Dana's confused expression, Jaleesa said, "You get a choice in this, too." Satisfied that the collar fit and wasn't restrictive, she sat on the edge of Dana's twin-sized bed. "Head down." Dana dropped her gaze. "Please crawl over here and take off my shoes." Dana was still fully dressed, but by the end of their evening, she would put those shoes back on Jaleesa's feet while fully nude.

Once the shoes were off and tucked out of the way, Jaleesa said. "You did well, ladybug."

Dana giggled softly but said nothing.

Jaleesa reached her hand down and commanded Dana to stand. Once standing, she grabbed the hem of Dana's blouse and pulled it over her head. Jaleesa sighed at the beautiful sight. Dana was a small woman, and her breasts were small as well, but the juxtaposition of her white bra against her deep brown skin was enticing. Jaleesa couldn't help herself. She kissed the lace bra line moaning with satisfaction. She lay Dana on her back and undid the button on Dana's slacks. A slow and deliberate down pull of the zipper while her gaze was locked onto Dana's made Dana's hips arch. Jaleesa took advantage of the movement and slowly pulled the pants off. She tossed the pants onto a chair near the dresser. The thong matched the bra, and Jaleesa took her time kissing the lace border. As expected, a hand reached down and touched her head. No, that would never do. But it had been expected. Jaleesa didn't reprimand. She simply stood and pulled her bag off the bed and onto the dresser. Two soft Velcro cuffs were pulled out and silently fastened on Dana's wrists.

"Color?" Jaleesa asked.

"Green," Dana said.

Jaleesa moved quickly and had Dana's throat in one hand instantly. "What did you forget?"

Dana swallowed hard. "Ma'am. Green, Ma'am. I'm sorry. It won't happen again."

Jaleesa pushed Dana away by the throat gently. Damn, she had hoped that lesson could wait until next time.

"Still green?"

"Yes, Ma'am," Dana said and took a big breath, letting it out slowly. She was nervous. That was okay. Jaleesa had had many nervous subs in her time.

Jaleesa reached underneath Dana and undid her bra. She pulled it off and tossed it on the chair. A spike of arousal hit her as she saw the hardening nipples. She kissed each one reverently and then backed off to attach the cuffs behind the head of the bed to the frame below. The fact that there was no headboard never stopped a woman as experienced as Jaleesa.

Wordlessly she reached down and shimmied the thong off her captive's body.

"Lovely," Jaleesa said as the scent of arousal hit her nostrils. She was still fully clothed and would probably remain that way this first time. She wasn't sure yet.

Jaleesa cupped one of Dana's breasts. "Do you see how easily accessible you are to me now?"

"Yes, Ma'am." Dana's voice was a bit raspy. Oh, yes, she was aroused.

Jaleesa cupped the other breast and then lightly, oh so lightly, pinched one nipple. Dana arched her back in pleasure. Jaleesa pinched the other. A light moan escaped as Dana's eyes fluttered shut. She liked pain, just like she'd said during their auction chats. How much, though? Where were her limits? Jaleesa squeezed both nipples harder. There was a slight whimper, but Dana handled it well. Jaleesa momentarily released the pressure and then smashed her fingers together. Dana yelped, and her mouth dropped open.

Jaleesa's mouth replaced her fingers as she kissed each nipple in turn. Gentle sucking peaked the nipples allowing for easy flicking with her tongue. The wonderful noises coming from her new submissive were music to her ears. One day they'd explore whether Dana could have a nipple-gasm. Time would tell.

Jaleesa left Dana's nipples and let her hand run down Dana's torso. Dana was very aroused, so Jaleesa didn't want to torture her for too long. Not during their first time together, anyway. Jaleesa moved down the bed and used both hands to yank Dana's legs apart.

"Ma'am," Dana cried and arched her pelvis.

"I can do whatever I want with you. I could even leave you spread-eagled like this for your roommates to find."

"Oh, please," Dana begged. "No, Ma'am. Please touch me, Ma'am."

Jaleesa smirked at Dana, letting her know she'd been teasing. It was all part of the fantasy for some. She ran both hands up and down Dana's inner thighs until one hand reached the swollen and eager flesh. Wet to the touch, Jaleesa's fingers began a wonderfully slow exploration of the fleshy outer lips, followed by a rolling and twisting of the inner. Twisting brought out more moans. Dana was a pain lover, indeed.

Jaleesa eased her index finger into Dana's well and inserted another when Dana didn't protest. She'd said she liked penetration, so Jaleesa was testing that theory. Three fingers in, Jaleesa thrust lightly. Dana moaned with each thrust. It was music to Jaleesa's ears. It had been so long since she'd pleasured a woman like this. She squelched her own moan at the thought and thrust harder. She leaned down and licked her own hand, now wet with Dana's arousal. "You taste so fucking good." She moaned in pleasure.

That got an even bigger response from Dana. It was almost a grunt. Jaleesa sucked the growing little pearl into her mouth. She held it between her lips and flicked it sharply with her tongue. Her fingers continued to piston in and out. Her tongue lashed the bundle of nerves beneath it. She sucked hard, then flicked, sucked, flicked. The hand pistoned. Dana's hips arched up high. She cried out as she came. Her legs tried to slam shut on Jaleesa, but she'd positioned herself precisely so that wouldn't happen. Okay, her hand was trapped, but that was expected. Dana's spasming center squeezed Jaleesa's fingers. It was a physical language that Jaleesa understood well.

She slowly pulled out and made her way up to Dana's heaving chest. She lay her hand on Dana's abdomen. Dana opened her eyes, but then they rolled back as an aftershock hit her. Watching a woman in the throes of orgasm was the most beautiful sight in the world. She couldn't have that with Tina. She swallowed that regret and focused on the lovely thing beneath her.

Jaleesa took her very wet fingers and coated Dana's lips. Without needing to be told, Dana licked it off. After a few more coatings of the lips, Jaleesa thrust one finger at a time into Dana's mouth for cleaning. She pulled her fingers out and kissed Dana properly. "You did well, ladybug."

"Mmm," Dana said, still catching her breath.

Jaleesa kissed her lips once more and stood up. She grabbed a towel out of her bag and threw it on the bed. She reached up to undo the cuffs around Dana's wrists and let them fall behind the bed. "These are to stay here."

Dana cleared her throat as she pulled her arms down and then rubbed her wrists. "Yes, Ma'am."

"But you are never to put them on yourself. I am the only one who can put them on you. Same goes for the collar. You can take it off, but only I can put it on." Jaleesa snaked two fingers underneath and pulled up gently. It was her subtle way of checking to make sure the collar wasn't too tight.

"Yes, Ma'am. Thank you." Her eyes fluttered with emotion as she tried to find words of gratitude.

"You're a beautiful woman, Dana." Jaleesa nudged her over so she could climb on the bed. She placed the towel over Dana's very wet center and shimmied up next to her. She urged Dana to roll on her side and lay her head on Jaleesa's chest. This way, Jaleesa could cradle her.

Dana purred when she did so. They lay quietly for a few moments until Jaleesa said, "I have to leave you soon."

Dana groaned her disappointment.

"But before I go, I want to give you a few instructions." Jaleesa had to lay down some ground rules that would help keep them both sane. Dana was prone to sub frenzy, and Jaleesa had to address it immediately. "There will be no blowing up of my phone. Before calling, you will always text me beforehand to ask if it's okay to call. I may not get back to you right away. That is no cause for panic. We're both working women. You understand that, right?"

Dana nodded. "Yes, Ma'am."

"I will get back to you eventually. But do not, and I repeat, do not send me idle chitchat in a text or call me because you're bored. Do not call me unless I instruct you to or say it's okay in a text message. Do you understand this so far?"

"Yes, Ma'am."

"Having said that, I would like a text from you every morning within an hour of you waking up. Also, you must answer my texts within three hours. If you do not do these things, I will consider this impertinence. And you will be punished. Now before you go getting any ideas. Punishments don't mean fun-ishments. You will not like the punishments you're given."

"Yes, Ma'am. I understand."

"Good. You're a good girl, Dana." Jaleesa nudged Dana to sit up so she could receive a passionate kiss. Jaleesa was so aroused when their lips separated that she almost lost her cool. "Nadu," she said, hearing the thickness of arousal in her own voice.

Understanding took a moment to permeate Dana's thoughts, but when it did, she leaped off the bed and got into the required pose. Jaleesa sat up, still fully clothed, and looked at her nude submissive kneeling on the floor. Dana's legs were opened wide, and her center was glistening nicely. Arousal hit Jaleesa again. At some point, not that night, but at some point, she would stroke herself to orgasm while Dana watched. Perhaps that would be a night of chastity for Dana but with many, many orgasms for Jaleesa. Oh, the possibilities.

"You're a beautiful woman, Dana." She'd already said it, but Dana needed to hear it again.

"Thank you, Ma'am."

"The way you have your hands resting downward on your thighs indicates that you're relaxed and in your pose. That's good. However, when you turn them upward. Yes, like that. It means you're signaling to me or any Dominant that you are willing to serve them in any way they wish. Is that understood?"

"Yes, Ma'am." Dana kept her hands facing upward.

"One day soon, I'll make use of that tongue of yours."

Dana's breathing became labored again as she said, "It would be my honor to give you pleasure, Ma'am. I've been told that I'm good at it."

Jaleesa chuckled. "Good to know." She stood up, tossed the towel in the laundry hamper by the closet, and said, "I bought these toys explicitly to be used on you and you alone. You can look at them, but you are not to try them out. They are for me to use on you. Understood?"

"Yes, Ma'am."

"Until we meet up like this again, you are allowed to touch yourself. You are not, however, allowed to cum. You can bring yourself to the edge, but not over. If you mess up, you will tell me. Remember that honesty thing?"

"Yes, Ma'am. This will be difficult."

"I'll text you some possible dates we can get together again. You may also suggest some."

"Yes, Ma'am."

"I require my shoes, Dana."

Dana crawled back, and it was all Jaleesa could do not to put her hands all over that warm eager body. She had to get back home. She had that dinner and conversation with Harriet to attend to. It was just as important as this liaison with Dana this afternoon. But with less moaning. Of course, she'd call Tina the second she got in the pickup. The poor woman must be dying to hear how it went. Jaleesa also wanted to reaffirm what she would offer Harriet. Jaleesa would have to have a similar, more in-depth conversation with Tina soon as well.

Dana slipped Jaleesa's shoes back on quickly and without fumbling. "Good girl," Jaleesa said and stroked Dana's cheek. Dana leaned into the caress. Yes, she was a good girl.

Jaleesa stood and said, "Nadu," and pointed. Dana crawled back and kneeled, chest out, hands face up on her thighs. "How do you feel about this evening? What is your color?"

"The deepest avocado green there ever was, Ma'am."

Jaleesa grinned. She was secretly pleased that Dana had remembered to finally use the code word they'd agreed on when they chatted on the auction site. "Avocado green for me, too." She took one step toward the closed bedroom door making a mental inventory of everything she needed to take back with her. It wouldn't do to make a smooth exit only to slink back in because she'd forgotten something. One time was enough to squash that faux pas from her repertoire.

"Stay in that pose until you hear me close the front door. And then I want you to throw on that robe and lock your apartment door. I need to know that you're safe."

"Ma'am?"

"Yes, ladybug?"

Dana giggled and said, "Will you please text me that you got home so I know you're okay?"

Ooh. Something stabbed at Jaleesa's heart. She couldn't recall any sub in her history of subs ever asking her to do that. Jaleesa cleared the emotion from her throat and said, "Of course." She took another step toward the door, turned, and said, "Goodnight, my little avocado. I hope you had a good birthday today."

"How did you know?"

"I know all," Jaleesa said with a chuckle and headed out the door.

Jaleesa heard giggling and then a faint, "I did, Ma'am. Thank you," as she shut the bedroom door behind her.

Chapter 22

Tina

Both Tina and Jaleesa were quiet as they traveled north toward Denton Heights. Jaleesa seemed intent on navigating the Saturday traffic while Tina was lost in thought. They were meeting Penni to do a bit of house hunting. It had been two weeks since Tina had her first weekend sleepover at Jaleesa's, and Jaleesa had her first date with Dana. In those weeks, Jaleesa met up with Dana a few more times. Tina was getting used to the idea of Jaleesa needing that kind of physical release, and Jaleesa seemed so much more settled and content afterward. Tina let herself relax. She was no longer waiting for Jaleesa to break up with her because she needed more sex. Tina surprised herself at how comfortable she was with the arrangement with Dana. She thought maybe she'd have regrets once things got going, but not so far.

Tina reached up and caressed her new necklace. She loved the sense of peace it gave her. It symbolized the commitment she'd made to Jaleesa the night before. They'd had many heart-to-heart talks about what a D/s relationship would mean for them, and it sounded like heaven to Tina. But before officially agreeing to be collared, Tina pounded Jaleesa with questions, scenarios, and what-ifs. Jaleesa handled them all well and not once made Tina feel stupid for asking. Harriet was there last night when they'd made it official. Tina had gotten down on her knees, even though Jaleesa didn't ask her to, and bowed her head. Jaleesa fastened the necklace around her neck. It was a gorgeous silver necklace with an infinity symbol swirled around a heart.

Tina thought Jaleesa would officially collar Harriet last night but that didn't happen. Jaleesa told Tina in private later that each collaring was special and needed to be separate. She would collar Harriet soon and even showed Tina the big-link silver necklace she would present to Harriet. It was incredible to see how Jaleesa and Harriet cared for each other. Seeing it firsthand was what made Tina unafraid to commit to Jaleesa in a similar manner. During the ceremony, though, Jaleesa made such a big deal about the communication aspect of their relationship that Tina wanted to tell her to stop, that she got it already. But she didn't say anything. Clearly, that was important to Jaleesa.

She felt so much love from the woman in the driver's seat that she kept thinking about how very different her life might have turned out if she hadn't asked for help way back when. And, in a way, Skeeter offering her heroin was the catalyst to asking for that help. The one small sane part of her that was left had recognized her boundaries, her limits. Tina smiled. Jaleesa was always talking about limits, hard and soft. It was an interesting way to look at life.

Tina stole a glance at Jaleesa's majestic profile. She had been doing well with her sponsor Elaina and faithfully read from and took notes in the margins of the AA Big Book just about every night. Tina had kept up with her own sponsor but thought maybe it was time to branch out and become a sponsor herself. Her sponsor had been encouraging her to do so for a while now. After all, she was over eleven years clean at this point, so maybe it was time. Overdue, probably. She'd have to talk it over with Jaleesa first. It was scary being responsible for other people. She didn't know how Jaleesa did it.

"Whatcha thinking about, bunny rabbit?" Jaleesa said. They had just taken the Denton Heights exit.

Tina didn't want to reveal her current thoughts, so she said, "More corporate types infiltrated the bank this week. Something's going down soon. I can feel it."

"Oh, yeah? Are Henderson's days numbered?"

"Could be. They totally see how often he leaves early. And I told them about Amber seeing him doing unsavory things in the parking lot with a woman, but I don't know what's happened with that. I think they're doing some kind of audit, too. I've had to show them my summaries for the last few months. And all this week, I've had a mentor. That's what we're telling Henderson. Mrs. Armstrong is nice and all. She's older, but boy howdy, has she been grilling me about JW bank protocol and all kinds of things having absolutely nothing to do with my particular job. I feel like I'm on trial, too."

"She probably has to make it look good, so Henderson thinks all of you are getting audited or evaluated. And to be fair, you have been doing a lot more than your job description. Am I right?"

"Yes, true."

"Maybe she's making sure things have been taken care of while Henderson wasn't doing them. Even Amber thought you were the manager."

"She did," Tina said with a laugh. "Can you imagine that? Me? Bank manager?"

"I can."

"What?" Tina scoffed.

Jaleesa pulled the pickup into a gas station but didn't pull up to the pumps. Her movements were quick and jerky as if she were mad. She threw the pickup into park and turned to face Tina. "Yes, I can see you as the bank manager. Tell me why you can't."

Tina scoffed again. "I don't know," she said with a shrug. "It's just not ever been something I've thought about."

"Why not?"

The entire conversation continued in that fashion—Tina attempting to explain herself and Jaleesa asking why or why not. The whole thing made Tina very uncomfortable, and said so, besides the fact that they would be late meeting Penni.

"Tina," Jaleesa said to get her attention. Her eyes expressed love and a wise confidence that Tina had come to trust. "You know what's worse than starting something and failing?"

"What?"

"Not starting it at all. Baby, I want you to do whatever you must to become a bank manager. If you have to take courses, I'll support you in that. If you have to work overtime, we'll work through that. In the least, I want you to explore the possibility. I don't want you to have any more regrets in life."

"What if I'm bad at it? What if I don't do a good job?"

"You? You're already doing most of that job now. The employees love you, and you lead well. But, sure, if things don't end up working out, then at least you tried. That is infinitely better than the regrets you'll have if you never try."

"This sounds like the pep talks you've been giving Dana about the landscape stuff."

"What can I say," Jaleesa said and waggled her eyebrows. "I want my women to be the best they can be. If I can keep my women happy, then I'm happy."

"You're 'women,'" Tina mocked. "I guess I'm one of your *women*, hmm?" She leaned over in such a way that Jaleesa understood she wanted a kiss. She got one and then got snatched into a hug.

"Baby," Jaleesa said after releasing Tina, "I just want what's best for you. So, let's find a house so we can get on with this nesting thing."

Five houses later, Tina and Jaleesa were weary. None of the houses Penni showed them so far were right for them. One was too small, and the second was too close to the neighbors. The last one they'd seen was out of their price range, but Tina understood that realtors always tried to stretch you. It was part of the process. She knew this because Penni had warned them about it beforehand. They followed Penni's car as she turned down a side street toward the last house on the list. Tina recognized the street.

"Baby, this is the street where I said I wanted to be your submissive."

"Well, by golly, it is," Jaleesa said with a goofy grin.

Tina laughed. They were both a little house-hunting drunk at that point. "Penni said this last one is within our budget but is a bit of a fixer-upper."

The neighborhood was a bit eclectic. There were one-story ranches and two-story houses like the one Penni was about to show them. A few cottages dotted the streets, along with a duplex or two. Some yards were pristinely manicured, and others had seen better days. The property Penni pulled up to was one of the latter.

"Don't judge a book by its cover," Penni said. She laughed and added, "I'm hoping once you get inside, you won't nope it out of there like you did on that third house. You didn't even let me get through my fixer-upper speech."

Tina laughed, saying, "Rats' nests tend to make me run."

"That one needs to be condemned," Jaleesa said seriously. Jaleesa was right. The roof had been falling in.

Penni looked rather serious when she said, "I'll make that recommendation to the board." She headed up what looked like a walkway, but it was so overgrown that Tina couldn't tell. "This roof is only ten years old," she said, referring to her notes. "So that shouldn't be a worry. And obviously, this jungle habitat can all be trimmed back," Penni said as she led the way. "You'll be parking in the garage anyway." She pointed, but Tina couldn't see through the overgrowth.

The deep red front door was cute with its stained-glass inlay above.

"You could clean up the overgrowth," Penni gestured to the sides of the front landing. She unlocked the front door. "Put a front porch in."

Tina reached for Jaleesa's hand as they walked in. The first thing that hit them was the staleness. Unlike the house they ran away from, this one wasn't dank or musty. It had more of an old stale smell as if the house had been shut up for a while and needed a good airing out.

"Carpets. Those would be replaced," Jaleesa said pointing to the well-worn dirty Berber carpeting covering the living room floors. "Penni, who lived here before?"

Penni checked her clipboard and said, "An older woman who lived alone. She was in her nineties when she passed."

"In the house?" Tina asked. She didn't want that kind of legacy in her first house.

"No, I remember the tour. They said she was in a nursing home for a while and passed there. Her son, who's in his seventies, wants the house sold. He lives out of state. Arizona, I believe."

"It's an 'as-is' situation, you said?" Jaleesa asked.

Penni nodded. "But there may be some things we can discuss with the son."

"Depending on the inspection, of course," Jaleesa said.

Tina was surprised Jaleesa was talking about inspections already. They hadn't even gone past the overlarge living room.

"Furniture included?"

Penni nodded again. "Yes. He said to toss or donate anything you don't want."

"Hmm," Jaleesa said. "The furniture looks old but in good shape. A bit of cleaning and restoration, and we're good."

They toured the rest of the house, and Tina was surprised at how deceptively big it was. Of course, everyone got a kick at how retro the décor and fixtures were. Jaleesa even quipped that the seventies wanted their house back, but then Penni said that style was coming back in vogue, so think twice before tossing anything.

The kitchen was dated. The yellow stove and oven matched the kitschy wallpaper, which was almost too much for Tina to bear. The laminate countertops were in surprisingly good condition, but the cabinets were worn and tired-looking, especially around the sink and stove. The window behind the sink and the windows near the kitchen table looked onto the overgrown backyard. The early afternoon sunlight gorgeously streamed through the dirty window giving it a homey feel. The back fence was rotting and falling, but Jaleesa reminded her to look at the potential. It sounded like she wasn't out and out rejecting the old house. And neither was Tina.

The massive house seemed to have "good bones," according to Jaleesa. When they stepped into an odd room on the first floor past the kitchen, Tina saw it had been set up as a formal dining room. The layer of dust on everything belied the fact that it hadn't been used in years. It was a good-sized, well-lit room. Tina shrugged. They would never use this as a dining room. An office for Jaleesa, maybe? No, it needed a door.

"Thoughts, love?" Jaleesa asked. "I see smoke pouring out of your head."

"A door could be put on this entryway, right?"

"Sure."

"It's out of the way. Plenty of privacy. This could be an office for you and maybe a bedroom space for Harriet?" She didn't wait for an answer. "Look. She could set up her bed here and her easel there. Oh, there's no closet."

"That's what armoires are for."

"And since there's no closet," Penni chimed in, "it wouldn't be considered a bedroom. And there's a full bath right here on the first floor she could use."

"Honey, it's perfect," Tina said and moved closer. Jaleesa automatically put her arm around Tina's waist, just as Tina had intended.

"So," Jaleesa said to Penni, "you're basically saying that this five-bedroom, three-bathroom house could really be a six-bedroom house."

"Sure. If you're willing to sacrifice this formal room space."

Jaleesa asked Penni to show them the kitchen area again. She turned to Tina and said, "Baby, the table in the kitchen is big enough for a crowd, don't you think? We wouldn't need a dining room."

"That table's bigger than my parents', and you've seen how big theirs is."

Jaleesa grinned at her. "Excellent."

Tina wanted to ask her what she was thinking but decided against it since Penni was standing right there.

"Let's tour the basement next," Jaleesa said.

"Perfect," Penni said. It seemed to Tina that Penni knew they were interested in the house, so she kept up her enthusiasm. "And then we'll go see the two-car garage. It even has two garage door openers. Finally, we'll go outside to inspect the yard and foundation."

After the basement tour was complete with a private eyebrow waggle from Jaleesa that Tina wasn't quite sure how to interpret, they headed through the garage and then out to the yard. Penni excused herself to go inside to make a quick phone call. They all knew she was creating space for Tina and Jaleesa to talk.

"Baby," Jaleesa said, pulling Tina into a hug. "I love this place."

"You do?" Tina put her head on Jaleesa's chest. "I know I was the one pushing for this, but it's kind of overwhelming."

"It is. I know. That front room would be perfect for Harriet. The primary bedroom suite is perfect for us. You can have your craft room upstairs in one of the remaining four bedrooms up there. And the yard is huge. Overgrown, yes, but that will simply be a labor of love. The house is near my new salon. And, bonus, it's near the main strip in town."

"And Rikki's coffee shop and the Indigo Café."

"Mm hmm. And the neighborhood seems to be fairly inclusive, too. I saw a few melanated neighbors as we drove in."

"Good," Tina said. She, too, had noticed the many and varied skin colors and nationalities on display as they drove the streets in the neighborhood. "So, I was thinking. Maybe it's not good for Harriet to be alone on the first floor at night. Maybe that large bedroom facing the backyard would be better."

"We'll let Harriet decide. How about that?"

"Yeah, best to let her pick."

"And if she chooses upstairs, you can make that space your craft room. If you want."

"Not your office?"

Jaleesa chuckled. "I'll have an office at the shop. I certainly don't want my home to become my second office."

Tina hugged Jaleesa harder. "So much to think about. And, hey, what was so great about the basement? It was just boring concrete packed with a lot of crap. We're going to have to deal with all that junk."

"Ahh, but there might be some treasures in there. We might be able to sell some of it to pay for our new suburban habit. And don't forget, with some cleaning and paint, we've got a great quiet place for impact sessions. Add in a few *custom* pieces of furniture, and I've got a playroom for Dana and me with a nice cage for you." Jaleesa kissed the top of Tina's head.

"Would you really build me one?"

"Anything you want, baby," Jaleesa said. "Hey, we haven't checked out that side of the house." She pointed to the far side of the garage. Jaleesa released Tina from her hold and reached for her hand. They picked their way carefully over the overgrown weeds, still dead from winter, and turned the corner. Jaleesa stopped abruptly. Tina saw immediately why she'd stopped.

"Baby," Tina gushed. "It's a sign."

Jaleesa nodded. Standing tall on an overgrown concrete slab was an upright basketball hoop and backboard. "Now, I'm the one who's overwhelmed."

"Do you want to go back through the house again?" Tina said. "To be sure?"

"I do. And this time, we'll take notes on everything that needs to be done."

"Got it." Tina held up her notepad. "A prioritized list. I won't make an offer if we find anything that would be a deal breaker."

"Excellent thinking, my love," Jaleesa said. "C'mon, let's go tell Penni to extend her phone call because we're going to be looking over this house for a while."

Tina's hand found its way into Jaleesa's, and she let herself be led around the garage and back to the front door. As she tried to imagine living there, she found it wasn't difficult, especially because she'd be living with the woman whose hand clutched hers.

~~~

It was late Tuesday afternoon. Tina sat in her office, trying to deal with a thousand different feelings. One of them was a good one. She'd met Jaleesa at her AA meeting last night and was floored by her awesome new haircut. Jaleesa said that Monday haircuts were good luck since Mondays were the start of the week, so a new haircut meant the start of a new life. Tina had never heard that folklore before, but if it helped them get off to an amazing new life together, she was all for it.

The cut was extremely attractive. It made Jaleesa look butch, and Tina told her so. It was the only word Tina could come up with. She ran her hands through the tapered cut and the low fade. The fact that she did that before the meeting in front of everyone totally signaled how close she and Jaleesa were now.

Tina sighed at the recent memory and fondled her commitment necklace. She wished she could keep that memory in the forefront, but truth be told, anxious thoughts were winning out. The anxiety over the offer they'd put in on the house Sunday afternoon vied for top billing on the anxiety list. The corporate people hovering over every action at the bank was a close second.

Jaleesa wouldn't let Tina put a bid on the house while they were still there in Denton Heights on Saturday. She said it was always better to sleep on things. When Tina woke in Jaleesa's arms Sunday morning, she wanted to make the offer immediately, but again, Jaleesa advised her to slow down. They had a sit-down breakfast that Harriet made, and all three of them talked over the details thoroughly. Finding nothing huge stopping them, Jaleesa still made her wait until mid-afternoon just in case they thought of something that would affect the offer. They didn't.

Harriet offered to pay a small monthly rent, and in exchange for room and board, she would also take on the role of chief cook and bottle washer in the new household. It was a role she had already taken on in Jaleesa's apartment. That was fine with Tina and more than fine with Jaleesa. They showed Harriet the pictures they'd taken of the house and yard, and she laughed at the overgrowth. She asked if they were sure there was a house in that jungle. It was nice to see Harriet joking around. It had been a while since Tina had seen this relaxed side of Harriet. Harriet mentioned an arts center in Denton Heights that she'd look into for a part-time job. Of course, as a convicted felon for cocaine possession, she might not be successful. The good news was that she was finally off probation and could move up to Denton Heights without worry.

Penni called Tina instantly once Tina texted her with the offer. Penni screamed into the phone how happy she was that Tina was finally getting settled and moving on. Tina hadn't realized how invested in her happiness Penni was, but it felt good to have someone championing their cause. They underbid the asking price, citing the need for significant renovations as well as the removal of the former owner's goods. Penni thought it was a reasonable and fair offer.

Penni said they'd probably hear something by the end of the workday on Tuesday as it was customary for the seller to respond within forty-eight hours one way or the other. Tina rechecked her phone. No response from Penni. It was already four o'clock with only one hour left of the workday. Oh, well. Maybe tomorrow.

Tina worked for a while, responding to emails from Corporate. The increased volume of emails was astounding now that they were under investigation. Thankfully, her mentor Mrs. Armstrong was busy in the back office doing whatever it was she did. Tina had no more scheduled customer appointments that day, so she stole a moment to recheck the JW Bank job listings for the millionth time. There were no openings at the two Denton Heights branches. Bummer. She was going to have to commute. It was a straight shot, so the commute wouldn't be too bad. And she'd be able to see her parents on the regular, so that was a plus.

With a sigh, she closed the job listings screen and let those thoughts go. If it was going to happen, it was going to happen. *Let go and let God*, she thought. She tapped her desk three times and said, "You're o-kay."

She clicked open a new browser screen and searched for the qualifications needed to be a bank manager at JW Bank. Jaleesa had asked her to look into it, and Tina knew she had to follow up or Jaleesa would not be pleased.

Tina saw motion in the lobby and looked up to see one of the corporate bigwigs locking the front doors after the final customer left the building. The drive-thru was also shut down, and the blinds were drawn.

Tina looked at her watch. Yep, it was quitting time. Research could wait until tomorrow. She powered down her computer, locked her desk, and stood up to shrug on her blazer.

Mrs. Armstrong appeared at her door and let herself in with the barest of knocks. Her gray hair was pulled back into an impeccable and impossibly tight bun. Her eyeglass chain was gold and accented her whole corporate look. She was an older woman who had that alpha thing down pat, just like Jaleesa—the alpha part, not the older part. Mrs. Armstrong left the office door open and said in a low tone, "Tina, yours was not the first complaint from this bank about Henderson's tendency to leave early. The Denton Heights east branch had similar complaints. Amber's was also not the first accusation of sexual harassment, but if I have anything to do with it, it will be the last."

Mrs. Armstrong stood in the doorway, effectively blocking Tina's exit. There was more movement in the lobby, and she said, "I'll need you to stay right here where you are."

Tina's heart sped up. Was she being accused of something? She sat down hard at her desk.

Mrs. Armstrong was watching the lobby. For what? Tina had no clue. And then she saw them. Two uniformed police officers entered the building, followed by two people in power suits. Tina tapped her desk three times in succession repeatedly. Another two officers were posted outside the front doors. When the officers passed her office, she breathed a sigh of relief. She now had the tiniest inkling of what Harriet must have felt that day when they came for her in her middle school classroom.

Mrs. Armstrong held her hand down and spread, effectively stopping Tina from moving, not that Tina was going to move. She was barely breathing. Through the open door, Tina noticed the tellers quietly huddled together, watching the drama unfold. Nancy looked at Tina wide-eyed and shrugged as if saying she didn't know what was happening. Tina shrugged back. She didn't know either.

It was only when Amber started cheering and clapping that Tina realized what was happening. A moment later, it was confirmed. Doug Henderson, bank manager of JW Bank in downtown Cincinnati, was under arrest. His suit jacket hung over his obviously handcuffed wrists as the two uniformed officers escorted him out of the building.

Amber stopped clapping and said, "That's right, asshole. I hope you get what's coming to you." A quick word from Nancy stopped Amber's taunts.

Once the corporate bigwig relocked the door after Henderson was escorted out of the building, Mrs. Armstrong turned around and took a big breath. "Are you okay?" she asked Tina. She shut the door to Tina's office.

"I guess so," Tina said. "I'm not exactly sure what just happened."

Mrs. Armstrong briefly put a hand on her own forehead as she blew out a sigh. She said, "Your former bank manager, Mr. Douglas Henderson, has been arrested on several charges. The sexual harassment charge stems mostly from the Denton Heights branch, but Amber's case pushed it over the top."

Tina had no words.

Mrs. Armstrong dragged a chair from behind the plexiglass partition and pulled it closer to Tina. She sat and said, "I championed long and hard for you, so I hope you'll say yes. In my time here, I've witnessed your kind, gentle, but firm leadership style. Tina, you have the knowledge, the smarts, and the love of these employees to be an amazing bank manager. I want to offer you a position as the interim bank manager of this branch. As manager, you would be in charge of every employee here and manage daily operations. I'll stay and mentor you for a couple of weeks, but I know you'll catch on quickly and won't need much from me."

Tina wasn't sure she understood. "Wait, what are you saying? You want *me* to run the bank?"

"Yes. We want you to be the face of this branch. Don't you pretty much run it now? You were the one who came up with that new promotion for the commercial accounts—quite successfully, I might add. You have also been instrumental in shoring up health and safety concerns for employees and customers."

Tina shook her head and shrugged. "I was just picking up the pieces and doing what needed to be done."

Mrs. Armstrong laughed. "That's exactly what a bank manager does, my dear. You're a hard worker. Believe me, Corporate knows you exceeded your sales goals by eight percent this past year. Your customer satisfaction ratings are through the roof, and your customers say they would use you again for their future needs."

"I'm just doing my job."

"And very well. I can see you're in shock, so let me add to it."

Tina laughed. "Oh, great."

"This is not to be general knowledge, but I'm sure I can trust you with it no matter your answer. As far as the rest of the employees know, Henderson was arrested for sexual harassment, which is true. But there's more."

"More?" Tina's heart dropped. What else had this scoundrel done? Oh, God. She had worked in the same bank with him.

"He has also been arrested for several bank crimes, including embezzlement and fraud. If you take the position, you will be debriefed about the details because you and I will be righting this ship." She sighed again. "Listen, Tina, I know this is a huge turn of events, and I wish I could tell you to think about it overnight and talk it over with your spouse, but I can't. I have to know your answer right now. If you're in, we can move you into the big office tomorrow morning. If you don't want the responsibility, although I think you'll be great—"

"I'm in," Tina interrupted. "I love this bank and the people in it. And you're right. I know what needs to be done. I think I can do it. With your guidance, of course. And a hotline to Corporate for my myriad questions." She chuckled to relieve the tension.

"You'll get all the support you need," Mrs. Armstrong said, looking relieved. "Deep breath now."

Tina did as instructed.

"We've held the employees back to let them know why Henderson was taken out in handcuffs." She looked into the lobby and gave one of the corporate types a thumbs-up. He threw her a thumbs-up back. "That's our cue. Are you ready to be introduced to your staff?"

Tina stood up. Her heart was pounding as she felt her entire body flood with heat. "One second." She closed her eyes and pictured Jaleesa hugging her, telling her she would be great, and telling her just to do it. "Okay," Tina said. "I'm as ready as I'll ever be." She blew out another sigh and followed Mrs. Armstrong into the lobby.

Tina widened her eyes at Nancy's confused-and-questioning expression but said nothing.

Mrs. Armstrong called for and got the employees' attention. "Thank you all for putting up with this circus these past few weeks. Gerald has already given you the details and the initial pep talk, but I wanted to dovetail on that by introducing you to someone." She looked around at all the employees.

Ahh, yes. Tina had seen Jaleesa do that. Mrs. Armstrong was making sure every employee felt seen and acknowledged.

Mrs. Armstrong put a hand on Tina's shoulder. "I would like to introduce you to your new interim bank manager, Ms. Tina Jenkins."

The lobby burst into applause and hoots of encouragement and joy. Nancy couldn't help herself and raced over to hug Tina tightly. "You'll be great Tina. You're already doing the job."

"Told you," Amber said from behind the counter. "That's my girl right there." The other tellers high-fived each other.

The other personal bankers, including Rusty McAllister, the grumpy curmudgeon, congratulated her and offered their help for whatever she needed. Tina thanked them and tried not to be overwhelmed by the overflow of attention.

OMG, thank God there's a meeting tonight. This thought came in between well wishes.

"Speech," Amber called out. Echoes of "speech, speech" filled the lobby.

Mrs. Armstrong stepped back and gestured to the spot where she'd been standing.

"Thank you, everyone," Tina said. "This is overwhelming, to be sure. For all of us, right?" She took in the head nods, and it relaxed her somewhat. "All I ask is that you keep doing what you've been doing for this bank. You all work incredibly hard." Murmurs of agreement filled the room. "I know. I see." Tina smiled at Amber and said, "It's going to take me a hot minute to figure out this new position, so please be patient and bear with me while I get my footing." More head nods affirmed that they were on the same page. "We want that community out there, which we are a part of, to know we've got their backs. We're here and will continue to be strong. And even though one bad apple infiltrated our ranks, we will continue to give them amazing and dedicated service as we've always done." There were more hoots and hollers, and Tina felt like she was giving a pep talk to her softball team before a championship game or something. "And, honestly, I think my first order of business is to get those dang bathrooms fixed." Mrs. Armstrong's laugh was the loudest among the cheers and clapping. Tina raised her fist in the air and pumped it once in acknowledgment.

"Okay," Tina continued. "We've been through a lot. I'll give you back to Corporate now, but I expect you all here bright and early tomorrow morning to start our collective new chapter."

"With bells on?" Amber quipped.

"It that's your thing, then sure," Tina shot back to more laughter from the employees. "Goodnight, everybody. And thank you."

She blew out a sigh as the employees clapped again.

"Oh, you're going to be fine, Tina," Mrs. Armstrong said, leading Tina back to her office while Gerard dismissed them to finish out their day.

Mrs. Armstrong shut the door and said, "I have a good feeling about you. Now that you've accepted this position, Corporate would like you to attend a five-day workshop for new bank managers. Two days are in Columbus at Corporate, but three of those days are virtual. I'll be back to cover while you're attending. The next one is in April, so you've got some time to get this place running efficiently the way *you* want it to be run."

"I'm overwhelmed." Tina hadn't been out of Cincinnati in over a decade, but Columbus wasn't that far away. She reached up and touched her necklace. Jaleesa would help her figure out how to do this.

"Go home. Take a bath. Have your hubby bring you a glass of wine, and go to bed early. You have a big day ahead of you."

Tina plopped in her office chair. She didn't have the strength to correct the woman about the hubby or the wine, but it didn't matter. "Yes, I do have a big day ahead. A big week. A big month." She laughed and then remembered her manners. "Thank you for all of your help during this—" She waved her hands around, trying to find the perfect word. "During this mess. And thank you in advance for your mentorship. I hope I make a worthy student."

"You will." And with that, Mrs. Armstrong opened Tina's office door and headed out. "See you tomorrow, bank manager."

Tina waved and took a moment to catch her breath. Holy crap. She couldn't wait to tell Jaleesa. And her parents, they were going to freak. All the excitement that afternoon made her a little late leaving, so she pulled out her phone to text her mother. She didn't get that far because Penni's text was, first and foremost, on her screen.

PENNI: You got the house!!!! He accepted your offer!!! Call me ASAP!!!

Chapter 23

Jaleesa

Jaleesa had way too much energy to bother with the elevator that Friday evening and took the steps two at a time. Dana's roommates' car was gone from the assigned spot, so the coast was clear for a glorious evening of sex and lovemaking. Yes, both. She wasn't sure what she had done to be so lucky, but she was grateful that three amazing women had fallen into her life. She loved them all in different ways. Each one bolstered and lifted her in ways she had difficulty expressing to them but would continue to try.

She slowed to a walk in the long hall heading to the apartment and smiled at the memory of Tina bursting with the news that the offer on the house had been accepted on Tuesday. Everyone at the meeting was very excited for her. The inspection of the new house would be this Sunday. Jaleesa was also proud when Tina confided more quietly about Henderson's arrest and her new job promotion. She was obviously nervous. The Columbus trip in April was freaking her out, so Jaleesa offered to go with her for the full two days. Miss Bessie was going to have to understand, and if she didn't, fine. Jaleesa would be quitting soon, anyway.

And then there was Dana. She was incredibly easy to be with. She was submissive by nature but could express her needs well in a strong voice. They'd had several play times together so far, and Jaleesa was getting to know her sexual submissive's proclivities. Different possible scenes with Dana ran through her head, and consequently, Jaleesa had been aroused all day long. So much so that she had to shower after work. The scenes didn't stop, though, and she was currently wet on arrival. Dana was not going to know what hit her once Jaleesa got her hands on her.

Jaleesa barely knocked once, and the door flew open. Dana ushered her in, locked the front door behind her, and flew into Jaleesa's waiting arms. Jaleesa lifted her off the ground, and Dana wrapped her legs around Jaleesa's waist. The sprite of a thing fit there so perfectly. Jaleesa kissed the woman senseless as they headed to Dana's room.

"Undress me," Jaleesa said simply as she put Dana back down. Dana's eyes lit up. She hadn't seen much of Jaleesa's body yet, only the crucial bits on occasion. But tonight was going to be different. Dana took her time and sent seductive glances to her Domme now and then. Although Jaleesa didn't ask her to, Dana folded each article of clothing carefully and stacked them on the dresser. She undid Jaleesa's bra and ran a stray hand over one of Jaleesa's breasts as if by accident. It wasn't. Jaleesa chose to ignore the transgression. She was too aroused to care at that point. Dana got down on her knees and lifted Jaleesa's foot to take off the shoe and sock. She repeated the motion on the other side. She shimmied closer, her head near Jaleesa's still-clothed center. She undid Jaleesa's pants button just as she looked up into Jaleesa's eyes. The lust Jaleesa saw in Dana's expression must have mirrored her own because she wanted to throw Dana on the bed and take her right then and there.

Dana eased down the zipper and pulled the pants off Jaleesa's long legs. Jaleesa stepped out of them and kicked them off to the side, not allowing Dana to fold them. Dana understood. The panties were next. Slowly, oh so slowly, Dana slid them down Jaleesa's legs. Jaleesa kicked them to the side as well.

Jaleesa wanted to grab Dana's mouth and shove it into her swollen wet mass of need, but she had other things in mind first.

"Nadu," Jaleesa said and used the hand signal she was teaching Dana.

Dana, still fully clothed, got into position. Jaleesa used the hand signal for closed legs because Dana had naturally spread her knees wide.

Although Jaleesa's body was gnawing for relief, she took a moment to show Dana her new collar. "This is a training collar," Jaleesa said. "The blue one was temporary. This black one signifies that we're making a commitment to each other." She clipped it on Dana's neck, and Dana reached up and stroked it lovingly. Jaleesa then reached into Dana's bag of goodies that Dana had obediently put out on display for their date and pulled out the extra pair of Velcro cuffs. One minute later, Dana's wrists were secured behind her back.

Jaleesa sat on the edge of the bed and splayed her legs open in full view. Dana licked her lips in anticipation. Ahh, little one, that is not going to happen just yet. Jaleesa moaned in anticipation as she caressed her own breasts with one hand and then ran the other down her body toward the spot that had been unrequited all day long. Dana's gaze followed Jaleesa's fingers. Jaleesa stroked herself, letting her sighs fall when they would. As Jaleesa's hand worked, her head fell back as a spark ignited in the distance.

"Ma'am, please," Dana begged. "Please let me." She groaned in frustration.

What to do. What to do. Jaleesa had originally planned to make Dana watch while she came, but that angsty invitation was too enticing to pass up. Jaleesa stood up and approached Dana slowly. She ran her thumb down Dana's lips, slipped her thumb inside, and then pressed Dana's mouth open by pushing on her bottom teeth. Jaleesa thrust two fingers in, inviting Dana to suck. She did, quite willingly, until Jaleesa yanked her fingers out. She moved closer.

"You know what to do," Jaleesa said, hearing the thickness in her voice.

Dana didn't have time for words as Jaleesa lifted one leg onto the windowsill behind Dana's head and pressed her center toward Dana's waiting tongue.

This was not the first time Dana had pleasured her orally, but it was the first time she'd done so without being satisfied first. Jaleesa arched her pelvis toward her submissive.

"Yes, yes, ladybug," Jaleesa purred. "That's my girl. Make me cum." A pre-orgasmic wave hit her, and she moaned. She grabbed Dana's head and pulled it tighter to her core. "Good, good girl." The words were cut off as she rode the edge, drawing out the sensations. She pressed Dana's mouth to her body and undulated her hips. Yes, yes, it was right there. Looking down at Dana's head moving to please her made Jaleesa's core clench.

Dana nibbled her way up Jaleesa's nether lips making Jaleesa shudder. Dana's flattened tongue smashed against Jaleesa's clit, causing a pre-spasm. Dana was skilled. Like she said she was. And she was good at learning what Jaleesa wanted, what Jaleesa needed. Jaleesa's moan lowered in pitch. The spark was back, getting larger. Dana flicked and sucked and licked so wonderfully sloppy that Jaleesa had no choice but to give in.

"Fuck," Jaleesa moaned as she came. "Good fucking pussy licker," she praised as Dana continued to lick slowly. She knew not to stop until told. "Stop," Jaleesa said but didn't pull away. Dana pulled her tongue back in. Jaleesa undulated a few more times over Dana's lips as the aftershocks coursed through her. She finally stepped back and leaned down to kiss the growing smile off Dana's lips. "Good girl."

The re-emerging smile growing on Dana's face pleased Jaleesa greatly. That boded well for the rest of Dana's evening.

"Stand." Dana did. Jaleesa unlinked the cuffs but left them on her wrists. "Clothes off." Dana complied. "Inspection pose." Dana clasped her hands behind her head, stood up tall, and widened her stance.

"Oh, the things we'll do together," Jaleesa mused as she ran her hands over Dana's body watching as nipples peaked or involuntary goosebumps appeared. Jaleesa's power center surged when Dana's throaty moan escaped when Jaleesa stroked an inner thigh. Jaleesa couldn't wait to move into the new house and get her basement dungeon set up. Of course, it would have to be carefully disguised for Tina's parents' visits. And her own parents, of course. She continued her inspection and wondered how Dana would react to wearing a tack bra. Maybe Jaleesa would make her wear it while cleaning the equipment after play. No, no—*before* play. Yes, that would be better. Dana would then sit on Jaleesa's lap. She'd make Dana suck her fingers on one hand while the other was busy down below fingering her until she squirmed. The tack bra, meanwhile, would make her aware of every movement. How positively sadistic.

And what about clothespin zippers? Would Dana like the feel when Jaleesa yanked the string causing the pins to fly off her skin one after the other? Her little Dana was only just beginning to understand the art of pain and pleasure. Jaleesa's power center was reaching maximum as she pictured giving Dana this gift.

She yanked Dana's hands down from the inspection pose, clasped them together in front, and practically threw the woman face down on the bed. "On your knees. Let me see you."

Dana complied and rested her forehead on the pillow. Her knees spread a little wider in anticipation. "Mmm, you're nice and wet for me, my young plaything. Just the way I like my women."

Jaleesa reached into the goody bag and found the harness. She strapped it on and then showed Dana the dildo she was about to be pummeled with.

"Please, Ma'am," Dana begged. "Please. I've been good. I haven't touched myself since our last time. I need release, Ma'am."

"I do love a sub that begs." Jaleesa maneuvered behind Dana on the bed, her gaze moving over Dana's petite athletic body. "You're beautiful, Dana."

Dana emitted a tight, strangled noise at the praise.

Jaleesa rubbed her hands over Dana's perfectly shaped ass, sucking air through her teeth in admiration. Anal training would begin this evening but later. Best to give Dana some relief first. She'd been celibate for almost an entire week, after all.

Jaleesa moved forward, jostling Dana on the bed. She grabbed two meaty handfuls of Dana's hips and let the dildo slide through her wetness. Dana jumped when the dildo grazed her clit, but this was not about Dana cumming right away. No, no, no. Jaleesa was going to drag it out long enough for her own spark to re-ignite.

She released one hip to guide the dildo inside the eager woman on all fours in front of her. Slowly, inch by inch, she entered Dana's body. Bottoming out, she stopped all motion letting Dana get used to the intrusion inside her.

After a moment, Jaleesa slowly pulled back, not quite letting the dildo fall out, and then slowly pushed back in. She kept up the slow pace for a while and then stopped all movement, much to Dana's dismay. She groaned at the betrayal. Jaleesa just laughed and reached for Dana's hips. She pulled Dana onto her shaft and then pushed her forward. Dana caught on that she was the one moving now. She rocked her body repeatedly, picking up speed until Jaleesa sensed her breathing quicken. Dana was close. Jaleesa grabbed Dana's hips and threw Dana forward off the dildo entirely. Dana didn't groan, though. She knew Jaleesa would satisfy her one way or another.

Jaleesa maneuvered Dana onto her back. Not an easy feat with Dana's wrists tied together. She unclipped them. She probably should have unclipped them first. Live and learn as they say. Jaleesa directed Dana to pull her legs up to her breasts and lift her hips with her own hands. Jaleesa moved in close and directed Dana to let her legs fall on Jaleesa's shoulders.

"Color?"

"Green, Ma'am," Dana said.

"Good. This anvil position only works if you're flexible enough. And I see that someone has been working on her flexibility like I asked."

"Yes, Ma'am," Dana said proudly.

Jaleesa grinned and leaned down to kiss her sub as one hand snaked below to guide the dildo inside. Dana inhaled sharply. Her arms wrapped around Jaleesa's back and dug in as Jaleesa thrust. Jaleesa's hips pumped at a steady rhythm. Jaleesa held her weight up with her arms but lowered herself to nibble on Dana's neck. She nibbled her way to Dana's shoulder and, finding a meaty part, latched on with her teeth. Fingernails dug into Jaleesa's back. But that was okay. She liked souvenirs from a night of lovemaking, especially the hidden mementos.

Dana was not passive. Her hips undulated as much as allowable by their tight position. Dana moaned. She was getting close. Jaleesa's power surged in her own body because she was the one causing that moan. A bolt of arousal ran through her, causing her head to roll away from the delightful shoulder she had been devouring.

"I'm cumming," Dana cried out and lifted her hips into the pounding.

Dana's cries were music to Jaleesa's libido, and she, too, felt the freight train of lust shooting through her. She smashed her mouth against Dana's in a furious possessive kiss and then came with a low moan. She continued to kiss her lover as she slowed her thrusts and then ultimately stopped. Jaleesa lowered her forehead onto Dana's as they breathed each other's breath. She was about to tell Dana she loved her but stopped herself. It was too confusing. She loved Tina. But she loved Dana, too. Just differently.

She smiled and laughed at their fervor, glad when Dana also laughed.

"So good, Ma'am," Dana said.

Jaleesa let Dana's legs down slowly, one by one, and then unstrapped the harness. She tossed it off the bed onto one of the towels Dana had been required to place on each side of the bed for moments like this.

Jaleesa lay next to Dana, who put her head on Jaleesa's bare breasts and sighed. They lay like that for a while, dozing and regaining their strength.

After a while, Jaleesa wasn't sure how long, she stirred when Dana's finger drew patterns on Jaleesa's bare chest. "Awake, ladybug?" she said to Dana.

"Yes, Ma'am," Dana said dreamily. "I'm glad I said yes to your crazy plan."

"Me, too."

"Is Tina still okay with it? With us meeting like this?"

"She is," Jaleesa said. "It still feels like some kind of grand experiment. One that we're all winning at."

"That's good." Dana sat up and said, "I'll get us some water. I forgot to bring some in."

"Nope." Jaleesa got out of bed. "I'll get them." She found Dana's robe and tried to put it on to no avail. It was way too small. Dana giggled as Jaleesa tried. "Oh, well." She threw her shirt on and left the room like Pooh bear on a water run.

When she returned with the waters, she didn't join Dana on the bed. She leaned against the dresser. "What aren't you telling me?"

"Ma'am?" Dana stopped drinking mid-swig.

"The boxes outside. Are you moving? Are your roommates moving? Again, what aren't you telling me? And before you answer, I want the truth."

"Yes, Ma'am," Dana said with a sigh. "Tee and Marie are moving out. They're going back to Columbus. Tee got a promotion or something. They're going to see if I can take over their lease here. And I guess I have to find new roommates now."

"No. You won't."

"But, Ma'am, I can't afford this apartment alone. I can barely afford to pay my share to them."

"Obviously, I need to talk this over with Tina. And Harriet. But I think the best thing for you is to come live with us up in Denton Heights."

"What?" Dana was clearly confused. "I can't live with you. Tina tolerates this arrangement of ours now, but having me right there under her nose all the time? She'd only resent me and then you, which would ruin everything. No, I'll find roommates. Maybe some college students. Women, of course."

Jaleesa made her way over to the bed removing her shirt as she went. "It was Tina's idea."

"What was?"

"You moving in with us."

"Say what? Naw."

"Yes, actually. Tina and I were looking at houses, and she said something about us needing to look at houses with more bedrooms because of Harriet and you."

"She mentioned me by name?"

"She sure did," Jaleesa said. "She joked about me having a harem, which is not exactly what it would be."

"But my job—"

"Is a crappy one, and you told me that the best landscape design program is at Phillips University in Denton Heights. Am I right?"

"Yes, as always, Ma'am."

Jaleesa scoffed silently. She was *not* always right. Far from it. "Sounds like we need a pow-wow with the boss, don't we?"

Dana giggled. "Tina rules the roost, huh?"

Jaleesa scoffed outwardly. "You'd better believe it." She reached for Dana's water and put it on the bedside table beside hers. "How would my little ladybug like some anal training this evening?" Before she let Dana react, she said. "Why am I even asking? She doesn't have a choice." Which was a lie because, of course, Dana had a choice in everything. Hopefully, Dana would do the right thing and let Jaleesa take care of her properly at the new homestead in Denton Heights.

~~~

Time sped up for Jaleesa that spring. Two months had passed since that fateful night she'd asked Dana to move in with them in Denton Heights, and it was now the third week of May. She'd closed on the strip mall and was deep into a million details of getting the salon ready. It would be another three weeks at least until she could have a soft opening. And currently, she was up on a ladder painting the high trim in the salon. Newly collared Harriet cleaned while Tina and soon-to-be-officially-collared Dana painted their way around the main workroom. Optic orange was not the color of choice, even though Tina had joked about that. Nope, soft painter's white was going up on the walls for now.

Tina's offer on the house had been accepted, and the inspection already done. It was determined that the old rundown HVAC system needed replacing, but the seller agreed to pay the closing costs instead of dealing with it. The closing date was set for early June, just a few short weeks away.

Yes, everything seemed to be happening so fast. It had only been six months since Jaleesa met Harriet, leading her to Tina, who led her to Dana. Jaleesa couldn't help wondering if Tina's desire to bring Harriet and Dana into the house had something to do with Tina missing out on the college experience of living in a dorm. Tina had confided to Jaleesa one evening that her addiction had taken so much from her, and she'd felt cheated out of basic life experiences. Jaleesa understood. Tina hadn't yet experienced that freedom and was yearning for it.

What was heartwarming was that any chance she got, Tina took walks with her dad and sometimes with her mom as well. It was a ritual they had long ago created to get Tina out of the house in a supervised manner. Jaleesa also knew the recent walks were a way for Tina to spend time with her parents since she would be moving out soon and changing all of their lives.

And then there was that night back in April in Columbus. Tina's corporate training had gone well, and she was nestled in the hotel room in Jaleesa's arms, safe and secure. Jaleesa was startled when Tina started to cry. Jaleesa finally coaxed out of her what was wrong. Basically, she was scared. Although she was excited about all the new things starting in her life, she was afraid of messing up.

Jaleesa softly encouraged Tina and reassured her that she would be okay. Tina tapped the back of her own hand three times. Jaleesa had seen her do this on many occasions, knowing it was some kind of coping mechanism. When questioned about its meaning, Tina said, "I tell myself, 'You're o-kay.' One tap for each syllable."

"Trying to convince yourself, huh? Is that what you say in your head? '*You're* o-kay?' Like someone outside of you is telling you that?"

"I guess."

"How about finding that strength I know is inside you and have your inner self tell you."

"Huh?"

"Say, '*I'm* o-kay.' Tell yourself."

Tina tapped three times and said, "*I'm* o-kay." She sighed contentedly. "That's very different, isn't it?" She tapped again. "I'm o-kay." She scoffed and said, "I like it."

"And you will be okay, baby." Jaleesa pulled Tina in her arms again. "I won't let anything bad happen to you."

Jaleesa came back to the present and snuck a peek at Tina and Dana from her perch on the ladder. They were seriously discussing Tamara somebody-or-other's third-place finish on a singing competition show they both watched. Tina and Dana both thought Tamara should have won and thought America 'got it wrong.' Plans were made to record the following season, almost like a pact between them.

Tina continued to amaze Jaleesa by being overjoyed that Dana would officially join them in the house. Tina and Dana had even squeed together like little schoolgirls when they met to talk things over. Even Harriet seemed happy that Dana was joining them. It was obvious that the older woman was fond of the twenty-six-year-old and said to Dana, "I'm glad you're joining our family." That made Tina tear up a little, and Jaleesa, too, she had to admit. It wasn't a typical living arrangement for most people. Still, the four women that were weeks away from moving into a five-bedroom house in Denton Heights were building their own version of a supportive family, and Jaleesa couldn't see her life going any other way.

Tina was fond of saying, "Let go and let God." Maybe Tina was right, and it was all due to divine intervention. If so, then this divine intervention also manifested when Jaleesa gave notice at Miss Bessie's salon. Jaleesa had managed to keep her new venture a secret by some small miracle, but Miss Bessie knew something was up and pulled her into the back office for a "chat." Miss Bessie was a regally composed older woman in her mid-sixties, wearing her graying hair proudly. When Miss Bessie asked why Jaleesa had seemed distracted, Jaleesa was honest. She told Miss Bessie about Tina and her new planned life in Denton Heights, which included opening her own salon. The divine part came when Miss Bessie leaped up and hugged Jaleesa instead of firing her on the spot and escorting her out the door. Miss Bessie then offered to mentor Jaleesa and gave her a dozen more tips, including how to hire employees and find those few trusted ones to give keys to. She'd had many different businesses in her lifetime and knew a thing or two.

"Don't ever leave the stockroom unlocked," Miss Bessie counseled. "You'll lose your inventory in a week. Learn from my mistakes." Jaleesa took notes on her phone and promised to invite Miss Bessie up before the grand opening for any last-minute tips. The last thing Miss Bessie said was that it was bad form to pilfer stylists from another salon. Jaleesa reassured her that she had no intention of doing so and that no one at Miss Bessie's shop knew anything about her plans. They all thought she was distracted by Tina, which was a pretty accurate assessment.

Jaleesa climbed down the ladder she'd been on while painting the trim near the ceiling in the new salon. They'd been at this since eight that morning, and it was nearing noon. She stretched her back. "Oof," she said, hoping to garner sympathy from at least one of the other three women working with her. Harriet shot her a sympathetic grin but then went back to cleaning and dusting the areas that Tina and Dana were painting their way toward. Cabinets and station mirrors were being delivered and hung early next week, so the painting had to be finished by then.

"You okay, baby?" Tina said with just the right amount of sympathy.

"Nope," Jaleesa said and pouted. "I haven't had a kiss from either of you in over an hour."

"Rock, paper, scissors?" Tina said to Dana, making everyone laugh.

"You go," Dana said.

"Oh, sure. Fine. I'll take one for the team." Tina groaned and lumbered toward Jaleesa as if it was a big chore.

"Hey," Jaleesa said. "I thought you loved me."

"Shut up and kiss me," Tina demanded. And Jaleesa did. She placed her hand between Tina's shoulder blades and pressed. Tina knew what was about to happen because she giggled. Jaleesa planted her foot forward and dipped Tina into a movie star kiss. When she pulled Tina back up, both Harriet and Dana clapped.

Tina fanned herself and said, "You are such a charmer." She then said, "Release me, woman. You and Dana need to get changed now so you won't be late."

"Yes, Ma'am," Jaleesa said and stood at attention.

"Yes, Ma'am," Dana echoed.

Tina scrunched her face at Jaleesa and added, "Text us when you get lunch, and we'll meet you at Rikki's, okay?"

"Sounds like a plan." Jaleesa turned toward Dana and said, "Clean up and meet me upstairs in the apartment."

Jaleesa grabbed her bag, winked at Tina, and headed out the back door to the landing leading to the apartment's outside steps. Once inside, she washed up in the bathroom, complete with brand new GFCI outlets installed in the entire building courtesy of the handyman she'd hired.

Jaleesa changed her clothes and said, "Come," when she heard a soft knock on the outside door.

Dana closed the door behind her and flew into Jaleesa's opened arms. The kiss Jaleesa got from her sub was passionate and searching. Jaleesa knew exactly what Dana needed. When the kiss ended, because Jaleesa ended it, she gave the Nadu hand signal. Dana immediately complied and knelt at Jaleesa's feet.

"How does the plug feel?" Jaleesa asked.

"Ready to come out, Ma'am, if I'm being honest."

"Go," Jaleesa said and pointed to the bathroom. "Clean it thoroughly and wrap it in the towel you brought. You may then undress completely. I know it's a little cold, ladybug, but unfortunately for me, you'll be fully dressed soon enough."

Jaleesa folded her painting clothes and placed them inside her bag, but only after pulling out the small goody bag she'd tucked inside that morning. Jaleesa knew their playtime would be limited in the coming months, so she'd devised a treat for Dana.

"Done, Ma'am."

Jaleesa entered the bathroom and closed the door behind her, just in case. Her heart fluttered when she saw Dana in inspection pose without being asked. "Very nice." Jaleesa ran her fingers over the tightening nipples on display. She reached into the goody bag and pulled out one of Dana's new toys.

"Ma'am?" Dana said, wary of the scary-looking device dangling from Jaleesa's fingers.

"Vibrating nipple clamps. You'll learn to love them."

"Meaning I may not love them now?"

"Precisely." Jaleesa waggled an eyebrow. She clamped one clip on and waited for Dana's gasp to subside before attaching the other. She dug out Dana's clean bra from her bag and asked Dana to put it on over the clips. In hindsight, they should have put the bra on first. Oh, well. Live and learn. Once the clips were attached and the remote-controlled battery tucked into Dana's bra, Jaleesa hit the remote.

"Ah," Dana gasped and folded in on herself as the vibrations took over.

"Fun, isn't it?" Jaleesa didn't have the heart to tell the poor woman that was the lowest setting. She'd find out soon enough, though, like in the car on the way to their meeting at Phillips University. Jaleesa turned off the vibration. "Humble pose, please."

Jaleesa tossed a folded towel on the floor for Dana's knees. She threw another out for Dana to lean on. Dana kneeled down, ass in the air, arms stretched out in front. Her forehead rested on the towel. Jaleesa moved behind her and rubbed lube into and around Dana's wrinkled penny. "Relax for me, ladybug. Good, good." Jaleesa pushed the new anal plug in and then smacked one of Dana's butt cheeks. "Mmm, I wish we had time for more, but we have a college to inspect. Someone has classes starting next week."

Jaleesa hit the second remote control, and the ass vibrator kicked to life.

"Oh, Ma'am." Dana fell out of her humble pose.

Jaleesa ignored the transgression and simply said, "Get dressed." She clicked the vibrator off, pocketed both remotes, and washed her hands. She headed to the door. "Lock up when you're finished. We're leaving in three minutes." She didn't wait for a reply and headed back down to the salon.

Two hours later, the four very tired women sat in Jaleesa and Tina's favorite section of Rikki's Coffee Shop, eating their late lunch and sipping coffee. Much to Dana's embarrassment, Jaleesa would hit the plug remote at inopportune moments, causing Dana to squirm. Tina and Harriet knew all about the hidden device and simply grinned. The nipple clamps were long gone, though. Jaleesa had Dana ease them off before going in to talk with the professor at the university. Any kind of clamp left on too long could be damaging, and Jaleesa only wanted to entice and enhance Dana's experience, not destroy it.

"These are good sandwiches," Tina said. "Queen City subs?"

Jaleesa nodded.

"I'm putting them on speed dial." Tina took a bite of her sandwich and rolled her eyes heavenward.

"How was the college?" Harriet asked Dana. "You met with one of the professors?"

"Yes, he was so nice," Dana said. "And the campus is gorgeous. It's a private university, but they do community outreach, like this certificate program. I have to get a book for the course. He said a used one is good enough. And then there's a bunch of drafting tools I'll need, like rulers, markers, and stuff." Dana whimpered as Jaleesa hit the remote control.

"Oh, honey, stop," Tina reprimanded.

"Okay," Jaleesa muttered and turned off the device. "You're no fun."

"Go on, Dana," Tina said, ignoring Jaleesa's pout. "What else did the teacher say?"

"He said real landscape professionals will teach us stuff, and if I pass, I'll get an official 'Landscape Design Certificate.'"

"Suitable for framing," Jaleesa quipped.

"Oh, great," Tina gushed. "We'll save a spot of honor on the living room wall, won't we, babe?"

Jaleesa nodded but then was concerned when Dana looked distressed. Was the plug bothering her? It was time for it to come out, anyway. "What's wrong?"

"I can't do all this," Dana said, looking down at her hands. "What if they find out I'm not good enough, or they go too fast, and I can't keep up? You know, like before."

"You're just scared, my little ladybug," Jaleesa said with a sympathetic smile. "And I personally know that you *can* do this. You're right there, Dana. You're at the door. You are the only one that can open it."

Dana nodded but didn't seem convinced.

"Look," Jaleesa continued, "if they go too fast, you'll raise your hand and ask questions. Too bad if they don't like that. You're paying for this course, right?"

"Yes, Ma'am."

"First thing, ask if you can record each lecture. They have an obligation to teach you in a way that you can learn." Jaleesa turned toward Harriet. "As a teacher, would you say that's correct?"

"Yes, mostly," Harriet said. "But the student has to put in an effort, too. It's a two-way street."

"We, all of us," Jaleesa said, "will catch you if you fall."

Tina and Harriet nodded their agreement.

"How about this," Jaleesa said to Dana. She had to get it out quickly because Rikki was heading their way. "We'll order that book tonight and start reading it together the moment it comes."

"You'll help me?" Dana asked.

"Of course."

"Us, too," Tina said and then looked up at Rikki.

"Hello, everyone," Rikki said. "It's always nice to see such friendly faces here."

"How ya doing, Rikki?" Jaleesa asked. Rikki looked pale. There were circles under her eyes as if she hadn't slept well. It must be the recent passing of her grandmother. No, it was an aunt. Maybe. Jaleesa couldn't remember. Tina would know. Tina was amazing that way.

Rikki shook a stray lock of hair out of her face, but Jaleesa recognized it as a head-clearing gesture. "Hanging in there, I guess. How's the salon coming?"

Jaleesa filled her in on the details but let Tina take over regarding the new house. Tina also introduced Harriet and Dana to Rikki, making Jaleesa feel bad. She should have been the one to do that.

"So, it's a real fixer-upper, huh?" Rikki asked Tina directly.

"Yeah, so if you know of any good handy persons...." Tina left it at that.

A commotion by the front door turned all their heads.

"Well, well," Rikki said. "A carpenter just walked in the door." Rikki beckoned them over.

Jaleesa recognized the older man but not the two younger men in tow. It was Master Seamus.

The smaller boyish-looking young man ran up to Jaleesa and said, "Are you Miss Jaleesa? Madison said you and your sub come here sometimes. She should be here any second. She said you were pretty, but wow. You're all so pretty."

"Billy," Seamus scolded. "Let me greet Miss Jaleesa first." He stuck out his hand and introduced himself. "Sorry, he forgets etiquette sometimes."

"No worries," Jaleesa said. "Pleased to meet you, Seamus." She then introduced her companions. This time she remembered. Yay. See? Not such a horrible Domme, after all.

"I've seen you both at Dominique's." Seamus pointed to Jaleesa and Harriet.

"And we've seen you, too," Jaleesa said warmly. "We're making Denton Heights our home now." She gave him a quick recap of their new life plans.

"Are you guys going to the Masquerade Ball next weekend?" Billy asked breathlessly. "Madison said you were." Without waiting for an answer, he said, "Papa, c'mon, you said I could get a brownie. Miss Lydia's putting out a fresh pile. Look!" He pulled on Seamus's hand. Jaleesa's suspicions were confirmed. Billy was a *little*.

"Duty calls," Seamus said. He turned to his other sub. "DeShawn, stay here with Miss Jaleesa until I get back."

"Yes, Sir," DeShawn said and stood still, his gaze down.

Rikki stood up, "I'd best get back." She blew out a sigh and laughed. "Brittany's working on her frothing techniques, and it just may be the death of me." She laughed again. "I'll come back over when Shasti and Madison get here."

"Sounds good." Jaleesa turned to Dana and said quietly, "There's the restroom. I'll need you to undo things. Understand?"

"Oh, yes, Ma'am," Dana said in relief. "Thank you, Ma'am." She picked up her bag and hustled away.

Everyone except DeShawn laughed, but Jaleesa detected a slight smirk on his face. He probably understood what was happening. Jaleesa resisted the temptation to hit the remote control as Dana made her way to the restroom.

Jaleesa patted the newly vacated seat. "Would you like to sit, DeShawn?"

"Oh, no, Ma'am. Thank you."

"It wasn't really a question. Please sit."

He did as asked but kept his eyes down. "Thank you, Ma'am."

"You can look up, young man." She'd called him 'young man' even though she judged him to be about Tina's age, early thirties—maybe late twenties.

"Thank you, Ma'am." He looked up at Jaleesa. He had the softest baby brown eyes she had ever seen on a brother. His mustache and beard were carved short and meticulously sculpted. His short fro was also meticulously groomed. Jaleesa wondered if his Dom required this groomed look or if it was his own personal choice.

"Miss Rikki said one of you three was a carpenter."

"Yes, Ma'am," Deshawn said. "I'm a carpenter. I work for Dom Silas at Silas Carpentry and Remodeling."

"Ahh," Jaleesa said. "So, you know your way around hammers?"

"Yes, Ma'am."

"Jigsaws, circular saws, routers, and sanders?"

"Yes, Ma'am," Deshawn said. "I use them on the regular."

"Miter boxes? Biscuit joiners? Framing squares?"

"Yes, yes, and yes."

"Ahh, but how about a two-person Tuttle tooth saw?" She grinned and waited.

Ahh, perfect. That did it. Deshawn broke into a smile and chuckled. "No, Ma'am, but Dom Silas has a two-person crosscut hanging in the shop for decoration."

"You did well, Deshawn." Jaleesa sat back and ate her last bite of sandwich. "I have a dining room with no door that I want to convert to a bedroom. Could you put a door in there?"

"Yes, Ma'am. Of course," Deshawn said. "I'd build sturdy framing and then put in any door you like."

"Hired," Jaleesa said. "We'll talk details later. We haven't even closed on the house yet."

"Thank you, Ma'am. And may I ask you something?"

"Of course. No need to ask if you can ask."

He exhaled an embarrassed laugh and looked down. "Are all these women your submissives?"

"Yes, they are. Does that surprise you?" Jaleesa wondered if her open affection for Tina and Dana confused people.

"No, Ma'am. Master Seamus has four of us."

"Ahh, yes. I think I knew that." Jaleesa recalled both Harriet and Shasti saying something about Seamus's many subs.

"Ma'am, it's just that I've never seen a sister in your role."

"Well now you have."

Deshawn's grin spread wide on his face. He looked at the floor by her feet, and Jaleesa wondered why. Did he want to kneel at her feet?

"Ma'am, do your subs pick on each other? Do you have to intervene and tell one of them to buck up and be a man?"

Jaleesa bit her lip at the part about being a man. Something was clearly bothering Deshawn, but it wasn't her place to butt into another Dominant's business. Unless there was abuse. She needed to tread carefully.

Tina had been in a deep conversation with Harriet about window coverings for the salon but reached over to squeeze Jaleesa's hand. She must have overheard the conversation. "Babe, we're going to get some brownies. Want one?" Was this Tina's subtle way of giving them privacy?

"No thanks," Jaleesa said. "Deshawn?"

"Oh, no, thank you, Ma'ams."

Jaleesa started to dig out her wallet, but Tina put her hand up, indicating that she had it. Jaleesa leaned toward Tina and got what she wanted and more. Tina kissed her fully on the lips and stroked her cheek lovingly. Harriet stood up and followed Tina to the front counter.

Dana came back with her bag tightly shut. Her expression was much more relaxed. Jaleesa indicated that she wanted Dana to sit on the floor at her feet. Dana did so and rested her head on Jaleesa's thigh. Jaleesa petted Dana's hair and smiled at her beautifully behaved submissive.

"No, my subs don't pick on each other," Jaleesa said, finally answering Deshawn's question. "We're in a household of mutual respect where the roles are clear. Granted, we haven't all lived together yet, but we will soon.

341

Does your Sir know that they pick on you?"

"Yes, Ma'am."

Ahh, she had guessed correctly. "And do you tell him all the details?"

"No, Ma'am. He's busy. He has Billy now, and a lot of his attention goes into being Billy's Daddy Dom."

"I see," Jaleesa said. "I would like you to tell your Sir everything that happens. But do so in calm moments when you've settled down, and the bully or bullies are not in earshot."

Deshawn looked down. "Yes, Ma'am."

"I need you to empower yourself, Deshawn. And, with your permission, I'll feel out Mr. Seamus about the matter."

A panicked look took over DeShawn's face.

"I'll tread carefully," Jaleesa said. "Mr. Seamus seems like a reasonable and caring Dom."

"He is, Ma'am," Deshawn said. "He chose me. I don't want to upset the apple cart."

"It's already been upset, hasn't it?"

He nodded.

"Words, please."

"Yes, Ma'am. Thank you for helping me and talking to Sir. And thank you for listening."

Jaleesa reached over and cupped his bearded chin. "You'll be okay," she said and was surprised that her tenderness brought tears to his eyes. He obviously hadn't had enough of that lately. She released him and let him look away to get his emotions under control.

She didn't have a chance to think about how to approach the subject with Seamus because the freight train that was Madison was barreling their way. Madison's and Shasti's faces lit up when they saw Jaleesa, making her heart leap. Yes, moving to Denton Heights was definitely the right move.

Tina had been right. Let go and let God.

Chapter 24

Tina

“**I** have things to say,” Tina announced to Jaleesa from the passenger seat of the parked pickup. Harriet and Dana had already gone in. It was mid-June, and they were at the Friendship Church for what was most likely their last meeting there. They had closed on and subsequently moved into the new house up in Denton Heights two weeks before and were settling into their new lives together. Harriet, Dana, and Jaleesa had moved all their things to the new house, but Tina was taking her time. She knew she was doing a slow band-aid pull when it came to leaving her parents' home, but she couldn't help it.

“Do you now?” Jaleesa said from the driver's seat. She turned toward Tina and reached for her hand.

“I know this is going to be hard for you,” Tina said. “I know from experience. But we're all here to support you.”

Jaleesa took a big breath and let it out slowly as if she knew not to pretend to be her usual tough and strong self in front of Tina. The soft opening of the salon would be in a couple of weeks, and Jaleesa was nervous, but it was a good nervous, unlike the nerves she had at the moment.

“Remember that the past is in the past,” Tina continued. “And you're no longer that person. We're making a great new life for ourselves. At the Masquerade Ball over Memorial Day weekend, it felt like that group of people could become lifelong friends. They understood our family and didn't bat an eye. No, it was more like they embraced us.”

"I felt the love, too," Jaleesa said. "And, unfortunately for Harriet, they wouldn't let submissives help out or do any service."

"Oh, I know," Tina said and grimaced. "She likes to keep busy in the background any chance she gets."

"Sometimes you have to step out of your comfort zone."

"She had all of us there to help her cope, though. Harriet adores you, Jaleesa."

"It's mutual. Sometimes you create your own family, don't you?"

"Mm hmm," Tina said. "And you know who else adores you? Madison. I'm happy Miss Shasti seems okay with that. It still feels weird to call them Miss, you know? Miss Shasti, Miss Rikki, Miss Rowena. When in Rome, I guess."

"It's a sign of respect."

"I liked it when you let Madison and Billy pull you onto the dance floor. You totally validated them."

"*Littles* are people, too," Jaleesa said. "They're people with ultra-big feelings. But I recall a certain Madison holding someone else's hand at that party."

Tina blushed. She hadn't been sure what to do when Madison reached for her hand during Rikki's touching speech memorializing her Aunt Matilda. It just seemed natural. "I don't know how you're so good at figuring out what people need, baby. You always seem to find a way to help."

"I'm not always right, but I like to think I have good instincts." Jaleesa cleared her throat and said, "Did Harriet tell you? She thinks she found us a new home group up in Denton Heights for meetings. They don't have mixed meetings, but they have some open ones, so we can continue supporting each other."

"That's so important," Tina said. "All the pieces are falling into place, aren't they, babe?"

"They are. Our respective parents find it strange that we're four women living in the same house, but they seem to understand that we're looking out for each other."

"I love our new house," Tina gushed. "My commute isn't too bad, either. A straight shot down 127 to I-75. I took 127 all the way the other day because the interstate was backed up."

"You did? Leaving fifteen minutes earlier has helped, right?"

"Yes. That was such a good suggestion." Tina took a deep breath and sighed. "I'm nervous."

"About what, honey?" Jaleesa kissed the back of the hand she was holding. "You're a great bank manager. And your evaluation isn't for another three months. You've got this."

"Don't remind me," Tina said. "No, I meant, I'm nervous for—" She pointed over her shoulder toward the church.

"You're nervous for me," Jaleesa said with a chuckle. "That makes two of us. Speaking of which, we should go in. Let me acclimate."

"Good idea. I think I was stalling for you."

Jaleesa smiled. "And I love you for it, Tina Jenkins. You have the key that fits my lock."

"Aww, babe. That's so sweet. Same goes for you." Tina leaned in for a kiss and got one. She murmured, "I love you, Jaleesa Whitmore."

"I love you back."

They walked into the church basement hand in hand. Kadesha was standing with Dana. She had an easy smile on her face. Good. Hopefully, that meant she was dealing well with Dana's unorthodox relationship with Jaleesa and Tina. It was good to see the two friends palling around.

Jaleesa walked up behind Dana and gave her a quick hug from behind. Tina's parents were due any minute, and Tina wasn't quite ready to explain her open relationship to them yet, if ever. Thank goodness both Dana and Jaleesa understood her apprehension and curtailed their PDA.

Jaleesa turned to Kadesha and said, "Guess who got an A+ on her capstone landscape design?"

"No way," Kadesha screeched and pulled Dana into a bouncing hug. "See? I told you to go for it."

"Now she just has to implement the design before the housewarming party in July," Jaleesa said.

Dana blanched. "I don't think I can finish it by then."

"We'll work together as a family to help," Tina said.

Harriet stroked Dana's arm as she nodded her agreement.

"Right," Jaleesa agreed. "And we'll only focus on what you deem most important. You're the one in charge. And Kadesha will help, I'm sure."

"Great," Kadesha said, rolling her eyes. "Do I have to get my hands dirty?"

The group laughed, and then Jaleesa pressed a quick kiss to Tina's forehead before excusing herself to greet Pastor Paul and Fran at the front of the room. Tina's nerves spiked. She was more nervous about Jaleesa's speech than she had been about her own. Adding to the nerves was that this would probably be their last meeting at the Friendship Church. It was bittersweet for Tina because this NA meeting had been her first after rehab. They'd seen her through her methadone days when she thought she wouldn't make it. They'd helped her get back on the path after her stupid relapse. Tina understood how important NA and AA communities were to her new little family. Living with Dana's youthful energy was uplifting. Harriet's steadfast presence was grounding. And then there was Jaleesa. She was Tina's rock.

Jaleesa put her arm around Tina's waist wordlessly as they moved to take their seats. Tina thought about her life before Jaleesa. She'd lived in cages of her own making. The cage of her parents' house. The cage of her pig trails to and from work. The almost literal cage of her bedroom and bed. And now, up there in Denton Heights, she had a different kind of cage—Jaleesa's. In Jaleesa's cage, Tina didn't feel confined. She felt safe. Knowing she had Jaleesa in her life, as well as Harriet, Dana, and her parents, Tina felt strong. *Strong* was a good word, but there had to be a better one. Empowered. Yes, that was the better word.

They sat in front of the podium in the same two seats they'd sat in the day Tina met Jaleesa. Tina felt loved, cared for, nurtured, and just plain nourished by the life she and Jaleesa were creating with Harriet and Dana. DeShawn had successfully put a solid wood door on Harriet's first-floor room, and she was all set up in there with an armoire and dresser for her clothes and an easel near the side window. Dana's room was so cute with her matching furniture and was the very first room they had painted. Tina wanted to make sure Dana was comfortable immediately in their unconventional setup. Tina and Jaleesa's primary bedroom was far from finished, though. They had yet to paint and were sleeping on a mattress on the floor. Their king-sized canopy bed was on order and would be delivered in the next three weeks or so.

"Your folks are here," Jaleesa said.

Tina stood up. "Mom, Dad," she called to them. They hustled to the front row and gave hugs all around.

"You'll do great, J-Dub," Tina's father encouraged Jaleesa.

"Thank you," Jaleesa said succinctly.

Tina's mother stood with an arm around Tina's shoulders. Tina tensed. Was her mother going to offer encouragement or what? *C'mon, Mom,* Tina willed.

Tina's mother released Tina and reached for both of Jaleesa's hands. Jaleesa looked a little startled but hid it quickly.

"Jaleesa," Tina's mother said, "you have been so strong and supportive of our baby." She glanced at Tina's father, who nodded in agreement. "Tina has never been happier since you came into her life. *Our* lives," she amended. "We've always wanted the best for her; by all accounts, she has that with you."

Tina's eyes flooded with tears. She blinked them away and was surprised to see her father getting emotional as well.

"We didn't get off to the best start," Tina's mother continued, "but we've examined our own ignorance and realized we hadn't given you a fair chance. I apologize for that. We'd been protecting Tina for so long that it would have been tough for anyone to break through the barrier we'd put up. Thank you for being you and giving us the time to come to our senses.

Thank you for giving Tina a new start in life."

Jaleesa wiped at her eyes, clearly affected by the apology. "Thank you. I appreciate your honesty."

Tina's mother sniffed back her tears and then put both arms out. Jaleesa responded in kind, and their hug solidified Tina's love for all things good in the world.

Tina's father wiped at his eyes and then grabbed the tissue box from the front table. Tina laughed when he passed it around. Oh, yes, they all needed one. Tina grabbed an extra because she knew she might not be able to hold it together during Jaleesa's speech.

"Thank you," Jaleesa said to Tina's parents again, and Tina didn't think it was only for the tissue. Jaleesa took a cleansing breath and lightened the mood by asking Tina's parents, "How go the Hawaii plans?"

"We're all set to cruise the Hawaiian Islands the weekend after your housewarming party next month," Tina's father answered.

"We'll drive you to the airport," Jaleesa offered.

"Aww," Tina said. "And look after the house."

The conversation was interrupted as Pastor Paul tapped on the podium to get the mixed AA and NA speaker meeting started. As she settled in, Tina realized that her parents hadn't taken a vacation since Tina's addiction started. That had been going on for thirteen years at this point. And that made her sad. They had all been hanging on by a thin thread for so long, hadn't they? Tina felt guilty as she realized her parents had also been in a cage—the one created by Tina.

Pastor Paul asked the crowd to join him in the Serenity Prayer, and afterward, Tina must have sighed or something because Jaleesa reached over, lifted her chin, and whispered, "I'll be okay."

Tina let Jaleesa think the sigh was simply nerves for her. The truth was that meeting Jaleesa had unlocked Tina's cage, which in turn unlocked her parents' cage. A smile crept up her face at that thought. This made Jaleesa smile. Jaleesa bopped Tina's nose and then gave her attention to Pastor Paul, who was introducing her as their June speaker.

As Jaleesa made her way to the podium, Tina couldn't help picturing Jaleesa at the grill flipping burgers in the backyard of their new home. It hadn't actually happened yet since they'd only been in the new house for a couple of weeks, but it felt like home. Tina made a mental note to buy Jaleesa a smart-looking yet functional barbecue apron befitting her status as head of household.

Speaking of things for Jaleesa to wear, Jaleesa looked resplendent in her casual black suit with its flattering nipped-in waist. Several shirts into dressing Jaleesa that afternoon, Tina finally settled on the cream-colored button-down with the cutaway collar. They'd tried a belt around the suit jacket, but Tina didn't like it, so off it went. Jaleesa had been so patient as Tina dressed her. Tina knew she could be bossy, but everyone in the household seemed to understand that this was Tina's love language. She was one part in charge and in everyone's business but also one part taken care of by the others. She truly was a switch, like Jaleesa said.

Tina's heart melted when Jaleesa looked at her from the podium before speaking. Tina gave her a nod of encouragement. *You got this, baby,* she sent telepathically.

Jaleesa cleared her throat and began. "Evening, everybody. My name is Jaleesa, and I'm an alcoholic."

"Hi, Jaleesa," the group, including Tina's parents, said back. They really were there to support Jaleesa.

"I am one year, five months, and fifteen days sober." The expected applause broke out in the room, bolstered by Dana and Kadesha hooting from their seats in the front row, causing a smattering of laughter.

Jaleesa smiled at them, effectively thanking them for their support. "When I asked Pastor Paul how to structure this speech, he said I had to get sober by seven o'clock." She pointed to the clock. More laughter followed. "I was a reluctant member of AA in the beginning. I didn't come here of my own will. A judge in a court ordered it."

Tina saw some heads nodding in understanding.

"I spent a lot of my time in those early days seething at the judge, resenting his very existence. But as you can see, I got beyond that. But let me back this story up to a point before that. I've had a lot of success early on in my life. The eldest of four kids in my family, I was expected to set the example. And I did. I got good grades, and I excelled at sports. One of those sports got me a near full ride to college, where I continued to excel."

She lifted her nose toward the ceiling and said in a self-deprecating manner, "I was a star. I set scoring records. I took my team to a championship win in my senior year. I was interviewed by newspapers and featured in women's sports magazines. Drinking back then had been celebratory. Casual. Managed." She looked back down. "Or so I thought." There were more head nods.

"But then I graduated, and all that attention to my greatness waned. I was invited back to alumni games and events for a few years. I was even asked to speak at one of the trustee luncheons. About four years after I graduated, I went to a home game. My old coach gave me a nice greeting, but none of the new assistant coaches had a clue who I was. Didn't matter, right? I was as big as life in that gym at that school. My coach asked me to stick around after the game so that I could say a few words to the team."

Jaleesa scoffed at herself. "It was a wonder that my head even fit through the door as I walked in after their game. My ego had become so inflated over the years that I wasn't prepared for what happened next." She cleared her throat, obviously choked up. "Coach introduced me to the team, and I greeted them, ready to instill wisdom from on high. And do you know what happened next? The hotshot standout of the team said, 'Who are you again?' It paralyzed me. How could she not know who I was? How could she not know of my greatness? Did she not sense that she was in the company of Blackwell College royalty? The other players on the team shrugged as if to say they didn't know who I was either. I was so thrown that I simply said, 'Great game, you guys. Good luck in the next one.' I turned to my coach, told him I'd be in touch, and hightailed it out of there."

Tina's heart ached for Jaleesa. She must have really been hurting.

"I never called my coach. I never went back to another game. Stupid, I know, but I haven't been back since that moment. The reality check I was thrown that day was my higher power's first attempt to get my attention. It did, but I got the wrong message. I needed the spotlight. I needed to be the sought-after friend, the life of the party, as we say. And I was. The drinking started in earnest. I never turned down an invite to go out. There was never a lack of camaraderie down at my twelve favorite watering holes around town. I got along with everyone, even at the biker bar on the other side of town. Drinking was our common denominator. I never realized until I got sober that I was trying to buy friends back then. 'Hey, drink with me,' I'd say, but what I was really saying was, 'Be my friend.'"

Tina noticed Dana and Kadesha nodding their understanding. She knew a lot about Dana's story and how she'd started drinking in middle school to fit in with the cool crowd, but she knew nothing about Kadesha's. And that was okay. It was her story to tell or not to tell, and although Tina was curious, it was none of her business.

"This went on for years," Jaleesa continued. "After a while, I developed a loyal group of drinking buddies. Some turned into girlfriends. But drinking and partying do not make for stable relationships. I somehow managed to keep a job. But weekend drinking started on Thursdays, quickly turning into Wednesdays, becoming a drink every evening after work.

"And then came that fateful night. My then-girlfriend and I were pulled over. I failed that fun little test on the side of the road. I spent seven days in a jail while they decided my fate. Rehab, ignition breathalyzer, and probation were my sentences. I was required to maintain sobriety. AA meetings like this one were required. I had to get paperwork signed by the leader every week.

"At my very first meeting, they gave me a newbie white chip. You know, the one that means you're headed down that long road toward recovery?" Jaleesa reached into her pocket and held it up. "At the time, I thought it was the stupidest piece of cheap white plastic. On one side is the

AA symbol, and on the other, that quote from Hamlet, 'To thine own self be true.' I was going to toss it in the bushes as soon as I got out of that meeting." Jaleesa paused for effect. She held up the chip again. "But I didn't. I told myself I'd throw it out when I got back to the apartment. Instead, I tossed the stupid thing in the top drawer of my dresser and forgot about it.

"Since I was required to attend the meetings, I'd settle into one of these uncomfortable fold-up chairs and obstinately and actively *not* listen. I was just biding my time until I could get the paper signed. If anything, my arrogance had me judging those wackos up there at the podium, telling of a time when they were out of control and doing stupid things." Jaleesa put her hands up to frame her face as if saying, 'Ta-da, you're looking at one of those wackos now.' A knowing chuckle murmured through the crowd.

"I didn't listen to their suggestions or their recommendations. I didn't absorb any of their wisdom. Nope. I wasn't like those people. I was going to do my time, pass their stupid sobriety tests, and then go back to living my best life, drinking and partying. How dare they take away my life's blood. I was the life of the party, damn it." Jaleesa rolled her eyes at her own misguided thinking.

"I finished my sentence. The judge cleared me, and I was free to go back to ruining my life. But I didn't. I truly think it was my higher power, but something made me rethink my life goals. I decided I'd go back to drinking a week from then. I was good for now. That week came and went, and I said the same thing. I turned down parties. I turned down drinks thrust at me during weddings. It was hard, but I was kind of arrogantly challenging myself. And you know what happened? I started feeling better. I was alert in the mornings. The other stylists and some customers pointed out how chipper and happy I seemed. I liked this feedback. I thought my then-girlfriend did, too."

Jaleesa cleared her throat. "Apparently, she did not. I came home from a long day at the salon only to find her stuff gone and a Dear Jane letter on the table."

There were a few polite groans from the crowd. Tina included.

Jaleesa acknowledged the sympathy. "Now, you would think," she said carefully, "that this would be an event significant enough to send me running out for a few of my former favorite beverages. It didn't. I dug in my heels even more. And it wasn't because I was fiercely guarding my sobriety. No, it was because I was furious that she would leave me. I was indignant and not going to let her have the upper hand. No way. If she couldn't handle a sober me, then buh-bye. If she needed the constant partying and fast life associated with that, fine. Go for it, but she'd be doing it without me.

"Yes, I was angry. Furious. This fueled another week of sobriety. And then another. Until I finally got fed up with it. I was tired. I wasn't proving anything to anyone. My ex was long gone. She wasn't coming back. My apartment was lonely. I'd spent Christmas day by myself. I went out, fully intending to stop at one of my favorite watering holes. I pictured the reception I'd get from my old drinking buddies when I walked in. But then I remembered the basketball team. They didn't know me. Would the same thing happen at the bar? Instead, I headed to a social club that didn't serve alcohol. But here's the thing. I fully intended to go to that bar afterward. I was going to drive home loaded. Already had it planned and everything.

"But remember that higher power thing? The one mentioned in the steps we're supposed to be working on? Well, that higher power put someone in my path that night. Someone who I now call a dear friend." Jaleesa looked over at Harriet. "That then-stranger needed my help. After I helped her, out of the blue, she said, 'Instead of a drink, maybe you need a meeting.' I was floored and confused. Did she know me? Turned out she had witnessed a stretch of my partying days and remembered me. Somehow, she figured out I was sober and took a pretty gutsy chance saying that to me." Jaleesa smiled at Harriet, patted her chest twice, and said, "It was a calculated risk, my friend, but you saved my life."

Harriet patted her own heart in response. Tina reached for a tissue from the box her father still held.

"The very next evening," Jaleesa said, "I went to that meeting she suggested. And at that meeting, I met a woman I now call my girlfriend." The look Jaleesa threw Tina made it clear to everyone how smitten she was. "She is amazing. She's the love of my life. God put her in my path. God put both of these women in my path who led me to more and more supportive and kind friends." Jaleesa smiled at Dana, Kadesha, and then at Tina's parents.

"Maintaining abstinence is hard. Willpower and determination alone won't work. You have to work the steps. You have to work with other people. Get. A. Sponsor. I am lucky to have an amazing one. She's taking me through the Big Book again. But for me, it's like going through it for the very first time." She scoffed at herself.

Tina loved this honest and self-deprecating side of Jaleesa. She wanted to rush up, pull Jaleesa into her arms, hug the stuffing right out of her, put it back in, and do it again.

"Steps eight and nine talk about reaching out to people you've harmed. So, I reached out to that ex-girlfriend recently."

Tina sat up straight. She didn't know this.

"Honestly, I didn't expect her to take my call. Or if she did take my call, I figured she'd just blow me off or tell me how boring I'd gotten when the partying stopped. Something like that. She'd make an excuse and hang up. But she didn't do any of those things. Do you know what she told me? She told me she left because she knew I was on the brink of changing my life for the better and that she would only hinder that. She snuck away because she knew I would try to get her to stay. Which is probably true," Jaleesa admitted. "She said she had to be tough and cold like that, so I could move on with my sobriety and find a better life than the one we'd made together. Although, honestly, I wished she'd found a better way to give me that life lesson. Then again, maybe the lesson had to be learned this way." Jaleesa looked up and pointed both index fingers up to God.

"Go to meetings," Jaleesa continued. "They're essential. Even to this day, a random thought will creep in about making a cocktail when I get home from work."

Tina inhaled sharply, hoping her parents hadn't heard it. She didn't know Jaleesa struggled like that. She seemed so put together all the time. Obviously, more checking in was needed. Living together was definitely going to make this much easier.

"Addiction is sneaky and underhanded," Jaleesa said. "Alcohol does not respect you. You could be going along, doing fine. Abstaining. And then addiction tries to tell you that you can drink like a normal person. 'C'mon,' it says, 'just have one drink after work. You're good. You don't have to get word-slurring, blackout drunk—just have one. Remember the good old days when you used to do that? You can do it again.'" Jaleesa scoffed and pounded the podium with each of her next three words. "No. You. Can't." She paused and added, "No, *I* can't. I won't delude myself into thinking now that I'm free from alcohol, I can take a drink without consequences. I cannot."

Jaleesa took a moment to regroup and then said, "Did I do that sweeping inventory of myself in step four? Did I understand how my self-centeredness, anger, and pride were handicapping me? Not at first, because I didn't take any of it seriously. It wasn't my fault I was in this stupid predicament. I blamed the judge, the cop, and I even blamed my ex for wanting to go to that stupid party in the first place. Never did that finger point where it should have." She shook her head and rolled her eyes at her own ridiculousness. "But bit by bit, I started listening to my higher power. It was pointing me toward the right people. I finally began that hard look at myself. And that, I'm afraid, is not something you ever finish doing. I had to be honest with myself because honesty is the catalyst for change. I had to surrender; give up my self-centered approach. The moment I became other-centered and started to genuinely connect to people was when it happened.

"This program works." Jaleesa did her 'Ta-da' pose again. She caught Tina's smile and nodded. "When you join AA, NA, or any other twelve-step program, you have instant family. You have people who understand what you're going through. They understand *you*. They help you get to a place where you can genuinely be proud of yourself again. Recovery is amazing. It's about looking inward, checking in with yourself, and staying grounded. For me, staying humble might be the better sentiment.

"One more thing, and then I'll wrap up. A while back, my girlfriend handed me a fifty-dollar bill." Jaleesa reached into her pocket and held up the bill. "She gave it to me so I wouldn't protest her removing the unhealthy foods from my kitchen that she thought might be making me sick." Jaleesa looked at Tina and said, "You didn't know that I kept this, did you?"

Tina shook her head, knowing her expression was one of amused confusion.

"Turns out she was right, and I feel so much better now. Anyway, I told another stylist the story about the fifty-dollar bill, and she went bananas. She told me that in numerology, fifty means something in your life is complete, and something new is beginning. She said it was clearly time for some aspect of my life to start fresh, and I needed to go for what I wanted."

Tina's jaw dropped open. Whoa. That freezer-cleaning incident happened right before Jaleesa came in to apply for the business loan.

"I chose to think of it as my higher power trying to get my attention. My life has certainly changed. My girlfriend is fond of saying, 'Let go, and let God.' She's right. When it seems scary to jump, that's when you jump. She showed me that. I would be stuck in the same place my whole life if I didn't listen to her advice. My biggest blessings are my recovery and the people I've met throughout my journey."

Pastor Paul made a comment about the time, and Jaleesa nodded. "I'll wrap up with this. Recovery starts with surrender. It starts with admitting there is a problem. Seeking help is the essential next step. Go to meetings, in-person or online. Find ways to engage with the people there. Come early for fellowship. Stay late. Volunteer to put the coffee out." She winked at Tina. "My focus has changed from me, me, me, everyone look at me, to one where I look at the people around me and figure out how to help them."

Jaleesa took a breath and said, "Keep coming back. It works—" She held her hands up to the crowd who finished the line, "—if you work it."

She leaned both elbows on the podium, quickly looked over all the rows, and quietly said, "So work it, 'cause you're worth it." She stood back up and said, "Thank you, everybody."

Tina leaped to her feet and clapped the loudest of everyone. When Jaleesa came within arms' reach, Tina scooped her up in a hug and said, "You did so well, baby. I love you so much."

Jaleesa let herself be hugged and then said quietly, "I love you back."

After the meeting, they stayed for a bit of fellowship. Well, they kind of had no choice. Everyone and her sister seemed to want to talk to Jaleesa about her speech. That did Tina's heart good, especially when she noticed her parents hovering nearby as if letting everyone know they knew the celebrity in their midst.

"That's good," Harriet said, nodding her head toward Tina's fawning parents. "They've come a long way."

"I know, right?" Tina said and stifled a yawn. It had been a long day, and they still had to drive home.

"She's on a good road," Harriet added.

Dana sidled up next to them. "I think we all are."

Tina linked arms with Harriet on one side and Dana on the other. "New beginnings, right? For all of us."

They all nodded their agreement.

Jaleesa blew out a sigh and widened her eyes at the sight of her family standing in front of her. "Time to go?" She widened her eyes even more as if to say there was only one correct answer.

"Yes," Tina said, except for the fact that there was one more thing.

Harriet stepped forward and handed Jaleesa a small white box with a red ribbon wrapped around it.

"What's this?" Jaleesa said and opened the box. Tina held her breath as Jaleesa pulled out the necklace. It was a thin gold chain with four charms hanging off it—T, H, and D.

Harriet's voice was shaky when she said, "One letter to represent each of us, Ma'am. We wanted to…" She closed her lips tight as emotion took over.

Dana picked up the slack. "We wanted to let you know that we're yours. That we're loyal to you and to each other." Her look took in Harriet and Tina.

Jaleesa looked toward the ceiling as she blinked back tears. Her smile took in each one of her subs in turn. "Thank you for putting your faith in me. You bolster me more than you could ever know. I'm the luckiest one here. You guys just collared me, didn't you?"

All three women nodded, and Jaleesa wrapped her long arms around them and squeezed until Dana protested that she couldn't breathe.

"Love hurts, ladybug," Jaleesa kidded but let them go. She handed the necklace to Tina and squatted so Tina could reach. Once the necklace was around her neck, Jaleesa touched each letter in turn. "Let's go home, family."

After a somewhat lengthy goodbye to Tina's parents, they piled into Jaleesa's pickup to go home. Once home, Tina and Jaleesa said quick goodnights to their equally weary housemates and headed to their new isolated bedroom.

"A bath for you," Tina proclaimed as soon as Jaleesa closed the bedroom door. She went into the bathroom to run the water.

"I'm too tired, babe," Jaleesa said as she undressed.

"Mm hmm," Tina said, having none of it. "Like I've told you many times, Jaleesa Whitmore, you are not invisible to me." She hoped Jaleesa understood the reference to the book she'd loaned Tina. "I need to give you aftercare. You're going to drop. I can see it."

Jaleesa narrowed her eyes as if wondering whether Tina truly had this power.

"You were quiet on the drive home," Tina explained. "You've been sighing since we got home where our wonderful bedroom oasis with jacuzzi tub and simulated candles await." She pointed to the battery-operated flickering candles she'd placed around the overlarge tub before they'd left. "So, if you don't mind unzipping my blouse, I will be joining you."

"Mmm," Jaleesa said with just the right amount of perk in her voice. She reached for the zipper and slid it down.

Tina smiled at Jaleesa as she slipped off her clothes.

Once they were soaking in the bath, Tina nestled against Jaleesa's silky, warm body. Jaleesa said, "Thank you for taking care of me."

"Jaleesa," Tina said, "I want you to know that I take you for who you are and who you are becoming. I've got your back, and I know you have mine. I think I understand this whole BDSM power exchange thing. We agree that we won't be invisible or indifferent to each other. You made a promise to look after me and all of us. And, in turn, we'll look after you and each other. It's a deliberate and spoken agreement."

"You're very wise, Tina."

"Thank you, baby. I mean, no one in this house is trying to force us into roles we're uncomfortable with. In fact, it's just the opposite. Harriet likes to please and to help out. She has the perfect environment for that now and seems really happy."

"That painting she made of the two of us is incredible."

"I know," Tina said. "She's so talented. And as soon as we paint the living room optic orange, it's going up in a place of honor."

"Color as yet to be determined," Jaleesa said with a chuckle.

"Yes, Ma'am," Tina said enthusiastically. "And we need Dana's certificate framed and mounted, too."

Jaleesa kissed Tina on the forehead and said, "You sensed my mood and reached out. Maybe I can accept that kind of help now. Before? I would have waved you off."

"You tried to."

"Sorry. I'm a work in progress, I guess." Jaleesa sunk lower in the water, causing a slight tidal wave. "I would have stoically maintained that I didn't need anyone's help. That I'm the one who helps others."

"And you still do, baby," Tina said.

Jaleesa mimed reaching into a shirt pocket and pulled out an imaginary key. She kissed the key and put it back in her pocket. Tina did the same.

Tina was about to make a grand statement about the symbolic meaning of locks, keys, and cages, but Jaleesa's soft lips on hers tore the words away.

~~~ The End ~~~

Newsletter Signup

Sign up for Danielle Grainger's newsletter to keep up with new releases. She also likes to recommend books to read (other than her own, of course).

Find the sign-up on Danielle's website: www.daniellegrainger.com

Reviews

Reviews help get my books into the hands of readers who enjoy books like this one. It's often difficult for readers of certain, err, tastes to find books they enjoy. Would you consider writing a review? Get the word out. Thank you for at least thinking about it.

Danielle Grainger

Addiction Resources
Alcoholics Anonymous Website:
aa.org

From the A.A. website: "Have a problem with alcohol? There is a solution. A.A. has a simple program that works. It's based on one alcoholic helping another.

Narcotics Anonymous Website:
na.org

From the N.A. website: "Our vision is that … Every addict in the world has the chance to experience our message in his or her own language and culture and find the opportunity for a new way of life."

Al-Anon Website:
al-anon.org

From the Al-Anon website: "Al-Anon is a mutual support program for people whose lives have been affected by someone else's drinking. By sharing common experiences and applying the Al-Anon principles, families and friends of alcoholics can bring positive changes to their individual situations, whether or not the alcoholic admits the existence of a drinking problem or seeks help.

Nar-Anon Website:
www.nar-anon.org

From the Nar-Anon Website: "The Nar-Anon Family Group is primarily for those who know or have known a feeling of desperation concerning the addiction problem of someone very near to you."

Asexuality Resource

The Asexual Visibility & Education Network
www.asexuality.org

From the AVEN website: "Welcome to the Asexual Visibility and Education Network. AVEN hosts the world's largest online asexual community as well as a large archive of resources on asexuality. AVEN strives to create open, honest discussion about asexuality among sexual and asexual people alike. Unlike celibacy, which is a choice to abstain from sexual activity, asexuality is an intrinsic part of who we are, just like other sexual orientations. Asexual people have the same emotional needs as everybody else and are just as capable of forming intimate relationships."

About the Author
Danielle Grainger

Dani is an instructor who currently resides in the southeastern USA with several pampered fur babies. She has always been an avid reader and ventured into writing after reading several novels she felt didn't accurately represent the BDSM lifestyle. With so many rampant misconceptions, she took a chance and crafted admittedly idealized versions of possible experiences. Dani hopes not only to entertain her readers but to enlighten and educate them as well.

Dani's Website:
www.daniellegrainger.com

Dani's Facebook:
facebook.com/danielle.grainger.7777

Dani's Instagram:
DaniGrainger84

Dani's Pinterest:
danigrainger84

Dani's Goodreads Page:
www.goodreads.com/author/show/19699760.Danielle_Grainger

Books by Danielle Grainger
THE DENTON HEIGHTS SERIES

The Denton Heights Series is the series that comes BEFORE the Bernadette Series. This group of books tells the stories of the beloved characters who populate the Bernadette Series world and live the BDSM lifestyle. We find out more of the origin stories of Madison and Shasti, Jaleesa and Tina, Marta and Shanice, Victoria (AKA Daddy Vic), and Lydia. The Denton Heights Series is basically the "Prequel Series" to the Bernadette Series.

Under Her Wing (Denton Heights Book 1)
(The Shasti and Madison Story)
A lesbian age-gap erotic romance with light BDSM aspects.

2023 GOLDIE FINALIST

Madison Kim finds herself on a bus headed to Denton Heights, Ohio, a suburb of Cincinnati. Her mother sent her there without notice to care for an elderly Korean woman Madison had never met. Madison is twenty-two-and-three-quarters years old, has a high school diploma, but isn't smart enough to go to college...so they tell her. Now she spends her time caring for Mrs. Park, going to the beloved Cincinnati Zoo, and watching movies on her outdated phone. She's not really sure why she's there, but she's taking it day by day. And then she meets strong nurturing Miss Shasti at a tea dance.

Shasti Balakrishnan has been looking for someone to call hers for more years than she cares to count. She wants a woman to love and care for in a nurturing Mommy Domme/little girl scenario. She's thirty-two and already a partner in a thriving medical clinic in Denton Heights, but truth be told – she's lonely. She thought she'd found a companion in Amber back in D.C., but that fizzled out once they realized they weren't what each other wanted—or needed. And then she meets adorably precocious Madison at a tea dance.
ISBN: 978-1-953734-10-5 (e-Book)
ISBN: 978-1-953734-13-6 (Paperback)

Danielle Grainger

In Her Cage (Denton Heights Book 2)
(The Jaleesa and Tina Story)

A lesbian/asexual interracial polyamorous erotic romance with BDSM aspects including Dominance and submission.

Jaleesa Whitmore is a lesbian Domme in and out of fast relationships fueled by sex. She doesn't understand addiction. Not yet, anyway. Although she had almost one full year sober, she was done with it. She was moments from heading down the familiar road of drinking that always made her feel good and filled that void. She was about to get her life back on its old track when a fateful encounter with a stranger, who would become a trusted friend, halted her downslide. She didn't know it then, but this encounter would not only lead her to a series of events and people that would change how she looked at life but how she approached it.

Tina Jenkins likes women but is asexual and afraid to try for another relationship. She does understand addiction. Just shy of eleven years clean of her opioid addiction following a dental procedure right out of high school, her parents carefully constructed and monitored everything in her world. It didn't matter that she was thirty-one years old and still living in the pink bedroom in her parents' house. It didn't matter that her mother now had to work from home, and her parents had to track her location and do routine searches of her bag, car, computer, phone, and room. None of it mattered because she was clean.

And then asexual Tina meets promiscuous Jaleesa. And everything changed. For both of them.

ISBN: 978-1-953734-28-0 (e-Book)
ISBN: 978-1-953734-29-7 (Paperback)

Within Her Grasp (Denton Heights Book 3)
(The Marta and Shanice Story)

A lesbian age gap interracial erotic romance with light BDSM aspects.

"Within Her Grasp" is an age-gap interracial lesbian romance that tells the tale of two women who had settled for unhappy lives. And then they meet.

White, thirty-something Marta Ingersoll was done with people. She just wanted to be left alone at work and at home, thank you. Her inside cat and the outside stray were all she needed. And her sister, Nora, too, of course. But that was it. And then, one fateful afternoon, her instincts to save a woman in obvious distress kicked in, and her life was shoved onto a strange new course.

Black, twenty-something Shanice Ward never got a break. Life had thrown challenge after challenge at the young woman, and this latest thing was too much, but it wouldn't stop. Woken up from a sound sleep by someone trying to remove her clothing, she shrieked for him to leave her alone. He didn't, but then, the most amazing thing happened. She discovered that superheroes were real, and one had just flown into her room to save her, and her life was shoved onto a strange new course.

ISBN: 978-1-953734-30-3 (e-Book)
ISBN: 978-1-953734-31-0 (Paperback)

THE BERNADETTE SERIES

Dr. Bernadette Garneau holds a Ph.D. in Mathematics and has just gotten out of a four-year relationship. Shortly after the breakup, she began an exploration of her repressed sexual desires. One message from a beautiful and powerful online Mistress and Bernadette leaps into the world of BDSM. The Mistress takes charge, and Bernadette reels in the heady power this stranger has over her. She has gotten a taste of the life, and she wants more. She needs more. Several online and in-person experiences with BDSM and Power Exchange have led to cravings she doesn't quite understand. A brief sexual exchange with an online Goddess unleashes an incredible pain to pleasure connection that she hadn't understood before. As she sifts through the posers and one-night stands, she hones in on what her submissive nature needs from a Domme. The Bernadette Series follows Bernadette's journey into the world of BDSM and her search for love and sexual satisfaction. As she said, "I want a monogamous partner who wants to not only love and nurture me but who also wants to drape me over her lovely couch and have her way with me."

Wrecking Bernadette (Book One in the Bernadette Series)
A lesbian erotic novel with heavy BDSM aspects featuring
Dominance and submission.

Dr. Bernadette Garneau holds a Ph.D. in Mathematics and is four months out of a four-year relationship. One good thing about breaking up is that Bernadette is free to explore her repressed sexual desires. One message from a beautiful and powerful online Mistress, and Bernadette leaps into the world of BDSM. Mistress Ciara takes charge, and Bernadette reels in the heady power this stranger has over her. She has gotten a taste of the *life*, and she wants more. She *needs* more.

ISBN: 978-1-953734-00-6 (e-Book)
ISBN: 978-1-953734-14-3 (Paperback)

(S)mothering Bernadette (Book Two in the Bernadette Series)

A lesbian erotic novel with heavy BDSM aspects featuring
Mommy Domme little girl

Dr. Bernadette Garneau's universe is pushing her toward change. Her initial experiences with BDSM and Power Exchange have led to cravings she doesn't quite understand. A brief sexual exchange with an online Goddess unleashes an incredible pain-to-pleasure connection she hadn't understood until that encounter. But after sleeping on it, she clearly understands that this Goddess would never be the long-term relationship she sought.

Disappointed, she wonders if she should just give up and move back to California to be closer to her family. That is until she meets Mama_Luvs, an online Mommy Domme. The woman is nurturing yet stern from the start and is just … perfect. And then Mama_Luvs wants to meet. Starry-eyed Bernadette packs for a New Year's Eve weekend, hoping that this time she's found *the one* – the one who wants to love and nurture her but who also wants to drape her over a couch and have her way with her.

ISBN: 978-1-953734-01-3 (e-Book)
ISBN: 978-1-953734-15-0 (Paperback)

Danielle Grainger

Becoming Bernadette (Book Three in the Bernadette Series)

A lesbian erotic novel with heavy BDSM aspects featuring
Dominance and submission

professor Dr. Bernadette Garneau has fallen in love with the world of BDSM. She has a nascent interest in the pain-to-pleasure connection, but she has yet to find partners interested in nurturing the soul within her body that they play with. Admittedly, she's had incredible sexual encounters with experienced Dommes, but all of them left her feeling cold for whatever reason. Most of them simply wanted a sadistic roll in the hay. Bernadette wants a strong Domme who will love and nurture her *before* flogging her on a St. Andrew's cross and *afterward* when her body is spent.

One afternoon, she finally musters up the courage to venture out and meet some new friends in the local BDSM community. In walks a tall, handsome butch woman with fantastic hair and a confident stride. When this woman asks Bernadette, "Are you collared," Bernadette truthfully answers, "No," and accepts a dinner invitation for that very evening. She is walking on stars when she gets home at 2 a.m. after an ethereal sexual liaison. On the one hand, she wonders who she is becoming – she's never been this promiscuous. And on the other hand, she wonders if this strong butch woman could finally be the Domme of her dreams.

ISBN: 978-1-953734-02-0 (e-Book)
ISBN: 978-1-953734-12-9 (Paperback)

Desiring Bernadette (Book Four in the Bernadette Series)

A lesbian erotic romance novel with heavy BDSM aspects featuring Dominance and submission.

Rikki Carmichael finally feels that deep D/s relationship she has been craving since her Aunt Tilda introduced her to *the life*. She embraced her dominant side early on but finding a suitable submissive woman who wanted more than a quick roll in the dungeon proved elusive. That is until Professor Bernadette Garneau arrived on the scene. Now collared and committed to Rikki, will Bernadette prove to be different, or will she turn out like all the others — fickle and full of lies and deception?

And will this perfect sub stay with her when she realizes Rikki's ship is sinking? She'd almost lost the coffee shop she owns when creditors came knocking down her door en masse seeking payment for debts that weren't hers. Rikki managed to keep her staff and most of her friends in the dark about it, but she has not been able to get out from under it. With high stakes all around, Rikki looks for the peace she is seeking within her relationship with Bernadette. If this one fails, it may be time to leave the life entirely and go live in a cabin somewhere isolated in the woods. But buying a cabin takes money – money she just doesn't have.

ISBN: 978-1-953734-03-7 (e-Book)
ISBN: 978-1-953734-09-9 (Paperback)

Danielle Grainger

Loving Bernadette (Book Five in the Bernadette Series)

A lesbian erotic romance novel with heavy BDSM aspects featuring Dominance and submission.

Bernadette Garneau, a beloved professor of mathematics, is a natural submissive. She likes structure and rules and finally found a way of life and a woman who would provide those things for her. The BDSM community she stumbled upon in Denton Heights, Ohio is where she found Rikki Carmichael, now her dominant partner and fiancée. Rikki is everything she's dreamed of. Yes, Bernadette found the captain of her ship. With Rikki's support and guidance, maybe other parts of her life can finally come together, too – like the respect she deserves but hasn't gotten at the university. Why won't anyone see that she deserves to teach those upper-level courses? And to move out of her closet of an office? What do they know that she does not?

Rikki Carmichael, the respected owner of Rikki's Coffee Shop in town, has finally found the woman of her dreams in super-smart and super-real Bernadette Garneau. Bernadette is a submissive who instinctively knows how to take care of Rikki and accepts Rikki's need to be in charge. Bernadette is the first submissive Rikki's ever had that wasn't solely out for her own gain. Once Rikki can climb out of the deep financial debt she's found herself in, she will finally make their engagement to be married public.

Miscommunication, faulty assumptions, and unmet expectations threaten this union seemingly made in heaven. When life comes at them hard and fast, they must rely on their bond and their loving self-made family of friends.

ISBN: 978-1-953734-08-2 (e-Book)
ISBN: 978-1-953734-11-2 (Paperback)